"I KNOW YOUR SECRET, MY LORD."

"You followed me?" Jaime's expression hardened and his face grew dark with menace.

Aleta's hand fluttered to her throat, her blue eyes wide with fright. "I-I wished only to warn you, my lord. I would never betray you."

Jaime grasped her narrow shoulders between his huge hands. A small cry of panic escaped Aleta's lips as he held her. The fire in his eyes was unmistakable. He let out a tormented groan and pulled her against him.

"Now that you know my secret, what will I do with you, my love?"

Then he kissed her. Hard. Demanding. To her deepest dismay, she felt the fire of his kiss leap into her soul. . . .

LORD of the NIGHT

CONNIE MASON

LOVE SPELL BOOKS NEW YORK CITY

LOVE SPELL®

March 1998

Published by

Dorchester Publishing Co., Inc.
276 Fifth Avenue
New York, NY 10001

ISBN 0-505-52254-3

The name "Love Spell" and its logo are trademarks of Dorchester Publishing Co., Inc.

Printed in the United States of America.

Prologue

London
July 1403

Standing proud and erect, he waved aside the black hood offered him by the hangman and bravely faced the huge crowd of jeering, laughing spectators, each vying for a prominent position from which to watch the hanging of one of the supporters of the deposed King Richard II. Many thought it a fit end for a leader of the rebellion in Wales. Instigator of the short-lived rebellion was Owen Glendower, who had proclaimed himself Prince of Wales in 1400.

After the unsuccessful attempt to seize the throne from King Henry IV, Welsh supporters of Owen Glendower were captured and brought to London for execution. Their property and assets were seized and all male members of their families sent into exile or slain. Though Welsh marcher lord Clarence Mortimer, a member of the family of natural heirs of Richard II, from the house of Mortimer, was not involved in the rebellion, his neighbor, Lord Grey of Ruthyn, and his son Evan

1

had accused him of conspiring with Owen Glendower and the Northumberlands.

Spurred by the condemned man's refusal to don the hood, the crowd roared in approval, pressing closer to the gallows to catch a last glimpse of the earl accused of treason. To the end Mortimer had proclaimed his innocence, but the evidence had been too overwhelming to be ignored by King Henry IV, who had acted with extraordinary vigor to put down the rebellion. For being staunchly faithful to him, Henry had rewarded Evan Grey with the Mortimer estates, one of the largest and richest in Wales.

Two retiring figures stood at the back of the crowd: a poor elderly peasant wearing a hooded cowl and a young boy garbed in coarse wool.

"Come along, Jaime, 'tis no place for you to be today. I shouldn't have allowed you to talk me into such folly. If you're discovered 'twill go hard on you."

The lad, no more than fourteen or fifteen, turned eyes as black as midnight on his companion. "I will stay until the end, Gaylord. My father would expect it of me."

Gaylord groaned in dismay. He didn't want the lad to witness the King's terrible vengeance. The King had decreed that following the execution, the body of the traitor was to be hacked into pieces and displayed as a warning to those who considered betrayal. He feared that the King's cruel justice would irrevocably damage the impressionable lad.

A mighty roar rose from the crowd as the hangman placed the rope around the traitor's neck. Obviously Clarence Mortimer was no coward, for he appeared calm as he stared over the heads of the pressing crowd. His dark eyes came to rest on the figures of a humble peasant and a small boy hovering at the edge of the crowd. Then, as if pleased by something he had seen, a smile tugged at the corners of his mouth and his voice rang out loud and clear as a hush came over the crowd.

"As God is my witness, I am innocent. I pray that one day I will be vindicated and my good name restored."

The spectators cheered in a show of approval for the condemned man's courage. Moments later the trapdoor opened and his body dropped into the bottomless pit of eternity.

From the edge of the crowd, the boy's body jerked convulsively as he watched the rope grow taut, bounce several times, then grow still. But the worst was yet to come. After the man was pronounced dead, the body was hacked into pieces and displayed on pikes to the crowd. His face darker than the blackest depths of hell, his expression fierce, the lad did not turn away from the grisly sight. His black eyes glowed hotly as he consigned the sight and words of the condemned man to his memory forever.

"Will you come away now, Master Jaime?" Gaylord asked, tugging on his sleeve.

"Aye, Gaylord, I'm ready to leave. But mark you well, I swear by all that's holy that I will avenge my father's death. Lord Grey and his son will suffer for what they have done to my father this day."

His words were uttered with such violent promise and grim determination that Gaylord paled visibly. Never in his entire life had he encountered such burning hatred in one so young.

Chapter 1

Criccieth, North Wales
1416

Icy, wind-driven sleet blew in from the sea, pelting the faces of the silent men working on the beach with salt and spindrift. They moved quickly and efficiently, unloading barrels from longboats rowed in from the bobbing ship anchored in the secluded cove beneath the cliff. After the barrels were unloaded and lined up on the beach, they were hoisted into wagons and driven up the cliffs along a narrow, winding path beneath a crumbling fortress whose dark shadow reached out like an ominous specter across the stark moonless landscape.

Atop the cliff, a shrouded figure mounted on a midnight-black stallion kept silent vigil. His ermine-lined cape billowed around him in wild disarray, giving him the appearance of a winged avenger.

On the beach below, one of the men spied him and pointed him out to his companions. Though many in the village knew of him, there wasn't one among them who would betray him.

Lord of Darkness, they called him.

Keeper of the ancient castle keep sacked and burnt long ago by Owen Glendower. Its high twin-towered crumbling keep, all that was left of the once-magnificent castle, perched on a rocky peninsula high above Tremadog Bay. At its back were the spectacular Snowdonia Mountains.

Master smuggler.

It was due entirely to the Lord of Darkness that the villagers had prospered during times of undue hardship caused by wars and famine. He conducted his business mostly through Gaylord, an aging man the Lord of Darkness trusted above all others.

Once the barrels were safely stowed in the wagon and dispatched up the narrow path to the castle, horse and rider wheeled abruptly and disappeared into the misty curtain of fog and darkness.

"Have the men been paid, Gaylord?"

Jaime Mortimer stood beside a blazing fire in the castle keep, the only section of the ancient castle still habitable. His face was half-turned from the light, casting his handsome features in bronze. His profile spoke of power and ageless strength, rigid and inflexible in character. Yet despite the enormous size of his muscular frame and intimidating bearing, his strong features held a certain sensuality, which many of the village maidens could attest to.

Hair as black as midnight, with eyes to match, Jaime Mortimer was a man few dared to challenge. But in the year 1416 he was a mystery to all but the villagers he had lived among since the age of fifteen when Gaylord had brought him to this isolated fortress by the sea that was too dilapidated and unimportant for King Henry V to bother with. Criccieth Castle had been in his mother's family for hundreds of years, but its antiquity and run-down condition had rendered it useless to the King.

When Gaylord had brought him here after the rebellion and his father's death, they had found the keep barely habitable, and throughout the years Jaime had developed a certain fondness for the windswept heap of rock and stone. Jaime knew from gossip that King Henry, the Greys, Lord Somerset, and their cohorts thought him dead these many years. But against all odds and with Gaylord's help he had survived, each year bringing him closer to obtaining his heart's desire. One day soon, he vowed, Evan Grey, Earl of Flint, would pay for his part in the death of Clarence Mortimer, and the title would be returned to its rightful owner.

"The brandy is stowed safely in the cellar and the men have been paid and dispatched," Gaylord said as he warmed himself before the fire. " 'Tis a good night's work, lad. 'Twill add greatly to your riches."

Jaime's brooding expression did not lighten as he stared moodily into the fire. " 'Tis time, Gaylord," he said absently. " 'Tis time I took charge of my destiny. Thirteen years have passed since my father's death, and his enemies have enjoyed their ill-gotten gains while I have lived in obscurity all these years, making my home in a crumbling heap of stone."

"At least you're alive," Gaylord pointed out. "Which is more than you'd be if the Greys and their cohorts had known where to find you."

"Henry IV is dead. These past five years the kingdom has been ruled by his successor, Henry V. For all we know, young Henry has no interest in seeking my death."

"Aye, but both Evan Grey and Lord Somerset would be interested to know that you're still alive. You're Clarence Mortimer's rightful heir; Grey stands to lose too much should you appear and attempt to reclaim your inheritance. I didn't save your life to see you toss it away, Jaime lad."

Jaime aimed one of his few genuine smiles at the old man. "Aye, Gaylord, I owe you my life. If not for your ingenuity I would have perished when the King's men came to claim the manor, or been exiled to France to be raised by strangers."

"As bailiff of Mortimer Manor I owed it to your father to keep his son safe," Gaylord said, squaring his narrow shoulders. "As long as I live, Master Jaime, I'll do my utmost to keep you from harm—or folly."

"Do you think I'm acting unwisely by pursuing my claim?" Jaime asked, frowning.

"Aye, I do. Take your riches, lad, and settle elsewhere. Find a wife, build your own manor, and make a new life for yourself."

"Bah, I have no use for a wife. Women are vain creatures, more trouble than they're worth. I use them to ease my loins when lust rages within me, but find little value in having the witless creatures around permanently."

"What of the fair Rowena?" Gaylord asked, rolling his eyes toward a closed door leading to an upper floor.

"Rowena can remain as long as she continues to please me. But as you well know, my friend, she will soon outstay her welcome."

Gaylord made a clucking noise deep in his throat. " 'Tis a pity you don't remember your mother. A gentle, loving creature she was, much loved and respected by your father. Had she lived you would have an entirely different opinion of women. And had your father lived you'd already be wed to Lord Somerset's daughter. You were betrothed to Aleta Somerset when the child was five and you eleven. 'Twas all done up proper, with legal papers signed by both parties."

"The lady is probably well wed, with several children hanging onto her skirts. She'd be eighteen by now, and you know as well as I that thirteen or fourteen is considered the appropriate age for a female to marry. Lord Somerset wouldn't wait for a traitor's son to claim his betrothed bride."

"There are other women available to wed," Gaylord suggested.

"Do you expect me to bring a bride back to this rotting pile of stone?" Jaime laughed harshly. "Nay, Gaylord, let it rest. I'll not marry, not until the Mortimer manor and estates are mine again."

Gaylord seemed to be mulling over Jaime's words before he finally came to a decision. "I wasn't certain if I should tell you this, lad, but I heard a bit of gossip tonight that might interest you."

Jaime smiled grimly. "I know you won't be satisfied until you've regaled me with your gossip, Gaylord, so say on."

Gaylord licked his lips nervously, then said, "Lady Aleta Somerset has been given to Evan Grey. Since you haven't been heard from in years, your betrothal has been declared invalid. Word has it that the wedding is to be performed at Windsor Castle in two weeks. King Henry has recently returned from the war in France and has given his permission to the match."

"Lord Somerset must be ecstatic," Jaime said dryly. "If his daughter has remained unmarried until now he must be frantic for a husband for the chit. Perhaps she's so ugly no man would have her."

"I hear she's fair to look upon," Gaylord responded.

"Your nose for gossip is remarkable," Jaime said dryly. He grew thoughtful. "I have a mind to foil Evan Grey's wedding plans, old friend."

Gaylord exhaled sharply. "What do you propose, Jaime?"

" 'Tis time for Jaime Mortimer to let the world know that he lives." His body was tense, his fists clenched at his side, and his eyes burned with the fires of hell.

Gaylord suffered a pang of fear for Lord Somerset's daughter. "The girl is innocent in all this, Jaime."

"She's a Somerset." Jaime's voice had a hard edge to it that did not bode well for Aleta Somerset. "The man was as deeply involved in Father's death as Evan Grey. He shared in Father's fortune with the Greys, a fortune that rightfully belonged to me. The entire family is blighted."

He turned abruptly, staring intently into the flames once again. A tense silence ensued, broken only by the sound of popping logs and snapping flames. When Jaime spoke again his voice was harsh, his face set in determined lines. "Find us some peasant garb, Gaylord. We leave tomorrow for Windsor Castle. I will go before the King a poor man and claim my betrothed bride. What have I to lose?"

"Your head, lad," Gaylord grumbled as he shuffled from the room. By now he knew Jaime Mortimer well enough to know that nothing would dissuade him once his mind was made up.

Windsor Castle

"Oh, my lady, you look wondrously fair," the elderly maid sighed as she adjusted her mistress's *hennin*, the conical-shaped headdress worn over the hair by ladies of quality. "Lord Evan is lucky indeed to be getting so ravishing a bride."

Aleta Somerset whirled before the mirror, pleased with her appearance on the day of her wedding. Her fitted dress was stunningly fashioned of rich scarlet brocade. A broad band of ermine encircled the bottom of the skirt and outlined the deep V neckline, shoulders, and wrists. Her *hennin* was covered with silk and draped with a veil of pure gold chiffon, which didn't fully conceal the wealth of silver-blonde hair which fell in soft lustrous waves to the middle of her back.

Short in stature, Aleta Somerset was as daintily fashioned as a China doll, with the face of an angel. Her eyes were as blue as periwinkles and her lips as lush as wild strawberries. In addition to her physical beauty, she carried herself with the haughty dignity of a highborn lady of wealth. Having had to wait so long to marry, she had been eager and more than willing to accept the very rich Evan Grey as husband and lord. It had been an embarrassment to be so old and still unwed. If not for that stupid betrothal to a traitor's son she would have already been mistress of a great manor and mother of several children.

"Oh, I do hope Lord Evan is happy with the match, Nan," Aleta said enthusiastically. "He is older and much more worldly than I."

"A man should be older and more knowledgeable than his wife," Nan said with a sniff, every bit as haughty as her mistress. "Besides, he's only forty-three. And why shouldn't he be happy? You are bringing him estates and lands in Wales that any man would envy. Thank the good Lord your father has finally gotten your betrothal to Mortimer's son set aside. No one has seen or heard from Jaime Mortimer since his father's death."

"I wouldn't know what the man looked like if he walked through the door this moment," Aleta said thoughtfully.

"If he's anything like his father he'd be a handsome man," Nan recalled as she straightened Aleta's veil. "But you know what they say. Like father, like son. He'd probably be a rebellious fanatic just like his father. You're much better off with Lord Evan."

"Is—is there anything I should know before the wedding?" Aleta asked, blushing. Since she had no mother she trusted Nan to inform her what would take place on her wedding night. She dreaded the bedding ceremony most but knew it was a ritual she couldn't avoid.

Nan's round face grew thoughtful, wondering if she should tell Aleta that most men were beasts when it came to rutting with a woman. As long as they enjoyed themselves they cared little for the woman's pleasure—if there was pleasure in bedding. Being unmarried all these years Nan had no idea as to the pleasure possible between a man and a woman. Then there were the husband's mistresses to contend with. If a married man didn't take a mistress he usually made do with servants or village women.

"Never having been married makes me a poor choice for information, my lady," Nan said slowly. "I can only relay what I've heard through gossip. Your husband will tell you what to do and what he expects from you. Mostly you will lie still and let him have his way. It will hurt the first time, but once you're with child he will leave you in peace and sport with servants or women from the village. I pray he won't bring a mistress to live in the house, for that would be most demeaning to you. But it isn't inconceivable that he would do so, and you should know what to expect should Lord Evan bring home another woman."

"Lord Evan will not take a mistress!" Aleta said with such fire and venom Nan feared the young lady was in for a nasty shock when the inevitable happened. Nan had heard much gossip about Lord Grey's insatiable appetite for women, which she had no intention of repeating to Aleta.

"It won't happen for a long time, my lady," Nan consoled. " 'Twill likely take a good while for the newness to wear off your marriage, and Lord Evan seems much taken with you."

Aleta lifted her chin stubbornly as she made a silent vow to do all in her power to keep Lord Evan from straying. She had waited a long time for marriage, and was thrilled with the advantageous match her father had made for her. Giving her reflection one last look, Aleta turned abruptly and started toward the door.

"I'm as ready as I'll ever be, Nan. Let's not keep Lord Evan and the King waiting."

The wedding was to be held in the King's private chapel, attended by family and friends. Henry V, unmarried and in his thirty-first year, had just returned from France, having led an extended war against Charles VI in order to be recognized as Charles's heir. The magnificent warrior king's ten thousand archers had shattered the French knights in 1415 and after being recognized as Charles's heir, Henry returned to England in triumph. After seeing to his own country's needs, Henry intended to return to France and wed Charles's daughter, Catherine.

Evan Grey watched with avid anticipation as Aleta walked into the chapel. She was small and dainty; Evan thought Aleta a fit bride for an earl. She was a trifle old, 'twas true, but she still had many childbearing years before her. Both he and Somerset had tried for years to get Aleta's betrothal to Jaime Mortimer set aside so that he might marry the heiress and increase his wealth. But more than that, Grey wanted to possess the Mortimer bride just as he now possessed the Mortimer estates and wealth.

Aleta smiled shyly at Evan Grey, thinking him quite handsome in his short forest-green velvet doublet with yellow silk-lined sleeves and cloth-of-gold undersleeves. Long tight hose hugged his muscular legs; one leg was encased in bright yellow silk and the other in gray. Soft leather shoes and belt completed the elegant ensemble. His blond hair was cut in the current style, close-cropped with the neck shaved to above his ears.

King Henry was similarly dressed in shades of royal purple. Some of the men present wore volu-

minous robes with long trailing sleeves in place of
hose and doublet but all were dressed for the occasion in silks, brocades, and velvets while the
women tried to outdo one another in the richness
of their clothing and their elaborate headgear.

Evan Grey quickly stepped forward to lead his
bride-to-be to the altar where the King and ancient
priest waited.

"You look lovely, my dear," he complimented
smoothly. Then he leaned close to whisper in her
ear, "But methinks you'll look lovelier without
your fancy clothes."

Aleta blushed to the roots of her golden tresses.
Just thinking about what went on in the marriage
bed made her giddy.

"We are ready, Sire," Evan said as he approached the altar with Aleta in tow. The aged
priest looked expectantly toward Henry and, at
the King's nod, cleared his throat to begin the
Mass.

Suddenly the door to the chapel burst open as
two peasants garbed in coarse tunics, leggings,
and wooden clogs shoved past the guards into the
King's private chapel. Dropping to one knee before the monarch, Jaime Mortimer looked up at
Henry and in a voice loud enough for all to hear
said, "Forgive me, Sire, but this marriage cannot
take place."

"Who are you and what's the meaning of this?"
Henry blustered angrily. "Can't you see we're in
the middle of a wedding? How did you get into
the castle?"

Aleta turned sharply, her eyes widening when
she saw the man who had burst into her wedding.
Peasant or noble, she had never seen a man such
as he.

Rising to his full magnificent height, Jaime looked over the assortment of wedding guests with a bored expression. "Forgive me for not dressing for the occasion, Sire, but I've been reduced to living in poverty since my father's death." His black gaze settled on Evan Grey, causing the earl to shift uncomfortably from foot to foot. "But if you'll hear me out, I think you'll agree that this wedding cannot continue."

"See here, knave!" Evan said, glaring menacingly at Jaime. "Be gone with you. What can a peasant possibly have to say that will stop this wedding?"

Stunned speechless, Aleta stared at the barbarian, angrier than she'd ever been in her life. How dare this common churl interfere with her wedding! Did he not know how long she'd waited to become a wife? He looked like a drab brown sparrow amidst a flock of colorful birds. She wrinkled her pert nose, as if offended by his barnyard odor.

Lord Somerset stepped forward, adding his considerable bulk in support of Grey's words. "Away with you, knave!" He motioned for the guards.

"Knave, is it, Lord Somerset?" Jaime said with quiet dignity. "I'll wager that my lineage is more noble than yours, my lord." He turned to the King, who appeared more curious than angry. "I am Jaime Mortimer, rightful earl of Flint and betrothed husband of Lady Aleta Somerset."

Evan Grey made a choking sound deep in his throat.

Lord Somerset gasped and clutched at his chest.

Aleta swayed dangerously as she fought to keep from swooning. How could this hatchet-faced giant be Jaime Mortimer? And if he truly was Jaime, why did he wait until now to claim her? Dear

Lord, was she to be denied the pleasure of a respectable marriage after waiting years to be claimed by a husband?

Finding his tongue, Somerset was the first to speak. "Impossible! Jaime Mortimer is dead. What proof do you have that you're Jaime Mortimer?"

"Sire, my lords," Gaylord said, stepping forward, "if you will allow me, I have the proof in my possession."

"Who are you?" Henry demanded, beginning to enjoy himself. He hadn't had this much fun since he returned from war.

"I am called Gaylord. I was bailiff of Mortimer Manor before the rightful lord was wrongfully accused of treason and put to death. I have the papers to prove my master's identity as well as the original betrothal documents between Jaime Mortimer and Aleta Somerset. As you well know, Sire, a betrothal is legal and binding."

"The man is obviously an impostor!" Evan Grey scoffed, slanting Jaime a malevolent glare.

"And the documents fraudulent as well," Somerset declared hotly.

"I would see the documents, knave," Henry said, holding out his hand. Reaching into his voluminous brown robe, Gaylord extracted two rolled parchments, placing them into the King's hands.

"I have preserved proof of my master's birth and betrothal throughout the years, Sire, and offer them to you now with the knowledge that you will see justice done."

Henry unrolled the fragile parchments one at a time, reading them carefully before looking at Jaime. "Where have you been these many years, Mortimer?"

"At Criccieth Castle in Wales, Sire, living in pov-

erty on my mother's ancient property while my
enemies occupy my lands and title," Jaime said
boldly. "But now 'tis time to claim my bride."

"The document can't be legal!" Somerset sputtered, fear lacing his heart. He had thought the
Mortimer heir long dead by now. After the father's death, he and the Greys had sent men
searching far and wide for the boy, but no trace of
him had ever been found. It was to prevent the
lad's turning up at an inopportune time in the future that had sent both him and Grey looking for
the boy.

"As you can see, Sire, everything is in order,"
Jaime stressed, sliding a glance at Aleta, who had
remained unusually quiet thus far. He hadn't seen
her since she was a headstrong toddler and was
quite struck with her beauty.

Suddenly Aleta raised her head, glaring at Jaime
in a straightforward manner, and the blazing hatred emanating from the azure depths of her eyes
stunned him. He quickly looked away, wondering
why it should bother him if the spoiled chit hated
him. Once she became his wife she'd have to obey
him whether she liked it or not.

"These documents could be forged," Henry
said, rubbing his smooth chin thoughtfully.

"Aye," Grey agreed with alacrity. "No doubt
they are, Sire. I suggest you throw this impostor
out on his ear and we get on with the wedding."

Henry wasn't fully convinced. He searched
Jaime's features, looking for some hint of the truth.
Though Henry was young in years, his short reign
was tinged with greatness and a good share of it
was due to his careful nature and astuteness.

"If memory serves, for I was just eighteen at the
time, your father was executed for his part in the

rebellion in Wales and his estate and title awarded to the Greys for their help in convicting the traitor."

"My father was innocent," Jaime declared with quiet conviction. "He neither condoned nor participated in the rebellion. His enemies, jealous of his wealth and position, conspired against him and accused him falsely."

"You have proof of this?" Henry asked sharply.

"Nay, no proof, Sire, but enough trust in my father's word to know that he would not lie to me. Before he was taken, he swore to me that he took no part in the rebellion but remained neutral despite his close ties to King Richard."

"The Mortimers were traitors," Grey spat heatedly. "Are you calling me a liar?"

"Aye, my lord, a liar and thief. You've stolen my birthright and now want my betrothed bride for yourself. But this time it won't work, my lord, for before God and my King I am claiming Aleta Somerset for myself."

Aleta's face drained of all color. "Nay! I will not! I will not marry an impoverished peasant without a shilling to his name. I want no part of a man who may be a traitor, just like his father."

Lord Somerset patted her hand awkwardly. "Don't worry, my dear, the King will put an end to this nonsense."

"If you have no further proof that the betrothal document is legal, Mortimer, I see no reason to delay or postpone this match," Henry decreed.

Jaime opened his mouth to offer vigorous protest but was forestalled when the old priest, who until now had remained quietly in the background, stepped forward. "If you will permit me, Sire, I may be able to solve this mystery."

The King looked puzzled but Gaylord, after searching the old man's face, smiled gleefully. "I think, Sire, that Father Lionel may indeed hold the key to the legality of the betrothal document."

Handing the parchment to the priest, the King watched carefully as the old man quickly scanned the document. When he finished, he held it aloft for the king to see, then pointed to a signature scrawled at the bottom of the page.

"I am the priest who officiated at the betrothal, Sire. See here, 'tis my signature. In the eyes of God and the Church the betrothal is legal, and as binding as if a marriage between the parties had already been performed. There can be no marriage today between Lord Grey and Lady Aleta Somerset."

A broad smile split Jaime's handsome features, softening the stern set of his square jaw and lending him an almost boyish look. He would have laughed aloud if Evan Grey wasn't glaring daggers at him and Aleta shuddering in obvious revulsion.

"I don't care what anyone says," Aleta declared venomously. "I won't be forced into a marriage with a penniless traitor's son."

Jaime turned his black gaze on Aleta and, frightened by the dark, brooding man whose piercing gaze seemed to penetrate the depths of her soul she drew her hand to her heart in a flutter of panic. Yet, strangely, she felt attracted to him in a way that she couldn't explain or understand. But instinct warned her that life with Jaime Mortimer would be like living in the worst kind of hell.

"You have no choice, my lady," Jaime said. His eyes glowed darkly as he turned to the King.

"What say you, Sire? To whom will you bestow the hand of Lady Aleta?"

"Sire, might I remind you that the Grey family has stood firmly behind you and your father at a time when others sought to restore Richard II to the throne," Grey said smoothly.

"And I, Sire, desire Lord Grey for a son-in-law," Somerset added.

"Sire," Aleta beseeched shakily, "I do not wish to wed Jaime Mortimer. I would have Lord Grey as husband." She shot Jaime a fulminating look, letting him know in a single glance exactly what she thought of his interference. Evan Grey possessed the wealth and position worthy of her, and Aleta had no desire to marry a man possessing neither land nor estates.

Deep in thought, King Henry drummed his fingers against his chin. In truth, he admired Jaime Mortimer for daring to interfere with the powerful earl Evan Grey. Just the size and girth of Jaime was intimidating enough to frighten most men. And if that wasn't enough, one had only to gaze deep into the burning depths of his midnight-black eyes to know that Jaime Mortimer was a man who would have his own way in all things. Henry was no fool. He realized that it wouldn't hurt to have a zealous young man like Jaime Mortimer in his camp, and he searched his mind for a way to resolve the touchy situation without making enemies of the Greys and Somersets. In the end it was Father Lionel who solved the dilemma.

"Sire," the old man began, speaking with the authority of his exalted station in the Church, "there can only be one decision in this matter. I remember Gaylord well; he was Lord Mortimer's trusted servant. If he says the man standing before us is Jaime Mortimer and has the birth records to prove it, then it is indeed the truth. Furthermore," he droned on, "since I myself officiated at the betrothal of Lady Aleta and Jaime, I declare it valid and binding. There can be no marriage between Lord Evan Grey and Lady Aleta Somerset unless Jaime Mortimer himself sets the betrothal aside and releases Lady Aleta."

Lord Somerset sputtered in indignation but Evan Grey was much more vocal in his disapproval. "Are you going to let this doddering old fool dictate to you, Sire? Anyone can see his memory is failing."

The frail old priest drew himself up within his rusty black robes of office and fixed Evan with a withering glance. "My memory is sharper than yours, my lord. Unlike you, I recall vividly what happened to Lord Mortimer—and what led to his demise."

"I'd be interested in hearing what you have to say, Father," Henry said curiously. "As for the marriage, the Church has spoken and I must follow the dictates of the Holy Church. I hereby declare the original betrothal between Lady Aleta Somerset and Jaime Mortimer valid."

Aleta gasped in outrage. "Nay! You cannot mean to give me to this—this peasant with the stench of cow dung on his clothing!" Never had she been so mortified in her life.

Jaime smiled grimly as his bride-to-be raved and ranted without cease. Finally, he had had enough.

"Cease, woman! No wife of mine will behave like a fishwife in my presence."

"Oh, you—you brute!"

"Sire," Jaime continued smoothly as he turned to Henry, "I have waited a long time for my bride while she has been growing older and her child-bearing years diminishing. If it pleases you, and since the priest and wedding guests are already present, I request that the marriage between me and my betrothed take place immediately."

Chapter 2

❦

"**N**ay! Nay! I implore you, Sire, do not force me to wed this man." Aleta's expressive face betrayed the fear she felt in her heart.

"You heard the priest, Sire, do you deliberately challenge the dictates of the Holy Church?" Jaime knew the King didn't dare defy the Church's authority but he wasn't certain Henry was agreeable to an immediate marriage.

"Sire, you cannot do this," Lord Somerset beseeched, aghast at the turn of events. "Obviously this man cannot support my daughter properly. Would you have her suffer because a landless pauper cannot provide for her?"

Evan Grey's hand hovered above his sword, as he desperately fought the urge to end the brash young man's life. "I wholeheartedly support Lord Somerset," he agreed tightly. "Had this traitor's son been interested in his betrothed all these years, he would have pressed his claim before now."

"What say you?" Henry asked, turning to Jaime.

"While your father was alive, Sire, I bided my time lest he recall my father's supposed crime and send me into exile. I had already lost so much I did not wish to be sent from the country of my

23

birth. As for supporting my bride, Sire," Jaime continued slyly, "does not my lady bring a rich dowry with her? As her husband it is my right to administer that dowry as I see fit. She will lack nothing while under my protection."

Henry suppressed a smile. He was coming to admire Jaime Mortimer more with each passing minute. He slid a sly glance at Lady Aleta, well aware of the reputation that preceded her. Her beauty was legendary but her fine temper was what made her truly memorable. In a day when women were expected to meekly accept their lot in life she continually raged against that which displeased her. She was spoiled and accustomed to having her own way and obviously needed a husband who could control her without quelling her spirit, for it was that very spirit that made her more than just another beautiful, vapid female.

"Since the Church has spoken through the venerable Father Lionel I will grant your wish, Jaime Mortimer." Evan Grey opened his mouth to protest but Henry silenced him with a slice of his hand. "You are correct in assuming your wife brings riches with her. All are enumerated in the betrothal agreement, as you well know.

"Among the various landholdings in Wales that will be yours upon your marriage is a large manor house not far from Criccieth that needs minor renovations before it is fit for occupancy. Included are several villages and farms from which you are entitled to collect taxes. As for the Mortimer title and estates now in Lord Grey's possession, I cannot return them to you without proof of your father's innocence."

"Then I ask a boon, Sire. Investigate the charges made against my father thirteen years ago. My claim is valid. Ask Father Lionel what he knows. My father was a respected man who would never betray his king. Many of his friends are still living; question them and perhaps you'll learn the truth of the matter."

Henry stroked his chin thoughtfully. "Aye, I'll do it, and let us pray that God's truth will prevail. Meanwhile, there is a wedding to celebrate. Are you ready, Father?"

"Aye." Though his voice was somber there was a definite twinkle in Father Lionel's eyes.

"Nay!" protested Aleta. "I know well the manor you wish us to occupy, and it is little better than a hovel. 'Twill take months of renovations to render it fit for occupancy. I beg you, Sire, postpone the marriage until that time."

"My bride goes with me to Criccieth," Jaime replied. "I have made the keep quite comfortable throughout the years, and my lady will not suffer undue hardship because of its condition. Furthermore, I will occupy no manor unless it is my ancestral home and my birthright is restored to me. Until my father's name is cleared and my title and estates returned to me, I will make my home in the castle keep at Criccieth. So will my lady."

Henry was becoming more and more intrigued by the young man standing before him. Nearly of an age, the king and Jaime were both bold, stubborn men determined to fashion their own destiny. The King had only one more question to ask Jaime. "Do you wish to change your clothing for something more appropriate before the ceremony?"

"Nay, Sire, I wish to remind those present that clothes do not make the man. I am still the son of an earl despite my lack of finery." In truth, he probably was wealthier and owned finer clothing than any man present, including the King. But it was a secret he intended to guard well.

"So be it." The King turned to the priest. "You may begin the ceremony, Father."

Jaime grinned, remarkably altering his dark visage and making him appear younger than his twenty-eight years.

"Wait!" Evan Grey cried, unwilling to accept the King's ruling. "I will not be a party to this farce. I ask permission to leave, Sire."

"Granted."

Turning on his heel, Grey strode angrily from the room. As he passed Jaime, he paused briefly and said for his ears alone, "Mark you well, Mortimer, you'll pay for this." Then he was gone, leaving a grinning Jaime in his wake.

Grasping Aleta's elbow, Jaime pulled her toward the altar. "We are ready, Sire."

The priest began the ceremony immediately while Aleta stood stiffly at Jaime's side, stunned by the unexpected turn of events. She had wanted this to be the happiest day of her life. But instead it had turned into a nightmare from hell. The priest droned the Mass and when it came time to give verbal consent, Aleta remained stubbornly silent. Jaime glared down at her in consternation. Aware of the stubborn set of her little pointed chin and mutinous expression, his grip tightened on her elbow. She opened her mouth and yelped. Taking her yelp for consent, the priest blithely continued. When Father Lionel pronounced them man and wife before God and the King, she was visibly shaken.

Turning her toward him, Jaime lifted Aleta's face with his thumb and forefinger and stared into

the burning depths of her blue eyes. His first
thought was to wonder what in the hell he was
doing claiming a wife when it was the last thing
he wanted. Was his hatred for Evan Grey and
Lord Somerset so great that he felt it necessary to
take out his anger on the daughter and betrothed
of his enemies? Lady Aleta was beautiful beyond
belief, and he deliberately hardened his heart lest
she embed herself where she was not welcome.
Yet despite his best intentions, he could not help
himself as he lowered his mouth and claimed his
prize in a passionate display that tickled the King
and enraged Aleta.

Aleta was shocked and angered when she realized Jaime was going to kiss her. She tried to pull
away, but he was too strong for her as he held her
chin in place and covered her lips with the moist
warmth of his mouth. His kiss was forceful, demeaning, yet thrilling in a way she'd never experienced before—or expected. It was as if he wanted
to put his brand on her before the King and those
assembled to view the marriage. When his tongue
shoved past her teeth into her mouth, Aleta acted
instinctively. She bit down on the offending ap-
pendage until she tasted the hot spurt of his
blood.

Jaime's eyes opened wide as he broke off the
kiss, giving no indication other than the lowering
of his expression that anything was amiss. Su-
premely satisfied, Aleta gave a shudder of distaste
as she turned away from her brawny husband.
Compared to her petite form he was a giant, and
if he wanted he could beat her or do her grave in-
jury. And no one would utter a word in her defense. But, to her credit, Aleta wasn't easily
intimidated. In her own time, in her own way, she

would have her revenge for being taken from a
man who would honor and cherish her and given
to a boorish peasant without a shilling to his
name.

It was a subdued gathering that assembled in
the great hall for the wedding feast provided by
the King. The only people who seemed to be having a good time were Jaime, Gaylord, Henry, and
the priest. A knot of people had gathered around
Lord Somerset, commiserating with the man,
Jaime supposed, while Aleta steadfastly refused to
share a trencher and cup with her husband. The
feast seemed to go on forever, but that pleased
Aleta, for just thinking about the bedding ceremony and what was expected of her sent chills of
apprehension racing down her spine. Even if her
bridegroom had been Evan Grey, the thought of
disrobing before strangers made her shudder with
dread.

"Are you cold, my lady?" Jaime asked, noticing
that her shoulders were quaking. Until now they
had had blessed little to say to one another. Jaime
seemed content to engage in conversation with
Henry, all but ignoring his bride, who fumed at
his side in impotent rage.

"Nay, my lord," Aleta replied coolly. " 'Tis my
way of displaying my distaste for you."

Jaime frowned. "There is nothing frightening
about me, Aleta; I am naught but a man. Do you
obey me and we will deal well with one another."

"I do not acknowledge you as husband." Aware
that she was treading on dangerous ground, Aleta
braced herself for the heavy hand of her new husband. When the blow did not come, she looked
askance at him, realizing that most men would

deal harshly with her for her brave but foolish show of open defiance.

"Are you deliberately trying to provoke me, my lady? Methinks you'd be better served if you sought to soothe the savage beast in me rather than deliberately let him out of his cage."

Aleta blanched. "Are you a beast, my lord?" For some reason she found it difficult to breathe. His feral expression did indeed resemble that of a beast of prey.

"Many would judge me so." His mirthless grin offered little hope for gentle treatment from him. Then, from the corner of his eye, Jaime caught a movement by the door. "Is that your tiring woman beckoning to you?"

Aleta turned her head and saw Nan motioning from the doorway. Her face turned bright-red, then drained of all color. When she began shaking uncontrollably, Jaime's black brows drew together in a frown.

"Do you fear me so much?"

"Fear you? Nay, my lord, I fear no man."

"Why do you shake, woman, if you do not fear me?" His voice was harsh.

" 'Tis the bedding ceremony I fear," Aleta said, gaining courage. " 'Tis a barbaric custom that allows strange men to look upon the unclothed body of a bride. I do not relish being subjected to scrutiny by lewd men who would inspect me for blemishes."

Until that moment Jaime hadn't given a thought to the ritual that usually followed the wedding ceremony. Having never had the opportunity to go to court or associate with the nobility, he wasn't aware that the bedding ceremony was so unpleasant an ordeal for the bride.

"Go with your tiring woman, my lady. I will be up directly." His face was expressionless, his voice giving no hint of what he intended.

Aleta turned and bid a shaky good night to the King, then hurried off after Nan.

"I envy you this night, Mortimer," Henry said, leering after Aleta with avid interest. "How soon before the bedding? 'Tis doubtful that so perfect a creature as your lady possesses a flaw anywhere on her body."

Henry wasn't the only man in the room expressing an eagerness for the bedding. Behind Jaime's back they wagered with one another as to the attributes of certain parts of her body.

"There will be no bedding ceremony, Sire," Jaime said with a hint of disgust. "I am a jealous man. It would not please me if anyone but myself looked upon the unclothed body of my lady."

" 'Tis all in good fun," Henry said, torn between disappointment and admiration. Few men were bold enough—or foolish enough—to voice his views before his King. Few men were so brave.

"Nevertheless, 'tis my wish that there be no formal bedding ceremony. Aside from Gaylord there is no one here I'd want to undress me and lead me to my bride. Those who would volunteer do so merely to leer at my lady wife."

"If that is your wish, Mortimer, then so it shall be," the King said with keen disappointment. "I will personally see that no man follows you to your wedding chamber." He motioned for a page to refill Jaime's mug. "Drink up, my young friend, you owe me your time for protecting your privacy. The deflowering will be better for the wait."

* * *

Aleta's face was flushed a rosy red, her body suffused with heat. Jaime's words, more than the thought of the bedding, had brought the warmth and trembling she was now experiencing. Aleta had just started up the stairs to the bridal chamber when her father materialized from the deep shadows at the base of the stairwell.

"Father, you frightened me," Aleta said, gasping.

Her father's face was dark with fury. "He won't get away with it, my girl! I have just spoken with Lord Grey and he assures me that you won't have to suffer Jaime Mortimer for long. We are already preparing a writ of annulment."

"A lot of good that does me now," Aleta complained. "I'm the man's wife, Father, and he will demand his rights tonight. Once he has bedded me I am all but useless to another man."

"Nay, not so, daughter. Lord Grey will still have you. He's told me as much."

"He would want me even though I am forced to submit to that smelly peasant who dares to claim me?"

"Aye, even then. So take heart, daughter, all is not lost. When we have gotten rid of Mortimer you will still be the lady wife of a rich and powerful earl."

"My lady, hurry," Nan pleaded from the top of the stairs. "We must prepare you for your lord."

"Go now," Somerset urged, giving her a little push. "Resist him if you can, but you must not allow him to possess more of you than that what is rightfully his. Hold yourself aloof, my girl, and persevere, for soon you will have a husband worthy of a Somerset."

Aleta stared at her father for the space of a

heartbeat before turning abruptly and running up the stairs. Nan waited for her at the door.

"Off with your clothes, my lady. Doubtless Lord Evan will be an impatient bridegroom."

Aleta froze. Did Nan not know that she had not married Evan? But how could she, when the tiring woman had been confined in the bridal chamber these past few hours. "Lord Grey will not enter the bridal chamber this night," she said softly.

"Of course he will, my lady," Nan scoffed when she heard Aleta give voice to such a silly notion. "Lord Evan will be unclothed by his friends and carried into the bridal chamber for the bedding ceremony and then it will all be over and you will be alone with your lord husband."

"I'm telling you, Nan, Lord Evan won't come tonight. Where have you been all evening?"

"Why, right here, my lady, preparing the bridal chamber. Is aught amiss?"

"Aye, Nan, there's much amiss. Something no one could have foreseen or expected. Jaime Mortimer showed up in the chapel in time to stop the ceremony."

"Jaime Mortimer! Lord have mercy on us. I thought the young man long dead. So there was no marriage, is that what you're trying to tell me?"

"Oh, aye, there was a marriage," Aleta said bitterly. "But not the one I expected. Father Lionel declared my betrothal to Jaime legal and binding, and the King saw fit to call off my marriage to Evan. You should have seen that arrogant knave," she fumed.

"Who? Lord Evan?" Nan asked, confused.

"Nay, Jaime Mortimer. He was dressed in peasant garb and smelled most foul. He's penniless and landless and the son of a traitor, yet the King gave me to him quite willingly."

"If Father Lionel declared the betrothal valid then the King had no choice," Nan said in an effort to soothe her distraught mistress.

"When the knave asked the King's permission for us to wed this very night, I wanted to die."

Nan's eyes bulged. "You were married to Jaime Mortimer?"

"Aye, Nan, and nothing Father or Lord Evan said would dissuade the King from granting permission. Henry even appeared to like the scoundrel."

"Oh, you poor little darling." The maid's voice was filled with pity as Aleta flew into her arms. Never had Aleta felt more miserable or helpless. It was a feeling she had experienced seldom in the past and she didn't like it.

"I can't do it, Nan, I can't let that vile oaf bed me. I'll fight him tooth and nail."

"Now, now, my lady, we'll think of something," Nan said, patting her back. "Mayhap I can sneak you out of the castle before your husband arrives. We can take refuge with my people until your father can free you from this onerous obligation Henry has forced on you."

Aleta's blue eyes sparkled with renewed hope. "Oh, Nan, aye, I knew I could count on you. If we hurry we can be gone before the bedding party is drunk enough to find their way to the bridal chamber. Gather my clothes, hurry, we must leave immediately."

Feeling no pain but not drunk enough to render him useless to his bride, Jaime rose somewhat unsteadily from his chair and bowed to Henry. "I

have partaken of your hospitality, but now 'tis
time to go to my bride lest she grows impatient
and seeks another."

Ribald laughter followed his words. And when
several men would have bounded after Jaime,
Henry stopped them with an outstretched palm.
Jaime had no idea what Henry said to the revelers
who would have followed him into the bedcham-
ber, but when he reached the foot of the stairs
there was no one behind him.

Jaime had one foot on the bottom step when
two stealthy shadows, illuminated by torches set
in sconces in the dark stairwell, were projected on
the stone wall. He could tell at a glance that both
figures were feminine. Naturally suspicious, Jaime
scooted into a dark niche, waiting until he could
identify the figures. Though both women were
cloaked and hooded, he had no difficulty recog-
nizing Aleta.

Nan led the way. "To the stable, my lady," she
whispered when they reached the foot of the
stairs. She hurried forward, carefully skirting
the great hall where the revelers still sat eating
and drinking. Expecting Aleta to be close on her
heels, she neither lingered nor looked back. She
would have been terrified to know that Aleta was
no longer behind her. Jaime had but to reach out
and grasp Aleta's tiny waist with one hand while
muffling her cries with the other. Her feet never
touched the stone steps as he dragged her up the
long spiral staircase into the room at the top which
he assumed was the bridal chamber. Before he set
her on her feet, he removed his hand from her
mouth and shut and locked the door, placing the
iron key someplace inside his voluminous garments.

"Were you going somewhere, my lady? If I didn't know better, I'd think you weren't entirely pleased with this match."

Aleta spat out the taste of his hand. "You know what I think about this marriage. 'Tis Lord Grey I want, not you. Why would you want a wife who considers you far beneath her in rank and manners?"

Jaime smiled in wry amusement. "Nay, my lady, you err, 'tis you who will be beneath me."

His play on words flustered her. She backed away, eyeing his peasant rags with distaste. "You disgust me."

Jaime's black eyes glittered darkly. He had every right to chastise his bride in any way he saw fit. Indeed, it was his duty to show her the error of her ways. He could beat her, but that hardly seemed appropriate for a wedding night, even though she undoubtedly deserved it. Besides, he rather liked a woman with fire.

"My lady, my lady, are you there?"

Aleta rushed to the door, then stopped abruptly, suddenly realizing that it was locked.

"Tell her you are all right." Silence. "Do it!" His voice was harsh and unrelenting.

"I'm fine, Nan."

"Why did you turn back?" Nan asked worriedly. "Open the door, we must hurry before it is too late."

" 'Tis already too late, Nan," Jaime called through the door. "Go seek your bed, your lady will have no need of you this night."

"Oh." A long silence ensued. "Is that your wish, my lady?"

"Tell her," Jaime hissed.

"Aye, Nan, do not worry, I am fine. Go find your bed."

"Aye, my lady," came Nan's reluctant reply.

"Now what?" Aleta asked nervously. Her eyes were riveted on the door, waiting for the men below to charge into the room to view the bedding ceremony. She steeled herself for the indignity that she assumed was to take place next.

Jaime's grin was as darkly compelling as the devil's. "Now, my lady wife, I'll try to forget that you wounded me grievously when you attacked me with your teeth and get on with the bedding." He followed the direction of her gaze and knew immediately the cause of her fear and confusion. "There will be no formal bedding ceremony," he told her tersely as he began stripping off the coarse woolen garments he wore. "Your beauty is for my eyes only."

Aleta's relief was short-lived when Jaime removed his short brown cloak and uncinched the rope around his waist, allowing his long-sleeved, hip-length tunic to drop to the floor. When he stood before her, clad only in tight woolen hose and those absurd clogs, Aleta gasped and turned away. His shoulders were more than twice the width of hers and his chest was darkly furred with fine black hair. His neck was thick and his biceps bulged in a vulgar display of power and strength. His massive torso tapered to a narrow waist taut with ropy muscles. It seemed indecent for a man to appear so blatantly, sexually masculine.

"Remove your clothes, my lady," Jaime growled in a guttural voice. "Or would you prefer I play ladies' maid for you?"

He reached out to her and was shocked to see that his hand was trembling. From the moment the priest had pronounced them man and wife he had thought of little else but bedding the haughty little wench. For all her tiny stature she was a feisty little baggage and he ached with the need to tame the streak of stubborn resistance that ran rampant through her body. For purely legal purposes, Jaime knew how important it was that their marriage be consummated. Other than using Aleta in a carefully calculated plan for revenge, he had no use for her—or so he tried to tell himself.

"I do not wish to bed with you," Aleta announced imperiously.

Jaime shrugged. "It matters little what you wish or do not wish." He grasped her *hennin* by its golden veil, pulling it off her head and tossing it aside. He sucked his breath in sharply as his action revealed the heavy curtain of silver-blonde hair tumbling past her shoulders to her waist. "Sweet Virgin," he muttered, captivated by the glorious mass of hair cascading down her back. It reminded him of moonlight shimmering on water. He grasped a length in his hands, amazed at the sensual pleasure it gave him as it slipped through his fingers like liquid silver.

Jerking from his grasp, Aleta backed away. Jaime stalked her relentlessly. "You cannot escape me, my lady."

"I'll scream."

He laughed. "Scream away. The walls are thick and the bridal chamber remotely located in the castle, as it should be."

"I will not submit willingly."

Jaime flashed a roguish grin. "I had considered beating you but hoped there would be no need for it. Do you force me to it, I will change my mind and probably enjoy it as much as the bedding."

Aleta's chin jutted out belligerently. "You are twice my size, but if you feel the need to strike someone with half your strength, then do what you must."

Despite Aleta's false bravado and haughty words, Jaime felt a grudging admiration for her foolish courage. But his admiration didn't extend beyond the fact that consummation was necessary to make their marriage binding. Fixing her with the black intensity of his eyes, he reached for her, and this time easily caught her. His thick fingers curled around her waist and he dragged her hard against the solid wall of his chest. It was the first time Aleta had been in intimate contact with the opposite sex and she was stunned by the intensity of his response.

"I don't want to hurt you, my lady," Jaime said, surprised to discover that he actually meant it. Brutality wasn't his way with women. He was a sensual lover, enjoying his encounters and taking pride in giving his lovers pleasure. Whether village girls, servants, or the Lady Rowena, he always made certain he made their times with him memorable. Though he considered most women vain, witless creatures, he had never found the need to mistreat them.

"If you don't want to hurt me, then let me go," Aleta beseeched. "You are much too large for me."

It took a moment for Jaime to realize what Aleta was hinting at and when he did lust surged through him, tightening his loins painfully. He leered at her.

"Before the night is over, sweetheart, you will see that what you are referring to is not only possible but highly enjoyable."

"Nay, I will never enjoy what you intend this night."

"Maybe not, my lady, but I will." Unerringly his lips found hers, and for the second time in her life, the first being after they had repeated their vows, Aleta felt the potent heat of a man's passion.

She expected Jaime's lips to be hard and punishing, but they were soft and coercive. She waited fearfully for the explosion of brutal passion, but found only the soft pervasive force of his desire. She wanted to hate the taste and heat of him, yet savored the warmth and sweetness. Then her father's warning suddenly came to mind and she stiffened her body and renewed her struggles. He had advised her to avoid surrendering to Jaime Mortimer, but she wasn't certain that was possible.

Jaime snorted disgustedly when he felt Aleta stiffen in defiance. "So be it, my lady. I truly wanted to be gentle with you, but you have made your choice." Picking her up by the waist, he tossed her on the bed, which was already turned down in anticipation of the bedding by the faithful Nan.

What Jaime had intended to be a rather cold, passionless consummation had suddenly turned into a heated battle of wills. And somewhere along the line his passion had exploded into an urgent need that was fast becoming an aching torment. Lord help him, he wanted the defiant little witch. And not merely for revenge, or because it piqued his perverse sense of humor to steal her from the man he hated above all others. He wanted Aleta Somerset because she had been meant for him from the moment of her birth. And because . . . Because . . .

Trapped on the bed, Aleta felt overpowered by

Jaime's strength. She uttered a small cry of despair as he slowly, without the slightest twinge of embarrassment, stripped off his hose and clogs. Nude, he appeared to dominate the room. Try as she might, Aleta could not turn her eyes from that blatantly sexual part of him that stood up in avid attention from its thick forest of black hair at the juncture of his thighs. It was the first time she had seen a fully aroused male. Or any nude male, for that matter. Her eyes grew wide with terror and she began silently reciting every prayer she'd ever been taught, for she knew a man such as Jaime Mortimer would surely kill her.

Jaime's arrogantly slashed brows tilted upward as he recognized the reason for Aleta's fright. "Give over, my lady, and I swear you'll come to no harm at my hands."

Her mouth went dry as she shook her head in a negative motion. "Nay. I will not accept you as husband." In a last-ditch effort to escape, she shot from the bed. But Jaime easily captured her and pinned her to the surface with his hard body. Then he began to undress her, slowly, deliberately, completely. When her last piece of clothing joined the growing pile on the floor, he raised himself above her and looked his fill.

"By the Holy Rood, you are lovelier than I imagined, sweetheart." Her skin was the purest alabaster, her breasts firm and rose-tipped, sized perfectly to fill his hands. Her tiny waist flared out deliciously at the hips, and at the juncture of her thighs her maiden's hair curled in golden tendrils atop a plump mound. "I had no idea what I was getting when I left Criccieth, but I would have had you were you so fat you waddled and had chin hair. Methinks I prefer you this way."

To Aleta his words served only to fortify her belief that Jaime Mortimer wanted her merely to thwart Evan Grey and her father, not because of that cursed betrothal of long ago.

"I find you monstrously ugly and disgusting, Jaime Mortimer," she blasted in her haughtiest voice.

"Methinks you protest too much." Jaime grinned as he ran his hands along the satiny surface of her skin. "I vow before the night is over you will think me quite remarkable—in every way."

"In a pig's eye!"

Chapter 3

S he beat against him, but he brushed away her hands as he would pesky gnats. He caught her hands, pinning them against her sides. "You are foolishly brave to talk to me in such a disrespectful manner, but I will enjoy teaching you how to be a dutiful wife."

She twisted beneath him frantically, realizing too late that her movements were stoking the fire of his passion. Effortlessly he secured both her wrists above her head with one hand while his other hand slowly cupped her breast and teased the nipple with the rough pad of his thumb. A mirthless smile curved his full lips when it rose to coral hardness.

When he lowered his head and took it into his mouth she stiffened and made a low gurgling sound deep in her throat. She cried out, and against her will she arched into the hot brand of his mouth as he fed voraciously on her.

He emitted a harsh, guttural cry, raised his head, and with his hungry mouth he found hers. His kiss was savage, almost brutal as he ravished her mouth with the hot thrust of his tongue. Aleta whimpered, the sound lost in the moist warmth of

42

his mouth. The man was an animal, never would she give him the satisfaction of knowing how frightened she was of him. She had been stunned and shocked when he had forced his tongue past the barrier of her teeth.

He lay upon her heavily, almost too heavy for her petite frame, and she gasped for breath. She cried out again, but this too was lost in the depths of his throat as he continued to kiss her, drawing her deeper into the liquid magic of his mouth and tongue. And still she fought him.

He drew back, smiling with cynical bitterness as his black gaze swept over her. "Yield, my lady."

"Nay, knave, how can I yield when I was meant for Evan Grey? I will fight you till the bitter end."

"Do you think your feeble struggles will thwart me from my goal? Nay, my lady, I will consummate this marriage so none can dispute my right to you or your fortune."

"I will not yield!" Aleta cried, grimly resolute.

Jaime's eyes burned hot and black as he laughed softly. "I do not need your cooperation, my lady." He moved against her, his face dark and determined, his body tense.

To her chagrin, Aleta could not turn her eyes from the stark beauty of his face. All planes and angles, his rugged masculinity had never been more pronounced or frightening. She felt her throat constrict as his maleness probed between her legs. She felt the tempest of his passion, his fire, his determination as he paused at the portals of her womanhood. She felt his body tauten, his buttocks flex. And then she felt the burning thrust of him into her virgin passage.

The pain came, swift and devastating, and she fought the scream that welled in her throat as

tears spilled from her eyes. Seeing her eyes darken
with pain, Jaime paused briefly, and when he continued, his movements were almost gentle. He began to thrust deep, deep inside her, until Aleta
thought she would shatter and die.

But she did not die. Not even when his tempo
increased and he stroked and thrust and his hands
found her breasts and his mouth whispered
against her lips, saying things she did not understand. When she felt pain become pleasure, she experienced a new kind of torment. Gritting her
teeth, she refused to show Jaime by word or deed
that he was affecting her in any way. Not even
when her body yearned for a lofty goal she was
only vaguely aware of and her flesh burned hotter
than the fires of hell to attain it.

Jaime felt the tension build in the body beneath
him and gave a cynical chuckle. Experienced in
the many ways of love, he knew the moment
Aleta's body softened and accepted him. Knew,
also, when the pain stopped and the pleasure began. And knew that he would bring her to climax
despite her vigorous protests and denials. That
thought brought his own release so close to the
edge that it took fierce concentration to keep from
exploding inside her. She was so small and tight
he deliberately held himself back lest he hurt her
beyond repair. Instinctively he knew that someone
as tiny as Aleta would need time to stretch enough
to accommodate all of him.

The longer Jaime thrust and stroked the greater
the pleasure Aleta felt, until she thought she was
going to burst. Daring to look into his face, her
breath caught painfully in her throat. His face was
stark with concentration, his head thrown back,
his throat arched gracefully. She thought him sav-

agely beautiful and more frightening than any man she had ever known. Then all thought slid to an abrupt halt as something inside her shattered, flooding her with such incredible splendor she thought she'd die from it. She bit her lip to keep from crying out and tasted the bitterness of blood.

Jaime knew the exact moment of her climax and allowed his own release to spill forth. Aleta felt the honeyed spurt of liquid fire warm her body and knew a despair far greater than any she had ever experienced before. Jaime Mortimer had taken something precious from her, something that she had intended to give to Evan Grey. She would never forgive him for that.

His breath still hammering in his chest, Jaime lifted himself from Aleta and lay down beside her, staring at the ceiling. A deep frown creased his brow as he considered the consequences of taking a wife who obviously despised him. Acting on the spur of the moment, he had raced to London and claimed Lady Aleta Somerset as his own, and now that the marriage was consummated he was saddled with a wife he wasn't certain he wanted. Though he had derived immense satisfaction from taking the woman Evan Grey wanted, he hadn't the slightest notion what to do with her. A wife was the last thing he had needed.

Turning to Aleta, he searched her face. Her cheeks were wet with silent tears and he was impressed by her ability to conceal the pain he knew he had caused her. Knowing that he had given her pleasure in the end, though, more than compensated for the remorse he might have felt over hurting her.

"Are you all right, my lady?" he asked kindly. Never let it be said that he was a brutal husband.

"Do I look all right?" Aleta snapped crossly. "You hurt me."

"I gave you pleasure."

"Nay, not so," she denied vehemently. "I obtained no pleasure from this brutal coupling. If you touch me again I swear I will find a way to kill you while you sleep."

Jaime's face grew dark with barely suppressed rage. "You are my lady wife. 'Tis your duty to obey me in all things."

"I will not!"

Angered by her daring, Jaime reared up on his knees, pinning her to the mattress with the black intensity of his eyes. No one, man or woman, had ever spoken to him in such a manner. Knowing that he should punish her and nip her rebelliousness in the bud, he drew back his hand, as if to strike her.

Aleta stiffened, aware that Jaime could do her real harm if he struck her, but she was unable to keep her temper in check. "Go ahead, knave, hit me," she dared. "You will gain no friends when I show up to break my fast with my face bruised beyond recognition. My father and the King are fast friends."

"There are places where bruises don't show," he said, his eyes raking her naked form ruthlessly.

Yet, staring down at her diminutive form, Jaime knew he wouldn't strike her. Not even if she goaded him beyond reason. It wasn't his way. Nor would he demand of her that which she was unwilling to give. Their marriage had been consummated; after tonight he no longer need bed her.

Aleta's chin jutted out and Jaime nearly laughed aloud at her bravado. When he lowered his fist and leaned back against the pillow, Aleta let out a shaky breath. She was so certain he was going to strike her she had steeled her body for the pain.

"Go to sleep, Aleta, you need not worry that I'll bother you again this night. Or any other night," he sneered derisively. "I have done my duty. The marriage is consummated, and after tonight you need no longer suffer my obnoxious presence in your bed. My mistress is installed at Criccieth Castle. Rowena has proven an accomplished lover, while you are too new and clumsy at love to satisfy me."

Aleta's mouth flew open. "You would humiliate me by keeping a mistress in my home?" she gasped, stunned. While she knew most men did not honor their marriage vows for long, she never considered that Jaime's mistress would live in her home.

"I would as soon send her packing, my lady; it is entirely up to you." He watched her closely, aware of what his words implied, and waited for her answer. She was such a fetching little creature he'd gladly send Rowena away if Aleta would become his docile plaything. She was his wife, after all, and her duty was to yield to him in all things.

Aleta's blue eyes burned hotly as she glared up at Jaime. "Keep Rowena. I care not if one or twenty women warm your bed, as long as it isn't me."

"So be it, my lady," Jaime said harshly. "But be forewarned. If you take a lover, it had better not be Evan Grey. On second thought," he amended, " 'tis better you remain chaste, for I will accept no bastard get under my roof."

Rising to her knees, Aleta began beating on Jaime's broad chest. "You—you disgusting animal! If all men are rutting pigs like you, I want no lovers. Get your heirs upon Rowena," she added as an afterthought. " 'Tis well that you not bring legitimate children into a family of traitors."

At that moment Jaime came closer to striking a woman than he ever had in his life. This tiny scrap of femininity had wounded him as severely as a man more than twice her size. She had a vicious tongue, and he seriously considered throttling her before she drove him insane. Any other man would have beaten her black and blue by now. Grasping her two wrists in one big hand, he flung her aside.

"Go to sleep, my lady, before I do you serious damage. You'll need your energy for the trip to Criccieth Castle. 'Tis the middle of winter and bitter cold."

Aleta eyed him warily. "Must we leave so soon?"

"Aye. We leave before your father and Lord Grey can band together and take you from me by force."

A hopeful look came over Aleta's face.

"Nay, lady, I can protect my own," Jaime declared when he noted Aleta's thoughtful expression.

Then he turned his back on her, pulled the cover over him, and promptly ignored her as if she didn't exist. Beside him, Aleta fumed in silent rage, hating him, hating what he represented and hating his flagrant disregard of her feelings. The man was arrogant, crude, and brutish. And his daring was beyond belief. Bursting into the castle, past the guards and into the chapel to interrupt her marriage to Evan Grey had been a reckless act, albeit one that had won the King's admiration. Obviously the man was not lacking in courage. It was his character that was seriously flawed. What made him think she'd want a traitor's son for a husband? Or that she'd meekly accept him as her lord and master? Nay, she told herself. Let Jaime Mortimer keep his mistress, for she'd fight him tooth and nail if he tried to bed her again.

Having come to that conclusion, Aleta reached for the blanket and settled down for the night, moving as far away as possible from the comfortable warmth of Jaime's big body. But no matter how desperately she clung to the edge of the bed, her mind still cringed from the knowledge that he had made her feel pleasure. How could that be? she wondered curiously. When he had forced his body into hers, the pain had been excruciating. She had fully expected to die from it, yet she knew the exact moment pain had turned to pleasure and her body softened and stretched to accept him.

She shuddered, trying to deny the incredible way in which her body had spun out of control as Jaime stroked and thrust inside her. Yet no amount of denial could make her forget the burning touch of his hands, the moist sweetness of his mouth, or the way he had drawn a response from her reluctant body.

And she'd never forgive him!

Sighing despondently, Aleta closed her eyes, realizing that until her father succeeded in freeing her, she was bound by law to follow her husband to his home, no matter how crude or humble it might be.

During the night the wind rose, howling through the narrow window with chilling effect. The fire died in the hearth and the room grew bitter cold. Unknowingly, Aleta moved ever closer to the warmth radiating from Jaime's big body, and when he felt her softness nudge him, he opened his arms, bringing her tightly against him. Still sleeping, Aleta sighed contentedly and snuggled deeper into his warmth.

Suddenly aware of Aleta's bare bottom pressing against his stomach and her breasts filling his hands, Jaime's eyes flew open. At first he thought she was awake, but the even cadence of her breathing told him she still slept. Keen disappointment surged through him when he realized that the coldness of the room had forced her to seek him in the bed, not the same need that filled his loins to near bursting.

But he would not take her. Nay, though his blood sang through his veins and his body suffered the torments of hell, he'd not take her again. He was upset with himself for enjoying her too much the first time, and he had neither the time nor the inclination to woo his lady wife. He didn't want Aleta Somerset for herself, he tried to convince himself, but for the pleasure obtained by denying Evan Grey something he so obviously coveted. And it was the lady's wealth and property he wanted, not her love or respect.

Carefully removing his hands from the taut mounds of her breasts, Jaime forced his thoughts from the woman in his arms and tried to remember how Lord Somerset and the Greys had plotted together to bring about his own father's death. He knew the elder Grey had died two years previously, but fortunately the son was still alive to feel the brunt of his retribution when it came. Finally he fell asleep, vowing that no woman, least of all his lady wife, would get in the way of his quest for revenge against those responsible for his father's shame and for stripping him of his birthright.

Aleta awoke to the certain knowledge that someone was staring at her. Her blue eyes flew open, meeting the black, enigmatic gaze of Jaime Mortimer.

"Good morrow, my lady," he drawled. His dark eyes raked her insolently. "I hope you slept well. I've been waiting for you to awaken."

His gaze settled on the tangled profusion of silver-blonde hair that spilled around her shoulders in wild disarray. She was a glorious sight, with her bare shoulders and tops of her full breasts enticingly displayed above the blanket she held to her chest. He tried to ignore the clamoring of his body.

Aleta blinked repeatedly, then frowned, annoyed that her husband was now clad in the same rough brown peasant garb he had arrived in the day before. "Have you no other clothes?" she asked sourly.

Jaime grinned impudently. "I am sorry my attire displeases you. But as you well know I have little wealth of my own. Although that will all change now, my lady, won't it?"

"Perhaps," Aleta allowed, giving him nothing. "But think you that either my father or Lord Grey will allow me to be spirited away by you? Nay, good sir, a way will be found to thwart your foul intentions."

Jaime's grin widened. "You are mine, Aleta, according to the law of the land and the Church. King Henry has sanctioned our union and the priest has blessed it. 'Tis my right now to bid you do I see fit, or punish you for defying my wishes.

It will behoove you, lady, to seek my good nature in all things."

Her eyes flashing dangerously, Aleta fumed in impotent rage. She knew so little of this imposing man, she feared angering him unduly. One blow of his huge hand could do her great harm. "We shall see, my lord," she said sweetly.

Jaime's smile turned sour, wondering how, in so short a time, had he allowed this slim slip of a girl to get under his skin so effortlessly and annoy him so thoroughly. " 'Tis time to break our fast, my lady. The King and his entourage await us in the great hall."

"I would bathe first," Aleta said imperiously.

"Aye, I expected as much. Your bath will arrive momentarily."

As if on cue a knock sounded at the door and Jaime moved to open it. A procession of servants entered, one hefting a large brass tub and the others carrying buckets of water. The tub was placed discreetly behind a screen and Aleta waited in the center of the bed until the tub was filled and all the servants had departed. Then she looked pointedly at Jaime, waiting for him to leave. When he stubbornly remained within the room, arms crossed over his massive chest, Aleta gave an exasperated sigh and said, "Am I to have no privacy?"

"Aye, my lady, all the privacy you wish. I will return for you in fifteen minutes." Turning abruptly, he strode out the door. The moment he stepped into the hall, Aleta leaped from the bed and disappeared behind the screen. Lingering outside the door, Jaime heard the splash of water, knew Aleta was safely ensconced in the tub, and reentered the room. He paused a moment beside the bed, staring at the bottom sheet. Then he stripped it from the bed and left the room without alerting Aleta to his presence.

Aware that Jaime would return for her in fifteen minutes and unwilling that he should find her unclothed, Aleta hurried through her bath. Peeking around the screen, she saw that the room was empty and quickly rummaged through her trunk, placed in the room earlier in anticipation of her marriage to Evan, for a dress. She chose a heavy velvet gown trimmed in fur with a high neckline and long trailing sleeves in a vibrant shade of blue. Jaime entered the room just as she tied the last of the laces at her waist.

"How nice to find a woman on time for a change," he remarked approvingly. "Perhaps there is hope for you yet, my lady."

Only her flushed face betrayed Aleta's anger. While she'd bathed, she had decided to hold her tongue until she learned what her father had planned for Jaime Mortimer, for surely he wouldn't allow her to be spirited away to some remote place to wither and die.

He held his arm out to her. "Shall we go? I'm famished." He leered at her. "I'm certain your hunger must be as great as mine, my lady."

Ignoring his remark, Aleta lifted her pointed little chin in the air and hurried out the door before him. His laughter floated to her through the deserted hall and winding stairway as he quickly caught up with her. Grasping her hand, he placed it in the crook of his arm.

They descended the steps together and entered the great hall amidst much noise and boisterous chatter. But the moment they appeared in the great arched doorway, all conversation and laughter abruptly ceased. A hush fell over the assemblage and all eyes turned in their direction. Cringing inside, Aleta sought out her father. She found him seated beside Evan Grey. Lord Somerset's face was ruddy and his eyes bore into them with such blatant animosity she felt seared by the sizzling heat of his gaze. Though she realized his anger wasn't directed at her, it still was disconcerting to witness her father's obvious fear and hatred for the man she must now call husband.

Shifting her gaze to Evan, the breath left her chest as his ferocious glare seemed to include her. His eyes were wild, his face mottled, turning his handsome features almost ugly. Aleta shuddered, suddenly frightened of a man she had hoped to marry. Jaime felt her shudder and leaned over to whisper, "Fear not, my lady, they cannot hurt you."

"Why would they want to hurt me?" Aleta snapped curtly. " 'Tis you they would like to skewer, my lord."

"Aye." Jaime grinned. "For there is no doubt in their minds now that you are truly my wife." Deliberately he directed his gaze across the room to the wide balcony overlooking the great hall.

Aleta looked puzzled as she followed his gaze. Her cry of dismay seemed to release the tension in the room and the laughter and conversation resumed, only now she knew that she had been the object of those sly glances and bawdy remarks. Her anger grew in leaps and bounds as she stared at the balcony in absolute horror.

Hanging from the railing, the blood-spattered sheet that had just recently adorned their bed gave mute evidence that their marriage had been duly consummated beyond reasonable doubt. Aleta's face flamed and then drained of all color as she turned stricken eyes on Jaime. "Is this your doing, my lord?"

The rage and condemnation in her eyes gave Jaime an uncomfortable moment, making him doubt the rightness of his decision to display the proof of Aleta's virginity. For a brief moment he questioned his motives to use Aleta to seek vengeance on Evan Grey and Lord Somerset. Then the image of his father's lifeless body swinging from the gallows put everything back into perspective. He'd do whatever was necessary to prove his father had been the innocent victim of a conspiracy instigated by the Greys and Lord Somerset.

"Aye, my lady, 'tis my doing," Jaime freely admitted. " 'Twas not done to embarrass you, but rather to prove to those present that our marriage has been consummated and none can challenge the legality of our union. Besides, 'tis the custom."

"You could have ignored the custom, my lord," Aleta bit out from between clenched teeth.

Then suddenly Henry seemed to notice them for the first time as he motioned them forward. "Ah, the newlyweds have decided to grace us with their presence. Come in, come in and break your fast with us."

"We are being summoned, my lady." Jaime smiled, dragging her forward. "Take that sour look off your face and try to act like a proper bride."

"When hell freezes over," Aleta hissed, hiding her true feelings behind the false smile pasted on her face.

"Come sit beside me," Henry said enthusiastically, noting Aleta's mutinous expression and envying Jaime the taming of so glorious a creature.

Though Henry had met young Mortimer only yesterday, he admired the young man for his audacity in coming to court dressed in peasant garb to claim his betrothed bride. Against all odds the fierce young man had defended his father's innocence and even managed to wring a promise from him to look into the charges that had sent Clarence Mortimer to the gallows. And even though it might incriminate two men he trusted, he fully intended to learn the truth and right a wrong if one had been done.

Seating Aleta on the King's right hand, Jaime settled in the chair beside her. Immediately a page appeared to pour their ale and another with a trencher of food for them to share. Jaime dug in enthusiastically, amusing the King. " 'Tis said vigorous exercise during the night increases one's appetite."

Lord Grey heard the King's remark and nearly choked on a piece of meat. His face grew dark with rage when Jaime merely grinned in response and winked at Aleta. Aleta pretended not to have noticed, but her rising color provided great amusement to those assembled around the table.

"Well, my friend, will you remain at court or must you return to Criccieth?"

"Is that an invitation, Sire?" Jaime inquired.

Aleta paused, waiting breathlessly for Henry's answer. She wanted desperately to remain close to her father and Lord Grey until they could find a way to free her from the odious peasant to whom the King had wed her.

"Aye, 'twould please us to have you at court, but 'tis no order that you do so."

"Then I must refuse, Sire," Jaime said regretfully. "I will take my bride to Criccieth Castle while you investigate the charges against my father."

"Pity," Henry sighed. " 'Twould be most pleasing to have someone like you about to amuse before I return to France to claim my royal bride. Since you have no men-at-arms we will provide you with a dozen good archers, all trusted mercenaries, to guard your bride on your journey home. You may keep them should they choose to remain in your employ."

Surprised, Jaime arched a dark brow. "Your generosity is much appreciated, Sire."

"Aye, but you have snared quite a prize, and we can't have Lady Aleta roaming the countryside without proper escort, can we?"

"Nay, Sire, and I thank you. My bride's life must be protected at all cost. With your permission we will leave as soon as Lord Somerset releases his daughter's dowry into my keeping."

"We will see to it this very day," Henry promised. "Go then, Jaime Mortimer, but know that before we depart for France we will summon you and give you the result of our findings concerning your father."

Jaime couldn't have asked for a better ending to his reckless intrusion into Windsor Castle. He had gained a wealthy bride and obtained the King's promise to investigate the false charges made against his father. Not only had Aleta added greatly to his wealth but he had also gained the King's ear.

Aware that she would soon be at the mercy of her fierce husband, Aleta grew panicky. "Sire! I do not wish to accompany my—my husband to Criccieth. I wish to remain at court and serve your lady wife when you bring her back from France."

"Pay no heed to my bride, Sire," Jaime said smoothly. "I fear she's distraught at the thought of leaving her family."

"Nay, not so!" Aleta cried. "I fear for my life. No one knows what this man is like or what he's capable of. He merely wishes to use me in retaliation for some imagined offense against his father years ago. Everyone knows Lord Mortimer was a traitor to the crown. 'Tis obvious the son is no better."

Jaime's black eyes bored into Aleta's in cold scrutiny. "I vow, Sire, that I would not harm a hair on my lady's head."

"Sire!" Lord Grey interrupted, jumping to his feet. "I know the Mortimer family better than anyone, and I tell you a grave injustice was done by giving the Lady Aleta into this crude oaf's keeping."

Henry frowned. "We obeyed the dictates of the Church. The marriage is not up for debate. As you can see—" He motioned toward the offending sheet hanging from the balcony. "—the marriage has been consummated. Unless Lady Aleta tells us otherwise." He turned toward Aleta. "What say you, my lady? Do you deny the proof hanging above our heads?"

Aleta wanted to lie, wanted to tell all who would listen that consummation had not taken place, but she could not. Jaime Mortimer had made her his by right of possession and against her will had given her pleasure. Though she despised him enormously, how could she deny what she had felt in his arms?

"Nay," she whispered, casting her eyes downward.

"What say you, my lady?" Jaime asked, pretending not to have heard her tremulous answer.

Aleta's head shot upward and she glared at him furiously. "Nay," she repeated, her voice rising on a note of panic.

"Bastard!" Lord Grey shouted, shaking his fist at Jaime. "You'll pay for this! Aleta belongs to me. You lost the right to her the day your father betrayed his king."

Jaime would have leaped to his feet and charged Lord Grey despite his lack of weapon had not Henry placed a restraining hand on his arm. "There will be no violence done in my hall. The marriage is done and 'twould be best, Lord Grey, if you accepted it. As for you, Jaime Mortimer, take your lady wife to Criccieth till tempers cool. We suggest you get her with child as quickly as possible. Only then will this furor die down."

Jaime disagreed, aware that the so-called furor would exist until either he or Evan Grey ceased to exist. But he wisely kept his own counsel. "Aye, Sire, we will depart at dawn tomorrow."

"Oh." This from Aleta, who knew a despair far deeper than any she had ever experienced in her life.

Chapter 4

The moment Jaime turned to engage the King in deep conversation, Aleta slipped unobtrusively from her chair and hurried from the hall and up the steps leading to the tower where she and Jaime had spent the previous night. No longer able to bear the sight of the sheet hanging from the balcony in plain view of the King and his court, she wanted desperately to escape from the intolerable situation. How dare that despicable peasant she had married make a public spectacle of her, she silently raged. Hadn't he already taken more from her than she was willing to give?

She was halfway up the winding stairway when she heard her name whispered through the air. So softly was it spoken that she thought it her imagination, until she heard her name called a second time. Thinking her father had followed her in order to have a private word with her, she paused to await his arrival. But it wasn't Lord Somerset who suddenly appeared; it was Lord Grey.

"Lady Aleta, I would speak with you in private," Lord Grey said softly.

Somewhat wary, Aleta waited, aware that she was tempting fate by doing so. No telling what her brutish husband would do if he caught them alone. Unlike Lord Grey, Jaime Mortimer was no gentleman. While Evan climbed the last few steps that would bring them together, Aleta had time to study him more closely. They had met on several occasions, but she couldn't recall ever really scrutinizing his features other than to concede that he was a handsome man who wore his thick blond hair shaved closely at the neck in a most fashionable manner. He was clean-shaven, as was the custom of the day, and somewhat stocky, but not fat. His tight gray-and-green hose revealed legs corded with muscles and his yellow tunic was clearly designed to conceal a slight paunch around his middle. Funny she hadn't noticed that before, Aleta thought curiously.

Though Lord Grey was an imposing figure in his colorful clothing, there was something about his light-blue eyes that disturbed her. Perhaps it was because she had never been alone before with the man. Or because he looked at her somewhat differently now than he had before she had wed Jaime Mortimer. Perhaps it was his calculating manner. Though she fought against making a comparison between Lord Grey and Jaime Mortimer, it was difficult not to do so. It was so very obvious that Evan Grey came up lacking when compared to the commanding physical presence of her husband.

"Lady Aleta," Grey whispered furtively. " 'Tis important that I speak with you before you leave. It matters not that Mortimer has bedded you, I still want you." Not exactly true but close enough. "Your father and I have already made plans to free you from that traitor's whelp. It must be soon, before he gets you with child and squanders your dowry, so be prepared to act quickly."

"Free me?" Aleta asked excitedly. "How? Where?"

" 'Tis best you don't know the details, my lady," Grey said in a hushed voice, "but it will be very soon." He grasped her hand, drawing her close. "You were meant to be mine, my lady. I own everything that once belonged to the Mortimers, and possessing you, the woman meant to be Mortimer's bride, is my ultimate goal."

Aleta's eyes widened as she tried to make sense out of his words. It sounded as if he wanted her merely because she was the last piece of Mortimer property he did not yet possess. She had been Jaime Mortimer's betrothed bride before Clarence had turned traitor, and marrying her would gain Lord Grey every last Mortimer possession. But that was silly, she tried to tell herself. Lord Grey wanted her because he had fallen in love with her, or so her father had told her. It was as simple as that.

"You don't know Jaime Mortimer," Aleta said breathlessly.

"Nay, my lady, Jaime Mortimer doesn't know Evan Grey." He smiled derisively. "I will make him sorry he ever showed his face at Windsor Castle. The crude knave hasn't a shilling to his name, while I am rich and powerful and firmly in the King's favor. Fear not, my lady, you will be mine."

He was so close Aleta could see the sudden flare of madness deep within his eyes. It seemed to burn right through her and she shivered. "I—I must go," she whispered fearfully. "We mustn't be caught speaking like this."

Grey's face hardened. "I will kill Mortimer for

daring to take what belongs to me." Suddenly his arms tightened around her, bringing her so close she could feel the ridges of his thick muscles beneath his tunic.

"Lord Grey, please," Aleta said, suddenly frightened. She would never have guessed that Lord Grey could act in so aggressive a manner. Until now he had always been a perfect gentleman in her presence.

"Take your hands off my wife." The words were softly spoken but carried such menace that Lord Grey's hands instantly fell away from Aleta's waist. Aleta flattened herself against the rough-hewn stairwell, chilled more by Jaime's glowering expression than from the damp stone wall pressing into her back.

"I was merely bidding your lady good-bye," Grey said smoothly. "If you recall, we were nearly wed until you so rudely interrupted the ceremony."

"I also recall that you have stolen everything that once belonged to the Mortimers," Jaime charged. "Taking my bride would have been the culmination of all your dreams."

"Rebellious dogs like you and your father deserve no consideration. You may have fooled the King but you haven't fooled me. You'll always be a traitor's whelp without a shilling to your name and undeserving of the Lady Aleta. Beware, Mortimer," he warned. "Watch your back, for Lady Aleta will not remain with you for long."

"I can protect what is mine," Jaime said ominously. "And I give you fair warning, never touch my wife again. I share with no one."

Aleta gasped, stunned by Jaime's crude remark. Did he think she'd bed other men? Nay, she silently vowed, she'd remain chaste for the remainder of her life before she'd give him the satisfaction of accusing her of infidelity. Hopefully, her father would obtain an annulment and free her from a marriage she found distasteful.

"We shall see, knave." Grey smirked nastily. "We shall see who wins the fair Lady Aleta." Bowing jerkily to Aleta, he turned and disappeared down the winding stone staircase.

The moment he was out of hearing Jaime swung around to face Aleta, his features dark with fury. "Be gone, woman, before I vent my spleen on you!"

"I have done nothing," Aleta defended herself stoutly.

"Nothing, you say? Nay, my lady, nothing but meet secretly with a man you would call lover if I allowed it. But hear this: whatever you conspired with Evan Grey this day will not come to pass. Now go, before I beat you for your insolence."

"You wouldn't dare!" Aleta hissed. But when he made a move toward her she was astute enough to turn and flee up the stairs. Fortunately, he did not follow.

Aleta carefully avoided Jaime the rest of that day, preferring to spend time with the castle ladies in the solar. They met for the evening meal, where she was forced to share a trencher and cup with him. But as soon as the meal was over she fled quickly to the tower room, praying she would be asleep before he joined her. Her prayers were answered.

Jaime pushed open the door, staring moodily at the tousle-haired beauty asleep in the bed. There was just enough fire left in the grate to see the provocative outline of her slim body stretched out beneath the blanket. Her hair was touched with fire, the silver-blonde tresses glowing like a thousand shimmering diamonds. She looked so angelic, lying with one smooth arm curled over her head, that Jaime was tempted to touch her to see if she was real. But he didn't.

Nay, he knew full well she was real. He had tasted her succulent flesh, invaded the tender depths of her sweet body and sparked a response in her that was anything but angelic. Just thinking about thrusting himself inside her again brought an ache to his loins and sweat to his brow and very nearly caused him to lose control of his senses. Only the strict discipline he had imposed upon his body throughout the years saved him from doing something he knew he'd regret.

Lady Aleta despised him. She had called him a crude peasant lacking in manners. She thought him a landless pauper and hated the way he had garbed himself.

And he wanted nothing from Lady Aleta. Not her body or her wealth or her scorn. He had taken her merely to thwart Evan Grey.

After convincing himself that any woman in his bed would do as well as Aleta, Jaime threw off his clothes and climbed into bed beside her, careful not to touch her. Nevertheless, he was excruciatingly aware of the warmth of her body and it was a long time before he finally fell asleep.

Aleta greeted the cold dawn with trepidation. Though she wasn't physically aware of it she knew Jaime had slept beside her last night, for the indentation of his head still remained on the pillow. But since his side of the bed was cold she knew he had arisen hours ago and was preparing for their departure. Just then the object of her thoughts entered the room.

"We leave in one hour, my lady. If you would break your fast first, I suggest you arise and make ready. I will see that your trunks are loaded on the wagon." Then he turned and departed before she could form a reply.

Exactly one hour later Aleta was mounted on her palfrey and ready to follow her husband through the bitter-cold countryside to his crude abode. Though she had no idea what to expect once they reached the crumbling ruins of Criccieth Castle, she knew she wouldn't like it. Fortunately her dowry was available to improve their circumstances if Jaime chose to use it for that purpose.

The twelve mercenary knights provided by King Henry were garbed in mail, carried crossbows, and looked fierce enough to frighten any enemy daring enough to attack them. They rode huge war-horses that snorted and pawed the ground anxiously. Jaime was nowhere in sight but Gaylord was there, driving a wagon she assumed carried her dowry. In addition to the chests of gold and silver there would be linens, bedding, some furniture, and various items all brides were expected to bring to their new homes.

Then abruptly Jaime appeared, albeit a Jaime she had never seen before. Resplendent in silver mail, wearing a jewel-hilted sword, velvet tunic, and flowing cape lined with thick fur, he was mounted on a huge midnight-black stallion finer than any Aleta had ever seen. He spotted her immediately bidding her father good-bye, and reined his mount in her direction.

"Be prepared to ride long and hard, my lady, for

Criccieth keep is a monstrous long way," he warned.

"I am a good rider," Aleta retorted. "I'll not slow you down."

"See that you don't."

He was about to ride away when Aleta called, "My lord, how did you come by such finery? Methinks you have dressed yourself above your station. Or has the King gifted you with his cast-off clothing?"

Jaime smiled grimly. "Your dowry contains sufficient gold and silver to garb myself in the finest cloth and ride blooded stock."

Aleta flushed, aware that Jaime Mortimer would never allow her the last word. She watched him as he rode away, a commanding figure seated regally astride a magnificent horse worthy of his immense frame. Then she had no time for further rumination as Jaime gave the signal and the mercenaries rode off with Jaime in the lead. After a final wave to her father, she had no choice but to follow, with Gaylord and the wagon bringing up the rear.

The pace Jaime set was indeed brisk, but Aleta had no trouble keeping up. When the wagon fell behind, Jaime split the men-at-arms into two groups, sending six back to travel with the wagon and keeping six with him and Aleta. That night they sought hospitality at Craven Manor, the home of the Bridewells, whose cool reception was not unexpected by Jaime. The Mortimer name was still despised in England. But since the Somerset name was a respected one, they were not turned away. Aleta slept in blissful solitude since Jaime chose to bed down with his men in the great hall.

The following days were a repeat of the first, with shelter sought each night in various dwellings along the way. At the end of the third day Aleta was so sore and stiff she could barely dismount without help. But she was determined not to ask Jaime to slow their pace for her sake. Though he had barely spoken to her since they had left Windsor Castle, she was all too aware of his avid scrutiny. She knew immediately when his eyes were upon her, for she could feel the heat of his burning gaze warm her body despite the bitter cold.

Aleta knew they had crossed into Wales when they passed through the town of Flint. Grey Manor—previously known as Mortimer Manor—was nearby; it had once been Jaime's ancestral home but now belonged to Evan Grey along with the family wealth. It was to have been her home upon her marriage to Lord Grey. She could tell by the closed look on Jaime's face that he still considered it his property despite everything and harbored a wealth of bitterness and resentment for its present owner.

Disaster struck after they crossed the River Dee west of Flint and entered into the Clwdian Range, as rugged and desolate a country as any Aleta had ever seen. They rode in a valley created by hills rising on either side of them. It was cold, bitter cold, and Aleta burrowed deeply into the warmth of her thick, hooded cape. A shout was her first inkling that trouble of any kind existed. Glancing to the left, she saw a party of a dozen or so men armed with crossbows and bows and arrows spilling over the summit riding sturdy Welsh ponies. They were crudely dressed in furs and their bearded faces were fierce enough to frighten the bravest of men.

"Welshmen!" Jaime cried as he rode back to join

Aleta. "Hang on, my lady." Jerking the reins from her fingers, he spurred his stallion forward. Nearly unseated, Aleta grasped the pommel and hung on for dear life.

He headed directly toward the opposite hill. Up, up they climbed, followed by the six men-at-arms. The wiry Welshmen were close on their heels, brandishing weapons and screaming wildly at the top of their lungs. Daring to glance back over her shoulder, Aleta saw that the men-at-arms had reined in to make a stand. Though badly outnumbered, they had vowed to protect Jaime Mortimer and his lady and intended to do so. Besides, if they could stop the Welshmen long enough their six companions who rode behind with the wagon would soon catch up with them.

Aleta clung tightly to the back of her palfrey as Jaime led them into the trees. When one of the Welshmen broke through the line of men-at-arms, Jaime stopped long enough to nock an arrow into the crossbow and take aim. His aim was true, felling the Welshman with an arrow embedded cleanly into his heart. They continued on. When they were out of sight and sound of the fighting, Jaime brought the horses to an abrupt halt.

"Wait here," he ground out harshly as he reined his stallion back toward the fighting.

"Where are you going?" Aleta cried, alarmed.

"Think you I would leave my men to fight without me?" Then he jerked on the reins, causing his mount to rear and paw the air before thundering off down the hill.

Sliding from the saddle, Aleta's legs turned to rubber as she clung to the animal for support. What if the Welshmen overpowered Jaime and his men? she wondered desperately. What then would happen to her? As quickly as that thought formed, another took its place. The only way Jaime would let the Welshmen get to her was if he was dead. The thought was not comforting.

Sinking to her knees, she allowed her fear free rein before taking herself in hand. She was no simpering maiden afraid of her own shadow, she chided herself. She was Lady Aleta Somerset, proud, defiant, and—and—nay, she was afraid. She'd heard about the fierce Welshmen who roamed the hills in search of prey, attacking and murdering travelers indiscriminately. She remained on her knees for what seemed like hours, until the cold seeped through her bones, until she was so chilled she felt as if she'd break if she tried to move. Then, suddenly, Jaime appeared before her, looking like the devil himself astride his coal-black stallion.

"They're gone," he said, dismounting. "The rest of the knights arrived and helped chase them off." When Aleta made no answer, or move, he stared at her curiously. "Did you hear, my lady? They will not harm you."

Aleta looked at him dumbly.

"We questioned one of the wounded," Jaime continued, "and learned that they had been paid to attack us. But since the man wasn't the leader, he didn't seem to know the name of the man who had paid them. But a name wasn't necessary, I know full well who is responsible for the attack upon us."

Aleta blinked but did not respond.

"God's blood, woman!" Jaime roared. "Are you daft?"

Numb with cold, Aleta began to shake uncontrollably.

Suddenly aware of the frozen ground upon which she had been kneeling, Jaime cursed violently, then swept her up into his arms. Sitting on a nearby log, he cradled her in his arms, wrapping his cape around her as she slowly warmed to his touch.

"You're nearly frozen," he chided harshly.

"I—I—feared you'd—be—be killed—and I'd be at the mercy of those—Welshmen," she said through chattering teeth.

"Do you have so little faith in me?"

"I hardly know you. What I do know of you is hardly trustworthy."

Jaime chose not to answer. Instead, he asked, "Are you ready to continue on?"

"Aye, I'm ready," Aleta said, suddenly realizing that she reclined most comfortably on Jaime's lap.

Two days later they reached the sea. Aleta could smell the tangy aroma of salt and sea long before she heard the crash of surf against the cliffs. Jaime rode back to join her. "We are nearly there, my lady." His lips curled into a cynical smile. "I hope you won't be too disappointed in my humble home."

"I know not what to expect," Aleta said acidly. "You appeared out of nowhere dressed like the meanest villein, and yet somehow I doubt you're as poor as you pretend. Who are you really, Jaime Mortimer? Peasant? Devil's spawn? Some evil lord of darkness? Mysterious changeling?"

"Aye, my lady, all of those," Jaime agreed quite affably. "And I promise that in time you will know me by each and every name you have labeled me." He spurred his horse, leaving an echo of mocking laughter in his wake.

The castle keep rose in stark relief against a gray sky from a pile of crumbled rock and stone. Behind it the sea, whipped to a fine froth by the howling wind, crashed against the cliff upon which it stood. At one time the castle must have been magnificent, Aleta allowed, but all that stood now was a crumbling keep surrounded by a partial curtain wall hardly worthy of the name. The castle and its remote setting appeared utterly desolate. A shudder slithered down Aleta's spine. It was obvious that the cliff behind the ruined castle and high wall surrounding it would have made it impenetrable had it survived the ravages of time.

Jaime saw her shudder and frowned. "I'm sorry it does not meet with your approval, my lady." His biting sarcasm was not lost on Aleta. "I am but a humble peasant bereft of land and existing solely on nature's bounty and God's will."

"Humble indeed," Aleta muttered, spurring her palfrey forward. His amused chuckle followed her all the way to the rubble that had once been the gate house, a grim reminder of the castle's earlier splendor. She halted, wondering what would happen next since the place looked utterly deserted.

"Welcome home, my lady," Jaime mocked with wry amusement.

They entered the inner bailey, followed by the men-at-arms, who she was certain must have been as bewildered as she. Once inside the curtain wall Aleta saw that the inner bailey wasn't quite as she had imagined it. She even recognized a semblance of order amidst the crumbling stone of the ancient castle. She was startled to see two small boys appear from nowhere to take the horses to the stable, which was set against one of the sections of curtain wall still standing.

Jaime dismounted quickly, then helped Aleta. "Wait here," he ordered. "I would instruct the men first."

There was nothing welcoming about the keep, Aleta decided as she studied the square, gaunt structure that rose four stories into the air. She could imagine what the inside looked like and shuddered to think about the conditions under which she would be forced to live until her father freed her from this despicable marriage. Certainly Jaime Mortimer wasn't lying when he said his circumstances were humble. Yet, despite its austere appearance, the keep had about it a look of haughty grandeur with its four large towers jutting out to protect walls that no longer stood.

On the lower levels the windows were no more than slits in the immensely thick walls. The windows on the upper floors were cut in the shape of large keys and a steep staircase on the outside of the keep led directly to the second floor. Aleta had seen a few castles in her time and this one appeared to be several hundred years old.

While Jaime was deep in conversation with the men-at-arms, the wagon loaded with their valuables rattled over the drawbridge, followed closely by the knights. Jaime went immediately to greet Gaylord, quite forgetting that Aleta was left standing outside in the cold. Suddenly, from the corner of her eye, Aleta saw a flash of color at the top of the staircase leading into the keep. Swiveling her head, she saw a woman poised on the top step.

Dressed in crimson velvet, the woman appeared young and attractive. She started down the steps, her hips swaying seductively beneath the clinging folds of her gown. As she drew closer, Aleta saw that she was indeed young and quite lovely. Her skin was as white as the snow atop the mountain and her hair as black as a raven's wing. The contrast was startling. She was tall and willowy, her figure curved in all the right places though not overly voluptuous. Her eyes were a curious shade of violet that hinted of dark secrets and a violent nature.

It didn't take long for Aleta to guess who the woman was. She was Jaime's mistress, the one he had called Rowena.

All too soon Rowena was standing before her, eyeing her with open hostility.

"So he arrived in time."

"I beg your pardon," Aleta said haughtily. Though she tried to appear calm and collected, she fought the instinct to pull every hair from the violet-eyed beauty's head.

"Jaime wouldn't have brought you to Criccieth if he hadn't married you," Rowena announced sourly. " 'Tis a pity. You'll not be happy here, my lady."

"Whether or not I'm happy is none of your concern."

"Aye, but it is, for you see I am the woman Jaime wants, not you."

"If he wanted you so badly, why did he travel all the way to England for me?"

Rowena shrugged. "He has his reasons."

Though Jaime hadn't bothered to tell Rowena his reasons, she wanted Aleta to think she was privy to all his secrets. She had raved and ranted when Jaime told her his intentions to travel to England to collect his betrothed, but little good it did her. She was told in no uncertain terms that she could leave or stay, whichever suited her. Of course she had chosen to stay, for she knew Jaime

Mortimer enjoyed her as much as she enjoyed him. And he had said many times that he wanted no wife. But she had no idea that Aleta Somerset would be so lovely or desirable.

Aleta fought hard to control her temper as she silently vowed to harangue Jaime until he sent his mistress away. Having the woman in her home, such as it was, was too humiliating to be borne. Even if she didn't intend to share her husband's bed it would be utterly contemptible of him to keep his mistress under the same roof as his lady wife. But Jaime Mortimer had never pretended to possess one shred of decency.

"Ah, I see you've met."

"Jaime!" Rowena squealed, throwing herself into his arms. "I've missed you so."

Jaime tried to hold Rowena at bay but it was near impossible, so exuberant was her welcome. He glanced at Aleta, noting the sudden leap of flame in the blue depths of her eyes. Her face had turned to stone and her fists were clenched at the sides of her tense body. Sighing hugely, he deliberately set Rowena aside.

"Greet my lady wife, Rowena—the Lady Aleta." Then, turning to Aleta, he said, "My lady, this is Rowena Howard."

Aleta stared hard at Rowena, then deliberately turned her back. " 'Tis monstrously cold out here, my lord."

Jaime's eyes sparkled with amusement. Aleta wasn't about to acknowledge Rowena; a grudging admiration flared into life somewhere in the vicinity of his heart. "Forgive me, my lady, you must come inside where 'tis warm."

He offered her his arm. At first Aleta thought to refuse but a glance at Rowena changed her mind.

The dark-haired beauty was glaring daggers at Aleta and if looks could kill, Aleta thought, she would already be dead. Raising her pointed little chin, she allowed Jaime to lead her up the long flight of stairs. She had no idea what to expect once she got inside the ancient keep and steeled herself to expect the worst.

The stairs led to the forebuilding in one of the towers and into a garrison room, which occupied the entire second floor. The wellhead was also on that floor. From there Jaime led her up another flight of stairs to the great hall and solar. Aleta was pleasantly surprised by the condition of the great hall. Though all else might be crumbling, the inside of the keep was in surprisingly good shape. A huge stone fireplace took up one entire wall, flanked by benches topped with cushions. Astonished, she looked at Jaime.

"Did you expect a hovel?" he asked, anticipating her unvoiced question.

"Aye, 'tis what I was led to expect. From your manner of dress I naturally assumed you were destitute. I hope you enjoyed your sham."

"No sham, my lady. My father was stripped of all his wealth before he was put to death, leaving nothing to me but his memory."

"But ..." She looked around, noting the little touches of luxury that adorned the hall. "How do you account for all this?" She swept the hall with one slim arm stretched outward.

Jaime merely smiled but Rowena, who had followed them into the keep, said, "I find the keep quite comfortable—and Jaime more than generous."

Aleta sent her a fulminating glance. "Perhaps you are unaccustomed to the finer things in life.

As for my husband's generosity, do not expect it to continue. I am mistress of the keep now." She'd be damned if she'd let the black-haired witch get under her skin. If Jaime intended to keep his whore under his roof, she'd just have to let the witch know who was mistress of the keep.

Rowena opened her mouth to fling out a scathing retort but Jaime forestalled her. "Have you hired help from the village in my absence like I asked, Rowena?"

"Aye, Jaime," Rowena said importantly, " 'tis done. I've engaged another cook, kitchen helpers, stable boys, and serving women. Will they be enough?"

"For the time being," Jaime said. "Later Lady Aleta can inform Gaylord as to how many other servants she might require. There are plenty of villagers glad to have the work. Go tell Cook that we will sup in two hours." He turned to Aleta. "Come along, my lady, I'll show you the sleeping chambers on the fourth floor."

As he led her up another flight of winding stairway, Aleta felt the heat of Rowena's violet gaze on her back. On the fourth floor he opened the door to a large chamber consisting of an inner room and small outer room overlooking the cliff and beach below. The outer chamber was largely empty but the inner chamber held a bed, table, and single chair. A stone hearth in the sleeping chamber spread warmth to both rooms. Several woven rugs were scattered about the sleeping chamber and the windows were covered with heavy tapestries to protect against the cold. The bed was enclosed in hangings rich in color and design.

" 'Tis far more grand than I expected," Aleta allowed. "Is it mine?"

"Aye, my lady. 'Tisn't so grand as Mortimer Manor or Somerset Castle but it's been home to me since I was a young lad. I'm merely biding my time here until Mortimer Manor is restored to me. Meanwhile, I'll have your trunks carried up." He turned to leave.

"My lord, wait."

He swung around to face her. "Have I forgotten something?"

"Aye," Aleta said tightly. "Rowena. I demand that you send her away."

Chapter 5

Jaime's arrogant black brows slashed upward. Regarding Aleta with wry amusement, he asked lazily, "You demand, my lady?"

"Aye," Aleta muttered, beginning to tremble. Despite his mild tone Jaime looked so fierce she nearly lost her nerve. Until she remembered that she was his wife and had every right in the world to make demands. "Aye," she repeated more firmly. "Send your harlot to live in the village if you must have her near, but 'tis demeaning to have her in my home."

"It pleases me to keep Rowena here." Actually, he didn't care one way or another whether Rowena stayed but he wasn't about to admit it to Aleta.

Suddenly, all the amazing control Aleta had shown these past days since her forced marriage to Jaime Mortimer fled as she flew at him. Doubling her tiny fists, she pounded on his massive chest, so angry at him, the King, and all who conspired to disrupt her life that she consigned them all to hell in the most graphic language she knew.

"Cease, my lady, before you hurt yourself!" Jaime roared, amazed at the strength in her spindly arms. Though he hardly felt her blows, he suspected she suffered more from her attack upon his person than he did. Not yet thirty, he was at the peak of his physical prowess. His tall body was lean and tough with well-defined muscles ridging his chest, neck, and shoulders like bands of steel. He realized how mightily her hands must sting from her blows and caught them easily in one large fist.

"How dare you humiliate me by keeping your harlot under my roof!" Aleta railed, furious at finding herself rendered immobile.

"And how brave you are to strike me, my lady," Jaime retaliated, his expression thunderous. "This is my home and I will do as I please. The Lady Rowena will remain as my guest."

"Lady! Ha! If Rowena is a lady then I am a queen."

Seeing her now, her silvery tresses flying about her in wild disarray, her cheeks blooming from her anger and her blue eyes shot with flame, he could well imagine her a queen. And what a glorious queen she would make!

He made one more try to subdue her as he drew her close, so close he could feel her warm breath fan his cheek. Just looking at her made him think scandalously lewd thoughts—delicious thoughts. Releasing her hands, he grasped the sweetly rounded cheeks of her buttocks and pressed her against him in such a manner that every part of her was touching every part of him.

Gasping in dismay, Aleta's mouth flew open. His loins were full and heavy and she grew lightheaded as she felt him boldly prodding against the softness between her legs. With vivid clarity she recalled their wedding night and how Jaime had

wrung a response from her despite the initial hurt
he had caused her. And how she had writhed beneath him as he thrust into her time and again,
turning that pain into pleasure so profound she
still shivered whenever she thought about it. She
had hated him then, just as she hated him now,
and had been glad of the fact that he intended to
leave her in peace after the consummation. But
that had been before she had seen Rowena. And it
rankled when she recalled his words on their wedding night.

You are too new at love, my lady, to satisfy me,
Jaime had told her with a careless shrug. *But at
least you amuse me.*

Aleta remembered how her face had paled at his
crude taunt and how her answer had angered him.
*I thank God that I am too inexperienced to satisfy you.
But if you are seeking amusement, perhaps you should
look elsewhere.*

Jaime had no idea what Aleta was thinking but
he was suddenly so hot for her he wanted to
thrust himself into her until she begged for mercy,
and this despite his resolve to the contrary. He had
always considered it a weakness to want any
woman so fiercely, yet here he was lusting after
Aleta like an untried boy. Originally his plan for
Aleta was to use her to exact revenge against those
responsible for his father's death, not to become
obsessed with the little witch, he told himself. Still,
he recalled clearly the tempting curves of her
smooth white body writhing in open enjoyment
beneath him and the virginal heat of her sheath as
he thrust himself inside her.

He remembered how sweet her mouth tasted,
how wet and tight and wonderful she felt as he
impaled her with his weapon. She had fought him

tooth and nail and refused to yield, but he had
stroked the fires inside her into brilliant flame and
in the end she had been conquered. Aye, conquered, he thought glumly. He had mastered her
body, perhaps, but not her will. Her proud, defiant
spirit had refused to bend.

"Release me, my lord," Aleta panted. She found
it difficult to breathe with Jaime pressed against
her so intimately. The part of him she feared the
most rose like a staff of tempered steel between
them.

Her mouth was slightly open, her lips moist and
inviting. Jaime could no more resist the urge to
kiss her than he could stop breathing. Lowering
his head, he seized her lips in undisguised enjoyment, his tongue exploring their shape and texture
before pushing past her teeth into the warm intimacy of her mouth. Aleta made a guttural sound
of denial deep in her throat as Jaime thoroughly
and with great relish explored the sweet confines
of her mouth. He held her so tightly that each
breath was painful.

Then abruptly his hands began to move over
her body, fondling her hips, her buttocks, roving
the length of her spine, and Aleta felt a hot flame
shoot upward through her insides. But as exciting
as his hands were, the aggressive thrust of his
rigid shaft between their locked bodies was even
more arousing. Their clothing was no barrier for
his violent arousal as he urged her closer and
ground his loins against her.

Suddenly she felt herself spinning away from
him and she grasped the bedpost to keep from
falling. He was breathing heavily and his black
eyes were narrow condemning slits as he glared at

her as if he held her responsible for what had just transpired between them.

"What manner of woman are you?" Dark and accusing, his eyes probed her very soul. "Only a witch could burrow under my defenses so quickly as you have done. You obsess me, lady, and I won't allow it."

Aleta's brows shot upward as she eyed Jaime warily. "I am no witch, and I neither want nor invite your attentions. What I do want is for you to send Rowena away. You owe me that much."

"I will send her away when it pleases me," Jaime said sourly. He was still very angry at himself for nearly losing control with Aleta. He had too much at stake to became a fawning bridegroom spellbound by his wife.

Aleta's face grew rigid. "If I must suffer your harlot's presence in my home, then do me the courtesy of keeping her out of my way. She will not be welcome in my solar. Nor are you," she added meaningfully.

Jaime smiled, but the smile failed to reach his eyes. "I told you on our wedding night that I would trouble you no more, my lady. Unless, of course, you still insist that I send Rowena away. Then I will be forced to use you in her stead. If that is what you want, then I will banish her immediately."

"Nay!" Aleta cried, backing away. "I will not allow you to touch me again. I pray that my father and Lord Grey will find a way soon to free me from this odious marriage. I—I do not want a child whose grandfather was a traitor, nor one who will inherit neither land nor wealth from his father."

"Whose child do you want, my lady?" Jaime

asked, his face taut with barely suppressed rage. "Never say it is Evan Grey's child you want, for I will kill you both before that foul deed comes to pass. You are my wife and shall remain my wife. Nothing your father or Grey can do will change that."

They stared at one another, the tension between them so volatile it was like a bubbling volcano, threatening to explode at the slightest provocation. They would have gone on staring at one another, both proud and unyielding, if Rowena hadn't burst in on them.

The sultry beauty stared at them in narrow-eyed jealousy as she entered the room. If ever she had seen a man smitten, it was Jaime Mortimer, and she liked it not. Aleta Somerset had everything while she had nothing. Her whole world had collapsed around her when Jaime had informed her of his intention to bring back a wife from England. Despite that, she had chosen to remain at Criccieth; the thought of Jaime bringing home a wife hadn't bothered her all that much, until she saw the enchanting Aleta and the way she had enthralled Jaime. Ever astute, Rowena interpreted the situation between husband and wife accurately. She hoped to work the animosity that existed between them to her advantage. That Aleta was an unwilling bride was obvious. That Jaime was ignorant of the sizzling attraction between them was even more obvious. There was just one other piece of information to be gleaned from their relationship before she could concentrate on keeping Jaime tightly bound to her.

"What do you want, Rowena?" Jaime asked sharply as Rowena stepped into the room.

"The lady's trunks, Jaime, are they to be taken to your chamber?"

"Nay, my lady will rest easier in her own chamber," he remarked dryly. "I'm sure she will find it less—stressful." His cynical gaze swept over Aleta in a most distracting manner.

Feeling enormous satisfaction, Rowena swallowed the smug smile that hovered over her full red lips. It was just as she had suspected! she thought jubilantly. Jaime might be taken with his bride's beauty but apparently not enough to want to share her bed, which suited Rowena just fine. Aleta's loss was her gain.

Rising above the raging lust that had plagued him the moment he had touched Aleta, Jaime bowed courteously, his smile mocking. "I will leave you to your solitude, my lady. Dinner will be in the hall below. I will send one of the servants up to help you." Whirling on his heel, he walked past Rowena and out the door without a backward glance.

Rowena took Jaime's exit as an invitation to taunt her nemesis. Walking further into the chamber, she paused before Aleta in open challenge. "Why aren't you sharing your husband's chamber? Methinks he is none too pleased with his lady wife. Your innocent ways and inexperience must surely repel a virile man like my Jaime. But do not fear, my lady, I will keep him happy and contented, just as I have done since the day we met."

"Get out of here," Aleta hissed from between clenched teeth. "It matters little to me who my husband beds. There's no telling about the tastes of peasants. As for me, I'm more particular than he. If he chooses to bed a harlot, then I am pleased to be relieved of the onerous chore."

Rowena's face grew mottled. She would have flown at Aleta in fury if she didn't fear Jaime's retribution. Though she knew he didn't particularly care for his bride, she was still his lady wife and deserving of his respect. She knew Jaime well enough to know he wouldn't allow Aleta to be mistreated by her or any of the servants. Instead, she used barbed words to wound her adversary.

"Your husband doesn't care for you, my lady. How astute of you to accept it so graciously. I will leave you to your unpacking. I haven't seen Jaime for many days and nights, and we have much lost time to make up for." Having imparted those cruel words, she bestowed a sugary smile on Aleta and sidled from the chamber.

"Bitch," Aleta muttered as she slammed the door behind Rowena. Let Jaime have his whore, she told herself, for soon she'd be with a man who truly loved her and wanted her for herself. Jaime had been certain the attack by the Welshmen had been instigated by her father and Lord Grey, and had she realized it at the time she would have made an effort to escape instead of cowering in the trees worrying over Jaime's safety. Which brought up another matter entirely.

She might want to be rid of Jaime Mortimer but she didn't wish his death. If she could communicate with her father she'd tell him she only wanted her freedom, not a man's death on her conscience. It surprised her that her father had resorted to desperate measures to free her from an intolerable situation. She would have preferred that he seek an annulment instead of using devious methods.

Before Aleta could tackle her trunks, one of the newly hired servants from the village appeared and timidly asked if she would do as maid to such a great lady. Her name was Bess and Aleta liked her on sight. Old enough to be Aleta's mother, Bess was pleasantly rounded with an amazingly wrinkle-free face and soft brown hair interspersed with gray. Her hazel eyes crinkled at the corners when she offered a shy smile and her friendly manner endeared her immediately to Aleta.

"I would be pleased to have you as my maid, Bess," Aleta said graciously.

"Do you wish to bathe before you sup, my lady?" Bess asked. "It would be no trouble to have hot water carried up. There's a tub in the master's room that can be brought in for your convenience and placed before the fire."

"I'd adore a bath," Aleta said with alacrity. "Is there time?"

"Aye, if we hurry." Then she was gone, and Aleta sat down on the bed to wait. Lost in thought, she glanced around the large austere room, thinking that it would be made much more comfortable once some of the furnishings she had brought with her as part of her dowry were in place.

Meanwhile, in his own chamber on the same floor of the small keep, Jaime paced back and forth in angry contemplation. Had he been foolish to ride to Windsor Castle and make his presence known to his enemies, since they had thought him dead all these years? By bringing attention to himself he might be endangering the activities of the Lord of Darkness, activities that had proven extremely profitable in the past. Yet he couldn't stomach the thought that Evan Grey would have possessed every last thing that had belonged to him once the Lady Aleta became his bride.

And some good had come from his rash action.

He had gained the King's ear and wrung a promise from him to investigate the charges against his father. Of course it wouldn't bring his father back, but it could restore to him all that the Greys had wrested from the Mortimers through treachery. Aside from that, there was the Lady Aleta herself to consider. Aleta was a prize any man would covet. Aye, she was an encumbrance, he had to admit, and not the docile wife he desired. And more importantly, there was always the fear that she might discover his illegal activities and endanger all their lives.

And yet—yet, having met his lady wife, he had to concede that she had certainly made his life more interesting.

Then there was Rowena. What perverse demon made him insist that she remain at Criccieth? he wondered. Upon reflection he decided he had done it to spite Aleta after she had claimed that she didn't want his child. Somehow her words had hurt him more than he would have ever imagined. Every man wanted an heir, even him. One day, he vowed, when his title and property were restored to him, he'd have a child, but not until then. Whether or not Aleta was the mother of that child remained to be seen.

Suddenly, in the midst of his pacing, the door to his chamber burst open and Rowena rushed inside. "Jaime, my lord!" She flung herself into his arms. "I have not had time to welcome you properly." Her arms went around his neck and she pulled his head down to meet her lips. But for some reason Jaime couldn't work up the enthusiasm to respond, despite the fact that he hadn't had a woman since his wedding night.

It wasn't that Rowena wasn't appealing, for she

had pleased him well since the first day she had come to the keep with her brother, seeking shelter on a stormy night. They had become lost in the blinding snow, and fortune had smiled on them when they arrived at Criccieth keep. Crumbling though it might be, there was a warm fire, food—and a handsome rogue named Jaime Mortimer. When Trevor Howard left Criccieth keep several days later, Rowena had remained. That was two years ago.

"Ahem. My lord, do I interrupt?" Gaylord stood at the door. Ordinarily the scene he had burst in upon wouldn't have fazed Gaylord, knowing Jaime and the hot-blooded Rowena so well, but since Jaime was now a married man, he thought it beneath Jaime to trifle with his harlot under his lady wife's very nose. His disapproving frown gave mute testimony to his feelings.

"Come in, Gaylord," Jaime invited as he unwound himself from Rowena's clinging arms. "Rowena was just leaving."

"But Jaime," Rowena said with a pout, sending Gaylord a baleful glance, "I haven't seen you in days and days and I missed you so. Send the old man away, you can speak with him anytime."

"Nay, Rowena, I would speak to Gaylord now. Go, we will have time together later, after we have supped." Though his words promised untold delights, his eyes lacked the warmth of conviction.

Still pouting, Rowena strode huffily from the chamber. Gaylord quietly closed the door behind her. "You tempt fate, my lord," the old man chided sternly. "God's blood, Jaime, you bring yourself no honor by flaunting your mistress before Lady Aleta. I questioned your wisdom before you married, but now that I have met your lady wife I question your sanity. Life will not be easy at Criccieth keep."

"Life never was easy, Gaylord," Jaime replied. "Surely you above all others know I have no time for a wife. I married Aleta to keep Lord Grey from having her. There is no love involved—on either side. You heard her, she despises me. She lives for the day her father will free her from this marriage and give her to Lord Grey. That day will never come."

" 'Tis dangerous having her here," Gaylord warned. "What if she discovers you're involved in smuggling? It will be the end of us, for if she truly hates you as much as she seems to, she'll not hesitate to betray you."

"I promise she'll not betray me!" Jaime vowed harshly.

"What about Rowena? So far she is ignorant of the identity of the Lord of Darkness, but what will happen if she finds out?"

Jaime smiled. " 'Tis only Aleta I'm unsure of, not Rowena. Rowena is the one woman I can trust."

"Heed me well, Jaime, you place your trust falsely."

"Nay, Gaylord, our secret is safe with Rowena."

"Do you intend to bed the woman beneath your lady wife's nose?"

Jaime scowled. " 'Tis my business and mine alone, Gaylord. You came here for a purpose—what is it?"

"The Lady Aleta's dowry. What should I do with the chests of gold and silver?"

"Place them in the secret room beneath the floor of the keep. I already have a substantial hoard of gold and silver earned from selling our smuggled

goods so I truly do not need her dowry. Nor do I
intend to claim the lands that came to me upon
my marriage to Aleta until I have won back my
rightful place in society. As for the household
goods, ask Aleta how she wishes to dispose of
them; they are hers to do with as she pleases."

"Aye, my lord," Gaylord said, disgruntled over
Jaime's callous disregard for his bride. Intuition
told him that Jaime wasn't as unaffected by Aleta
as he pretended. But the lad was stubborn, and it
would take a miracle to bring them as close as a
husband and wife should be. And keeping
Rowena underfoot wasn't going to help matters
any. After sending Jaime a censuring look, he
turned and left the chamber.

Jaime was already seated at the table in the hall
when Aleta joined him for the evening meal.
Rowena was there too, seated on Jaime's left. Aleta
slid into the empty seat at Jaime's right. Looking
down the long table, she smiled and nodded at the
knights who had accompanied them from England. They smiled back, all of them quite taken
by their employer's lovely lady. There were even
some disapproving looks aimed at Jaime when
they realized that Rowena was his mistress. It was
obvious they thought he showed enormous disre-
spect by seating her at the same table as his lady
wife.

"You're late," Jaime grumbled as he pushed his
trencher closer for Aleta to share. He thought she
looked quite fetching in a deep-blue gown and a
golden-veiled *hennin* all but covering her shimmering tresses. When he stared at her overlong,
Rowena frowned in annoyance and tried to distract him.

"Jaime, tell me about your journey to England. Did you see the King?"

Jaime turned to Rowena but his mind was still on Aleta. Though Rowena was undeniably lovely, Aleta's golden beauty far surpassed Rowena's sultry darkness. "Aye, I saw the King."

"What does he look like?"

Jaime frowned, unaccustomed to judging other men's looks. "Perhaps Aleta can best describe the King. What say you, my lady, can you describe King Henry for Rowena?"

Aleta did her best to comply, though she'd rather have concentrated on her food, which was surprisingly delicious. "Henry is young and quite comely," she allowed graciously. "His hair is dark and clipped short in the current style." Here she paused, eyeing Jaime's unfashionably long hair with open disdain. "Some call him the warrior king, and indeed he has proven himself a fierce defender of England. He is to return to France and marry soon."

Rowena was sorry she had asked the question, for while Aleta was talking Jaime seemed unable to take his eyes from her. To counteract the potent pull Aleta had on Jaime's senses, Rowena slid back her chair and whispered loud enough for all to hear, "My lord, I will leave you now and await you in your chamber." Then she sidled from the hall before Jaime had time to recover from the shock left in the wake of her words. He never imagined she would be so bold.

"Do not linger on my account, my lord," Aleta said sweetly. "I would hate to have your whore grow anxious. As you can see, I am still enjoying the delicious meal prepared by your excellent cook. Gaylord will stay and keep me company."

"Indeed, my lady," Gaylord agreed, sending Jaime a disapproving glare.

"I shall do as I please," Jaime thundered, settling himself back in his chair. "And it doesn't please me to retire so early. Finish at your leisure, my lady, and I will see you to your room."

And linger she did. In fact, Aleta was certain it was the longest meal in history. But as all things must, it came to an end and she indicated that she was ready to retire. Jaime leaped to his feet to assist her. Taking her arm, he led her toward the stairs. They wound their way up the spiral staircase in tense silence.

When they reached her chamber, Jaime bowed courteously and said, "Tomorrow you may explore the keep at your leisure. It isn't a large one, so you'll have no difficulty finding your way around. I'm certain either Gaylord or Rowena will show you around if you'd like." He stared at her hard for a moment, then turned and strode off down the hall toward his room.

Aleta watched him walk away, power emanating from every virile inch of him, painfully aware that he was going to Rowena. Some devil in her made her call out, "Good night, my lord, I wish you joy of the night and all that it brings to you," Then she entered her room and closed the door quietly behind her.

Jaime froze in mid-stride but did not turn. When he heard Aleta's door close he continued on to his room. Rowena was waiting for him, just as she had promised. Curled naked in the center of his bed, she stretched languorously, displaying her ample charms enticingly.

"You've kept me waiting, my lord." Her full lips curved into a charming little pout.

Jaime's brow furrowed. He was strangely un-
moved by her blazen sexual display, and he had
no idea what was wrong with him. Two weeks
ago he wouldn't have hesitated a moment to take
full advantage of what Rowena freely offered. But
now ... God's blood! he swore to himself. Aleta
was a witch capable of stealing his manhood!
Rowena was opening her arms, inviting him to
participate in the lustful pursuits they had enjoyed
time and again in the past, but to his utter disbelief and heartfelt disgust he felt no stirring in his
loins. No urgent need driving him. He turned
away and walked to the narrow window, pushing
aside the tapestry that covered the opening so he
could look out. What he saw on this nearly moonless night far out into the bay pushed all thought
of Rowena aside as he whirled away from the
window and strode from the chamber.

Rowena was stunned. "Jaime! Where are you
going?"

"I have business to attend to," he flung over his
shoulder. "Go find your own bed, I may not return
this night."

"You're going to her!" Rowena accused hotly.
"Can't you see that your wife doesn't want you?"

Her words were lost on Jaime, who had already
started down the stairs. Gaylord met him at the
foot of the stairs, on his way up to find him.
"You've seen the ship," he said anxiously.

"Aye, 'tis a week early. Summon the men, we
must give the signal and meet them on the beach
below. The tide will soon run out and 'tis dangerous for them to linger so close to shore."

Aleta couldn't sleep. Her mind was filled with
images of Jaime with Rowena, doing all those

wonderfully arousing things he did to her on their wedding night. Finally, during the darkest side of midnight, she rose and reached for the flagon of ale Bess had left at her bedside in case she thirsted during the night. If not for the burning embers in the hearth, the room would have been as black as pitch. As she drank her ale, Aleta became aware of noises drifting through the eerie night from the beach far below the keep. Curious, she made her way to the window. Pushing the tapestry aside, she gazed down on the windswept beach where breakers were pounding against the shore.

Lights. Many, many lights dotted the beach and Aleta watched in utter fascination as the lights moved freely about the narrow strip of sand below the cliffs. Far out in the bay she could see the winking lights of a ship, growing bright and dim in turn as the vessel rode the undulating waves. She watched so long her feet grew numb from the cold. And when she went in search of her slippers and returned, the lights were gone and the beach was blanketed in total darkness. Had she imagined the lights? she wondered. What could possibly be taking place down there at this time of night? When no answer became clear, she returned to bed to ponder the mysterious phenomenon. It was nearly dawn before she fell into a fitful sleep.

Jaime returned to the keep just as the sky turned from the deepest purple to mauve. The smuggled goods had been safely stored away in a secret room beneath the bottom floor of the keep and would be distributed to area merchants later. But now, after the long night's toil, all he could think of was a few hours of much-deserved sleep. He was still sleeping soundly when Aleta left her chamber the next morning and entered the great hall. The only person present was Rowena, who was eating by herself in splendid solitude. Taking a seat at the table, Aleta did her best to ignore the sultry beauty.

"Good morrow, my lady," Rowena said cheerily. "If you're wondering where Jaime is, wonder no more. The poor man had a most tiring night and is still abed." Though she had no inkling of Jaime's actual labors during the strenuous night, it fed her ego to let Aleta think she and Jaime had spent the night together in romantic pursuit. "Your husband is a magnificent lover—so strong, so tireless. But then I suppose you already know that." She sighed dreamily.

"If he is so tireless, what are you doing up so early, Rowena?"

Rowena sent Aleta a quelling look. "I have responsibilities here. I must instruct the servants in their duties." She rose to leave.

"Normally all responsibility inside the keep falls to the lady of the manor," Aleta replied haughtily. "As the master's whore you have little to say in the running of the keep."

Rowena gasped in outrage. "I am more to Jaime than his whore! And since I hired the servants I will instruct them."

Aleta's stubborn little chin rose in the air. "I think, Rowena Howard, that you place too much importance upon your place in the keep. Please confine your duties to the master's bed."

Rowena glared murderously at Aleta. "You will be sorry for those words, my lady." Then she flounced from the hall, leaving Aleta fuming in impotent rage.

So her husband and Rowena had played bed games all night, Aleta thought furiously. It served the rogue right if he couldn't get himself out of bed today. Not that she wasn't grateful to Rowena for performing a duty she had no intention of performing herself, she tried to tell herself. For all she cared, Jaime could sport with his mistress all night, every night.

And yet . . . The hurt was still there. The hurt and resentment and shame. It stirred within her heart like a giant claw, plucking at her pride and leaving her naked and vulnerable.

Stubbornly Aleta refused to acknowledge another stirring in her heart—this one even more humiliating and painful.

Chapter 6

$\sim\!\!\sim\!\!\infty\!\!\sim\!\!\sim$

Two weeks later Aleta was once again awakened during the night by strange doings below on the beach. But she rarely saw Jaime alone to question him. They met at the evening meal, where Rowena was usually present, fawning over Jaime until Aleta felt sick to her stomach.

Little by little Aleta had taken over the reins of the household, as she had been taught to do by her mother before she died. It delighted her no end to see the servants come to her for orders instead of depending on Rowena. Some of her success in the household had been due to Gaylord, she acknowledged, for he had told the servants in no uncertain terms that Aleta was the lord's wife and mistress of the keep.

Having the servants call Jaime lord was puzzling to Aleta. In truth, Jaime was no lord at all but a peasant stripped of his title and wealth, yet they treated him like he was a god and insisted upon calling him by a title he no longer held and certainly didn't deserve.

When Aleta had been at Criccieth a month and once again noted unusual activity on the beach below the keep, she decided to question Bess on the matter. When the tiring woman entered her chamber the following morning, Aleta asked her conversationally, "How long have you lived in the village, Bess?"

"All my life, my lady," Bess answered, pleased by Aleta's attention.

"You must know everything that occurs," Aleta continued innocently.

"Oh, aye, my lady, there's not much that gets by Bess Leland."

"Are you married, Bess?"

"Aye, my lady, these past twenty years to a good man named Daffid. We have three boys, all grown and married, and seven grandchildren."

"How do your husband and boys make their living?" Aleta asked curiously. "When I rode through the village it appeared quite prosperous."

A closed look settled over Bess's plain features. "They manage, my lady."

"And the other villagers? Do they depend on the sea for their livelihood?"

"The sea, my lady?" Her face lit up. "Oh, aye, the sea. They most surely do make their living from the sea."

"Do they engage in frequent night-fishing?"

Bess frowned, puzzled by Aleta's line of questioning. "Nay, my lady, not so much."

"I thought perhaps it would explain the lights I've seen sometimes on the beach below the cliffs late at night. Have you noticed them?"

"Lights on the beach?" Bess was a simple soul, not given to deviousness or lying, so when Aleta's question caught her off guard she answered without hesitation. "You must mean the lights that appear when the Lord of Darkness . . ." Suddenly her hand flew to her mouth and her eyes grew wide with alarm. "Oh, my lady, pay no heed to my ramblings. Daffid always said I talked too much."

"Nay, Bess, I am most interested. Who and what is the Lord of Darkness?"

"He is no one, my lady, just an old wives' tale I heard at my mother's knee." Turning abruptly, she busied herself with chores, making it abundantly clear that the subject was closed. Aleta sighed, realizing she'd get nothing more from Bess. But she was determined that sooner or later she'd get to the bottom of the strange occurrences on the beach.

That evening Rowena was late arriving in the hall for the evening meal. Taking advantage of her absence, Aleta asked Jaime if she might go riding, since a break in the weather was producing most pleasant days.

Jaime stared hard at her for a moment, then said, "Aye, my lady, as long as you take two men-at-arms with you. Tell Gaylord the day before you wish to ride and he will arrange it for you."

"Two men-at-arms!" Aleta gasped, annoyed. "What danger exists in so desolate a spot?"

"Danger exists everywhere, Aleta," Jaime said softly. *Indeed*, he thought but did not say, *each time I am with you, I place myself in grave danger of succumbing to an emotion that has no place in my life at this time*. "But since I doubt either your father or Grey would dare risk the King's wrath and show up on my doorstep, 'tis safe enough to ride. Lord Grey is too fond of the pleasures found at court to bury himself in the country."

"You're so generous, my lord," Aleta shot back sarcastically. "If it is safe, then why must I have a guard? Are there other dangers I should know about?"

"What dangers are you referring to, my lady?" Jaime kept his expression purposely bland, but inside he was seething. What did Aleta know?

"Am I the only one in the keep to notice those strange activities taking place late at night on the beach?"

His eyes narrowed and his back became ramrod-straight. "Strange activities? I fear you are being fanciful, my lady. I have noticed nothing unusual. Perhaps 'tis merely fishermen you heard or saw." His eyes clung to hers, analyzing her reaction to his simple explanation.

She lowered her eyes. "Perhaps," she allowed, not at all convinced.

Then Rowena arrived and the subject was dropped. But not forgotten. Aleta remembered it because she had vowed to get to the bottom of the mystery, if there was one. Jaime remembered it and cursed himself for having given Aleta the chamber overlooking the beach. He should have installed in her the smaller, safer room facing the mountains. How was he to know she was such a light sleeper?

This past month had been a busy one for the Lord of Darkness. Two ships had arrived with contraband goods and his secret room was near to bursting with smuggled items. He intended to get rid of most of them soon, but now that Aleta had stumbled upon his activities he was in a quandary. If she had noticed the activity on the beach she was bound to hear the men moving the goods from the keep to the waiting wagons. Noises carried within the old stone walls, and the slightest scrape of a barrel or cask was certain to arouse her suspicions. The longer he pondered the dilemma the more the answer eluded him. He certainly couldn't afford to have Aleta involved in his illegal activities. Nor could he allow her to discover his secret and betray him and nearly every man in the village.

"You are quiet tonight, my lord," Rowena said, sidling so close to Jaime he could feel the heat of her body penetrating his clothing.

Jaime hadn't shared her bed since he had brought home a wife, and it puzzled and frightened her. She knew from servants' gossip that Jaime wasn't bedding Aleta and couldn't imagine what was keeping him celibate. It wasn't like the virile, lusty lover she knew so well to eschew the sensual side of his nature.

Jaime sent Rowena a blank look, so caught up in thoughts of Aleta that for a moment he forgot Rowena was still living in the keep. Nothing about her seemed to please him of late. She was too tall, her breasts too large, her dark sensuality too blatant—all these and more made her unappealing to him. He really should send her away, he thought, but felt pity for her.

Rowena had insisted that she had nowhere to go since her brother had pledged himself to one of the minor barons somewhere in Wales. Jaime decided to instruct Gaylord to find Rowena's brother and send Rowena to him forthwith. But that still did not solve the problem at hand. Somehow he had to keep Aleta occupied during the nights it would take to move the smuggled goods from the keep. Suddenly he smiled, remembering something he had nearly forgotten. It would take some work but it could be accomplished.

Two days later Aleta looked out the window and saw the approach of a glorious day. She made plans immediately to ride, only she wasn't going to take men-at-arms with her. She was perfectly capable of taking care of herself, she thought defiantly. Jaime could rant and rave all he wanted; she wouldn't be ordered around like a small child. She hurriedly donned a green velvet riding dress, snitched a substantial snack from the kitchen, and left the keep before anyone was aware that she was gone. Fortunately neither Gaylord nor Jaime were in the keep and she had deliberately arisen before Rowena was up and about in order to avoid answering questions.

The inner bailey was deserted, so she assumed the knights were out with Jaime somewhere. She went directly to the stable where one of the stable boys saddled her palfrey without protest. Minutes later she rode from the keep, happily munching an apple. She meant to explore the village first, then ride out into the countryside where signs of spring were evidenced in the budding trees and tender shoots of new grass springing up through the rich black soil.

The village shops and outlying cottages appeared to be in good repair, with thatched roofs and walls intact. She greeted goodwives out sweeping their doorstoops and visited merchants, amazed by the quantity and variety of goods available in a country so recently ravaged by war. Everywhere she went she was given a warm welcome, offered a cool drink, and treated with the courtesy due a lord's wife, though Jaime was no lord. When the sun was high in the sky, she left the village and rode out into the open countryside. She stopped beside a bubbling brook to eat the bread and cheese she had pilfered from the kitchen, seating herself atop a flat rock while her horse grazed nearby.

Replete, Aleta rose to leave, intending to ride back to the keep. The thunder of hooves brought her spinning around. Squinting into the sun, she saw a rider mounted on a powerful steed approach at a reckless speed. Her first thought was to flee. It could be Jaime coming after her, she realized, and in a fine rage for having been deliberately disobeyed in the matter of the guard. But as the rider drew closer she realized it wasn't Jaime. He wasn't riding that fierce black stallion Jaime was so fond of and he was dressed in colorful attire which her husband avoided with a passion.

"Aleta!"

She recognized the voice immediately.

"I've been riding this way every day for the past two weeks, hoping to find you alone."

"Lord Grey!" Stunned, Aleta watched warily as his steed drew to a halt before her. "I thought you were in London."

"Nay, my lady, I have been in Wales nearly as long as you. I'm on the King's business, but you are the primary reason I am in Wales, Aleta." His penetrating gaze seemed to pierce her.

Aleta blushed, embarrassed by the naked hunger in his eyes. "What business does Henry have in Wales, my lord? She hoped her question would serve to turn his attention on something other than herself.

"Smuggling business, my lady, but that doesn't concern you. The King is being deprived of much-needed revenue, and I, as official tax collector of the area, am responsible for bringing the smugglers to justice."

"Smuggling!" Aleta exclaimed. Something connected in her brain. Something that needed further thought. "How terrible. Do you have any leads?"

"Nay, my lady, just suspicions. And a name that makes no sense. But enough of unpleasant business," he said, dismounting and clasping her hands in his. "Your father and I have been worried about you. That brute doesn't mistreat you, does he?"

"I am fine, my lord, truly. But what of my father? Is he well?"

"Aye. He stayed behind in London to pursue your annulment. I still want you, Aleta." His bold eyes swept her face and body in a most disconcerting way. "Come away with me now, my lady. I will take you to Grey Manor. 'Tis highly defensible and I have enough men to protect you from Mortimer should he be foolish enough to come after you. I'll wager that once you are in my home, he will agree to an annulment readily enough. For all his faults, Mortimer is a proud man who will not want you back after you and I have—er—after you are in my possession."

Aleta was stunned. What Lord Grey was suggesting was immoral, yet she couldn't help thinking that Jaime would be glad to be rid of her and not bother to fight for her. Why should he want her when Rowena performed all the necessary duties of a wife? Besides, he hadn't enough men to challenge Evan in battle.

"I doubt my husband would miss me," Aleta revealed, trying to keep the hurt from her voice.

"Do I detect a note of regret?" Grey asked, frowning. "Do not tell me you've grown fond of that crude peasant."

"Fond? Nay, never say it, my lord. He wants me merely as a means to gain his own ends, whatever they might be. I want a man to love me for myself."

Grey's eyes gleamed slyly as he drew Aleta closer. "I love you, my lady, I have always loved you. You need an older, wiser man to protect you and treat you gently, not some young hotheaded whelp who would misuse you and squander your fortune. The King was remiss in giving you to Jaime Mortimer, but I shall remedy that."

To impress his words upon her, he drew her roughly against him, crushing her lips with a fervor that belied his promise of gentle treatment. His lips were hard, his tongue a rapacious dagger as it stabbed hot and insistent past the barrier of her teeth into her mouth. His hands grasped her hips, dragging her against him with such force the breath was slammed from her.

His kiss shocked her. Had she ever really known Lord Evan Grey? she wondered, suddenly frightened by his brutal display of power. She moaned, trying to convey her displeasure over his careless handling, but Grey mistakenly thought her aroused by his ardor and increased the pressure of his mouth.

Nothing could stop him now, Grey thought gleefully as he ravished Aleta's tender mouth. He and Aleta would ride away from this place to his home where he would keep her for his pleasure, satisfied that he finally had everything that had once belonged to the Mortimers, whom he had good reason to despise. Once her father had obtained an annulment to her marriage to Mortimer, he would marry her and take possession of her fortune. After he tired of her and her looks had faded from constant childbearing, he would leave her safely in the country to care for his offspring while he sported with his mistresses in London.

He was about to break off their kiss and help

her mount her horse so they could ride away when he happened to glance behind Aleta and see Jaime glaring at him from atop his magnificent black beast. He froze, his hands sliding away from Aleta's hips. Stunned to find herself free, Aleta reeled backward. She caught her balance and righted herself just as Jaime spurred his mount and plucked her from her feet, placing her on the saddle before him. Aleta let out a cry of dismay as she felt his arms bruise her rib cage. She hadn't even known Jaime was anywhere nearby.

His arrogant black brows were set into a straight line, his jaw was clenched and his mouth taut with threat. "Had I known you intended to meet your lover I would have confined you to the keep, my lady," he said grimly.

Aleta swiveled her head to glare mutinously at him. "I have no lover."

"Maybe not, but you would have had my arrival been delayed a moment more. Lord Grey was so hot for you he would have taken you on the ground if I hadn't interfered."

"You despicable knave!" Aleta cried, raising her hand as if to strike him.

"Go ahead, my lady," Jaime dared, "but be prepared to suffer the consequences."

His warning did not go unheeded. Though backing down wasn't her style, Aleta thought it prudent at this time. Her hand dropped to her side but she continued to glare at him with murderous intent. Smiling ruefully, Jaime turned his attention to Lord Grey.

"What are you doing in Wales, Grey? I thought the country held little appeal for you."

"I'm on the King's business," Grey said, in full control of himself again. "Of course you'd know nothing of the smuggling going on in the area, would you?"

Jaime laughed humorlessly. "Smuggling? Nay, I know nothing of smugglers. But I suppose chasing nonexistent smugglers is as good excuse as any for being where you don't belong. The land you're standing on happens to belong to me. The castle and attached land, worthless though it may be, was deeded to me by my mother. It is the one thing you cannot take from me. Listen well, Grey: if I ever catch you near my wife again, I'll kill you."

"You don't deserve Lady Aleta," Grey sneered, backing away cautiously. Something in the young man's expression sent fear coursing down his spine. He'd never seen such cold, ruthless eyes. Without armed men behind him Grey hadn't the courage to challenge Jaime. "She despises you, you know," he continued, striking at Jaime with barbed words. " 'Tis me the Lady Aleta wants. I will have her yet, Mortimer. In my bed, on her back, begging for my attention." Without waiting for Jaime's reaction, he vaulted onto his steed and bolted away.

"Coward!" Jaime spat. "It appears your would-be lover is afraid to stand and fight for you, my lady."

Aleta couldn't believe her ears. Lord Grey's crude language shocked her greatly. She was beginning to doubt he was the gentleman she'd assumed him to be. And why hadn't he stood up to Jaime? Was he the coward Jaime claimed him to be or had he merely been acting with prudence? Whatever his reason, she hadn't expected him to turn tail and run, leaving her to face her husband's wrath alone. And just one look at Jaime's glowering expression told her how greatly she had angered him.

"As for you, my lady," Jaime said, turning his chilling gaze on her, "you have gone too far this time. I fear you must be taught a painful lesson." Releasing his grip on her rib cage, he pushed her rudely to the ground. He quickly dismounted before she could rise, planting a booted foot in the middle of her stomach to hold her down. Though she knew Jaime to be a hard man, she had never considered that he would actually hurt her.

"What are you going to do?" Fear shivered through her when he withdrew his riding crop from his belt and slapped it against his palm in a threatening manner. "You wouldn't dare beat me!" Aleta challenged bravely.

"You have more courage than sense, my lady," Jaime sneered. "I'll do whatever is necessary to keep you from straying again to meet your lover. If I hadn't passed through the village and learned that you were out and about alone, I wouldn't have known you planned to betray me with my enemy."

"You're a fool, Jaime Mortimer!" Aleta shrieked as she tried to lift Jaime's foot from her middle. He reacted by exerting more pressure. Aleta gasped for breath, certain now that he meant to kill her. Who would stop him? "I might hate the idea of being married to you, but I'd never betray you."

"Say on, lady," Jaime said sarcastically. "Why is it I don't believe you?"

"Because you're a disgusting oaf who wouldn't know the truth if it stared you in the face."

"You go too far," Jaime warned in a voice so low and menacing Aleta's face drained of all color. Suddenly the weight of his foot lifted, but instead of freeing her he merely flipped her onto her stomach. She heard the riding crop swish against his thigh and steeled herself for the first painful bite of the whip.

But Jaime wasn't satisfied to beat her through the layers of her clothing, it seemed, for he pulled the cape from her shoulders, grabbed a handful of material at her neck, and ripped downward. Aleta moaned in protest when cool air whispered against the bare skin of her back.

Jaime had every intention of beating his wayward wife, not enough to hurt her unduly, but certainly enough to make her think twice before disobeying him again. But the sight of her vulnerable back, so white and smooth and unblemished, brought a cry of raw anguish from his throat. At that moment beating Aleta was the very last thing he wanted to do.

Goosebumps rose on her exposed flesh while her clenched fingers plowed furrows into the musty earth. Her eyes closed tightly and Jaime saw her body tense, waiting ... Waiting ... She had no idea how profoundly the sight of her bared flesh was affecting Jaime, or that Jaime had never in his life struck a woman. All she knew was that she had angered him beyond redemption and he fully intended to punish her. When no blow fell after what seemed like hours but was in reality just moments, Aleta gathered her courage and swiveled her head to stare at him. The riding crop, once raised in anger, now trailed on the ground. And Jaime was staring at her so raptly she felt her flesh sizzle. She drew in a ragged breath, more frightened by the raw hunger in his gaze than she had been by the riding crop.

"Get up!" he thundered, stepping back so she

could rise. When she was slow in doing so, he
reached down and dragged her to her feet. Then
she was in his arms, crushed against the hard wall
of his chest, unable to move, to breathe, to think.

The moment Jaime set his hands on her Aleta
had stiffened and begun to struggle. Then his
mouth came down brutally on hers. His kiss was
intentionally bruising as he ruthlessly took what
he wanted, what he had been hungering for from
the very moment of their meeting. The consummation of their wedding vows had merely whetted
his appetite for more of his entrancing wife. Yet he
had deliberately held himself aloof, knowing how
much she despised him. He had thought that having Rowena in the keep would satisfy his lust, but
he had been curiously unable to avail himself of
his mistress's charms.

Aleta's lips parted helplessly beneath Jaime's furious onslaught. Blood thudding violently in her
temples, she battled to escape from the punishing
brutality of his kiss, but all her struggles were in
vain as Jaime's enormous strength easily subdued
her. His hands slid the length of her back, pressing
her buttocks against his loins, letting her feel the
powerful thrust of his aroused manhood. Then his
hands came up to her breasts, testing their weight
in his palms, rubbing the nipples in a most erotic
manner with the pads of his thumbs.

Dragging her mouth away from his, Aleta
sobbed and cried out, "Nay, not here! Not on the
ground like an animal!"

Through the haze of passion he heard her and
let loose a string of curses that seared the air
around them. "Why not, lady, you were willing to
couple on the ground with Lord Grey."

"Nay, not so!" Aleta denied. "Please, my lord."

It was her shaky plea that did it. But instead of
finding herself released from his arms, she was enmeshed more tightly in his embrace as he
wrapped her cape tightly about her, swept her
from her feet, and lifted her onto his saddle. Before mounting behind her, he grasped her palfrey's
reins. Digging his heels into his stallion's flanks,
they shot forward. But instead of heading back toward the keep, Jaime reined his mount toward the
wooded hillside.

"Where are you taking me?" Aleta asked,
alarmed. Did he intend to take her into the woods
and kill her?

"Where we won't be disturbed," Jaime said.
Suddenly he smiled, not one of his sarcastic grins
but a true smile, more devastating than if he had
struck her.

"I won't allow you to beat me, my lord," Aleta
warned. She didn't understand this Jaime. If he
wasn't being surly or nasty she didn't know how
to react to him.

"I have no intention of beating you, my lady.
There are more pleasant things we can do."

"You are no longer angry with me?" Aleta asked
curiously.

"Angry? Anger doesn't begin to describe what
I'm feeling right now."

A chill swept over Aleta. Then suddenly they
plunged into the forest and the chill was enhanced
a thousandfold. He seemed to know exactly where
he was going. After fifteen long, tortuous minutes
in which Aleta clung desperately to the saddle to
keep from being thrown while traversing over un-
even ground and dense forest, they came abruptly
to a small clearing. And in the center of that clear-

ing sat a small cottage. Jaime leaped from the horse and held his arms out to Aleta.

"Come, my lady, 'tis time to pay for your willfulness."

She slid into his arms and down his length, every corded muscle in his huge body coming in violent contact with her softness. She felt his arousal, still enormous and pulsing after their ride through the forest.

Placing a hand against her back, he shoved her none too gently through the door. Aleta hadn't known what to expect, but certainly not a room made comfortable with the addition of several pieces of furniture and a bed of furs. There was even a cheery fire burning in the hearth. She swung around, eyeing him narrowly.

"Whose cottage is this?"

"Mine, my lady. It's been made ready for your visit."

"My—visit? I don't understand."

Jaime smiled, removed the cape from her shoulders, and tossed it aside. He had thought of this cottage, built by his mother as a sort of retreat before her death, when he was searching his mind for a way to keep Aleta from hearing the wagons carrying off the smuggled goods in the dark. He would need but a night or two in which to accomplish the removal, and had suddenly recalled the cottage. He had hired help from the village and ordered it scoured thoroughly and stocked with food in anticipation of Aleta's visit. He had intended to bring her here even if he had to carry her bodily. And that's very nearly what he had done.

The wagons were set to arrive at the keep tonight after midnight, and he had intended telling

Aleta this very day that they were going off for a short visit with a neighboring baron. Only there would be no baron, just this cottage where Jaime planned to keep her until the contraband goods had been safely delivered. Then he had ridden through the village and learned that Aleta had been out riding alone. At first he had been angry; then his anger had turned to fear. What if someone should accost her, or harm her? He would never have forgiven himself if something happened to her.

"What don't you understand, my lady?" Jaime mocked. " 'Tis simple enough. Your doting husband wishes to spend time with you alone." Actually, his intention had been for Gaylord to stay at the cottage with her.

Aleta didn't believe him for a minute. "Don't lie, my lord. Tell me the truth. Why have you brought me here? I know you want me no more than I want you."

"You're wrong, my lady. In a very short time I'm going to show you exactly how much I want you." It had never been Jaime's intention to make love to Aleta once he brought her here, but all that had changed the moment she was in his arms. He wanted her. He had always wanted her. And he damn well was going to have her. If she was so damn eager to give herself to Grey, then he felt no compunction about using her to sate the enormous lust for her that had been gnawing at him.

Her eyes wide with fright, Aleta turned to flee out the door. Jaime caught her easily, dragging her sharply against him by winding his hand in the long strands of her silvery hair and tugging. Tears came to her eyes as she fell heavily against him. "Brute," she mouthed. "Knave! Satan!"

"Aye, my lady, all of those." Seizing her flailing arms in one huge fist, he lifted her chin with the other and claimed her mouth in brutal possession. When he released her his expression was dark and hungry, his eyes bold and assessing. "I want no other man in your thoughts when I take you. Forget Evan Grey—there is only me, your husband, and no one else will ever have you but me."

"You cannot control my mind!" Aleta challenged. His hands on her shoulders were like vises and she swallowed hard, realizing too late that she risked much by deliberately taunting him.

"Perhaps not, but right now 'tis only your body I'm interested in."

She backed away. "You promised! Where is your honor? Isn't Rowena enough for you?"

"My honor lies in the grave with my father, stripped from me by Evan Grey and men like him who coveted all that my father owned. You should know better than to believe a man who has lost everything but his pride. Yet neither pride nor honor saved my father from an untimely death. Nay, lady, you cannot shame me; I will take what I want."

"Will nothing change your mind?" Aleta whispered shakily.

"Nay, my lady. Take off your clothes. I suddenly have a great need to see you naked in the daylight."

Chapter 7

Stunned by his brutal manner and crude remarks, Aleta deliberately turned her back on Jaime, forgetting that her shredded dress bared more of her than she was willing for him to see. She started violently when she felt the roughness of his hands on her bare back, felt the searing flame of his touch. When he lifted the silver curtain of her hair and pressed his lips to her vulnerable nape, the heat was unbearable.

"Do you need help getting out of your clothes, my lady?" His words rasped warmly against her neck. "I intend to finish what I started."

"Nay, you cannot!"

"Aye, I can. You are my wife. I would take advantage of what you offered Lord Grey."

"I offered him nothing." Aleta feared he meant to hurt her, to punish her for being found with Lord Grey.

"Didn't you, lady?"

Once again his lips pressed against her flesh and she could feel herself flushing all over. She fought his embrace. "You accuse me falsely, sir."

Abruptly he turned her in his arms, holding her tightly against the stirring in his loins as his lips

came down on hers. His kiss continued, deep and
soft, until Aleta's struggles ceased. Only then did
he draw back slightly and slowly begin to undress
her. Her dress fell away from her breasts and a
strangled groan escaped from between Jaime's
tightly clenched lips. Their bodies were still
pressed closely together and the sudden lurch of
his manhood against her soft belly brought to him
a different, wildly intense emotion that suddenly
had nothing to do with anger or punishment.
Jaime stared at her intently, searching her face,
seeking an answer to the potent emotion that
raged through him.

With ridiculous ease he freed her from her dress
and underthings, locking her in his hungry embrace, so tightly the breath slammed out of her
chest. And when he kissed her again she reacted
to the subtle difference in him. Her lips softened,
deliberately seeking the invasion of his tongue,
and her body molded to his, no longer fighting
against his potent caresses. She knew instinctively
that he wouldn't hurt her, and recalled with tortuous delight the night he had made her his wife.
Though she had fought him when he hadn't hurt
her, he had given her pleasure. And Lord help her,
she wanted that pleasure again.

Jaime burned with fever. Nay, he was chilled to
the bone. Never had he desired a woman quite as
desperately as he wanted Aleta. God's blood, she
was his own wife, and he felt like a besotted lad
with shaking hands and knees. Those were the
kind of feelings he had tried to avoid in the past.
It rankled to think that Aleta considered him a
crude bumpkin whom she had been forced to
wed. It was Evan Grey she wanted, not him, never
him. Yet she was his wife—and he wanted her.

Impatiently Jaime sought her soft breasts, seized
by a primitive desire stronger than life itself. His
fingers stroked, caressed, teased, feeling her
breasts tauten and throb beneath his touch. She
trembled, her loins contracting almost painfully at
the sudden jolt of hunger clawing at her belly. He
had awakened her to passion once and her body
hadn't forgotten it. She recognized immediately
the source of that clawing ache pulsating deep inside her and groaned in despair.

Her groan seemed to ignite something inside
Jaime as he dropped to his knees, lavishing kisses
over her breasts, her belly, lower, until a terrible
fear seized Aleta. He was moving so close to
something so private she couldn't believe he
meant to—meant to . . .

"Jaime, no!" She grasped his hair, trying to raise
him to his feet, but he seized her wrists in one
hand and held them behind her as he continued
his dazzling path downward. When he reached
the golden triangle at the juncture of her thighs,
he stopped for a breathless moment, looked up at her,
and grinned. Then he was parting her, his tongue
seeking the sweet heat between her pale thighs. At
his probing touch Aleta screeched, surging helplessly against the rough stroking of his tongue.

Despite her protests, Jaime was relentless, con-
tinuing his glorious torture until Aleta writhed
and cried out in sweet agony. His control all but
shattered, Jaime swept her up in his arms and
carried her to the bed of furs. Following her body
down on the soft surface, he was so aroused he
tore open his hose in a frenzy of need, and with a
hoarse cry of pleasure buried himself deep inside
her with all the hungry fervor of a man beset by
demons.

"God's blood, Aleta," Jaime gasped, feeling her tighten around him. "I can't help myself. You've bewitched me, lady. I didn't want this to happen, but I can't say I'm sorry. Hate me when it's over, but let me love you."

Aleta couldn't have stopped him even if she wanted to. The moment he had thrust inside her, the erotic sensation of hot flesh sliding against hot flesh made her forget all the reasons she had ever hated Jaime Mortimer. When his powerful body began thrusting, driving, again and again, seeking ecstasy, she felt her own body responding when she had thought it impossible to do so after being nearly torn apart only moments ago. And when his mouth sought her breast, suckling vigorously, then laving the turgid tip most lovingly, Aleta went crazy beneath him.

"Jaime, please!"

"Ah, sweet, you don't know how I've longed to hear you speak those words."

Then he was plunging, rising above her, plunging again, hurtling her into rampant ecstasy.

She cried out his name.

Somewhere in the deep recesses of her brain she heard him shout, felt the hot splash of his seed, and knew he had reached a reward as great as her own. For a long time afterward they lay locked together in total exhaustion. Finally rousing herself, she moved away from him. She was stunned to realize that such a wanton, violent coupling could have given her such pleasure. How could they have traveled from intense anger and rage to abandoned oblivion so swiftly? Her body still tingled and ached—he certainly hadn't handled her gently—and the guilt she felt over succumbing so eagerly and experiencing such ecstasy mortified her.

"Regrets, my lady?" Jaime asked softly. He had seen the play of emotion upon her expressive face and knew exactly what she was thinking. She still thought him unworthy of her and felt shamed over taking pleasure from their fierce lovemaking. Deliberately he placed a leg over her to keep her from rising.

"I regret the day you showed up at Windsor Castle." Her voice was bitter. A hot flush stained her cheeks and she hastily sought to hide her nakedness from him.

"Nay, lady, you need not cover yourself from me." He pulled the fur from her fingers. "I don't like hasty couplings. I wanted to enjoy you at my leisure, but I hadn't reckoned with my anger, or a hunger so fierce it was eating me alive. I thought that possessing you would finally put the demons riding me at rest, but I was wrong. Satisfying those demons will probably take the rest of my life. At the very least the rest of this day."

"I won't be humiliated again."

Jaime eyed her narrowly, taking in her furious blue eyes, the wild tangle of golden hair, the defiant tilt to her chin and the angry color staining her cheeks. She was magnificent. Her lips were red and swollen from his kisses, her body flushed, her glorious hair curling in wild disarray around her shoulders, and he wanted desperately to make love to her again.

"Humiliation has nothing to do with what I want to do to you, lady." His voice seemed to reach out and touch her, moving like a warm breath against her flesh.

There was something noble and splendid about

this man, she suddenly realized, with his stark, bold features and proud bearing. If he hadn't shown up the way he did and forcibly demanded that she wed him, there might have been a chance for them. Under any other circumstances she might have even admired the man for his strength of conviction and steadfastness in defense of his father. But his callous taking of her on their wedding night and flaunting of their stained bedding for all to see the next morning was unforgivably crude. And now this. He had made her feel things she didn't want to feel, do things that had shamed her.

"What are you thinking?" Jaime asked, noticing her preoccupation. His eyes dropped to her heaving breasts. Reaching out, he touched a finger to her right nipple.

Aleta jerked as if scalded. "I'm thinking that I want to leave here."

He moved on to the other nipple, apparently fascinated by the nub of rosy flesh as it rose against the pad of his fingertip. "Tomorrow. Or the next day," Jaime promised absently.

"Nay, I won't be used again by a crude peasant! I want nothing to do with a man who dishonors his wife by keeping his mistress in the same house."

Jaime went rigid. "I have not dishonored you."

"Liar! Why didn't you let Lord Grey have me? I find you despicable." She watched warily as he began removing his clothing. Unbidden, her eyes fell to his rampant sex as he tossed his hose aside and posed naked over her, a magnificent specimen of potent masculinity. He was so handsome it took her breath away.

He leered at her. "I find you entrancing, my

lady. Spread your legs and welcome your husband."

Aleta gasped in dismay. "Your vulgarity offends me. I am your lady wife, not your harlot."

Grim-faced, he lowered himself atop her, making her aware of his arousal. But Aleta was determined not to lose her soul to him again. If he felt anything for her, anything at all, she might have felt differently. But she knew she was just a pawn to Jaime, albeit a desirable one, and he was a virile man with an enormous appetite for sex. Yet, though she knew he was a scoundrel, when he kissed her she felt the thrill of excitement curl through her.

Raging anger consumed Jaime. An anger directed at himself. He knew that Aleta felt nothing but contempt for him, yet he couldn't keep his hands off her. Her powerful allure had ensnared him, enraptured him, until he craved her sweet flesh with an all-consuming hunger that rode him relentlessly. But he had no time to dwell on his anger now—not now, with his lovely wife undulating beneath him so sweetly. There would be time for regrets later—much later.

"Aye, my lady, my wife," he answered. " 'Tis something I hope you'll not forget in the future."

Hungrily his mouth fastened on hers, kissing her again and again, his delving tongue probing deeper and deeper. And suddenly Aleta's body was no longer her own, but an extension of Jaime's, to do with as he pleased. It pleased him to rub against her sinuously as he kissed her, touching her everywhere, making her crave the warm heat of his hands, his lips, his tongue.

A grim smile curved Jaime's lips. It pleased him to know Aleta was aroused, perhaps not as aroused as he but aroused nonetheless. And he certainly couldn't deny his condition, not with his manhood throbbing and pulsating between their twisting bodies. But he wanted more from Aleta than forced arousal, he wanted to hear her whisper to him of her need, to tell him she desired him—he wanted her soul. Slipping a knee between her thighs, he deliberately rubbed it against the sensitive flesh where her legs met. Aleta moaned, nearly wild for release as she grasped his invading knee with her thighs and pushed against it hard.

"You want me," Jaime whispered against her ear as he ground his knee against her sex. "Ride my knee, my lady."

"Nay!" she cried, driven nearly wild by the arousing motions of his thrusting knee but refusing to allow herself the pleasure he offered. She fought to gain her wits as she struggled against the hard drive of his relentless knee, determined not to fall victim to his lust. She pushed against the solid wall of his chest, lashing out with all her strength to dislodge him. Her resistance fazed him not at all, making him all the more determined.

"Say the words, Aleta, say them!" His voice was harsh with need.

"Nay!"

Abruptly he removed his knee, replacing it with his hand as he cupped her mound. Carefully, with great relish, he slid a finger inside her, then another, while rubbing the tender bud of her desire with the pad on his thumb.

Aleta shrieked. "Damn you!"

"Is that all you have to say to me, my love?" His fingers moved inside her with relentless abandon as he bent his head and raked her nipples with his teeth.

Aleta's control snapped. "I want you, Jaime! Please, I can stand it no longer!"

Fully as tormented as she, he removed his hand instantly, sliding full and deep inside her—deeper still, until she thought she would burst, so incredible was the pleasure. His passion-glazed eyes glittered down at her, watching her face as his thrusts grew almost frantic. He knew the moment ecstasy burst inside her, knew by the tenseness of her body, the surprised look on her face and the wild keening that slipped past her soft lips. Then he knew no more as his own climax took him to paradise—and beyond.

They stayed at the cottage two days and two nights. Each night Jaime made love to Aleta with all the furor of a man possessed. And each day he cursed himself for falling victim to Aleta's allure.

It frustrated and angered Aleta that she had begun to accept—nay, anticipate—Jaime's lovemaking. Though they had little to say to one another during the day—during those times they weren't making love, the moment he looked at her in that special way a trembling took hold of her. His piercing black eyes had the power to turn her legs rubbery, and when he touched her, she was lost. Then he would lead her to the fur pallet, undress her slowly, and love her to distraction.

It was while Jaime lay with Aleta in his arms, relaxed and sated, that Aleta brought up the subject of the late-night occurrences on the beach. Her question caught him totally off guard.

"Who is the Lord of Darkness, Jaime?"

She felt his body tense as he turned his head to

stare at her. "Where in the world did you ever hear such a name?"

"It doesn't matter where I heard it. Who is he? Or what is he?"

"An old wives' tale," he said dismissively. "Forget it."

"Lord Grey said he was hunting smugglers. Do you think there really are smugglers in the area?"

"Nay." His voice betrayed no emotion. "I've heard nothing of smugglers. Even if there were smugglers, they have nothing to do with us." Adroitly he changed the subject. "I've decided 'tis time to return to the keep. We'll leave tomorrow."

For the space of a heartbeat she searched his face for answers he seemed unwilling to give. "Why *did* you bring me here, my lord?"

He was quiet a long time. "I wanted you to see a place that my mother loved."

There was some truth in his words, but Aleta couldn't decide just how much.

"And I thought we needed the time to get to know one another."

"Will I ever know you, Jaime?"

"Probably not," Jaime admitted dryly. "Since I am a peasant without wealth or property—your words, my lady, not mine—you'll probably never understand me. Nor I you."

"You have Criccieth."

He laughed harshly. "Aye, a crumbling pile of stone."

"We could always live on one of my properties. They're yours now. One has a manor house that we could live in quite comfortably."

"Perhaps one day, my lady, but not now. We will live at Criccieth keep until the King removes the stigma of traitor from my name and returns my birthright to me."

"That might never happen," Aleta warned softly.

"Then I will make you a promise, Aleta. If the King finds no evidence to clear my father's name, I will release you from your wedding vows. If Grey still wants you he may have you."

Aleta gasped. "You would let me go?"

He searched her face, his eyes so dark they were like looking into the devil's lair. "If it is your will."

Though neither realized it, they had reached an unspoken understanding in this isolated setting where they had explored the limits of passion. Jaime had brought Aleta to the cottage in order to keep her from learning about the smuggling operation, and had discovered that a woman of fire existed beneath her angelic appearance. Her temper was stunning, but so was her passion. He had learned that Aleta hated and loved with equal vigor.

Aleta had discovered far more about Jaime. She learned he could be fierce yet tender, rough yet gentle, and stubborn to a fault. Despite his words to the contrary, inside his massive frame dwelled a fierce pride driven by a relentless thirst for truth.

They left the cottage the next morning.

Rowena was waiting at the bottom of the steps when they entered the bailey. "Where have you been?" She launched herself at Jaime, her lips pursed into a pout. "Gaylord said you had taken Aleta somewhere but refused to tell me where." Her violet gaze rested accusingly on Aleta.

Gaylord appeared at the top of the steps and started down to join them. When he reached the bottom he nodded at Jaime. Jaime knew immediately that the keep had been successfully emptied of contraband and payment stored safely in the secret room. He returned the nod before answering Rowena's question.

" 'Tis as Gaylord said, Rowena, Aleta and I have been visiting a special place these two days."

Rowena's mouth turned downward. "You've never taken me to a special place."

"So I haven't," Jaime said distractedly as he set her aside. He went immediately to Aleta and assisted her down from her mount. He decided to speak with Gaylord immediately about finding Rowena's brother, for he was truly becoming weary of her. It no longer seemed necessary to keep her around merely to taunt Aleta. His wife may have thought him a crude peasant, but he wasn't as heartless as she would have liked to believe.

Since returning from the cottage, Jaime realized that he must steel himself against Aleta's bewitching allure. To allow her knowledge of the devastating effect she had upon him would give her profound power over him. With that kind of power it would be so easy for her to gain his trust and betray him and the villagers.

Once inside the keep Aleta headed directly for her room, but Jaime stopped her with a hand on her arm. "I have decided to remove you to another room. One closer to mine. Your things have already been moved."

She could read nothing from his expression, so had no idea she was being moved because Jaime wanted her away from the beach side of the keep. Since it would do little good to protest, she followed him in silence to the chamber he had as-

signed to her. Once inside she regarded him evenly, one golden brow raised in question. The room
had to be one of the smallest in the keep.

It boasted only one window, which overlooked
the bailey and remnants of the curtain wall.
Granted, the mountains in the distance were
breathtaking, but other than that the room had little to commend it.

"I thought the view of the mountains would
please you," Jaime explained tersely.

"I'd rather face the sea."

"I want you here, Aleta," Jaime said softly.

Aleta searched his face, seeking the truth. What
she found was a look so hooded she had no idea
what Jaime was thinking. But the searing flames in
his dark eyes stole her breath away. The flames
seared through her, warming her breasts, her hips,
invading that womanly place between her thighs.
When he looked at her like that, she sizzled and
burned and forgot that she had been wedded to
this peasant against her will. What she did recall
were those magical nights in the cottage deep in
the woods where the hard cynical man she had
known turned into a tender lover any woman
would die for.

Any woman could love.

Jaime ignored Aleta's dismay as he pointed out,
"The chamber has been made comfortable with
the addition of your belongings. I think you'll find
it quite adequate. Now if you'll pardon me, my
lady, I have business to conduct with Gaylord."
He turned abruptly.

"My lord, wait. I—I thank you for showing me
the cottage."

Her words nearly brought him to his knees.
"The pleasure was all mine, my lady." Then he

was gone, leaving the chamber as swiftly as his legs would carry him. If he had remained with Aleta another moment he would have pulled her into his arms, kissed her with all the fervor of a man possessed, and laid her down on the bed.

Who would have thought such a feisty bundle of feminine beauty could have made such a lasting impact upon his life in such an amazingly short time? Certainly not him. Taking a wife at this time of his life, when his very existence was uncertain, had been a foolish move. And though rich enough through his own efforts, he was a man without inheritance or title to call his own. His name was still despised in England and unless the King's investigation, assuming there was one, vindicated his father, little hope existed that his birthright would be restored to him. Yet here he was, desperately wanting Aleta when his energies should have been directed toward clearing his father's name and regaining his property from those who had falsely accused his father.

Originally, marrying Aleta had merely been an end to a means, a way of depriving Evan Grey of something he wanted. But unfortunately the little vixen had somehow slithered her way beneath his skin without him realizing it was happening. Jaime knew that Aleta cared nothing for him. That she considered him a crude peasant with no manners or refinement. Little did she suspect that his wealth was equal to or greater than that of the richest man in the kingdom. And if he had anything to say about it, she'd never know.

Jaime had met greedy women before and was repelled by their need for wealth and property. Aleta could very well be one of those women. But he owed it to his father's memory to deny utterly, in both mind and body, his response to Aleta. He couldn't afford to be distracted by his delectable wife at a time when danger existed in many forms. Allowing Aleta to steal his heart and soul was a luxury not meant for him. His gut told him she'd betray him in a minute if given the opportunity.

Clearing his head of all his confusing thoughts, Jaime went in search of Gaylord. He had assumed that the removal and delivery of the smuggled goods had proceeded without incident, but wanted to hear the details from Gaylord. It was the first time since their operation had begun that the Lord of Darkness had been absent.

Meanwhile, Aleta's thoughts brought her to a startling discovery. The moment Jaime had strode from her chamber, the reason for being removed from her large comfortable room to this smaller one struck her forcibly. It wasn't because he wanted her close, nay, she denied hotly, he wanted her tucked away where she couldn't observe the strange happenings on the beach. The view from this chamber gave her little opportunity to spy on the illegal activities taking place on the beach below. But now that she was aware of the lengths Jaime would go to keep her ignorant, she was more determined than ever to learn exactly what was taking place on those dark nights. If her suspicions were correct, the King would be most interested. So would Lord Grey.

During the following days and nights Aleta became more convinced than ever that Jaime was lying when he said he had moved her into the small room she now occupied because he wanted her close. Not once since their return from the cottage had he attempted to make love to her. Night after night she waited in the lonely darkness of her room for Jaime to come to her. In fact, he seemed to have forgotten her completely. He was ever polite when they met, and seemed pleased that she was settling in at the keep, but not once did he indicate either by look or word that they had once been as intimate as any man and wife could be. Only one reason for his lack of attention came to mind.

Rowena.

Jaime was bedding Rowena and didn't need her. Yet, to Jaime's credit, he seemed as oblivious to Rowena as he was to her.

Rowena knew her time at Criccieth was reaching an end. Gaylord had already told her he had started a search for her brother at Jaime's request and as soon as he had been located she would either be sent to him or he would be asked to come for her. But as long as she was still here, the clever brunette decided to use her cunning to convince Jaime not to send her away. She had already discovered that creating dissension between Jaime and Aleta made life much more interesting and might even cause an irreparable rift. She knew Jaime wasn't bedding Aleta and felt confident that if she could get into his bed one more time she would make it so memorable for him he couldn't bear to send her away.

Rowena started her campaign immediately, invading the solar to do so even though Aleta had warned her that she wasn't welcome. She had devised a shrewd scheme and couldn't wait to put it into effect.

Aleta was totally absorbed in a tunic she was mending for Jaime and didn't hear Rowena enter, so she was startled to find the brunette standing before her.

"You aren't welcome here," she said tightly.

"Since we seldom speak, I thought you wouldn't mind this one time."

"Have you something important to say?"

"Aye, I think so." She smiled maliciously, sending goose bumps up Aleta's spine. "I believe I am with child."

The tunic fell to Aleta's feet; she made no move to pick it up. "Is—is it Jaime's child?"

"Do you doubt it?"

"Does Jaime know?"

"Not yet. I thought you should be the first to know."

"How kind of you. What would you have me do?"

Rowena's eyes gleamed spitefully. "Leave, my lady. Leave your husband to me. If he wanted you, he wouldn't get his children on me."

A strangled sob caught in Aleta's throat. How could Jaime do this to her? "Forgive me if I don't appear thrilled with your announcement, but learning that my husband's mistress is expecting his child isn't exactly—heartwarming." Her voice faltered. Suddenly she leaped to her feet, brushing past Rowena with all the dignity she could muster. She was much too hurt to listen as Rowena spoke glowingly of her pregnancy.

Jaime was puzzled by Aleta's absence at supper that night. Deeply engrossed as he was in conversation with Gaylord concerning the evening's shipment of contraband brandy, he dismissed her absence. Without Aleta's sharp intelligence and keen perception to hinder them he and Gaylord could converse privately in low tones. Rowena seemed involved in thoughts of her own, which suited Jaime fine. When he left the table much later, he went directly to his room, hoping to get a few hours' sleep before the darkest hours of night, when the men from the village would await the Lord of Darkness on the narrow strip of beach below the keep.

Lying in her lonely bed, Aleta's head pounded, thinking about the child Rowena carried. She had heard Jaime's footsteps as he passed her room on his way to bed hours ago, yet still couldn't force her mind to release the devastating knowledge that Rowena was pregnant with Jaime's child. The hurt tore into her like a double-edged blade, twisting and grinding until the pain was unbearable. She should be the one bearing Jaime's child, not Rowena. Even though she might despise her husband, no other woman had the right to give him heirs. In the deepest depths of her mind, Aleta realized that somewhere along the way her thinking concerning Jaime had become confused.

If she hated Jaime so much, why should she care if another woman bore his children?

She hadn't expected the terrible anguish that ripped her apart and made sleep impossible.

Nor was she ready to admit that an emotion stronger than any she had ever known had found a place in her heart.

Chapter 8

No amount of rationalizing gave Aleta the peace of mind she needed to drift effortlessly into sleep. Brisk air fragrant from the sea wafted through the window slit. A slim sliver of moon pierced the nearly total blackness of the night. Tossing restlessly, she threw aside the covers and rose from bed. Since sleep was impossible, she walked aimlessly to the window and gazed down into the inner bailey. Her mind was so distracted it took several moments for her to notice the movement in the bailey somewhere in the vicinity of the stable.

The lone figure of a man emerged from the small enclosure, leading a midnight-black stallion. In the meager light he appeared as an illusive specter blending into the violet shadows of the keep. Behind him his powerful mount danced nervously, his hooves sounding sharply on the hardened earth of the bailey. The man turned to soothe the high-strung animal, his long hair swirling around to obscure his face. The man's identity came to Aleta instantly. She knew of few men in this day and age who wore their hair long.

Only Jaime.

From the moment she had seen him she had known it was Jaime, though her mind tried to deny it. There was no mistaking his tall, muscular frame. As the dark figure moved silently through the bailey, Aleta came to a swift decision. She realized that the only way to discover the truth about the late-night occurrences below on the beach was to observe them personally. Pausing just long enough to throw a dark cape over her shoulders and slip on her shoes, she left her chamber. She offered a prayer of thanks for the flares left burning in the wall sconces along the spiral stairway as she hurried down the narrow stone steps to the third floor, then continued down to the second floor.

Aleta went directly to the flight of stairs that bypassed the first floor and led immediately into the bailey yard. She had used the outside stairs countless times and had seen the other set of stairs inside the keep leading down to the first floor where the stores were kept but had never ventured down there. There had never been a reason to do so. She paused briefly at the top of the outside staircase, saw that the bailey was now empty, and hurried down. Just as she reached the bottom, she caught a glimpse of Jaime mounting his stallion and riding toward the cliff side of the keep that overlooked the beach. She hurried after him, carefully picking her way across the bailey to a narrow path winding downward to the beach. She came to an abrupt halt when she saw Jaime poised at the edge of the cliff. Another man stood beside him. Jaime held a lantern aloft, waving it from side to side.

Fearing she'd be seen, Aleta crouched down behind a bush, watching raptly as Jaime waved the lantern several more times before handing it back to his companion. Then both men started down the steep path leading to the beach. Aleta waited a few minutes before approaching the cliff's edge, where she crouched on her stomach so she wouldn't be outlined against the horizon. What she saw stunned her.

An answer to Jaime's signal was being returned by a ship anchored in the bay. Aleta could make out its dim shape but little else. Since the tide was in, the ship was closer to shore than she had ever seen one venture before. Then, incredibly, dozens of lanterns appeared on the beach, and it wasn't long before Aleta saw a rowboat leave the ship. A short time later it bumped ashore, assisted by men on the beach who began unloading its cargo of barrels while it was still in shallow water. Another boat appeared, and another, each one making several trips until the narrow strip of beach was stacked high with barrels.

Aleta shook from cold, but nothing short of death or discovery would make her abandon her perch high above the beach. The sky was just turning from deepest purple to mauve when Jaime spoke earnestly to a man from the ship and all the rowboats departed. Aleta wondered what would happen next when she heard the creaking of wheels behind her. She flattened herself on the ground and held her breath as two wagons appeared at the top of the cliff and started down the steep incline. She allowed herself to breathe again when the wagons passed by without noticing her.

Once the wagons reached the beach, a frenzy of activity ensued as the barrels were quickly loaded into the wagons. She could see more clearly now in the murky dimness of early dawn, and every man on the beach, including Jaime, was bending his back to the loading of the barrels. When one of the wagons was fully loaded it started its arduous journey up the steep trail. Rather than risk discovery, Aleta decided to return to the keep. It was imperative that she arrive before the men started unloading the barrels or she'd be unable to slip back to the keep without being seen. As slow as the wagons were she knew she'd have plenty of time to reach the keep ahead of the smugglers.

Smugglers. The word frightened her. Smuggling was illegal, a crime punishable by death. What must Jaime be thinking to involve himself in so dangerous a pastime? Didn't he know he was deliberately depriving the King of much-needed revenue and placing himself and the villagers in jeopardy? Something had to be done, she realized, before Jaime ended up at the end of a rope. Not to mention the poor villagers, who had families to support.

She reached the keep a good ten minutes before the first wagon arrived. She waited on the second floor, watching from the window slit as the men unloaded the barrels and rolled them inside the first floor of the keep. When she saw Jaime ride up on his black stallion she turned tail and ran up the two flights of stairs to her chamber. Pacing back and forth restlessly, Aleta knew she couldn't let the matter rest now that she had discovered Jaime's secret. Something had to be done.

And soon . . .

But what?

Exposing Jaime's illegal activities to the authorities was certainly an option. Ignoring the whole matter was another, albeit a cowardly one, and she was no coward. Or . . . She could confront Jaime openly, advising him that she was fully aware of his illegal activities, and obtain his promise to stop immediately. To Aleta's chagrin, the choice wasn't difficult. She didn't want to see Jaime hang. And since she couldn't ignore the matter, she chose to confront him openly. Her decision made, she was finally able to sleep. She'd need all her wits about her if she was to convince Jaime to give up smuggling.

Jaime sought his bed about the same time Aleta returned to hers. He fell asleep immediately. This night's work had been exhausting but their profit would be enormous. The captain of the ship had said he'd have another cargo of fine brandy two weeks from today, and the villagers were eagerly looking forward to its arrival.

Jaime's first inclination had been to curtail their smuggling for the time being, since the King's men were hot on their trail. But the prospect of one more rich cargo had been too tempting to refuse. He had polled the men and they had opted for one last haul before retiring for a time and going back to farming. His last thought before he slept concerned Aleta and how his secret activities were making her suspicious. He wished he could trust her but feared that he could not.

The sun was already high in the sky when Aleta awoke later that morning. When Bess tiptoed in a short time later, Aleta noted that the serving woman was as bleary-eyed as she was. And why not? Aleta thought wearily. Her husband and son were probably among those men working through the night unloading contraband goods. And good wife that she was, she had waited up for them. Though Aleta had to bite her tongue to keep from blurting out that she knew what the men were up to, she refrained from questioning Bess. She wanted to confront Jaime first, to make him aware that he and the villagers were playing a dangerous game.

No one was in the hall when Aleta entered. She went directly to the kitchen for her breakfast and when she learned Jaime had ridden out with the men-at-arms she knew what she had to do. After downing her meager fare, she took the winding stairway all the way down through the garrison to the first floor where the stores were kept. If she had expected to see dozens of contraband barrels from last night's escapade, she was sadly disappointed. There were sacks of flour, barrels of ale for their own consumption, and various other foodstuffs, but no sign of the smuggled goods from the ship.

Aleta was astounded. She had seen the men unload the barrels and carry them up inside before she returned to her chamber. Had she been dreaming? Surely not. And then the thought occurred to her that there was a secret room. It defied logic to keep smuggled goods out in the open, but finding a hidden room would be nearly impossible. Scanning the walls of the keep, she saw nothing that remotely suggested a secret opening. Then her gaze fell to the floor, suspecting a trapdoor of some sort. When she noticed a suspicious section of floor nearby she dropped to her knees to inspect the thick wooden planks. That's how Jaime found her, upended, so to speak, with her hands searching the floor and her backside raised in the air.

"Are you looking for something?"

"Oh." Aleta blinked in surprise as she sat back on her heels. "What are you doing here?"

"This is my keep, remember?"

She rose to her feet, brushing dirt from her skirt. "I—I was checking supplies." Her chin rose defiantly. " 'Tis my duty, you know."

"Since when were you so conscientious about your duties?" Jaime taunted. "I could name some duties you'd do anything to avoid."

Aleta flushed. She had assumed it was Jaime who was avoiding *her*.

"What manner of supplies did you expect to find on the floor, my lady?" Jaime probed relentlessly.

Steeling herself for an unpleasant encounter, Aleta realized there was no time like the present to confront Jaime about his smuggling activities. Dragging in a steadying breath, she blurted out, "I know your secret, my lord."

Jaime's dark brows etched upward. "What secret are you referring to, my lady?"

" 'Tis no use pretending, Jaime. I saw you last night. I followed you to the beach. I know what you and the men from the village were doing. God's blood, you could all be hung!"

Jaime's expression hardened and his face grew dark with menace. "You followed me to the beach, my lady?"

"Aye, you and that great black stallion of yours. I can understand why they call you Lord of Darkness. I saw the ship anchored in the bay and the rowboats filled with contraband."

"You followed me to the beach?" Jaime repeated, his voice rising dangerously. Never had Aleta seen such a ferocious look on his face. His stance was so menacing she felt compelled to retreat a step. "You do well to fear me, my lady," he hissed, "for you have deliberately spied on me. Have you already notified the authorities?"

"I did no such thing!" Aleta protested, outraged. "But it would serve you right if someone did betray you. What you and the villagers do is wrong. The King's law is justifiably severe toward smugglers. You and your friends are depriving the King of much-needed revenue."

"So he can wage wars on foreign soil?" Jaime spat. "Henry should pay more attention to his subjects. No one came to my family's defense when my father was wrongly accused and I was deprived of my title and property. Nay, my lady, I fled in fear of my life. If not for Gaylord I would not be alive today."

"Why would anyone wish harm to a child?" Aleta questioned.

"Ask your father that question. Aye, and Evan Grey. But all that happened long ago. The subject now concerns you, my lady. Needless to say you have placed yourself in the midst of a very dangerous situation. What am I to do with you now, my lady?"

"Wha-what do you mean?"

"You are now privy to secret information. Information that could mean the lives of myself and nearly every man in the village."

Aleta gasped, realizing that she had unwittingly placed herself in peril. Jaime loomed over her bigger than life, his visage so fierce and threatening she feared for her safety. A husband could do almost anything he pleased with his wife—beat her, imprison her forever, kill her . . . Her hand fluttered to her throat, her blue eyes wide with fright.

"I—I wished only to warn you, my lord, nothing more. You are my husband. I would never betray you."

"Wouldn't you, my lady?" Jaime asked, not at all convinced.

"Nay, Jaime, truly. I hoped to persuade you to stop your illegal activities immediately."

"And if I didn't agree? What then?"

"N-nothing, my lord," Aleta stammered as she retreated another step.

Relentlessly, Jaime followed. "Why don't I believe you, my love?"

The chill warning in his voice sent shivers racing up her spine. "I would never tell a soul you are the Lord of Darkness or that you and the villagers are involved in smuggling. Does no one know your true identity?"

"Everyone in the village knows my identity, but I trust them implicitly. The name is used merely to confuse the King's men. But now that you know my secret, my lady, I no longer feel safe. Too many lives are at stake to risk discovery. What will I do with you, my love?"

Both Jaime and Aleta were so engrossed in their argument, neither noticed the figure hovering in the shadows halfway down the stairway. Rowena, finding herself alone in the keep, had wandered about looking for someone. When she heard voices wafting up the staircase from the storage area she grew curious and started down the stairs. The moment she recognized the voices of Jaime and Aleta she stopped and listened. Thus she was privy to everything that was being said. When she had heard enough to incriminate Jaime and nearly everyone residing in the village, she turned and fled back up the stairs. There was much to think about before deciding how best to use the damning information.

Aleta felt the black intensity of Jaime's eyes rest on her and her heart beat a furious tattoo against her breast. She knew—*knew*—he meant to do her bodily harm and she turned to flee, racing up the stairs as fast as her legs could carry her, her long hair flying behind her.

"Stop!"

She kept on going. Faster, faster still, until her heart slammed against her rib cage and her legs were barely able to move. Up, up through the second floor, past startled servants, to the third floor where people were moving around the hall, to the fourth floor and the safety of her room. Near collapse, panting from lack of breath, Aleta reached the door, sobbing in relief. Flinging it open, she raced inside and slammed it behind her, whirling around to turn the iron key in the lock. She screeched in fury when Jaime placed a hand against the door before the latch engaged and shoved it open, sending her flying.

She blinked in dismay as he stepped inside the chamber and slammed the door shut with his booted heel. "Did you think to escape me, my lady?" Bending low, he dragged her to her feet.

"Don't you dare lay a hand on me. My father will have an army at your door if you hurt me."

Jaime frowned. "I do not intend to hurt you. Merely to warn you. Should you take it into your head to betray me you will suffer dire consequences."

"You—you are threatening me?"

"Aye. Heed me well, lady, for I promise your punishment will not be to your liking."

Aleta blanched, knowing full well that Jaime meant to do away with her if she betrayed him.

Jaime did not enjoy frightening Aleta but he had no choice in the matter. He knew that she'd do anything to find her way back to Evan Grey, even if it meant betraying her husband. If it led to his execution, so much the better, for then she'd be free to marry the man of her choice. But he couldn't let that happen. There were too many lives at stake besides his own. Nearly every man in the village had participated in the smuggling operation at one time or another, and he couldn't allow them to be arrested and taken from their families.

"I am still your wife, my lord," Aleta reminded him with as much courage as she could muster. "You owe me respect."

"Respect! Respect works both ways. You've never hidden the fact that you despise me. You have called me peasant and traitor's son so many times I have not the fingers and toes to count them."

Aleta's temper exploded. Perhaps she was being imprudent but she could not help herself. How dare Jaime blame her for his problems. If he hadn't shown up to disrupt her wedding to Evan Grey, she'd have no knowledge that Jaime Mortimer even existed. She decided to attack Jaime from another direction.

"How could one respect a husband who sets his whore above his own wife? I have asked you to send Rowena away, but you have steadfastly refused. Am I expected to assist at the birth of your bastard?"

A stunned look came over Jaime's face. "I have no bastards."

"You will after Rowena delivers her child."

"You lie!"

"Nay! Rowena is carrying your bastard. She has told me herself."

"God's blood, then 'tis Rowena who lies," Jaime spat. "She is slim as a rail still and I have not touched her since before we were wed."

Aleta gasped in dismay. "How can that be? 'Tis you who lies."

"I do not lie, lady," Jaime said fiercely as he grasped her narrow shoulders between his huge hands. His eyes, as black as sin, impaled her. With a start she realized he was telling the truth. The knowledge stunned her.

Aleta flinched, feeling the power that coiled within him. "I—know only what Rowena told me. Loose me, knave, you're hurting me."

At the moment, releasing Aleta was the last thing he wanted to do. He hadn't touched her since they had made love in the cottage for fear of reawakening the dormant passion he harbored for the beautiful little witch. He had deliberately kept his distance, refusing to unleash the lustful giant dwelling within him, knowing full well how she felt about him. He had deliberately suffered the pangs of hell rather than bed Rowena, who was more than willing. There was no accounting for the way he felt about Aleta, and rather than risk his soul and all he strove for he had deliberately avoided her.

Then too there was the terrible struggle with his conscience. Lord knew he wanted Aleta. He burned to taste her sweetness again, but surrendering to his yearning was not in his plans. Not now, not when he was so close to obtaining all that had been lost to him. Aleta was a pawn, he tried to tell himself, nothing more. He could allow himself no weakness where she was concerned, lest it destroy all he had worked and planned for these many years.

Unfortunately Jaime's body worked independently of his mind, and all his good intentions melted away as he felt the sweet warmth of her soft body beneath his fingertips. Instead of releasing her, he let out a tormented groan and pulled her hard against him. His hands slid downward, over the fragile bones of her spine, molding the rounded cheeks of her buttocks with his palms and pressing her against the pulsing hardness of his loins.

A small cry of panic escaped Aleta's lips as Jaime held her against him, the fire in his eyes unmistakable. She felt undulating waves of heat and energy emanating from the tautly coiled muscles of his body and knew that he wanted her. Then he kissed her. Hard. Demanding. His mouth bore down on hers, forcing her lips apart with the relentless sweep of his tongue. Only her pride remained now to protect her against surrendering completely to his will. And soon, Aleta realized, not even her pride would be enough to save her from Jaime's passionate assault. To her deepest dismay, she felt the fire of his kiss leap into her soul and burn away her resolve.

With a surge of gladness Jaime felt her body soften and mold against his. Lifting his head, he smiled down at her. Suddenly free of his mouth, Aleta fought desperately against her body's betrayal. It galled her to think that his touch had the power to destroy her mind. Edging backward, she glared up at him and hissed, "Bastard! Why are you doing this to me?"

"I don't know," he replied, just as puzzled as she. "Are you a witch? I find myself in the uncomfortable position of wanting no other woman but you. If you were honest, you'd admit that you want me in the same way. Does your body burn for my attention, my lady? Does your mouth yearn for my kisses? Does your soft sheath grow moist at the thought of my thrusting blade buried inside you to the hilt?"

The blatant sexual content of his words turned her cheeks to flame. And to her dismay she felt a tingling start at her spine and stab with relentless fury between her thighs. And when his hands came up to cup the soft fullness of her breasts, she was certain he could feel her distended nipples beneath the material of her dress. He could. The pads of his thumbs found them easily as he massaged them to painful sensitivity. Her stifled moan made him even more bold as he moved his mouth over one nipple, licking it through the material. The friction of coarse material over erect nipple brought another moan from Aleta's lips as she pressed against him.

"Oh, lady," Jaime groaned as he swept her from her feet and carried her to the bed. "I want to submerge myself in you so deeply you'll think I've pierced your soul."

His hands worked on the fastenings of her gown with amazing ease as he methodically undressed her. Aleta's hands flew to his wrists as she tried to stop him. But her meager effort went unheeded as Jaime shoved them aside and continued relentlessly, not stopping until he had stripped her bare.

"Your beauty never ceases to amaze me," he

whispered reverently against the pulsing heat of her throat.

"I—stop, please. I can't think with your mouth on me."

"You're not supposed to think, my love, only feel. I want you to feel everything I do to you."

"Bastard," she gasped, even as her arms closed around him, as her mouth lifted to his and her body arched against the hardness of his body.

"Aye," he agreed, giving her a roguish grin.

Freeing himself, he rose above her long enough to remove his clothing before straddling her. He bent, his mouth caressing hers. Just when Aleta thought she had experienced the ultimate caress, his lips slid down her neck, moving sensually over her shoulder, her collarbone, her breasts, where he suckled and licked until Aleta thought she would lose her mind. She cried out in surprise when he flipped her over, his lips whispering hotly against the ridges of her spine.

"Your skin is as soft as velvet," he groaned raggedly. His kiss pressed against her buttocks and Aleta cried out when his hands touched her intimately, sweeping with aching tenderness between her thighs. "You're all pink and white and golden."

Abruptly he turned her over again, prodded her legs apart with his knees, and settled between them. When Aleta looked up he was staring at her, his eyes so dark and fathomless it was impossible to read meaning into them. Sitting back on his haunches, he let his hands caress her, touching her everywhere. Then his fingers found her and a slow grin curved his lips.

"You're ready for me, my lady." Reaching for her hand, he brought it between her legs, letting her feel the moisture gathered there. Then abruptly he removed her hand and placed it on the hard pulsing length of his sex. "Just as I am ready for you."

Aleta's eyes widened, amazed that something so immensely hard and erect could feel like the slickest satin. Instinctively her fingers curled around him, growing bolder as she stroked him experimentally.

Jaime nearly flew off the bed. "God's blood, Aleta, you drive me wild." Then he was on his knees, burying his head between her legs, taking possession of her with his mouth and tongue.

"Jaime, no!"

He raised his head and smiled. "Oh, yes, my love, definitely yes. I want to savor every inch of your delectable flesh." Then he returned to his sensual feast, grasping her hips and holding her in place as he ravaged her with his mouth and tongue.

The torture was unbearable. Aleta's body alternately burned and shook from chills as Jaime lavished her with the most intimate loving possible between man and woman. She wanted to rage against this unfair intrusion upon her body, but she feared if she did he would stop—and then she would die. Never had she felt so helpless or totally consumed by another human. His tongue lashed her ruthlessly; his mouth found the tiny nub of intense pleasure nestled in a golden nest and nipped and sucked until her tormented cries filled his ears with sweet music. Her climax came upon her like a startling, soaring explosion. Like bursting stars, and darkness shattered by piercing light.

While she was still vibrating from the force of

nearly unbearable rapture, Jaime thrust into her, intensifying the feeling. Screaming, she clutched his shoulders and arched against him. He thrust deep inside her. Deeper. So deeply she cried out again at the savagery of his assault. This time she climbed heights so dizzying she felt her soul leave her body. Vaguely she heard Jaime shout, felt him stiffen, felt the hot splash of his seed against the walls of her womb. Then she knew no more.

Moments later—or was it hours?—Aleta opened her eyes to find Jaime staring at her. His expression was thoughtful, his dark eyes narrowed as if contemplating some great mystery.

"Why do you do this to me," Aleta asked shakily, "when you know you are stronger and more experienced than I? How can I resist when you manipulate my body to your will?"

"I don't know," Jaime replied softly. His eyes were troubled. "I have only to touch you and my senses leave me. Believe me, I don't like it any better than you do." He was frowning now, trying to come to grips with his feelings, but the thunder of his heart was much too loud to hear the warning voice of his conscience.

Aleta knew she was treading on dangerous ground, but while Jaime was in a contemplative mood she had to try one more time to convince him to give up smuggling.

"Jaime, my lord, I beseech you, listen to me. You must give up the dangerous game you're playing. Lord Grey is bound to find out sooner or later that you're responsible for thousánds of pounds of lost revenue."

"Will you tell him, my love?" His voice was low and menacing and his eyes glowed darkly with accusation.

"I? Nay, not I," she denied hotly. "I seek only your promise to desist immediately. I like not what you are doing."

"Then forget it, Aleta. Forget what you saw last night. I warned you that you wouldn't like the consequences should you betray me and I meant it. But just to be on the safe side, you will move your belongings into my chamber immediately. I want you nearby at night where I can watch you."

"What about Rowena?" Aleta asked belligerently.

"I care nothing for Rowena. I will confront her concerning the tales she is spinning. But it matters little what she says or does, for she will be leaving when I can spare the men to take her to her brother."

"Truly?" Aleta asked, startled. It couldn't be soon enough for her.

"Aye, truly," Jaime concurred. "One woman in a keep is enough for any man. Now," he said, his eyes gleaming wickedly as he leaned over her, "enough talk. I find I am inordinately famished for another taste of your sweet flesh."

Grasping her by the waist, he slid to his back and lifted her atop him. Aleta's blue eyes widened as he placed her astraddle his loins, the erect rod of his great sex prodding between her thighs.

"You're insatiable," Aleta whispered shakily as she began to warm to his touch.

"Aye, where you're concerned. Put me inside you, my love, I need to feel the sweet heat of you surrounding me again."

Lulled by the deep seductive resonance of his voice, Aleta couldn't have protested even if she had wanted to. Grasping his erect staff, she lifted herself, then pushed downward with her hips. She gasped aloud as he slid full and deep into her, stretching her until she thought she would burst from the fullness. Then her thoughts were scattered as Jaime grasped her buttocks and shoved her hard against him, moving, thrusting, withdrawing, bringing her to the very brink of madness. But all too soon it was over, and she felt the heat of his great sweat-slicked body pressed against her as she collapsed atop him. Despite the sunshine streaming in the window, she closed her eyes and slept.

Chapter 9

Jaime did not sleep. Easing Aleta off of him, he pulled a cover over her and slipped from the bed. He paused in his dressing to stare down at her, amazed at the powerful emotion that raged through him. She consumed him utterly, wringing him inside out and stealing his senses. He hadn't truly wanted a wife, yet without Aleta his life would suddenly lose something very precious. Granted she was willful, quarrelsome, and disobedient, but making love to her gave him enormous pleasure.

She looked so innocent, Jaime thought as he gazed down on her, with her silvery hair framing her lovely features like a silken halo. Though petite, her body was perfectly formed, with breasts just the right size to fill his hands.

If only she didn't hate me, he reflected bitterly. Sighing regretfully, he quietly left the chamber. In the hall he encountered Bess and told her to move Aleta's things into his room, that henceforth Aleta would sleep in his bed. Rowena happened to enter the hall while he was instructing Bess as to his wishes and she turned a bilious shade of green.

She waited until Bess left the hall before turning on Jaime.

"So you're bedding the cold bitch," she hissed. "You promised that your marriage wouldn't affect our relationship. You said you were marrying Lady Aleta to thwart Evan Grey. Though I failed to understand your need for a wife when you had me, I trusted you. Yet you have deliberately avoided me these past months. Has the Lady Aleta cast a spell on you, Jaime? Has she unmanned you with her witchcraft?"

"Don't speak of witchcraft," Jaime warned ominously. " 'Tis dangerous to mouth blasphemous words where anyone might hear. If you recall, I made no promises. I said you might stay or leave, whatever your pleasure. You chose to stay."

" 'Twas my understanding that you'd not replace me in your bed. You have treated me most callously since bringing that pallid excuse for a lady to the keep."

Jaime's expression hardened, which should have warned Rowena. "Keep your foul mouth off of my lady wife. You aren't fit to wipe her shoes. You have deliberately lied to her and I demand that you cease."

Rowena's eyes grew round. "Lied? Nay, Jaime, I did not."

His eyes narrowed dangerously. "Tell me truly, Rowena, do you carry my child? It can be confirmed easily enough. I have only to send for the village midwife to prove or disprove your claim. It will go hard on you if I find you have deliberately lied to my lady. Tell the truth now, and I will see that you are escorted safely to your brother with more than enough coin to compensate you for your services."

"You are sending me away?"

"Aye. 'Twas wrong of me to keep you here after I wed. Aleta is my wife; this is her home."

"You would send away a woman who is carrying your child?"

"Nay, I would not. Are you carrying my child? Think carefully before you answer."

Frustrated, Rowena gnawed her bottom lip. She wanted to fly at Jaime in a fine rage, to rail at him for letting her languish while he took another woman to his bed, to scratch his face to shreds to make him less desirable in the eyes of his wife. She wanted to lie, to tell him she was carrying his child. But she did none of these. She had seen the result of Jaime's temper often enough in the past and feared having it directed at her. Even though she still wanted Jaime, would always want him, she knew he would punish her severely if she lied about a baby and then failed to produce one.

"Nay, I do not carry your child."

"I knew it could not be, but I wanted you to admit it. I wanted no bastards and always took care to produce none. Had you continued with your lie, I would have sent you from here with nothing but the clothing on your back."

Rowena gulped, realizing how close she had come to making a grave mistake. "Don't send me away, my lord," she pleaded prettily. "Let me stay near you. Perhaps one day you will have need of me."

"Nay, Rowena, I will not need you—not now, not ever. But unfortunately I have not the men at this time to accompany you on your long journey, so you will remain until I can spare an escort for you. When you leave here you will find I have been most generous with you. In the meantime, do not aggravate my lady."

Rowena's temper flared. "You think I care about riches? Nay, Jaime, 'tis you I want!" Her violet eyes narrowed dangerously. "Think twice about sending me away, my lord." Her thinly veiled warning went over Jaime's head for he had no inkling that Rowena knew things that could prove disastrous to him.

"When the time comes you will leave."

Turning on his heel, he strode from the hall, leaving Rowena fuming angrily. At that moment she hated Jaime as she had never hated another human being. Even more than she hated Aleta. She smiled slyly as an idea took root in her brain. When she left the hall she was still smiling. No one stopped her when she saddled a horse later that day and rode from the keep.

Aleta was miserable. She hated having to lie beside Jaime night after night, feeling the warmth of his body pressed intimately against hers, knowing that she had only to reach out and he'd respond instantly. Each night when he came to bed she pretended sleep. But when he undressed in the dim light of the hearth she watched through slitted eyes, recalling how warm and vibrant his flesh felt beneath her hands as he thrust into her. He was immense, his thighs like twin oaks and his massive chest rock-hard with sinew and muscle.

This night was no different than the others. He had come to bed late as usual, undressing by the light of the dying fire. Feigning sleep, she watched, her eyes clinging for a breathless moment to his groin where his manhood, huge and heavy even at rest, sprang from the dark forest between his legs. Her breath slammed against her chest. He was magnificent!

Realizing where her thoughts were taking her, Aleta lifted her eyes to his face. Strong and bold, there was a proud nobility about him that could not be denied. Her gaze settled on his full lips, recalling with a flush of pleasure how he used them to tease and taunt, how the moist warmth of his mouth made her body hum with contentment. And his hands. Lord, those huge hands and the wonderful things they did to her made her heart pound and her body tremble.

"Do you see anything you like, my lady?"

"Oh." Aleta's eyes widened. She had no idea Jaime was aware that she had been watching him. Her whole body turned rosy and she was glad Jaime couldn't see her. "I wasn't looking at you."

"Weren't you?"

"Since when could you see in the dark?"

"I do not need daylight to know when your eyes are upon me, my love. They leave a trail of fire wherever they linger."

"Conceited oaf," Aleta grumbled, deliberately turning her back.

A chuckle rumbled from Jaime's chest as he crawled into bed beside her. "Do you want me, Aleta? I'd be glad to oblige. 'Tis no sin to feel desire. It can happen even when one professes to hate the other."

"I feel no desire for you, my lord," Aleta denied stiffly. "I feel insulted by the way you treat me. I demand my own chamber. I cannot abide sharing a bed with you."

"And I cannot trust you, my love. Go to sleep," he advised, sighing wearily. "I will not sicken you

by imposing my will on you. I will not make love
to you unless you wish it."

"That day will never arrive," Aleta said smugly.

"I predict it will arrive sooner than you think."
The implicit promise in his voice troubled Aleta.
He was so sure of himself, so absolutely certain
she would beg him to love her. He had already
robbed her of her pride; did he want her soul?

The days sped by with unaccountable haste and
Aleta was grateful that Jaime had spoken to
Rowena, for the sultry brunette seemed to be
avoiding her. Jaime had told her that he would
send Rowena away soon and she couldn't wait for
that day to arrive. Meanwhile, she knew with absolute certainty that Jaime wasn't sharing
Rowena's bed, for each night she felt his warmth
beside her. Aleta also knew that Rowena wasn't
pregnant, for Jaime had told her that Rowena had
deliberately lied about the child in order to vex
Aleta.

And true to his word, Jaime hadn't attempted to
make love to Aleta again. Nor had she extended
an invitation, no matter how desperately she
yearned for the warmth of his caress and the heat
of his mouth on her body.

Two weeks had passed without incident since
that day she had confronted Jaime about his
smuggling. About that time she began to notice
his preoccupation. He was gone from the keep for
longer periods of time and didn't come to bed until very late at night. And he conferred with
Gaylord for hours on end. She thought his behavior strange until she recalled his words about the
next shipment of brandy due to arrive two weeks
from the last. She counted back, realizing that the

ship carrying the contraband brandy would arrive almost any day now. The thought frightened her. What if something should go wrong? What if something happened to Jaime?

During the past few days Aleta had been allowed to go riding in the company of one of the men-at-arms. Today, as she considered the ramifications of Jaime's illegal activities, she decided to take advantage of the lovely day and go for a brisk ride. She was better able to think with the wind at her back and the sun in her face. Since Jaime always left two men at the keep when he rode out, Aleta hurried to the bailey, hoping one of them would accompany her. She was in luck. One of the knights, Sir Nigel, promptly offered his services. He and the other eleven men-at-arms who had accompanied Jaime to Wales had willingly remained with him. To a man they liked and respected Jaime Mortimer, and since Jaime was able to pay their wages they had gladly stayed on.

Early summer was glorious in the Welsh mountain country and Aleta and her escort rode for miles, until Sir Nigel suggested they return before it grew dark. Reluctantly Aleta agreed. But when Sir Nigel turned his mount, the hapless animal stepped in a hole, lost his balance, and reared, throwing Sir Nigel to the ground. The animal's hoof struck the knight in the head and Sir Nigel sprawled in a lifeless heap on the ground. Aleta leaped from her palfrey and tried valiantly to revive the poor knight, to no avail. Since he was too heavy for her to lift and he showed no signs of regaining consciousness any time soon, she realized it was up to her to get help for the injured man.

She remounted and would have ridden furiously to the keep when she noticed a party of men approaching swiftly from the east. She paused in indecision. She couldn't ride away now, not when the riders could be of help to Sir Nigel. She waited patiently for the men to reach her. She nearly turned and rode off when she saw it was Lord Grey, accompanied by a dozen or so armed men.

"Aleta," he hailed, looking from her to the prone form of Sir Nigel. "What happened?"

"My escort fell and was struck in the head by his mount. He needs help. I can't get him back to the keep alone."

"My men will lift him and you can lead his horse back to the keep. Unless, of course," he added quickly, "you don't wish to return to the keep. I've been worried about you." He searched her face for signs of abuse and was almost sorry when he saw none.

"I must return," Aleta said. "Jaime will be expecting me. I'm surprised to find you still in Wales, Lord Grey. How is the King?"

"The King is furious," Lord Grey revealed. "The smuggling continues and we haven't a clue who is behind it. We have only a name. Lord of Darkness. Do you know anything about it, my lady?" he asked slyly.

" 'Tis merely a myth," Aleta said, her voice shaky. Lord Grey couldn't know anything, could he? "The man does not exist. I know this for a fact."

"Do you, my lady? I think you know far more than you're willing to divulge. Perhaps this Lord of Darkness won't be so lucky next time."

The note of warning in Lord Grey's voice and the malicious gleam in his eyes frightened Aleta. What did he know? Abruptly she turned to watch two of Grey's followers drape Sir Nigel across the saddle. "Be careful," she cried when he started to slide off.

The motion must have revived Sir Nigel somewhat, for he groaned and opened his eyes. Seeing Aleta surrounded by strange men, he rallied and tried to draw his weapon, but his strength failed him.

"'Tis all right, Sir Nigel, I am in no danger," Aleta assured him. "How do you feel? Can you ride?"

Still groggy, Sir Nigel hoisted himself upright in the saddle. "Aye, my lady, I can ride well enough. Let us be off."

He had recognized Lord Grey from seeing him at court and was worried about Aleta's safety. He grew suspicious when he heard Grey say, "I like it not that you are going back to Mortimer, Lady Aleta. You know I would protect you."

"I must return, Lord Grey. Tell my father that I—that I look forward to seeing him again."

Sir Nigel tensed. His employer had warned him about Grey and had instructed that he be driven off if he was seen within the borders of Criccieth. But Sir Nigel was sorely injured, and alone. There was little he could do but escort the Lady Aleta from danger as quickly as possible.

"Then I bid you farewell, my lady. But heed me well, it will be but a short time before we meet again. Your father sends word through me that delivery is at hand. And much thanks, my lady— your information will be of tremendous interest to the King."

Puzzled, Aleta stared at him hard for a moment, the meaning of his words escaping her. Then she spurred her palfrey and he shot forward, followed by Sir Nigel, weaving drunkenly in his saddle.

Aleta had hoped that Jaime wouldn't be told of her encounter with Lord Grey, but her hopes were dashed when Jaime questioned her closely that evening at supper.

"Did you enjoy your ride this afternoon, my lady?"

Aleta sent him a quelling glance, fully aware of what he was leading up to. "How fares Sir Nigel?"

"Well, except for a sore head. Have you nothing to tell me about your encounter with Lord Grey?"

"There is nothing to tell," Aleta insisted.

"For your sake as well as mine, I hope you are telling the truth, my lady. Sir Nigel appeared quite disturbed by what he had heard. Are you certain you have nothing to tell me?"

"Nothing," Aleta repeated earnestly.

That night Jaime did not come to bed and Aleta awoke abruptly several hours after she had fallen asleep with the certain knowledge that something was amiss. She knew that it was time for the ship to arrive with smuggled brandy, and wondered if Jaime was already below on the beach with the village men. Since the window to Jaime's chamber overlooked the beach it wasn't difficult to check her suspicions. Rising from bed, she shoved aside the tapestry and peered downward. Sure enough, dozens of lights were blinking on the narrow crescent of land. It was a moonless night, dark and impenetrable, perfect for the kind of activities Jaime was engaged in. Yet something wasn't right.

She felt it in her bones.

The very air screamed of danger, and Aleta's keen intuition sent her messages she couldn't ignore. Turning abruptly, she raced toward the door, an unnamed terror prompting her to warn Jaime of some unseen, unknown danger. That she should even care at all gave her a moment's pause, but she quickly pushed her doubts aside when she thought of all the villagers whose lives could be in jeopardy.

And Jaime. Though she tried to deny it, she didn't want Jaime hurt or taken prisoner. He was too vital and alive to perish at so young an age.

When she reached the door a curse flew from her lips. It was locked from the outside! "Damn you, Jaime Mortimer!" Her voice trembled with rage as she raced back to the window, reaching out and shaking her fist at the man who was the bane of her existence. "Your misplaced trust could cost your life, not to mention the lives of half the men of the village!" She had no idea when Jaime had locked the door but supposed it was when she had dozed off shortly after she had gone to bed.

Peering downward, she watched in trepidation as a hazy mist rolled in from the sea, nearly obscuring the tiny figures scurrying about on the beach. Though she couldn't see the ship through the fog, she knew instinctively it was anchored out there in the bay. Then she happened to glance to the left, toward the winding path that led down to the beach, and her blood froze in her veins. She saw men on horseback, too many to count in the dim light, carefully descending the steep incline. Her worst nightmare had materialized!

She opened her mouth, screaming a warning down on the scene from hell, knowing full well that she couldn't be heard. Held captive in the chamber, Aleta could do nothing but watch helplessly as Evan Grey and his men descended upon Jaime and his band of smugglers. Then she lost sight of them as the path curved sharply. She saw them again when they charged out onto the beach in a surprise attack. The fog prevented her from viewing much of the actual fighting but she heard the cries and din of battle.

Transfixed, she stared out the window. Her misery intensified as the cries continued for what seemed like hours. Only when the first blush of dawn colored the eastern sky and the fog lifted was Aleta allowed her first clear glimpse of the beach and sea beyond. The ship was gone but she could see Grey's men poking around on the beach among the barrels. She thought she saw a body or two stretched out on the sand but the rest of the smugglers seemed to have melted into thin air. There was no sign of Jaime or his great black stallion. Turning away from the window, she threw on her clothes and waited for Jaime to return—if he returned.

It was mid-morning before she heard someone outside her door. Rushing to the panel, she cried out, "Jaime, is that you!"

"Nay, my lady, 'tis Bess."

"Have you the key, Bess?" Aleta asked anxiously. "Please unlock the door."

"The key is in the lock, my lady."

"God's blood, Bess, open the door! Is my husband in the keep?"

The door opened and Bess stepped inside. Her eyes were red-rimmed and misty, as if she had been crying.

"What is it, Bess? What has happened?"

Mopping her eyes, Bess ignored the question as she began tidying up the room.

"You can tell me, Bess—I know all about the

Lord of Darkness and what he and the village men do down on the beach in the dead of night."

"You know, my lady?" Bess asked, astounded.

Aleta nodded gravely. "Something happened last night, didn't it?"

"Someone warned the tax men." Bess sniffled. "If it wasn't for a secret passage through a cave leading to the top of the cliff, all the men would have been slain or taken prisoner. But the Lord of Darkness is a wise man and took great care that there was another way up the cliff before he chose that particular stretch of beach for his operation. If someone hadn't seen the tax men coming down the cliff, 'twould have been disastrous. My man was sorely wounded, my lady, but thank the good Lord my son returned safely."

"Four good men were killed and many others wounded," Jaime said as he strode through the open door into the chamber. He nodded curtly at Bess. "Leave us, Bess. Go home and see to your man." His face was carved from stone, his voice harsh with recrimination as he turned his relentless gaze on Aleta.

Bess turned and fled from the room, aware of the storm brewing within Jaime Mortimer's massive form. She didn't want to be around when it erupted into full fury.

Jaime strode to the door and carefully closed it behind Bess, then he turned on Aleta, scowling darkly.

"Why did you do it, my lady? Do you hate me so much that you would endanger the lives of dozens of men trying to support their families in this ravaged land?"

Aleta's blue eyes widened and she was seized

by a terrible anger. "You accuse me of betraying you?" she asked tautly.

"The facts speak for themselves, my lady. You were alone with Evan Grey. Sir Nigel told me he was unconscious for a time and when he awakened you were deep in conversation with Grey. You also knew when the next ship was expected and had sufficient time to tell him. I should have expected it," he said bitterly. "Did you tell him my name? Will the King's men be coming for me?"

"You're a great fool, Jaime Mortimer," Aleta bit out angrily.

"Deny it if you can," he challenged. His voice sounded almost hopeful, but when Aleta remained mute, glaring at him defiantly, he knew a despair few men had ever known. By her very silence she had given him the answer he sought. Of course Aleta was guilty, he reasoned, else she'd be protesting vigorously.

Aleta's chin rose mutinously. Never would she give Jaime the satisfaction of seeing her grovel. Of course she was innocent, but what good would it do to protest? He wouldn't believe her no matter what she said; he had already judged her guilty and condemned her.

"Have you nothing to say, my lady?" Jaime prompted. He wanted desperately to hear her defend her innocence even though his heart told him she was guilty.

"I deny or admit nothing, my lord. Think what you will, for you have already judged me. I always suspected you were without compassion, and you have just proven it. You're an arrogant bastard, Jaime Mortimer. You should have heeded my warning and given up smuggling." Deliberately she turned her back on him.

A terrible rage seized Jaime. Flinging her around to face him, he grasped her narrow shoulders and shook her violently. "You sorely tempt me, my lady. Because of you, four good men are dead and many gravely wounded. If not for the fog we would have all been taken. But fortunately we were able to slip away by another route. Because of you a cargo of fine brandy is lost." His shaking was so severe her teeth rattled and her eyes rolled back in her head.

"G-go a-ahead, k-k-kill m-me!" she said defiantly as she sought to keep from swooning.

"You challenge me still?" Jaime roared as his rage escalated. But he stopped his ruthless shaking nevertheless, holding her upright between his huge hands.

Gasping for breath, Aleta's brazen eyes met his. "I will always defy you, my lord, so long as you accuse unjustly."

"Why did you do it?" Jaime raged.

"You tell me," Aleta returned, closer to swooning than she had ever been in her life.

"You want Evan Grey. 'Tis no secret that you wanted to wed that base scoundrel. 'Twould please you to see me slain."

Aleta blanched. "Nay."

"I warned you you would not like the punishment should you betray me." He held her still, like a captive dove whose fragile bones he could easily crush beneath his big hands.

"Do your worst, my lord, I will not beg for mercy. But know this: you will never know for sure if I am innocent or guilty of betraying you."

Jaime's temper exploded. "Only a witch could try my temper so. Perhaps Rowena is right, perhaps you truly are a witch and should be burned at the stake. But fear not, my lady, I will beat the evil out of you."

Jaime acted so swiftly Aleta was stunned when he grasped her by the arm and ripped her gown down the back from neck to hem. Then, lifting her off her feet, he threw her across the bed, face-down. When she dared to look over her shoulder, Jaime's remorseless gaze was riveted on the bared flesh of her back, buttocks, and legs. He was frowning fiercely when he drew his riding crop from his belt and slapped it across his thigh.

When he raised it into the air, Aleta closed her eyes and mentally girded herself for the first sting-ing blow. She heard the whip swish through the air and saw the downward plunge of his arm. The slash of the whip sounded like thunder in her ears and she jerked in surprise when the brutal blow did not touch her. It landed instead on the bed be-side her, shredding the counterpane as it would have her tender flesh.

The next sounds Aleta heard were Jaime's stran-gled groan and the whip striking the floor. She tried to rise but the force of his body as he fell upon her pinned her to the bed.

"God help me," he beseeched earnestly, "for I cannot bring you pain no matter what you have done. 'Tis better that I keep you imprisoned in my chamber forever than mar your lovely flesh." Ris-ing slightly, he turned her over, looking deeply into her eyes. "What are you, my lady, that I can-not bear to cause you pain?"

"Your wife, my lord," Aleta answered softly.

His eyes gleamed like polished onyx as they fas-tened on hers. "Aye."

The hot caress of his breath warmed her flesh

where it brushed her face. His mouth hovered over hers, tantalizingly close.

He knew he should punish Aleta, but his mind utterly rejected the thought of causing her pain. He wanted her. He wanted her at night when he slept beside her but was too disciplined to succumb to his need; he wanted her during the day when she moved like a small graceful nymph about the keep; and he wanted her all those times in between when he recalled how wonderfully sweet and fresh she smelled and how thrusting into her gave him such incredible pleasure. Just thinking about her burned him inside out. Having once tasted her, he wanted her again and again, like the fine brandy men craved.

Aleta held her breath, aware that Jaime was going to kiss her and wanting it despite his anger and her anger and all that stood between them. Yet when his mouth touched hers, she placed her hands against his rock-hard chest, determined to avoid the kiss. But his hands had tunneled into her hair, holding her still for the hot plunder of his mouth.

Aleta moaned, aware of his hard-muscled thighs spanning her slim hips, of the great pulsing length of his sex prodding her belly through the confines of his hose. And as his mouth fell on hers, she became aware of the utter devastation of his kiss. A fierce growl of denial swept upward from her throat as she felt the persistent sweep of his tongue part her lips and ravish her mouth.

"Nay, my lord, not like this," she implored. She wanted his tenderness, not his anger.

"Aye, my lady, you're mine. Yield, for I'll have you despite your resistance."

"I cannot!" Aleta cried, twisting beneath him.

His voice was harsh with need. "You can."

With a swift rending of material he tore the tattered remnants of the gown from her, baring her to his touch. Then his hands were on her body, caressing the fullness of her breasts, his fingers playing on her nipples, making them harden. His lips left her mouth, his tongue tracking a moist trail of fire from her jaw to the cleft between her breasts, where his dark head rested a moment as he kissed and licked first one hardened nipple then the other. When his hand slid between their bodies and his fingers tested the slick passage between her thighs, Aleta cried out, acknowledging her surrender.

This man—her husband—this compelling, infuriatingly arrogant man had the power to reduce her to ashes. Why? she wondered distractedly. It was Evan Grey she wanted, wasn't it? Why did Jaime have to be the one to make her body thrum and the blood sing through her veins? She had tried to hate him. Lord knew she had reason enough to despise him and his high-handed treatment of her. He didn't love her; that wasn't his reason for claiming his betrothed bride.

Then her thoughts splintered as Jaime's mouth and tongue replaced his fingers, sending her soaring to the pinnacle of ecstasy. When she floated back to earth, Jaime had stripped and was kneeling between her outstretched thighs, waiting for her senses to return so he could begin his tender torment all over again.

He began stroking her and Aleta wondered when she had lost the will to fight. When had loving one another become necessary to their well-being?

When had love replaced the hatred in her heart?

Chapter 10

Dizzy from Jaime's kisses, Aleta's thoughts scattered. A gasp escaped her lips at the sudden parting of her thighs. She jerked in response when she felt the bold thrust of his fingers inside her, and the heat begin to build again. He stroked her. Intimately. Then abruptly withdrew. Aleta moaned in protest.

"Do you want me to continue, my lady?" The seductive whisper of his voice sent her reeling in despair. Why must he torture her?

Resist, she told herself. "Nay, my lord, never!"

His fingers returned, opening the soft petals of her womanhood and nurturing the flower within most diligently. "Tell me, my lady. I will not grant you release until you tell me what you want."

Unable to speak, Aleta shook her head from side to side in vigorous denial. When he bent his dark head and taunted an erect nipple with his teeth, she hovered on the verge of madness. But Jaime was relentless, knowing exactly when to cease his tender torment and when to begin anew. She could feel his sex, huge and distended against her thigh, and was turned inside out by a terrible need she was too shamed to put into words.

"Jaime, please."

"Aye, my lady, I *will* please you, as soon as you say the words."

"Damn you! I want you!"

"Where?" Jaime prodded.

"Inside me!" Aleta screamed. "I want you inside me!"

Suddenly every sensation was magnified as Aleta felt the intensity of Jaime's dark eyes on her. She felt the hard hair-roughened texture of his chest and legs as he lowered himself atop her. Felt the fire of his passion-glazed eyes burn a path along her skin. Was aware of the weight of his body pressing her into the softness of the bed. Felt her thighs stretch to accommodate his huge bulk and wondered if she would split in two as he grasped her outstretched legs and rested them atop his shoulders. Her eyes closed, then flew open when the huge pulsing length of him thrust inside her—deep, so deep she feared she couldn't take all of him.

But she could.

His hips flexed again and again as he thrust and withdrew, shuddering with each deep penetration. Never had he experienced such profound bliss. The tightness of Aleta's sheath held him securely in the cradle of her loins as he cried out, "God's blood, my love, you're so incredibly hot and tight I could perish this instant and never attain a paradise as profound as the one I'm in now!"

His hips pumped faster. More furiously. Until he felt Aleta cry out and tremble beneath him. Then the storm within him crested, unleashing a tumult of raw ecstasy. A great shuddering seized him.

Aleta felt the hot splash of his passion bathe her womb and knew no more. She must have slept, for when she opened her eyes Jaime was fully dressed and staring down at her with a peculiar expression in his eyes.

Was it anger? Aleta wondered distractedly. If so, his anger was unwarranted, for she had done nothing. She had tried to warn him, but the locked door had prevented her from reaching the men on the beach. Did he truly believe she had betrayed him to Lord Grey? Did he hate her for it? She thought he did, which made it extremely difficult for her to remain in the keep. If he had made love to her because of tender feelings for her, she might have forgiven him, but she knew that he had taken her in lust, not love. Nay, never love. Whatever purpose she served in his life had nothing to do with that tender emotion that had stirred her heart against all odds. She was merely an integral part of a plan to seek vengeance for his father's death, that much she had learned. She could not live with the knowledge.

Jaime's eyes narrowed as he searched Aleta's lovely features. How could he have allowed a woman to become so important to him? he wondered. When had Aleta found that soft place inside his heart that he had protected most diligently? How could he fall in love with a woman who despised him? Easy, he answered himself as his eyes filled with the beauty and sweetness of her. Aleta was like no other woman. She was his wife, his love, yet he dared not reveal his feelings, for to do so would make her more powerful than his fiercest enemy. And still she would despise him. There was no solution to his dilemma.

Aleta watched Jaime carefully. She knew he didn't trust her and wondered what he intended to do with her since he had been either unable or unwilling to beat her. Their eyes met and clung, and in that brief encounter words that could have changed the course of their lives were left unsaid.

Jaime was the first to look away. "You are forbidden to leave the keep for any reason." Nothing in his voice hinted of the tender lover of just moments ago.

"For how long?" Aleta challenged.

"Until I say otherwise."

"And if I refuse?"

"I will lock you in your room."

"Am I allowed in the bailey?"

"Nay, you are not to leave the keep."

"Am I a prisoner?"

"Call it what you like, my lady, just know that I will keep a watchful eye on you from now on. 'Tis most unfortunate that you failed to reveal the identity of the Lord of Darkness."

"How do you know I didn't?"

"If you had, Lord Grey would be here now to place me under arrest. What stopped you, Aleta? Why didn't you tell him I was the Lord of Darkness?"

Aleta refused to be baited. She merely repeated the words she had spoken before. "I told him nothing." She had already proclaimed her innocence; she had nothing more to say. Jaime had drawn his own conclusions.

Enraged by her silence, Jaime knew he had to leave or do something he'd be sorry for later. He'd already been seduced beyond redemption by the alluring temptress and couldn't let it happen again. "You may rest easy knowing I will no longer share this room with you," he groaned out remorselessly. "When I'm with you, I forget that I have dedicated my life to clearing my father's name and avenging his death. Naught will ever be more important to me than seeking retribution for the betrayal of my family. Not even you, Aleta." Turning abruptly, his angry strides carried him from the chamber.

For the next several days Aleta rarely left her chamber. Her mind was in turmoil. She was embarrassed and shamed by the way she had wantonly responded to Jaime's lovemaking. She recalled vividly how she had whimpered and begged him to take her, how her cries and gasps had urged him on, how desperately she had clung to him when he had driven her to the brink of madness and beyond.

How much she was beginning to love him.

The situation was impossible. With each passing day, Aleta realized that remaining with Jaime meant surrendering her pride and losing her soul. She decided to leave and made secret plans to join her father in London. Lord Somerset was a powerful man with high-placed friends and Aleta knew he would protect her from Jaime. But the restrictions Jaime had placed on her movement gave her little opportunity to leave. Twice she had saddled her mount and rode from the keep and twice she had been stopped and returned. Once by Sir Nigel before she left the bailey and once by Jaime himself. Jaime's face was thunderous when he had intercepted her as she rode from the keep. Now, on this last attempt, she had actually gotten beyond the curtain wall before Jaime came pounding after her.

"I warned you what I would do if you left the keep," he said sternly. "The first two times I let you go with mere warnings, but you have sorely

tried my patience. Just remember, being locked in
your chamber is your choice. You should have
obeyed me, my lady. Just where did you intend to
go? Were you rushing off to provide Evan Grey
with the identity of the Lord of Darkness? Do you
intend to share his bed? Forget it, my lady, you belong to me and I share with no one."

"You can't keep me here against my will, Jaime
Mortimer," Aleta hissed. "What will the King say
when he hears I am a prisoner in my own home?"
She smiled sweetly. "I suspect he'd be greatly relieved to catch the smugglers."

Jaime smiled grimly. "You had your chance to
give away my secret, my lady. You will never have
another."

Aleta had been locked in her room over a week
now and in that time the only two people she had
seen were Gaylord, who brought her meals, and
Bess, who cleaned her room while Gaylord stood
outside the door to make certain Aleta did not
leave while Bess was occupied. Gaylord didn't like
the idea of Aleta being confined to her room and
had protested to Jaime, but Jaime was adamant.

"Would you see us all hang, old man?" Jaime
asked, scowling fiercely.

"Nay, Jaime, your lady wife would not betray
us."

"Think you not? She already has. Have you forgotten the night Grey and his men killed four of
our comrades?"

"How can you explain the fact that Aleta did
not reveal your identity to Lord Grey?"

"The woman's actions are beyond comprehen-
sion," Jaime concluded. "There is no accounting
for her failure to divulge my name."

"I can think of one," Gaylord suggested slyly. "Perhaps your lady wife has grown—fond of you."

Jaime laughed harshly. "Aleta despises me."

"And you care nothing for her. Am I correct?"

Jaime remained mute, staring at Gaylord as if the man had lost his mind. "What difference does it make?"

"Are you bedding Rowena?"

"Nay! I have no desire for the woman."

"Does Aleta know you love her?"

Jaime tensed. Was he so obvious? "Your mind plays tricks on you, Gaylord. I do not love Aleta. You know full well I have no time for games of the heart. My every waking moment is consumed with bringing Grey to justice."

"Tell that to someone who doesn't know you so well," Gaylord chided. "I will guard your lady but I do not like it. Search your heart well, Jaime. I suspect you will discover that you are not as immune to Lady Aleta as you pretend. Tell her how you feel and you may be surprised by her response."

Rowena was thrilled by the turn of events. Not only were Jaime and Aleta no longer sharing a room, but Aleta was being confined to her chamber. Though no one knew for certain, Bess had hinted that Aleta was the one who had told Lord Grey about the smuggling taking place on the beach below the keep. After her anger had cooled, Rowena was glad Jaime had escaped unscathed and was even sorry she had betrayed him. But to her credit she hadn't revealed the identity of the Lord of Darkness. Somehow she couldn't bring herself to divulge Jaime's secret, insisting to Lord

Grey that she knew nothing except what she had overheard concerning the arrival of the smugglers' ship. She had chosen to keep that last vital bit of information to herself. But if the need arose, she would use it to her own advantage.

Meanwhile, Aleta was growing desperate. A virtual prisoner, she feared Jaime would let her rot in the confines of her chamber. Was there no escape? She found a solution in a most unlikely place.

One day Rowena couldn't resist planting herself outside Aleta's door and taunting her. The first time she called through the door she received no response from Aleta. Then, after careful thought, Aleta changed her mind, deciding to see what Rowena had to say. Perhaps the sultry brunette might even be convinced to help her, she thought hopefully.

"Have you come to gloat, Rowena?" Aleta called through the door.

"Perhaps," Rowena admitted cheerfully. "While you are locked in your chamber I am free to come and go as I please. But do not fear, my lady, I will take good care of your husband while you are confined. Gossip has it that Jaime is monstrously angry with you. What have you done?" she asked innocently.

"I have done nothing," Aleta alleged. "And you are welcome to my husband if he'll have you."

"I do not need your approval."

Aleta heard Rowena's footsteps as she turned to leave and was suddenly inspired. "Rowena, wait! I—I have a proposition for you."

"Proposition?" Rowena asked. Her interest was definitely piqued. "What kind of proposition?"

"If you were to help me escape from the keep

you would have my husband all to yourself. Wouldn't that please you?"

"Aye," Rowena said with alacrity. "But little good it would do me. Jaime would be so angry he'd kill me."

"He doesn't have to know it was you who helped me. Plead innocence, he'll believe you. He knows you hold no love for me."

"It could work," Rowena agreed, suddenly eager to comply. "What would you have me do?"

"First you must steal the key from Gaylord and let me out of this room. Then you must distract the men-at-arms so I can saddle my horse and ride away without being challenged. Can you do that?"

"Distracting the men is easy," Rowena said with conceit. "They all are smitten with me, and I have amused myself with them on more than one occasion."

"I'll bet you have," Aleta muttered beneath her breath. Aloud she said, "Will you do it?"

"You promise not to come back?"

"There is no reason to return," Aleta said bitterly. "Jaime does not want a wife."

"Then I'll do it. When I've managed to steal the key from Gaylord, I'll come for you. Be prepared—I already know where the old man keeps the key."

A sigh trembled from Aleta's lips. She had no idea why she should be so distressed over leaving a man who wanted her merely to keep someone he hated from having her. True, Jaime craved her body, but he didn't care enough about her to trust her. And she couldn't live under those conditions. Ignoring the fledgling love she felt for Jaime was the most difficult thing she had ever done.

Later that morning Jaime unlocked the door to

Aleta's room and stepped inside. It was the first time she had seen him in several days and she drank in the sight of him. Surely there was no man in the kingdom to compare with Jaime Mortimer.

Jaime knew he had made a mistake in coming to Aleta's room the moment he saw her standing before him, looking like a fragile bird ready to take flight. But he had to make certain she was faring well under the restrictions he had placed upon her. Gaylord had told him she was physically able, but he had to see for himself. He was leaving that very afternoon for Flint and wanted to see Aleta before he left. His trip to Flint was necessary in order to learn if Evan Grey was playing some kind of cat-and-mouse game with him. If Grey knew he was the Lord of Darkness, why wasn't he coming to arrest him? It seemed inconceivable that Aleta would tell Grey about the smugglers and deliberately omit the most important piece of information. Did she care more for him than she was willing to admit?

"What are you doing here?" Aleta challenged. "Have you come to release me from this prison?"

"And good day to you too, my lady," Jaime replied sarcastically. "I see your deposition hasn't improved any."

"What do you expect when I am confined against my will? Do you plan to keep me imprisoned forever?"

Jaime's good humor dissolved. Aleta had a way of bringing out the worst in him despite his good intentions. "I had thought I was being quite lenient with you, my lady. Most husbands would have been swift to punish. Betrayal is a most grievous offense."

"Are you so certain I betrayed you? What you

did is against the law—anyone could have betrayed you for a price."

Jaime frowned. What Aleta said made sense, yet he knew none of the villagers would risk betrayal, for to do so would be cutting off their own nose to spite their face. He trusted every one of his knights, most of whom knew nothing about his smuggling activities, and Gaylord was as faithful as the day was long. Nay, Aleta was guilty as sin, he decided. Yet . . .

A small doubt remained.

"As certain as I can be. But that's not why I'm here. I'm leaving for a day or two. Half my men will remain at the keep and the other half will accompany me."

A frisson of apprehension slid down Aleta's spine. "Where are you going? Will you be in danger?"

"I go only as far as Flint," Jaime revealed. A hint of a smile curved his full lips. "Do you fear that I won't return, my lady? Or perhaps rather that I will return. Fear not. Gaylord will attend to your needs. As for danger, I cannot say. I do not go to seek trouble, merely information. Since I rarely leave Criccieth keep and few people know of the existence of Jaime Mortimer, I expect to return without incident."

Aleta stared at him hard, then deliberately turned her back. "Fare thee well, my lord."

"What! No farewell kiss?"

She spun around to face him, hands on hips. "A kiss, my lord? Nay, I think not." Just the thought of Jaime kissing her set her heart pounding. One touch was all it would take to produce the humiliation and shame of total surrender. If he cared for her the tiniest bit she would at least have that to soothe her tormented soul, but she had never heard one word from him concerning his feelings.

Jaime recognized immediately his mistake in coming to see Aleta. Fortunately he succeeded in keeping a tight rein on his emotions when he wasn't around her, but when she was a touch away his resolve melted. His groin felt full and heavy, his legs weak. A familiar ache began low in his gut and flooded his loins. He wanted to reach out and drag Aleta into his arms, to kiss her until she returned those kisses with wild abandon, to thrust into the tightness of her hot sheath until it grew moist with his juices and hers.

He wanted to love her.

Aleta recognized the look on his face and cried out in panic, "Don't touch me!" She felt the heat of his body, smelled the musky masculine scent that belonged exclusively to him, and knew that if he touched her she was lost.

Wrapping his hands in the abundance of her hair, he pulled her hard against him. His kiss was not gentle. It was fierce, hungry, demanding. Her knees buckled. In one graceful motion he swept her off her feet and carried her to the bed.

"God help me, for I can't help myself," Jaime groaned moments before he stripped them both naked.

Nude except for a sheet pulled up to her chin, Aleta lay in bed, staring up at the ceiling. Jaime no longer lay beside her. He had departed after an exhausting two hours that had left her bruised and hurting, and not just from his passionate assault. His departing words were indelibly inscribed upon her brain. "Aleta, my love, my heart and mind are at war where you're concerned. If you could but love me, who knows what our lives would be like? They say a fine line separates love and hate. On which side of that line do you dwell, my lady?" When she would have answered him, he shook his head and said, "Nay, my love, do not speak, for I already know the answer."

The great stupid oaf, Aleta silently ruminated. *Can he not feel how my body welcomes him? Does he not know how my heart embraces him?* That fine line between hate and love had been crossed long ago, but he was too dense to see it. And what about *his* feelings? Could he not say he cared for her? That he trusted her? She sighed despondently, wondering why the distance between her and Jaime could be easily bridged in bed but nowhere else. Granted they were both stubborn. They both had more pride than sense. And she knew full well that Jaime's quest to clear his father's name took precedence over all else—even love.

Over the voices in her head, Aleta heard a scratching at the door. "Aleta, 'tis I, Rowena. I have the key." Without waiting for an answer, Rowena turned the key in the lock and quietly stepped inside. She saw Aleta in bed, noticed her clothes scattered about the floor where Jaime had flung them, and her eyes blazed with fury. "What are you doing in bed in the middle of the day?"

Aleta bit her lip to keep from blurting out the truth to Rowena. She feared that Rowena would become so incensed after hearing the truth that she'd refuse to help her. But Rowena was astute enough to figure it out for herself.

"The room reeks of sex," she observed, glaring at Aleta. If looks could kill, Aleta would have been dead. " 'Twas my understanding that Jaime was avoiding you. What did you do to entice him?"

"This wasn't my idea," Aleta complained. "Forget it, I'll be leaving here soon anyway. Is everything arranged?"

"Aye," Rowena said sourly. "Jaime's leaving has simplified things. The men-at-arms are in the hall eating their noon meal and your horse is saddled and waiting for you in the stable. I'll distract the two men guarding the bailey while you lead your palfrey outside the curtain wall. Have you any idea where you will go?"

"Aye, I go to London to my father."

"Get dressed," Rowena said crisply. "I must get the key back into Gaylord's keeping before he misses it. Be assured the guards will be occupied while you make your escape. Since we are unlikely to meet again, my lady, I bid you farewell. Do not fear, I will care most diligently for your husband."

Aleta waited until Rowena closed the door behind her before leaping out of bed and struggling into her clothes. From under the bed she removed a satchel holding a few items of clothing and personal belongings she had made ready earlier. Then she left the chamber, peering down the darkened hallway before exposing herself. When she reached the winding staircase, she hurried down them as fast as her legs could carry her. She nearly panicked when she reached the third floor and heard voices coming from the hall. But by keeping to the shadows she was able to continue down the stairs unnoticed. Another moment of fear came when she had to descend the outside staircase into the bailey.

Miraculously Rowena had managed to distract the two knights, for they were nowhere in sight. A few more steps and she was in the stable. Aleta grasped the trailing reins of her palfrey and led him into the bailey and past the curtain wall. Once outside the curtain wall she mounted swiftly and rode away as if the devil himself was after her. She had no idea that Rowena left the keep a short time later, riding furiously in the direction of Grey Manor.

Evan Grey sat at the long wooden table in the great hall of his sprawling manor house that had once belonged to the Mortimers. Seated around him, his men-at-arms were devouring huge quantities of food and drink. But Grey seemed oblivious to the magnificent abundance of food as he scowled into the ornate gold cup containing his ale. How had the smugglers escaped his ambush? he wondered angrily. When the fog had lifted, only four smugglers remained on the beach among the barrels of brandy. And since they were all dead he was unable to learn the identity of the Lord of Darkness. Not that he didn't have his suspicions.

He cursed himself for not forcing more information from Rowena. Though she had insisted she was merely a simple village girl who had overheard information vital to the King, Grey knew there was more to her story than she had admitted. Aye, he had since learned that she was Jaime Mortimer's mistress. Which gave him pause for thought. He had first considered the possibility that Jaime Mortimer was the Lord of Darkness. But if that were true, why had his mistress betrayed him?

A commotion at the doorway caught his attention and he was surprised when the very lady he had been thinking about burst into the hall. Two knights were hard on her heels.

"My lord, I wish to speak with you," Rowena cried as the men caught up with her. " 'Tis most urgent."

"Let her enter," Grey said, motioning Rowena forward. "Are you alone? 'Tis dangerous for a lady to be out so late without an escort."

"I am alone, my lord, and have ridden a great distance." Her disheveled appearance lent credence to her words. Her hair was tangled from the wind, her clothing awry, and her face and neck smudged with dirt splattered from beneath the flying hooves of her mount. She looked on the verge of collapse.

"Sit, Rowena, and refresh yourself with food and drink," Grey said, sliding his trencher before her.

"Nay, my lord, there is no time. You must act swiftly if you wish to catch the bird in flight."

"Bird in flight?" Grey repeated. "Are you referring to the smugglers? Do you have word of further activities in the area? Say on, my lady."

"The bird I am talking about is the Lady Aleta," Rowena said, lowering her voice. "She has left Jaime and is fleeing to London. If you hurry you can catch her on the road. 'Tis full dark now and if she hasn't stopped in the woods for the night she will surely be hindered by darkness."

"Lady Aleta has left her husband?" Grey asked, delighted.

"Aye, she can no longer abide him and seeks sanctuary with her father in London. I know you were to wed the lady before Jaime claimed her and thought you'd be interested in hearing my news."

" 'Tis a long way to London," Grey mused. "Doesn't Lady Aleta realize the danger in traveling alone? Why didn't she come to me for succor? I can't believe the bastard has let her go without a fight. I will kill him if he has hurt her."

"Jaime left the keep, he doesn't know she is gone. I know not where Jaime has gone, only that he will not return for a day or two."

"I suspect you are not displeased by Lady Aleta's sudden departure," Grey observed slyly. "I have since learned that you are not a simple village girl as you claimed. You are Jaime Mortimer's whore."

Rowena looked surprised.

"Did you think I'd not seek information about you after the great service you have done me? My men were quite thorough. They learned you still reside in that great rotting hulk once referred to as Criccieth Castle. And since you are still there I can only assume you are servicing Mortimer."

Rowena wisely kept her silence, refusing to admit or deny anything Lord Grey said.

"Have you more information concerning the smugglers? A pity they escaped so handily. I'd pay well to learn the identity of the Lord of Darkness."

"Nay, I know nothing about the Lord of Darkness," Rowena lied. "Rumor has it that the smugglers have decided to cease their operation until the furor dies down."

"We will catch them," Grey vowed with a hint of menace. "And when we do they will all hang for their crimes."

"What do you intend to do about Lady Aleta?" Rowena asked abruptly. She didn't want to talk about the smugglers, she wanted to make certain

Aleta never returned to Jaime. And a man like Evan Grey was determined enough to make certain Aleta never saw Jaime again.

"I intend to ride immediately," Grey said, rising and calling for his men to join him. "Refresh yourself, Rowena. I will have a chamber prepared for you. Before you leave tomorrow I will see that you are rewarded generously for this night's work."

Thrill to the most sensual, adventure-filled Historical Romances on the market today...

FROM ◨ *LEISURE BOOKS*

As a home subscriber to Leisure Romance Book Club, you'll enjoy the best in today's BRAND-NEW Historical Romance fiction. For over twenty-five years, Leisure Books has brought you the award-winning, high-quality authors you know and love to read. Each Leisure Historical Romance will sweep you away to a world of high adventure...and intimate romance. Discover for yourself all the passion and excitement millions of readers thrill to each and every month.

Save $5.⁰⁰ Each Time You Buy!

Each month, the Leisure Romance Book Club brings you four brand-new titles from Leisure Books, America's foremost publisher of Historical Romances. EACH PACKAGE WILL SAVE YOU $5.00 FROM THE BOOKSTORE PRICE! And you'll never miss a new title with our convenient home delivery service.

Here's how we do it. Each package will carry a FREE 10-DAY EXAMINATION privilege. At the end of that time, if you decide to keep your books, simply pay the low invoice price of $16.96, no shipping or handling charges added. HOME DELIVERY IS ALWAYS FREE. With today's top Historical Romance novels selling for $5.99 and higher, our price SAVES YOU $5.00 with each shipment.

AND YOUR FIRST FOUR-BOOK SHIPMENT IS TOTALLY FREE!
IT'S A BARGAIN YOU CAN'T BEAT! A Super $21.96 Value!

◨ *LEISURE BOOKS*   A Division of Dorchester Publishing Co., Inc.

GET YOUR 4 FREE BOOKS
NOW—A $21.96 Value!
Mail the Free Book Certificate Today!

4 FREE BOOKS

A $21.96 VALUE

Free Books Certificate

YES! I want to subscribe to the Leisure Romance Book Club. Please send me my 4 FREE BOOKS. Then, each month I'll receive the four newest Leisure Historical Romance selections to Preview FREE for 10 days. If I decide to keep them, I will pay the Special Member's Only discounted price of just $4.24 each, a total of $16.96. This is a SAVINGS OF $5.00 off the bookstore price. There are no shipping, handling, or other charges. There is no minimum number of books I must buy and I may cancel the program at any time. In any case, the 4 FREE BOOKS are mine to keep—A BIG $21.96 Value!

Offer valid only in the U.S.A.

Name _____

Address _____

City _____

State _____ *Zip* _____

Telephone _____

Signature _____

If under 18, Parent or Guardian must sign. Terms, prices and conditions subject to change. Subscription subject to acceptance. Leisure Books reserves the right to reject any order or cancel any subscription.

A $21.96 VALUE

4 FREE BOOKS

Get Four Books Totally FREE — A $21.96 Value!

▼ Tear Here and Mail Your FREE Book Card Today! ▼

PLEASE RUSH
MY FOUR FREE
BOOKS TO ME
RIGHT AWAY!

Leisure Romance Book Club
P.O. Box 6613
Edison, NJ 08818-6613

AFFIX
STAMP
HERE

Chapter 11

Aleta rode until darkness closed over the land and she could no longer see the road. Since she was reasonably certain no one was following her, she led her palfrey into a copse of trees, unsaddled him, and curled up in her cloak on the mossy grass. Fortunately the night was mild, but Aleta would welcome the day she crossed over the River Dee into England where the Somerset name was respected and she'd have no trouble finding refuge at the various homes along the way. She realized that some might consider it odd that she was traveling without escort, but few would dare question an earl's daughter. With that thought she closed her eyes and fell deeply asleep.

Evan Grey returned to the manor when darkness hindered his search for Aleta, realizing that he wouldn't be able to see her if she passed him in the night. He knew Aleta couldn't have gotten far, so at first light the following morning he and ten of his men rode furiously toward London. He intercepted Aleta shortly after she had left the copse where she had spent the night.

Aleta saw the riders and a terrible fear seized her. Had Jaime discovered her absence already and come looking for her? Spurring her mount, she charged down the road, oblivious to the shouting going on behind her. But her palfrey was no match for the powerful war-horses ridden by Grey and his men. Grey caught up with her easily, grasping the reins and pulling her to an abrupt halt. A surge of relief pounded through Aleta when she saw it was Lord Grey stopping her flight and not her irate husband, for she knew that Jaime would be enraged when he found her gone.

"Lady Aleta, what are you doing so far from home? Does your husband care so little for you that he sends you out without an escort?" Grey thought it best to act as if he had met Aleta by chance, not because Jaime's whore had told him Aleta had left her husband.

"I—I go to London, Lord Grey, to my father. I'm sure Jaime would have sent an escort with me had he known I wanted to leave, but I left rather abruptly." A dull red crept up her neck. Did Evan know she was lying? "Jaime was away on—business; I left before he returned."

"Left or ran away, Lady Aleta? Have you finally come to your senses about that peasant you married? After our last conversation, I could have sworn you were infatuated with the traitor's son. If not for risking the King's wrath I would have gathered an army and taken you by force. Fortunately your father is close to winning an annulment from the highest court in the land. I still want you, my lady, despite the fact that Jaime Mortimer has bedded you." He jerked on the reins, turning her mount in the direction from which they came.

"Where are you taking me?"

"To Grey Manor. The house is a virtual fortress. Mortimer hasn't the men to launch an attack."

"Nay, my lord, I do not wish to go with you. I prefer to go to my father."

"You will come with me whether you like it or not, Aleta," Grey said in a voice that brooked no argument. "Your father will thank me for keeping you safe while he procures your annulment. Once you are free he will betroth you to me. I expect you to show proper gratitude for having been rescued from that interfering bastard who thinks he's good enough to marry an earl's daughter." He leered at her, giving her ample warning of what he wanted from her. Aleta suppressed a shudder of revulsion. Suddenly Even Grey no longer seemed as attractive as he once had.

"I'd much rather go to my father," Aleta told him. "Please release my reins so that I may be on my way."

Grey smiled diabolically. "Nay, my lady, you are mine now. Everything that once belonged to Mortimer is finally within my grasp. I wanted to kill Mortimer when he showed up to claim you. He will never get you back."

"Is that the reason you want me, Lord Grey?" Aleta asked coolly. "Why is it so important that you claim everything the Mortimers once owned?"

Grey's face hardened. " 'Tis a long story, my lady, and I won't bore you with it. Clarence Mortimer was a traitor and deserved to die."

"Not according to Jaime," Aleta contended. "I've changed my mind, my lord, I no longer wish to marry you."

Grey threw back his head and laughed uproariously. "How droll. It matters little what you want. Your father and I have already agreed upon the terms. Once the annulment is granted, Mortimer will have to return your dowry and it will be mine."

"I was forced into my first marriage, I will not be forced into a second," Aleta said with grim determination.

" 'Twould seem your husband failed to tame you, Aleta. I shall endeavor to remedy his oversight. Perhaps we should start before the annulment, just to demonstrate that I am a better man than Jaime Mortimer. You do understand what I want, don't you, my lady?"

"Nay, my lord, I certainly do not understand. You aren't the man I thought you were. Perhaps Jaime was right after all. Perhaps his father wasn't the traitor everyone claims."

A swift shadow of anger swept across his face. His whole demeanor was growing in severity. This was an Evan Grey Aleta had never seen before. "Heed me well, my lady: keep your opinions to yourself. You will find me a most generous husband if you obey me in all things. All I require of you is that you satisfy me in bed and bear my children. I do not need your opinions or criticisms."

Before Aleta could form a reply, Grey spurred his mount. Aleta's horse followed and she clung to his flowing mane in an effort to remain upright. No further conversation was possible as Grey's men swept Aleta toward Grey Manor at a furious speed.

Grey Manor was every bit as formidable as Evan said. Not as old as Criccieth keep, it stood on a slight rise surrounded by a deep moat. A thick wall circled the perimeter and a stone gate house stood guard at one end of the drawbridge, which was now lowered to allow their entrance. The manor itself was more imposing than any Aleta had ever seen. Inside the walled enclosure stood a chapel, thatched barn and stable, piggery, smithy, kitchen with elaborate chimney, and a fenced-in garden. A well stood in the middle of the yard.

"What do you think of my manor, my lady?" Grey gestured with a proud sweep of his hand.

"*Your* manor, my lord?" The haughty arch of her brow effectively conveyed her contempt.

"Aye, *my* manor. Everything that once belonged to the Mortimers is now mine. The manor, the serfs, the land as far as the eye can see, and all the wealth the family had accumulated down through the years—and you, my lady. Soon this will all be yours, Aleta."

"I don't want it," Aleta said pointedly. "Nor do I want to remain here with you. It wouldn't be right, I am a married woman."

Grey dismounted, jerking her none too gently from the saddle and pulling her hard against him. "You won't be married for long, my lady, so you may as well get used to me." He ran his hands brazenly over her back and buttocks in a bold display of ownership. Aleta struggled to free herself but Grey merely laughed and pulled her closer.

"My desire for you has never waned, my lady. Can you feel how much I want you?"

Aleta flinched, feeling the thrust of his thick manhood against her belly. "Please, Lord Grey, release me. Your men are watching. If we are to be wed you must show me respect, at least in front of your retainers."

Aleta's mind worked furiously. Though she had no intention of wedding Lord Grey, she thought it made sense to let him think she was amenable to his plans. At least until she could find a way to es-

cape or get word to her father. Surely her father
wasn't in agreement with Lord Grey, was he? Why
had she ever left Jaime? she lamented. After seeing
and listening to Evan she knew there was absolutely no way she would ever marry the man. She
preferred being Jaime's prisoner to ending up as
Evan's wife. Had she remained with Jaime she
might have convinced him in time to trust her.
Maybe he'd never love her, but her own love
would have been enough to sustain her.

Grey's hands dropped to his sides and he
stepped away from Aleta. "You are right, my
lady," he concurred. "I want no gossip to follow
you into our marriage. I will endeavor to contain
my ardor until we are wed." In a voice meant only
for her, he added, "Except when we are in private." Then, more loudly, "Come, my lady, I will
show you to your chamber. 'Tis the best in the
manor. I hope you will like it."

Inside, the manor was as opulent as the outside
indicated. Rich tapestries hung on the walls and
the carpets beneath her feet felt thick and plush.
The great hall was every bit as magnificent as the
one at Somerset Manor and possibly as grand as
the King's own Windsor Castle. As she passed
through immense rooms hung with vivid paint-
ings and rich draperies and hangings, Aleta could
picture Jaime, dressed in satin and brocade, strid-
ing within these walls. He belonged in a setting
such as this, she mused as Evan led her up a
winding staircase.

"Your chamber, my lady," he said as he flung
open the door to a set of two huge rooms. The first
was a solar, complete with spinning wheel and
cushioned chairs. But it was the inner chamber
that brought a gasp from Aleta's soft lips.

It was definitely a lady's room, decorated in soft pastels with silk and satin hangings and carpets so thick her feet sunk in up to her ankles. " 'Tis—'tis most impressive," Aleta said for want of a better word.

"I'm glad you like it, Aleta. One day I will join you in yonder bed. If your annulment isn't forthcoming soon I may forego the ceremony in favor of the consummation."

Aleta's face flamed. *Over my dead body!* she thought angrily.

Mistaking her flushed face as an indication of her pleasure, Grey growled deep in his throat and pulled her close. "That notion seems to please you, my lady. Did Mortimer teach you things about yourself you never knew before? Did he make you writhe and cry out?" His grip tightened. "I despise him for taking your virginity, but who knows, maybe he did me a favor. How experienced are you, Aleta? Did he teach you to crave a man's touch, to desire the thrust of a man's body inside yours?"

Aye, Jaime's body! her mind cried. *Not yours! Never yours.*

Evan leered wolfishly at her before lowering his mouth and covering hers in a hungry kiss. His lips were hard and demanding and Aleta struggled to escape his unwelcome kisses. She didn't want this. She didn't want Evan! She knew that now, knew it with every fiber of her being. Leaving Jaime had been a terrible mistake. Lord Grey's kisses made her cringe in revulsion while Jaime's kisses sent shivers of desire racing through her. If she could return to Criccieth keep right now, she would do so with the knowledge that Jaime was the only man she could ever love.

Suddenly Evan shoved her away. "You'll have to do better than that, my lady, if you wish to please me." Was there a hint of menace in his voice? Aleta wondered as she scrubbed her lips with the back of her hand. She hated the taste and scent of him.

"I do not wish to please you, my lord," she dared to say. "I wish to return to my husband. Or continue on to London to join my father."

"You will remain in my protection until your annulment is forthcoming," Grey said sternly. "Unfortunately I must report to the King personally concerning the smugglers."

Aleta's spirits soared. "You will take me with you?"

"Nay, you will remain here under guard. My steward, Sir Gillan, can be trusted to follow my orders to the letter. You are not to leave your chamber during my absence. A guard will remain outside your door at all times. But do not think your husband will fight his way inside these walls, for I have a sizable army at my disposal and intend leaving most of them here to defend the manor and—" He leered at her again. "—my most prized possession. When I return we shall see how much your crude lover has taught you. Until then, try not to miss me too much."

Whirling around, he strode out the door. Aleta stared after him in consternation. Evan's words led her to believe she could expect no help from her father. Indeed, her father had been in favor of the match between herself and Evan from the beginning. She waited a few minutes, then walked to the outer chamber and cautiously opened the door, thinking to flee before anyone knew she was gone. Immediately a burly guard blocked her path.

"Is there something you wish, my lady?" he asked respectfully.

"I—I wish to leave," Aleta demanded with as much authority as she could muster.

"My orders are to keep you within these rooms until Lord Grey returns from London. A maid will attend you directly, but meanwhile, please return to your chamber."

Her face flushed with anger, she spun on her heel and returned to her room, slamming the door behind her. How dare he! she fumed in silent rage. How dare Lord Grey kidnap her and keep her against her will. Immediately her mind turned to thoughts of escape.

Glancing toward the two windows, she saw that both were barred against intruders. But even if she did manage to escape this room, the drawbridge and moat presented a formidable obstacle. *Jaime,* she silently implored, *what have I done?*

Jaime returned to the keep in a lighthearted mood. His journey to Flint had provided him with the information he had sought. People on the street needed little prodding to talk about the smugglers reported to be operating in the area. Most were supportive of the illegal activity that robbed the King of revenue. The English were universally despised by the Welsh and any activity that deprived King Henry of the coin needed to finance his foreign wars had their wholehearted support. Many of the townspeople called the Lord of Darkness a hero, speculating on his identity and lauding his daring exploits. That none appeared to know his identity boded well for Jaime.

One man, claiming to be a relative of one of Lord Grey's knights, told Jaime that Lord Grey had no idea who the Lord of Darkness was. After that conversation Jaime decided there was nothing more to be learned in Flint and had returned to the keep. He was anxious to see Aleta again. She had created a wanting in him that plagued him both night and day. He needed to see her again, to make sure she was all right.

To love her.

And he was most anxious to learn why she had betrayed him yet deliberately withheld information about the Lord of Darkness.

Jaime knew something was wrong the moment he entered the keep. Gaylord met him at the door, a worried frown creasing his wrinkled features. "Something has happened, Gaylord, what is it?"

"Aye," Gaylord said, fully aware that Jaime was going to be furious. Since there was no way to soften the blow, he blurted out, " 'Tis your lady, Lord Jaime."

Jaime blanched. "Aleta? Has something happened to Aleta? Out with it, old man, I want the truth!"

Gaylord's shoulders sagged. "The truth is, I don't know what happened to Lady Aleta. When I brought her breakfast the morning after you left, I found her gone. 'Twas most strange, Jaime, the door was locked and the only key was in my possession."

"Gone? God's blood, man, where could she have gone? Who let her out?"

"I don't know, Jaime, truly. I have questioned everyone in the keep but learned nothing. To my knowledge the key to her chamber was safely hidden and never left my chamber. That same morning her palfrey was discovered missing from the stable."

"What of the men, have they searched for my lady?"

"Aye, they left immediately, but found no trace of her. I had assumed she'd go to London, to her father, but she was not found on the London road, nor had any of the travelers seen her."

"How long has she been gone?" Jaime asked tightly.

"Three days now, my lord Jaime."

"God's blood, my lady could be dead by now, or kidnapped by fierce Welshmen!" The anguish in his voice was terrible to hear. "Why, Gaylord? Why did she leave?"

"Search your heart for the answer, Jaime," Gaylord advised with a hint of censure.

"I know where the Lady Aleta has gone." Rowena's smug voice startled Jaime and Gaylord. They had been so intent in their conversation that neither had seen Rowena approach.

Jaime whirled on her, his face a mask of fury. "What do you know about this, Rowena?"

"N-nothing," she stuttered, realizing that she had made a grave error by speaking. But it was too late to back down now. "I sometimes spoke with Aleta through the locked door," Rowena admitted. "She—she confided that she hated being locked up and longed to escape so she could go to Lord Grey."

"Why would Aleta confide in you?" Jaime scoffed. " 'Tis no secret that you hated my lady."

"We are both women, Jaime. Confidences come naturally."

"So Aleta said she wanted Grey, did she?" Jaime questioned closely.

"Oh, aye, Jaime, she very much wanted Lord Grey."

"And you let her out of her room so she could go to him," he charged.

"Nay, nay, I would not disobey your orders. I don't know how she escaped. Question your men-at-arms, they admired her greatly. Perhaps one of them unlocked her door in exchange for—favors," she hinted slyly.

"Liar!" Jaime shouted, grasping Rowena's arms and shaking her until her teeth rattled. "Tell me the truth, wench. You released Aleta, didn't you?"

"Nay, Jaime, I did not!"

"Perhaps a beating will loosen your tongue," he threatened. Deliberately he withdrew his riding crop from his belt, making a great show of testing its strength against his palm.

Rowena licked her suddenly dry lips. Would Jaime really beat her? She must have been stupid to let Aleta talk her into releasing her. She should have known that Jaime wouldn't believe her, but she had been so anxious to be rid of Aleta that she had lost whatever sense she possessed. When Jaime raised the whip high in the air, Rowena's courage fled.

"Nay, Jaime, don't hurt me! Aye, I unlocked your lady's door, but only after she begged me to set her free. I was not lying when I said she wanted Lord Grey. You will find her there now, in his manor, in his bed. She hated you and couldn't wait to get to him."

"Bitch!" Jaime thundered, shoving her away from him. She stumbled and fell against a table. He gave her a black-layered look as she righted herself.

"Does the truth hurt, my lord?" Rowena asked

spitefully. "You've always known your lady preferred Lord Grey."

"Get out of here, Rowena, before I do you serious harm."

"You need me now, Jaime, don't send me away." She sidled close, pressing against him in a most provocative manner. "Have you forgotten so soon how your body responded when I pleasured you? I can make you forget Aleta, if you allow it."

"Be gone with you!" he ripped out impatiently.

Rowena bit down hard on her lip. "You don't mean that, Jaime."

"I have never been more serious." His lips thinned and his eyes were so black they reminded her of the darkest hell. "You have one hour to pack a small bag and leave the keep. You are no longer welcome in my home."

"You'd send me away? Alone? With nothing but a small bag?"

" 'Tis not what I intended, Rowena, but you have left me no choice. Gaylord will tell you where to find your brother and see that you have sufficient coin to seek lodging along the way. Expect nothing more from me."

Rowena's face was a glowering mask of rage as shock yielded to fury. "I will leave, but you haven't heard the last from me." Abruptly she realized that anger would get her nowhere with Jaime and decided to change her tactics. "But I am a reasonable woman," she continued in a placating tone. "I will give you a week to change your mind. I am well acquainted with your fierce temper. When it cools you will realize that sending me away is a mistake. You can find me in the village. But if I do not see you by the end of seven days," she added ominously, "you will be sorry for treating me so shabbily." Whirling on her heel, she strode away.

"I fear you have made a powerful enemy," Gaylord warned, having been privy to the entire exchange.

"Rowena can't hurt me, she knows nothing," Jaime returned shortly. "I should have sent the bitch away long ago but I was concerned over her welfare. I doubt not that she is perfectly capable of taking care of herself. Let her brother deal with her, I wash my hands of her. See that she is gone within the hour."

"Aye, Jaime," Gaylord said, not at all convinced they had seen the last of Rowena. "What of the Lady Aleta? Do you truly think she has flown to Evan Grey?"

"I believe it," Jaime said bitterly. "As Rowena so aptly put it, my lady has always preferred the wealthy Lord Grey to a peasant with dung on his shoes."

"You are no peasant, Jaime. Your blood is every bit as noble as your lady's. You come from noble loins. Your ancestors count a king among their forebearers."

"Tell that to my lady," Jaime said sarcastically.

"Will you let Grey have her?"

"Nay!" Jaime shouted. His expression grew so fierce Gaylord took an involuntary step backward. "Aleta is mine. She was meant to be mine from the moment of her birth and shall remain mine. Evan Grey has taken all else from me—he will not have my wife."

"You haven't the manpower to attack Grey Manor," Gaylord reminded him.

"If you are referring to Mortimer Manor," Jaime corrected, "I do not intend to storm the fortress.

No one knows better than I that the manor is impenetrable. Have you forgotten that I spent my childhood behind those stone walls?"

"I have forgotten nothing, Jaime."

"Then you will recall that the manor is honeycombed with secret tunnels and that as a child I played often in those dark passages."

"God's blood, Jaime, I *had* forgotten. My mind grows dim with age."

"*I* have not forgotten, old friend. I remember every nook and cranny of those winding tunnels. While I was growing up at Criccieth I played mind games to keep my ancestral home clear in my memory. Each night before retiring I would search my brain and memorize each entrance and exit to all the secret passages within the manor. Every nook and cranny of Mortimer Manor is as vivid to me as it was when I lived there."

Gaylord stared in amazement. He had always known Jaime was a remarkable man; it had been proven to him many times in many ways. "How will you get past the wall? I doubt they will lower the drawbridge for you."

Jaime grinned cheekily. "Simple. One of the tunnels leads to a small cave in the side of a nearby hill. If you recall, the entrance is well hidden by shrubbery; only someone who knows it is there would find it. The tunnels were built when the manor was constructed as a means of escape should the manor be attacked or surrounded. I will wait until dark to make my way inside the manor."

"It could work," Gaylord mused thoughtfully. "If the tunnels aren't blocked after all these years and the Lady Aleta agrees to leave with you."

Jaime's expression hardened. "She will leave

with me whether she is agreeable or not. She may prefer Grey but she is my wife." He did not reveal the soul-wrenching anguish he suffered when Rowena told him Aleta had fled straight into Evan Grey's arms.

He hadn't meant to fall in love, but his heart and body had worked independently of his mind. Before he knew it Aleta had ensnared him so completely there was no escape. Having once unleashed the sweet wonder of her passion, no other woman could ever satisfy him.

"Be prepared to bind and gag her," Gaylord warned. "One cry from your lady and Grey and his henchmen will have your head."

"Do not fear, Gaylord, I have no intention of being caught. I shall depend on you to see that Rowena leaves the keep as I have directed. I do not want her to know what I am planning."

"I will personally escort Rowena to the village," Gaylord promised. "What about the men-at-arms? Do you take them with you?"

"Nay, I go alone. Tell no one of my plans lest word reaches Grey. Leave me now, my friend, while I prepare for my venture into Mortimer Manor. 'Twill seem like old times, Gaylord."

Aleta slipped into the nightdress the maid held out to her, then curtly dismissed the woman who had been assigned to see to her needs. The only reason she had donned the nightdress was to allay suspicion. No one must know she harbored thoughts of escape. She knew the guard was still posted outside her door, for she had caught a glimpse of him when the maid left. He looked even more fierce than the man left to guard her door the day before. She prayed that Evan would be detained in London longer than expected, at least until she had found a way to escape. It was ironic that she had exchanged one prison for another. Right now she'd have given anything to be languishing in Jaime's chamber instead of living in fear of Evan's return.

By now Jaime would have returned to the keep, she reflected. Had he been angry when he found her gone? Did he miss her? Had he gone looking for her? Did he even care that she had left? Was Rowena comforting him? She had never imagined that picturing Rowena and Jaime together would hurt so deeply, but she had only herself to blame, for she had literally handed Jaime to Rowena on a platter. She must have been insane to think she could forget a man like Jaime Mortimer.

When the night grew so dark that she could barely see her hand before her face, Aleta crept to the door in the outer chamber. She had deliberately stayed awake, praying that her guard would fall asleep and leave her room unattended. The door opened noiselessly beneath her fingertips and she peered out through the crack. Dancing shadows played upon the walls, produced by light from a torch placed in a sconce in the darkened hallway. Her spirits soared when she did not see the guard. Creeping out into the hallway, she took a step forward, prepared to run like the wind, but no one challenged her. Suddenly, a giant shadow was cast upon the wall as the guard appeared like magic from a darkened corner.

"Do you wish something, my lady? I will summon your maid."

"Oh, you frightened me," Aleta gasped shakily as she searched her mind for a logical explanation for her midnight foray. "I could not sleep, and thought a cup of warm milk would help. But do not bother waking Hilde, I have changed my mind."

"Whatever you say, my lady." He stared at her hard and Aleta suddenly realized she was standing in her nightdress. Though buttoned to the neck, limned in the flickering light it was sheer enough to give him a tantalizing glimpse of the curves beneath the thin material.

Turning abruptly, she fled into her room, closing the door behind her. Her cheeks were flaming, her heart pounding like a trip-hammer. Without Evan in the manor to protect her she was at the mercy of her guards. The thought was sobering.

Since escape seemed unlikely this night, Aleta reluctantly sought her bed. She closed her eyes, but sleep would not come. Then a tiny noise, hardly more than a scrape of stone against stone, captured her attention. Her eyes flew open as she peered into the darkness, seeing nothing. Yet all her senses were alive and tingling. Her instincts warned her that someone had entered her chamber. She felt it with every fiber of her being. Sensed it so keenly her mouth opened in a silent scream. A shudder of dread slid down her spine as a hand clapped over her mouth.

She felt an odd sensation deep in the pit of her stomach when a low, husky voice whispered close to her ear, "Do not scream, my lady, or I will be forced to resort to drastic measures."

Chapter 12

Reeling with shock, Aleta was so stunned she couldn't have screamed even if she had wanted to. There was no possible way Jaime could have gotten into her room. Unless he could evaporate and materialize at will. The windows were barred, the guard never left his station outside her door, and she had been in the chamber three days without finding a way out.

The pressure on Aleta's mouth eased and Jaime's harsh whisper warned her, "If you value your life and that of your lover, do not cry out."

"Nay, Jaime, I would not cry out," Aleta gasped breathlessly. If it hadn't been pitch-black in the chamber Aleta would have seen Jaime's eyes widen in disbelief.

"Come," he urged. "Make no sound."

She was out of bed in an instant, searching for the dress she had removed earlier.

"God's blood," Jaime hissed impatiently, "what are you looking for?"

"My dress," Aleta whispered back.

"Forget it, there's no time. I'll buy you all the clothes you need." Roughly he grasped her arm and pulled her forward.

"Where are you taking me? How did you get in here? Are you a magician?"

"Save your questions for later. Never say you don't want to come with me for I'll take you from here forcibly if I must. Even if Grey has bedded you, you are still mine, Aleta, and I won't let him have you. If I had found him in your bed tonight I would have killed him."

"I didn't—" The words died in her throat as Jaime pulled her toward a seemingly blank wall and stopped abruptly, causing her to run into him. "Wha—"

She stared in consternation as Jaime reached forward and turned a wall sconce a certain way. A surprised yelp escaped her lips when she heard the same dull scraping noise she had noticed before. She could hardly believe her eyes when a section of wall turned slightly, revealing a hidden passage.

"Oh. That's how—"

"Quiet!" Jaime hissed as he took her hand and pulled her after him.

Earlier he had placed a torch in the sconce in the secret passageway and Aleta could see the gaping tunnel stretching endlessly before her. When he turned to retrieve the torch he must have released the catch on the hidden panel for it slid smoothly shut.

"How did you know . . . ?"

"I lived the first fifteen years of my life in this keep," Jaime explained before she completed the sentence. "I know every nook and cranny by heart. My father showed me these tunnels when I was still a toddler. I played in them often, pretending I was a knight of old escaping a fierce siege. Do not cry out to your lover," he warned harshly, "for sound carries in these passages. We must pass by Grey's chamber and beneath the moat before we are safe."

"I would not . . ."

"Tell me no lies, my lady," Jaime cautioned sternly as he led her through the maze of tunnels. It amazed Aleta that he knew exactly which turn to take without becoming hopelessly lost. She squawked in panic when something furry ran over her foot. A squeeze of Jaime's hand warned her to silence and she forced a calm she didn't feel.

When she heard the rush of water she stopped abruptly, refusing to budge.

" 'Tis only the moat," Jaime said with a hint of impatience. "The tunnel runs beneath it in one place. Be careful, the walls leak water and the floor will be slippery till we pass beyond the moat."

Slippery wasn't the word for it, Aleta thought with a grimace as her bare feet slid and skidded through murky puddles oozing green slime. At one point she lost her footing and would have fallen if Jaime hadn't thrust the torch into her hands and swept her up into his arms. By now she was chilled to the bone and shivering, and she welcomed the heat of his big body. She could tell by the way he acted that he was angry with her, but she couldn't blame him. She had sought to escape an intolerable situation, but the one she had inadvertently leaped into was far worse than the one she had left.

They continued on for what seemed like miles, winding and turning in various directions until Aleta feared Jaime was lost. Once they had passed beyond the moat she had expected to be set on her

feet, but Jaime continued to carry her, as if loath to
set her down.

Jaime was indeed loath to release Aleta. Now
that he had found her, he never wanted to let her
go. She felt so good in his arms, all warm and soft,
that losing her now would have been just as great
a tragedy as losing his father had been all those
years ago. His expression grew fierce when he
considered that she had left him for another man.
But he'd be damned if he'd let Evan Grey have
her. He didn't care how much Aleta despised him,
he still wanted her. Would always want her.

Would always love her.

Damn her!

Damn her for putting him through hell. For testing his patience. For turning him inside out. For
leaving him for another man. For making him love
her.

Aleta clung to Jaime with one hand and the
torch with the other as he carried her through the
tunnel. Dawn was still hours away when they
emerged from the narrow passage into a large
chamber barely high enough to stand in. Jaime set
her on her feet.

"You'll have to crawl through the cave entrance," he cautioned. "Wait for me on the other
side. I'll join you as soon as I douse the torch. The
light could easily be seen from the manor and I'd
prefer your absence not be discovered until morning. By then we will be nearly home."

He shoved her toward a small round opening;
Aleta dropped to her hands and knees and
crawled through. She filled her lungs with the
scent of fresh, clean air as she waited for Jaime to
appear. Then she saw him. He had emerged from
the opening and was piling brush and stones in

front of the entrance until it was completely hidden from view. When he finished he said nothing, merely taking her hand and leading her into a nearby woods. His huge black stallion snorted softly in welcome and then Jaime was lifting her onto his broad back. She felt him settle in the saddle behind her and an instant later they were on their way to Criccieth keep.

Sometime during the night Aleta fell asleep, supported by the strength of Jaime's arms and the comfortable bulk of his big body. She did not see the expression on his face or hear his voice as he whispered into her ear, "Rest well, my lady, for when we return to the keep you have much to account for."

They traveled all night, and when the light of day revealed how skimpily Aleta was dressed, Jaime removed his cape and placed it over her shoulders. Though her stomach rumbled from hunger, they did not tarry to find a bite to eat.

"Persevere, my lady," Jaime advised, "for 'tis too dangerous to stop along the way. By now your lover knows you have flown and has ordered his army out to find you. Once we are at Criccieth I doubt he will risk Henry's anger and attack."

Aleta's temper flared. "How dare you call Lord Grey my lover! I did not go to him willingly and I certainly did not allow him in my bed."

"Did you not?" Sarcasm made his voice harsh. "I was amazed to find you alone in your bed."

"For your information, Lord Grey wasn't even in the keep. He left for London immediately after he brought me to his manor. The King had summoned him to report on the smugglers."

Jaime gave her a hard, searching look. "Am I to

assume you told him I am the Lord of Darkness? Should I expect a visit from the King's tax men?"

"Why can't you trust me, my lord?"

"Why did you run to Grey, my lady?" Jaime shot back.

"I did not. Who told you such a blatant lie?"

Jaime frowned, not at all sure now that Rowena had spoken the truth. Just then the keep came into view and conversation came to a halt as the men-at-arms rode out to meet them. In fact, there were so many men-at-arms that Aleta wondered where they had all come from.

"Is all well, Lord Jaime?" Sir Giles asked as he slanted a censuring glance at Aleta.

"Aye, Sir Giles. As you can see, I have my lady back. Have you followed my orders?"

"Aye. We have recruited men just like you directed. Many more will arrive soon. Word has been spread that a wealthy Welsh baron is taking men into his service."

"Wealthy?" Aleta questioned, sending Jaime an oblique look.

"Did you not know, my lady? Smuggling pays very well. I did not need your dowry, nor have I spent any of it. 'Tis yours to do with as you please."

"Did you say *wealthy?*" Aleta repeated angrily. "Why did you let me think you were a landless pauper?"

Jaime shrugged. "It seemed expedient to do so at the time." His explanation did little to appease her. "Pauper and peasant were your words, not mine. Besides, my land was stolen from me; I truly am landless."

Aleta had the grace to flush, realizing the truth of Jaime's words. She had insulted him time after time, ignoring the fact that his blood was as noble as hers and unaware that his ill-gotten wealth was probably equal to her own father's. But how could she have known that he was rich when his clothing and circumstances indicated that the opposite was true?

Her thoughts scattered as they rode past the curtain wall into the bailey, where more men-at-arms awaited them. Jaime dismounted and lifted her to the ground. "Go to your chamber, my lady, I wish to speak with my men. Gaylord will see that you are provided with food and a bath."

"I won't be locked in again."

"Do I have your promise not to run to Grey the first chance you get?"

"I want nothing to do with Lord Grey. I abhor the man."

Jaime's eyebrows shot upward. "Do you, my lady? Why don't I believe you? Go, Aleta, you are free to roam wherever you please in the keep. If I lock you in your chamber you will just coax someone to let you out. Obviously you had little difficulty convincing Rowena to release you."

Aleta froze. "How do you know Rowena released me?"

"I forced her to confess. After she told me you were fleeing to Grey."

"So that's why you're so eager to believe the worst," Aleta said bitterly. "Did Rowena comfort you in my absence?"

Jaime's black eyes were dark with fury. "I sent her away. She will trouble you no more."

"You—you sent her away?" Aleta was astounded. Having Jaime all to herself was a thrilling prospect. Now all she had to do was make him love her.

"We'll talk about it later, Aleta. Much later, after my temper has cooled. I fear I won't be able to control my anger if we speak now. But be warned, my lady, I will expect a full explanation from you."

Aleta stared at him hard, then turned and fled into the keep. After a meal and a bath, she was so exhausted she curled up in the bed and fell into a sound sleep. When Jaime arrived two hours later she was still sleeping. He did not awaken her. But he stood over her an inordinately long time staring at her, wondering what was so special about her that made him want her above all other women.

Her long silvery hair circled her head like a bright halo, giving her a sweetly angelic look. Yet she had proven time and again she was no angel. Her features were soft and feminine, her complexion peaches and cream. Her body was truly fashioned by the gods, he reflected. Small, but ripe and lush, and so alluring it was difficult to keep his hands off her. Reluctant to awaken her from a much-needed nap, Jaime slowly turned and walked away.

Aleta awoke refreshed and ready to face her husband's wrath. Glancing out the window slit, she saw that she had slept the afternoon away. She put on her prettiest dress, a coral silk cut low to show off her high bosom. Deciding against the *hennin*, she brushed her hair until it shimmered like silvery moonbeams and let it hang unfettered to her waist. But all her careful preparations were unnecessary, for Jaime was not in the hall to partake of the evening meal. Only the faithful Gaylord was at the table to greet her, and those of the knights who weren't occupied with duties.

"I trust you are well, my lady," Gaylord said solicitously. "You had us all worried."

"Even Jaime?" Aleta asked lightly.

"Aye, Jaime more than anyone."

You mean angry, Aleta silently contradicted. So angry that he was avoiding her lest his temper cause him to do her serious harm. Why did he always try to do his best to destroy her love? Didn't he realize she cared for him? Obviously not if he believed she had gone of her own accord to Lord Grey. She finished her meal quickly, excused herself, and went to her room. She wasn't at all tired after her long nap so she lit a candle and sat staring into the flickering flame until Bess came to help ready her for bed.

"How is your husband?" Aleta asked the tiring woman as she helped her on with her nightdress. "I hope his wounds are healed."

"My man is recovered, my lady," Bess said nervously. She had heard all the gossip about Aleta having betrayed the smugglers and feared saying anything that might endanger them.

Aleta was astute enough to realize Bess's dilemma and immediately sought to soothe her fears. "I did not betray your men, Bess. I would never do such a terrible thing. Had I done so I would have betrayed my own husband. Do you think I am capable of such an ignoble act?"

Bess searched Aleta's face, and obviously found her answer. "Nay, my lady, I did not believe the gossip spread by Rowena. Many of us believe you incapable of such deceit. But when Lord Jaime locked you in your chamber everyone believed you were being punished. Rowena fanned the flames with her malicious gossip. But if you swear you are not guilty I will believe you."

"I swear it, good Bess."

"What is it you are swearing to, my lady?" Startled, both Aleta and Bess whirled to face Jaime, who had entered the chamber noiselessly and now stood with his wide shoulders braced against the doorjamb.

"Leave us, Bess," Aleta told the tiring woman. "I wish to speak to my husband in private." She could wait no longer to tell Jaime that she was sorry that she had left, that she had never intended to end up as Lord Grey's prisoner, that she cared for him, only him.

Bess flung a sympathetic look at Aleta before she scooted from the room.

When they were alone, Jaime moved away from the doorway and quietly closed the door. Aleta stood her ground at the foot of the bed, dressed in virginal white and looking as fragile as a butterfly.

"Have you been avoiding me, my lord?" she asked softly.

"Perhaps," Jaime admitted, facing her squarely. They were standing mere inches apart, so close he could feel the soft caress of her breath whisper over his cheeks. Suddenly his thoughts fractured into a million pieces as a giant hand reached into his chest and squeezed the breath from him. He took an involuntary step backward, realizing he would never be able to think straight while he was close enough to touch her. And there were so many things he wanted to ask Aleta, so much she needed to explain.

Abruptly Aleta turned and perched on the edge of the bed. She knew what Jaime wanted to ask and forestalled his question. "I did not intend to go to Lord Grey when I left here, my lord."

"Where did you intend to go, Aleta?"

"To London, to my father."

She could tell by his expression that he did not believe her.

"Why?"

"Would you be happy locked in a room?" Aleta charged. "You make love to me, yet care nothing about me. Then you accuse me of betraying you. You prefer Rowena to me. I couldn't bear it."

"Prefer Rowena to you?" Jaime repeated, astounded. "Nay, my lady, never! I swear by all that's holy that I have not touched Rowena since before we were wed."

Aleta's eyes widened. Jaime had told her before that he hadn't bedded Rowena but she hadn't believed him. A solemn oath was another matter. An honorable man would never give a solemn oath unless he meant it. And even when she thought she hated Jaime she believed him an honorable man.

" 'Tis your turn for confession." His voice was low, intense, his expression taut. "You've never hidden the fact that you prefer Evan Grey to me. Is that why you rushed into his bed the moment you were free?"

The tension between them was drawn as tightly as a bowstring as she returned his intent gaze. "I give you my solemn oath that I did not flee to Lord Grey, nor did I share his bed. I was going to London when he intercepted me. It was as if he knew the exact moment I had left Criccieth and was waiting for me."

She could tell by the look in his eyes that he wanted to believe her, but something deep inside him refused. "It matters not, my love," he said huskily. "Needless to say, I would have risked anything to get you back. I'll never let you go, Aleta."

"Perhaps I no longer want to leave," Aleta said huskily.

"Why this sudden change of heart?" Uncertainty made his voice harsh.

Aleta bit her lip and looked away. "It—it wasn't so sudden."

Grasping her pointed chin between thumb and forefinger, he forced her to look into his eyes. They were black as sin and ruthlessly compelling. "What are you trying to tell me, Aleta? That you suddenly find yourself overwhelmed by my charm? Me, a destitute peasant? Do I no longer smell of dung and horseflesh?" His voice dripped with sarcasm.

"I haven't thought of you as a peasant for a long time." She made a disgusted sound deep in her throat. "You're as dense as you are stupid."

"Stupid! Dense! Is that all, my lady?"

His roar would have intimidated the hardiest soul, but Aleta was no fainthearted lady. Though her chin trembled, her voice did not falter. "Nay, my lord, there is more."

His expression was thunderous. "Say on, my lady."

"You are braver than any man I know. Sometimes your arrogance is unbearable, but you always treat the men who follow you with respect. You are honest and trustworthy, except in regards to me," she added, flashing him a sad little smile, "and handsome."

Jaime stared at her as if she had lost her mind. "What about dense and stupid?"

"That too. Only a dense man would fail to see

that his wife cares for him and no one but a stupid one would refuse to trust her."

Jaime's heart slammed painfully against his rib cage. He wanted to believe Aleta. Wanted to trust her with his whole heart and soul. And yet— Was she merely mouthing what he wanted to hear in order to keep the truth about her and Grey from him?

"I want to believe you, lady." He stepped closer, so close the heat of her body seemed to scorch him. He reached out, almost afraid to touch her, fearing she'd go up in smoke and blow away. Had he dreamed her words because he wanted to hear them so badly?

"Jaime." She swayed toward him, and then she was in his arms, held so tightly against his heart she felt its strong beat as if it were her own.

"God's blood, Aleta, no man has ever wanted a woman as badly as I want you."

"Then take me, Jaime, I'm yours."

His gaze swept over her face and searched her eyes, and the prolonged anticipation was almost unbearable. The heartrending tenderness of his gaze added a new element to this complex man she had married. Against all odds he had unlocked her heart and soul and she'd never be the same again. His lips hovered over her mouth, his tongue tracing the fullness of her lips. He kissed her with his eyes before he covered her mouth hungrily. Rising to meet him, she parted her mouth to the hot ravishment of his tongue. He crushed her to him, kissing her mouth, her chin, the racing pulse at the base of her throat.

His hands were shaking as he unbuttoned her nightdress, baring her breasts to his questing fingers. His mouth burned a blazing trail to one white globe and his tongue caressed the sensitive swollen nipple. Aleta cried out in wonder. His hands slid over her silken belly, sweeping her nightdress over her hips with a subtle twist of his wrists. He would have picked her up and carried her to the bed if Aleta hadn't stopped him.

"No, not yet," she pleaded, denying him his heart's desire. "I—I want to touch you in the same way you touch me." Shocked by her own boldness, she lowered her eyes.

Jaime smiled uncertainly. "Touch away, my love. But I'm not certain how much I can take."

"Persevere, my lord," she teased, "as you have taught me to do."

Her hands slipped beneath his tunic, raising it above his head. Eagerly Jaime assisted her, slipping it from his arms and tossing it aside. "Now what, my love?" he asked huskily.

Smiling with wicked delight, she explored his chest, her fingers lingering in the silken mat of black hair before roaming over the broad expanse of his shoulders and back. His muscles jumped and tensed beneath her searching fingertips and a moan slipped past his lips. "Now, my lord," she said, giving him a saucy grin, "I want to taste you."

Jaime's gasp sounded like an explosion as her mouth covered his male nipple; the tip of her hot little tongue lashing it relentlessly. Jaime started to pull away but Aleta grasped his hips, imprisoning him in a helpless web of seduction. When her small hands untied the laces of his hose and pushed them over his hips, his rod pulsated, hard and stiff between them. His body was so beautiful, looking at it pushed Aleta into aching arousal. She looked deeply into his eyes for the space of a heartbeat before dropping to her knees before him.

Her kisses fell like soft rain against his stomach. Jaime exhaled sharply, trying to lift her to her feet, but she shook her head and shoved his hands away. He reacted violently when her fingers curled around his throbbing erection. But when her lips touched him he cried out in genuine agony.

"God's blood, my lady, desist lest I embarrass myself!" He pushed her aside roughly, then quickly stepped out of his boots and hose. When he turned to her again, the diabolical gleam in his eyes sent Aleta's breath slamming from her breast. "Now, my love, 'tis your turn."

His hands worked swiftly, whipping the nightdress over her head until she stood as naked as he. His swift intake of breath told her exactly how much her body pleased him. His arms enveloped her, the clean masculine scent of him intoxicated her. When his lips covered her mouth she was instantly transported to paradise. Then he dropped to his knees, grasping the firm mounds of her buttocks as he held her in place for the hot lash of his tongue.

She was hot; she was cold; she was both at the same time. Scant moments before she was whirled away to oblivion, she was lifted high in Jaime's arms. He carried her to the bed, where they fell in a wild tangle of arms and legs. Then he was torturing her with the same sweet torment she had lavished on him only moments before.

His mouth trailed fire over the highly sensitized flesh of her breasts, belly, and inner thighs. The thrust of his finger inside her created a honeyed flow within her that culminated in the moist aching depths of her most secret place. Her plea came on a ragged sigh. "Jaime, please, now."

But his owlish grin told her he wasn't finished with her yet. A puzzled look came over her face when he pulled her to a sitting position and plopped her onto his lap. Bracing his back against a stack of pillows, he lifted her to face him, eased her legs apart so she was straddling him, and thrust deeply inside her. The sensation was so incredible Aleta cried out.

"Do you like that, my love?"

His hips flexed, at the same time shoving her down onto him, sending his member so deep inside her that a loud gasp and nod of her head was all Aleta could manage. Then he was pumping wildly, his head thrown back, a look of profound ecstasy on his handsome face. When he lengthened his strokes and bent forward, taking her nipple into his mouth, she felt herself vibrating with the beginning of her climax. With a hoarse cry, almost a shout, Jaime shoved her down hard upon him and unleashed the hot spurt of his seed deep inside her. The feel of his warm liquid bathing her loins sent a shattering sensation through her and she knew no more.

Aleta came back to her senses slowly, still held securely against Jaime's chest, her buttocks cradled in the well of his hips. And he was still embedded deeply within her. "I've never experienced anything so incredible," he whispered against her lips. His voice was shaky, his tone incredulous, as if unable to believe what he had just experienced. "I never thought I'd fall . . ." His sentence ended abruptly as he stared hard at Aleta. If he told her he loved her now, would she laugh at him?

She had insisted that she didn't want Evan Grey,

that she cared for him, but did she really mean it?
Was now the right time to provide her with the
kind of leverage that a confession of love would
allow?

Aleta's eyes widened. It sounded as if Jaime was
going to say that he loved her. What had stopped
him? "Finish your sentence, Jaime," she said softly.
"What is it you never thought you'd do?"

Thinking quickly, Jaime blurted out, "Still want
a woman so desperately after I've just made love
to her." She felt his manhood stir inside her and
moved her hips experimentally. It was the wrong
thing to do. Suddenly she was on her back and
Jaime was pushing her thighs apart. "This time
will be slow and easy."

It was. He loved her with aching tenderness.
Though Jaime realized there was a new dimension
to his lovemaking, he deliberately repressed the
impulse to blurt out his feelings. If he wasn't careful, Aleta would have him forgetting all about his
vendetta against Evan Grey and those men who
falsely accused his father. She'd have him lolling
about in wedded bliss, settling down and yearning
for heirs. Maybe one day, he reflected, but not yet,
not until justice was served and his father's name
cleared.

Aleta felt a stabbing pain pierce her heart. Either
Jaime was being deliberately obtuse or he truly
cared nothing for her. She knew so little of men;
perhaps all men were capable of tenderness
whether they loved or not. Jaime saw the
wounded look in her eyes and compassion compelled him to say, "You must know I care for you,
my lady. Do not ask more from me. Not now. Not
when I'm so close to obtaining my life's goal.
Know that I want you, Aleta. You belong to me.

You have always belonged to me. Can we not start
from there and see what the future holds?"

"Is there a future for us, Jaime?"

He searched her face. "You tell me. Can you forget Evan Grey? Can I trust you with my life? You
do hold my life in your hands, you know. If you
betray the Lord of Darkness, my life is forfeit."

"Nay, Jaime," Aleta whispered urgently. "I am
yours. I will not betray you."

If Jaime hoped for more, he exhibited no disappointment as he pressed her down onto the soft
surface of the bed.

Chapter 13

Meanwhile, dark forces were at work in London. These forces, led by Lord Somerset, threatened to tear Aleta's tenuous happiness apart. While Aleta and Jaime were enjoying a fleeting moment of bliss, Lords Grey and Somerset were closeted together in Lord Somerset's London town house, deciding their fate.

"I have beggered myself handing out bribes to the judges," Lord Somerset said sourly. "But my perseverence has been amply rewarded. The highest courts in the land have ruled in my favor. They have declared the betrothal between Aleta and Mortimer invalid and set aside the marriage. I am now free to betroth her to another."

" 'Tis about time," Grey complained. "Lady Aleta has been with Mortimer far too long for my liking. On what grounds has the betrothal been declared invalid?"

Somerset smiled thinly. "On the grounds that Mortimer waited overlong to claim his intended bride and that I was justified in believing him dead all these years. I took the liberty of having a betrothal document between you and Aleta drawn

225

up. After you have signed it, I'm off to Wales to collect my daughter."

With a flourish he handed the paper to Lord Grey, who perused it briefly before using the ink and quill sitting on the desk nearby to affix his signature. Lord Somerset heaved a sigh of profound relief once the pact was signed. He and Grey were both so deeply involved in the execution of Lord Mortimer that fear of betrayal by Grey made his becoming Somerset's son-in-law desirable as well as practical.

Aleta stood by the narrow window in the great hall, watching avidly as Jaime trained with his men. Bare to the waist, his torso slick with sweat, the thick muscles cording his arms and neck flexed tensely beneath the smoothness of his suntanned flesh. His tight hose did little to hide the massive strength of his thighs and calves, and Aleta grew faint just thinking about that hard muscular frame possessing her pliant body. But despite the fact that Jaime was nearly twice her size he had never hurt her. During the past days his gentleness had nearly compensated for his lack of words proclaiming his love—nearly but not quite.

Recalling his patience in bringing her to the highest pinnacle of sensation the previous night, Aleta's face grew flushed and her knees shook. She nearly jumped out of her skin when Bess, who had just entered the chamber, spoke.

"He's quite a man, isn't he, my lady?"

"Oh, Bess, you startled me!" Aleta said, her hand going to her throat. She turned back to the window. "Aye, Bess, I doubt there is a man like Jaime in the entire kingdom."

"If I remember correctly, my lady, when you arrived you couldn't stand the sight of Lord Jaime."

" 'Tis true," Aleta mused thoughtfully. "I thought him an ignorant peasant with the manners of an animal. I wish I knew what his feelings were where I'm concerned. I'm not stupid, Bess, I know Jaime's purpose in marrying me was to keep Lord Grey from having me."

"Perhaps at first, my lady," Bess said astutely. "I think Jaime cares more for you than you realize."

Aleta's face brightened. "I hope you're right, Bess."

Bess didn't respond; her attention was focused on a group of riders approaching the keep.

"What is it, Bess?" Aleta asked, noticing Bess's distraction.

"Company, my lady." She pointed toward the north and the riders just appearing over the crest of a hill.

Aleta gasped. There appeared to be a great many men, over one hundred. "I must warn Jaime!" she cried, flying from the room. But by the time she reached the bailey Jaime had already seen the riders and sent his men scurrying to arm themselves. Not that it would do much good. The crumbling walls couldn't possibly keep out the large number of men converging on them.

Aleta met Jaime at the top of the stairs as he entered the keep. "Jaime, who are they?" she cried fearfully. "Is it Lord Grey? Surely he wouldn't disobey King Henry and attack, Jaime, would he?"

"Who knows? Come," Jaime said grimly as he grasped her wrist and pulled her after him. "I must arm myself to meet our visitors. You are to remain in the keep while I deal with them."

Aleta grew breathless trying to keep up with

Jaime as he pulled her up several flights of stairs to their chamber. Once inside she helped him don mail over his tunic and arm himself with sword and crossbow. Times had changed since knights of old had encased themselves in coats of armor so bulky it took six men to lift them aboard their warhorses. Now armor consisted of fine mesh much lighter yet just as strong as the metal plates of old. When he was fully clothed he pulled Aleta into his arms, kissed her hard, and left quickly. Aleta followed, unwilling to cower out of sight until she knew who the enemy was. Jaime seemed unaware that she was close behind him.

By the time he had reached the steps leading into the bailey, the riders were close enough to see their pennants. Aleta let out a startled cry when she recognized the Somerset rose and lion. It was her father! She couldn't let Jaime battle her father—one of them could be killed. But she saw that fighting was exactly what Jaime intended as his men rallied around him.

"Jaime, nay! 'Tis my father. Don't kill him!" Recklessly she rushed down the stairs, running past a startled Jaime into the midst of Lord Somerset's small army.

"Aleta! Come back!"

But Aleta was past hearing as she reached up to stop her father's horse. Jaime's breath caught fearfully in his chest when the great animal reared and would have trampled her but for Lord Somerset's expert handling. Was Aleta so anxious to see her father that she'd risk death to reach him? Had she been waiting for Lord Somerset to arrive with his army and take her from him? He had hoped his fledgling friendship with King Henry would have put a stop to both Grey and Somerset's efforts to take Aleta away by force. Perhaps Henry was too enmeshed in his own problems to keep his barons under control.

Lord Somerset swung from the saddle, his face a mask of fury. "What in the devil are you trying to do, daughter, get yourself killed? Lord Grey would not be pleased to learn his future wife was trampled beneath the hooves of my mount." He passed a critical eye over her slim figure. "You are well, I trust?"

"Aye, Father, very well," Aleta said, recalling how intimidating her sire could be. "What are you doing here? Why have you brought an army if you've merely come to visit?"

"Is that all the thanks I get for spending a fortune getting this unfortunate misalliance between you and that traitor's son set aside?"

"Why are you so sure Lord Mortimer was a traitor, Father?" Aleta asked, searching his face. "Perhaps a mistake has been made."

"You dare question my integrity!" Somerset thundered. He raised his arm, intending to backhand her for even hinting that he was somehow involved in Mortimer's death. It wouldn't do to have his own daughter question his innocence. It was enough that Jaime Mortimer had raised doubts in the King's mind. Fortunately Henry was too involved in other matters to concern himself with something that occurred in Wales long ago.

"Touch her and you're a dead man." Jaime's voice hardened ruthlessly, his warning implicit as he grasped Somerset's arm in his iron fist. When he loosed it, Somerset's arm flopped ineffectually to his side. "Aleta is my wife; you no longer have authority over her. I vow you will never raise your hand to her again."

Somerset looked from Jaime to Aleta, surprised by the degree of Jaime's possessiveness. "Save your vows, Mortimer," Somerset sneered, "they'll do you little good now." He reached inside his doublet, withdrew an official document, and waved it beneath Jaime's nose. "Your marriage to my daughter has been declared invalid and I have betrothed her to Lord Grey. 'Tis most fortunate that your seed has failed to sprout in fertile soil," he taunted. "The Mortimer strain never was a hardy one." He laughed scornfully. "But you can be certain, knave, that Lord Grey will soon have Aleta's belly swelling with his get."

Aleta paled. "Father, what are you saying? Does the King know about this? Surely he would have had to sign the papers."

"The papers are signed," Somerset said slyly. " 'Twas easy enough with his mind so distracted with France and his bride-to-be. I acted as swiftly as I could, Aleta, knowing it was what you wanted. Lord Grey told me how you sought his protection when you left this great oaf of a husband." He glared at Jaime, his expression contemptuous.

A multitude of emotions assailed Jaime. Had Aleta been planning this all along, biding her time until her father arrived? Had she deliberately lied when she insisted that she did not seek Grey's protection when she had left him? More importantly, why had Aleta acted like she enjoyed his lovemaking, responding with such wild abandon that he had begun to believe in her?

Aleta knew exactly what Jaime was thinking and it wasn't true. "Nay, Jaime, it isn't so! I may have wished for an end to our marriage at one time but not since—since . . ."

"Enough, daughter!" Somerset roared, sending her an oblique look. " 'Tis done. Gather enough clothing for your journey to London. Mortimer can send the rest along later with your dowry. We leave at once."

"Nay!" Aleta's voice trembled with fear.

"Aleta is going nowhere with you." Jaime's voice was soft but edged with steel.

"Look about you, Mortimer," Somerset advised with a sweep of his hand. "You and your men are outnumbered. If you choose to fight, lives will be lost and I still will have my way. Do I give the signal for attack, Mortimer, or do you let my daughter leave peaceably?"

Jaime's face hardened. He knew his men were prepared to fight, even against odds as great as these, but could he ask them to die for a woman as false as Aleta?

Aleta read the indecision in Jaime's eyes and knew he was as close to dying as he would ever be. He didn't stand even a remote chance of successfully routing an army as large as the one her father had brought with him. She wanted neither Jaime nor her father slain on the battlefield. Either death would destroy her.

Lord Somerset recognized Aleta's reluctance to initiate a fight over her and sought to take advantage of it. "I would speak in private with my daughter," he said with cool authority.

Jaime's face grew mutinous. "I will not allow it."

"Please, Jaime," Aleta pleaded, hoping to diffuse a potentially disastrous situation. "I—I wish to speak to Father alone."

Jaime gave her a hard, searching look, nodded, and walked away. His short, jerky steps betrayed his great anger. Taking Aleta's arm, Somerset led her out of earshot of his men-at-arms. When he whirled her around to face him, his face was set in rigid lines, his mouth nearly white with rage.

"What an ungrateful wretch!" The words hissed through his teeth in a heated outburst. "What you need is a good beating to pound some sense into you. But I'll leave that to Lord Grey. Perhaps he can make you behave more respectfully toward your father. I promised I'd do all in my power to gain your freedom. Why are you acting as if you had never wanted it?" He looked at her narrowly. "What has the bastard done to you?"

"Things have changed, Father. Jaime is not at all what I thought."

"God's blood, you've fallen for the knave!" Somerset all but shouted.

"I—I think Jaime and his father have been terribly wronged," Aleta defended stoutly. "I can't—nay, I *won't* leave. Not now, not ever."

"So, 'tis true," Somerset sneered contemptuously, "you do care for him. Lord Grey will soon rid you of your infatuation. I can't begin to understand why, but Lord Grey still wants you despite the fact that you've been used by Mortimer. And I can't afford to have Grey as an enemy. We're in this together."

"In what together?" Aleta asked curiously.

Somerset frowned. "It matters not to you. Will you leave here of your own free will or shall I order my men to destroy Mortimer and render this heap of stone into rubble? I can do it, you know, I've twice the men at my command. No quarter will be given, Aleta. Once I order my men into battle, no man will be left alive. Is that what you want? Think hard, my dear, before you answer."

Aleta didn't have to think very long or very hard. She loved Jaime too much to see him cut down in the prime of life. Perhaps by her own father. "I will go with you," she said shakily, "but I refuse to marry Lord Grey."

"Nay, Aleta, I will have your promise to wed Lord Grey before I leave here. Otherwise it will be as I described."

Defeat weighed heavily on Aleta's narrow shoulders. Its crushing responsibility nearly beat her into the ground. But in the end she had but one choice and she made it.

"Aye, Father, it will be as you wish."

Somerset smiled grimly. "Tell him."

Her feet were leaden as she turned and walked slowly to where Jaime was standing, followed closely by her father. When she opened her mouth to speak, her voice faltered. Snorting disgustedly, Somerset nudged her in the ribs. "Tell him, daughter, tell him what you just told me."

The pink tip of Aleta's tongue darted out to moisten her dry lips. Jaime seemed mesmerized by the simple act. Reluctantly his eyes swept upward to meet hers when her halting words drew his attention.

"I—wish to—accompany my father."

"Tell him why, Aleta," Somerset prodded ruthlessly.

Jaime's expression did not change, waiting for her to continue. Aleta gave her father a startled look but he merely nodded, conveying his wishes that she continue.

Please, Jaime, don't hate me, Aleta silently entreated as she spoke the words her father forced her to say. "Before I left London I—I begged Father to pursue an annulment and I haven't changed my mind."

"Tell him about your betrothal to Lord Grey," Somerset said with cruel satisfaction. He wouldn't be satisfied until Jaime Mortimer was utterly destroyed. If he pursued his efforts to delve into his father's trial, it could mean disaster for him, Lord Grey, and Lord Barlow, who had shared in Mortimer's wealth.

"Father, I—"

"Tell him, Aleta," Somerset commanded. His hand, which had been resting on her arm, squeezed so tightly Aleta flinched from the sudden pain.

"I'm going to marry Lord Grey!" Aleta cried out. " 'Tis what I've wanted from the beginning. This marriage was never my idea. So you see, my lord, there is really nothing for you to fight for."

Jaime's dark gaze raked insolently over her slim form. "Indeed, my lady, as you say, there is nothing to fight for. Forgive me for thinking otherwise. I've known from the beginning that you consider me less than dirt beneath your feet. Good-bye, my lady, I wish you and Lord Grey joy of one another."

Sweet blessed Virgin, how could he let her walk out of his life? a voice inside Jaime cried. Did the months they had spent together mean nothing to her? Perhaps those wondrous nights they had lain in one another's arms were easily forgotten by Aleta, but they had been indelibly etched upon his heart and mind.

"Jaime!" She reached out but he had already turned away. Snatching her hand back, Somerset grasped her shoulders and none too gently shoved her toward the keep.

"Get what you'll need for the journey," Somerset barked. Jaime did not look at her as she climbed the stairs to the keep, her shoulders slumped despondently. Nor did she hear her father say to Jaime, "You can see my daughter despises you, Mortimer. If you're smart, you'll bury yourself in your crumbling keep and leave Aleta in peace."

Aleta hurried to her chamber, sobbing all the way. She didn't want to leave Jaime, but neither did she wish to see him destroyed. Bess was waiting for her, her face stricken. "Oh, my lady, I heard everything. What will you do?"

"I must go with my father, Bess," Aleta choked.

"But you can't, you love Lord Jaime!"

"Father will destroy Jaime if I do not do as he says. I know him, Bess, he will do it. He's immensely wealthy and has an army at his command. Jaime couldn't possibly win against such overwhelming odds."

"I—feared you meant what you said out there in the bailey. But I should have known you'd never leave of your own free will. Stay, my lady, Lord Jaime will protect you."

"Nay, good Bess, I cannot risk my lord's life. Besides, you heard my father. An annulment has already been issued, I am no longer Jaime's wife. Now quit your sniffling and help me pack a small bag for the trip."

Jaime was nowhere in sight when Aleta returned to the bailey. Her mount was already saddled and waiting for her and Lord Somerset wasted no time in tossing her into the saddle. If Aleta had hoped for one last look at Jaime before she left forever she was sadly disappointed. With a motion of his hand, Somerset and his small army rode from the bailey, sweeping Aleta with them. She looked back but once, her face twisted into a grimace of agony.

Jaime watched the procession from the window slit of the hall, his expression unreadable, his eyes bleak with a kind of emptiness he had never experienced before. He watched until he could no longer see Aleta amidst the crush of men-at-arms surrounding her.

"She did not want to leave, Lord Jaime."

Jaime started violently, unaware that Bess stood behind him. His expression hardened. "You did not hear her words, Bess. Do not try to soften the blow of her leaving. 'Twas her choice. Had she chosen to stay, I would have fought to the death to defend her."

"Aye," Bess said softly. "That's what she feared. My lady did not want your death, Lord Jaime, she wanted your life. The only way to protect you was to leave with her father. She loves you. Besides," she reminded him gently, "she is no longer your wife. Lord Somerset has seen to that."

Jaime whirled on Bess, his face a mask of rage. "Aleta is my wife and will always be my wife, even though she does not love me." *In my heart I still love her*, he thought but did not say. "Nay, good Bess, make no mistake. Aleta has always wanted Evan Grey, and now she has what she wants. Do not speak her name to me again." Turning abruptly, he strode away.

The next day Rowena returned to the keep. Gossip had reached the village where the sultry brunette was staying and she wasted little time in insinuating herself into Jaime's life once again. She found Jaime sitting morosely before the hearth in the hall, staring without purpose into the fire that had long since burnt to ashes. Rushing to his side, she dropped to her knees before him.

"Jaime, I am here. I will not leave you like that faithless bitch you married. Let me help you forget the woman who betrayed you. It will be just like old times, Jaime, you'll see."

Jaime scowled at Rowena, not nearly as pleased to see her as she had hoped. "Leave me in peace, Rowena, I am fit company for no one right now, least of all you."

"Do not send me away, my love, I can ease you and make your nights more bearable."

He sent her an oblique look. "Do as you please, Rowena, it matters not." Turning away, he continued his brooding perusal of the cold hearth. Having won the right to remain in the keep, Rowena did not push her luck. She knew in time Jaime would turn to her for comfort, and after that it would only be a matter of time before she persuaded him to make her his wife.

The days passed slowly. But to Rowena's chagrin Jaime made no effort to bed her. In fact, he seemed unaware that she was residing in the keep. He drank excessively, often falling asleep sitting in the hall with his head resting on the table and a flagon of ale clutched in his hand. His men worried about him and Gaylord was beside himself with anxiety. Never had he seen Jaime in such pitiful condition. He racked his brain for ideas to bring Jaime out of his despondency, but when word reached them that Aleta and Lord Evan were to wed soon, he feared Jaime would lose his tenuous hold on reality.

He nearly did. Jaime's anger was awesome to behold as he went on a drunken rampage that lasted nearly a week. Desperate to pull Jaime from the brink of insanity, Gaylord suggested that they return to smuggling. The old retainer had received word that a ship carrying fine brandy and French lace had just left France and if they were interested they had but to signal with lights and the ship would lay offshore. To Gaylord's relief Jaime seemed receptive to the idea, and plans were set into motion. The villagers were notified and in the following days Jaime seemed to pull himself together, drinking less and spending long exhausting hours training with his men, though they had never been included in his illegal activities.

The ship's arrival and the reappearance of the Lord of Darkness after months of inactivity heralded a new era of smuggling, one which Jaime embraced with a vengeance. He took chances where others demurred; nothing was too daring or impossible. When word reached London about the resurgence of smuggling along the Welsh coast, the King dispatched a small army to help Lord Grey quell the vicious outbreak. But each time the troops arrived on the beach, the smugglers had already disappeared into thin air. In order to plague the King's men, the Lord of Darkness constantly changed the rendezvous place so that the revenuers never knew where to look next.

Aleta found herself a virtual prisoner in her father's home in London. She was allowed few visitors, except for Evan Grey. The King had left the city before she arrived and wasn't due back until after her wedding to Lord Grey. Aleta felt certain that had Henry known of her father's nefarious plan he would have intervened. But since the monarch was due to depart shortly for France to claim his own bride, his barons had already assumed partial control of the country. She was doomed. Marriage to Evan Grey, after experiencing the pinnacle of passion with Jaime, was a travesty. Only one man had the ability to ignite a flame within her soul.

Aleta had been in London over two weeks when Lord Grey came to call. When she refused to see him, her father ordered her from her room, then conveniently left them alone to speak in private.

Grey's taut smile warned Aleta that he was still angry with her for disappearing from his manor under mysterious circumstances. "This time you will not escape me so easily, my lady," he warned ominously. "When we are finally wed you will obey me in all things or suffer the consequences. But I'm curious to know how your peasant lover spirited you from my manor."

"We flew out the window," Aleta said with scathing sarcasm. "I do not wish to marry you, my lord, I want to return to my husband."

Grey's temper exploded. "Flew out the window, indeed! Keep your secret, my lady, it matters not. Didn't you hear your father? You are no longer wed to that penniless knave. You are mine, my lady, just as everything that once belonged to the Mortimers is now mine."

"I don't understand your animosity toward Jaime," Aleta said curiously. "Why do you hate the family so much?"

"You are very perceptive, my lady." An evil sneer twisted his lips. "One day I will tell you about the hatred that drives me."

"Lord Mortimer wasn't really a traitor, was he?"

Grey's expression grew furious. "Enough! I will speak no more of the Mortimers. I have come to discuss our wedding, Aleta. 'Tis my wish that we wed one month from today."

"Nay!"

"Aye. Henry has ordered me back to Wales, but I will return in time for our wedding."

"You go to Wales?"

"Aye, and this time the Lord of Darkness will not escape me. Rumor has it the knave has returned to smuggling, only this time he won't get away with it."

Aleta's heart skidded painfully against her rib cage. Didn't Jaime know how dangerous it was now to engage in smuggling? Lord Grey was determined to capture the Lord of Darkness, and if Jaime became careless he'd find himself swinging from the end of a rope.

Grey watched the play of emotions sweep across Aleta's lovely features and grinned delightedly. He couldn't wait to have her spread beneath him, bestowing upon him everything she had once given to Mortimer. Thinking about her naked body draped across him made him harden with desire and yearn for his wedding day. Suddenly it occurred to him that he needn't wait, that no one would fault him for anticipating his wedding day, least of all Lord Somerset. Catching her by surprise, he reached out and dragged her hard against him. Aleta squawked in protest, pushing against him with all her might.

"Do not fight me, Aleta, for I mean to have you before I leave for Wales. We are nearly man and wife. What can it hurt to sample what you've freely given that bastard who took you away from me?"

His mouth slammed down on hers, punishing, angry, taking out all his frustration on her vulnerable lips. When his tongue forced her mouth open and ravaged the tender insides, Aleta nearly retched. Loathing and disgust surged through her and when his hands tore away her bodice to torment her breasts, she reacted violently.

"I'll scream for my father," Aleta panted, fending off his hurtful caresses.

"Scream away, my lady," Grey taunted hoarsely. "He will not come to your defense. We are both in agreement that you need to be tamed, and 'twill give me great pleasure to begin immediately."

Realizing that no help other than her own ingenuity was forthcoming, Aleta renewed her efforts to free herself from Grey's onerous advances. His strength, fueled by raging lust, was enormous compared to hers. When he bore her to the floor and fumbled with the strings of his hose, Aleta reacted instinctively. Raising her knee, she smashed him in the groin. Her well-aimed blow rendered him immediately impotent as he rolled on the floor in agony.

Leaping shakily to her feet, Aleta stared down at him for a brief moment before turning and rushing from the room. Gasping for breath, his face a mask of pain, Grey shouted after her, "You'll pay for this, you bitch! Wait until we're married—I have ways of making you beg for my attention. And not all of them will be to your liking."

Fear lent wings to her feet as Aleta fled from the room, past her startled father and up the stairs to the safety of her chamber. Locking the door behind her, she collapsed on the bed, shaking and sick at heart. How could she allow this travesty of a marriage to take place? she wondered despondently. How could she *not* allow it when obviously she had no say in the matter? She feared Lord Grey would make her life a living hell, yet there was absolutely nothing she could do to stop the wedding.

That horrendous thought made Aleta's stomach roil and the gorge rise in her throat. Reaching beneath the bed, she retrieved the chamber pot just in time to empty the contents of her stomach.

Chapter 14

Rowena was growing desperate. During the weeks since she had returned to the keep Jaime had all but ignored her. She knew he had become involved again in smuggling and had even watched him leave the keep in the dead of night upon occasion. And just this morning she had inadvertently overheard a conversation between Jaime and Gaylord. They had been standing at the corner of the bailey and Rowena had come upon them suddenly, scooting into a crevice of the ruined wall when she heard their voices.

"The ship will lay offshore tomorrow night, Jaime," the old man was saying. "Do you want a signal given? Mayhap 'tis best we do not tempt fate. The number of revenuers have been doubled and 'tis said Lord Grey is returned to Wales to put a stop to the smuggling. Rumor has it he wants the Lord of Darkness badly."

"Damn Grey to the deepest pit of hell," Jaime muttered darkly. "The man isn't smart enough to catch the Lord of Darkness without a betrayer in our midst to warn him. Since the Lady Aleta is gone we have nothing to fear."

"You accuse the lady falsely," Gaylord charged. "She is no traitor and I believe in her innocence."

" 'Tis no matter, Gaylord, that part of my life is over and done with. I live for danger and adventure now, and the exoneration of my father's name. What say you we travel to London to see the King after our venture tonight?"

"Then we move tonight as planned? I will notify the villagers to meet at North Beach where the cliffs give way to sandy beach. As for London, I seriously doubt your intentions are to visit the King. If you hope to see Aleta, I fear you will be disappointed. Her marriage is to take place within the month."

"Fear not, Gaylord, I go to London to see the King and for no other reason." His words belied the hungry look in his eyes.

They parted soon after that, leaving Rowena with much to think about.

Jaime sat in the hall a long time that night, hating the thought of facing his bed without Aleta in it to welcome him. He saw Rowena moving about the hall, trading laughter with his men-at-arms, and wondered why he hadn't availed himself of her services. Lord knew he needed a woman. Not too many months ago he had been satisfied with Rowena, but today the sultry beauty didn't appeal to him. How could he bed her when he'd had a woman like Aleta to love? Witch that she was, Aleta had rendered him useless to any other woman. How could she have left him so easily after all they had shared together?

Resting his head on his arms, Jaime recalled with yearning all those memorable nights they had explored one another's bodies until passion exploded with a burst of incredible sensation. He had wanted her then and he wanted her now. Wanted her despite the fact that she cared nothing for him. Despite the fact that she had betrayed him.

He wanted to hate her. Lord knew he had tried, but his heart rebelled.

Rowena watched Jaime closely as she moved about the hall. Though she flirted outrageously with the men-at-arms, Jaime seemed unaware of her presence. On more than one occasion she had had to make do with one of the knights when it was really Jaime she wanted. But not this night, she decided. Nay, this night she would be waiting for Jaime in his bed, wooing him with her supple body. Hurrying from the hall, she went directly to Jaime's chamber, undressed quickly, and slid naked between the sheets.

Jaime reeled to his feet, not quite as sober as he would have liked. He had consumed just enough ale tonight to deaden the ache of Aleta's loss. The stairs seemed endless as he negotiated the winding passage to his chamber, and when he finally entered the darkened room he threw off his clothes and flopped into bed. Weary to the bone, he pulled the cover over his hips and closed his eyes. The healing fingers of slumber soothed his aching body, lulling him to sleep.

Several minutes passed before Jaime realized that the fingers trailing fiery tracks across his skin were flesh and blood, having nothing to do with the dreamy state of his senses. His eyes flew open, suddenly aware of a small warm hand roaming across his back and buttocks. He groaned in dismay as that hand grew bolder, slipping between his thighs to cup and caress his manhood.

Rowena cooed in delight as her intimate touch brought Jaime to instant erection. Still groggy from his nightly bout of drinking, only one name came to the tip of his tongue.

"Aleta."

Turning abruptly, he reached for her, bringing her nude body hard against his. He groaned again, reveling in the warmth of her flesh and the way the hardened tips of her breasts pressed against his chest. His hands found the moistness between her legs and he rose above her, so eager to thrust inside her that his entire body trembled like a boneless mass of tissue and muscle.

Rowena frowned, eager to oblige Jaime but conceited enough to want him to know it was she he was bedding, not Aleta. "Jaime, 'tis I, Rowena. Love me, my lord, love me well."

Jaime's eyes flew open. It was too dark to see Rowena clearly but he recognized her voice. "God's blood, Rowena, what are you doing in my bed?"

"You need me, Jaime," Rowena whispered against his lips. "You've not had a woman since your—since Aleta left. Let me ease you. Remember how it was between us?"

Her hands slipped between their bodies, seeking the object of her desire. She inhaled sharply when she found he had shriveled considerably in the last several moments. Driven by desperation, she slid down his body. Jaime gasped and cried out when he felt her wet lips close around him. Rowena would have been shocked to know that Jaime's cries weren't the result of profound bliss. Though Rowena had performed the same intimate act many times in the past, this time it actually repelled him. Only when Jaime shoved her rudely away did Rowena realize that her attentions weren't welcome.

"Had I wanted you, Rowena, I would have summoned you," Jaime said harshly.

"If you hadn't fallen into a drunken stupor these past weeks, you might feel differently," Rowena charged. "I've never seen you in this condition, Jaime. That cold bitch you married is the cause of all your problems. Consider yourself lucky to be rid of her." Her hand slipped down to cup his sex. "I can make you want me."

This time when Jaime shoved her away he was less than gentle, giving an extra push with his foot that sent her slithering to the floor. "Have done, Rowena, I was finished with you a long time ago. I must have been insane to allow you back in the keep when I want you not. Begone from my life, woman! Find yourself another man to play whore for. When I arise on the morrow, I'll expect to find you gone."

"Jaime, you don't mean that." Rowena was shocked. How could she have made such a terrible mistake? She had been positive Jaime would welcome her back into his life and bed once he realized he could not have Aleta.

"Aye, Rowena, I have never meant anything more."

Picking herself up from the floor, Rowena searched for her clothes. Grasping them to her breast, she glared daggers at Jaime. "You'll be sorry," she said ominously. "I've warned you before, Jaime, but this time I mean it." Whirling on her heel, she fled from the room, unconcerned with her nudity. She departed early the following morning. Gaylord reported seeing her whipping her mount into a fine froth as she fled into the hills.

Evan Grey paced the length of the hall in his fine manor, his angry strides carrying him from one end to the other. No matter which beach he and his men patrolled, they found that the Lord of Darkness had moved his operation to another. Was there no end to the man's incredible audacity? He wanted the knave, wanted him badly enough to remain in Wales when he should be in London bringing his bride-to-be to heel. Aleta had sorely injured him during their last meeting, and he owed her a good beating for her unforgivable treatment. If Jaime Mortimer hadn't entered their lives those long months ago, Aleta would already be his bride and swelling with his first child.

His dark thoughts were interrupted by his bailiff. "My lord, there is a young lady at the door demanding entrance."

"At this early hour?" Grey said, scowling. "Tell her we have more servants than we need."

"I am no servant, my lord." Rowena stood in the doorway, having grown tired of waiting.

Grey's brow lifted. "Ah, Rowena, come in, my lady. What news have you for me this day?"

Rowena waited until the bailiff left before speaking. "News I think you'll pay well for, my lord," she said slyly. After betraying Jaime, Rowena feared his retribution and needed money to take her far from his grasp.

"Nothing was mentioned about reward before," Grey complained sourly.

"Ah, my lord, but this time I bring you the identity of the Lord of Darkness and where he can be found this very night. Does that information not merit reward?"

"You know the identity of the Lord of Darkness?" Grey was incredulous. And so eager for the information he was willing to pay anything. "You will find me quite generous, my lady," he said smoothly.

Rowena's voice hardened. "How generous, my lord?"

"Mercenary little bitch, aren't you?"

"A woman in my position can't afford to be otherwise."

Grey gave her a hard, searching look, then said, "Wait here."

Rowena watched narrowly as he turned and disappeared up a winding flight of stairs. He was gone a full ten minutes before he reappeared, placing a small cloth bag into her hands. Rowena hefted the bag, peeked inside, and grinned hugely.

"Does it satisfy you?"

Rowena nodded, indeed satisfied. "You are most generous."

"The name, Rowena. Apprehending the Lord of Darkness will be quite a feather in my cap."

A sudden pang of guilt gave Rowena a difficult moment. How could she betray a man she had once loved so passionately? Then she recalled the callous way in which he had cast her from his bed and his life, and her resolve hardened. She owed Jaime Mortimer no loyalty.

Her throat was suddenly so dry she had to force the words past her parched lips. " 'Tis Jaime. Jaime Mortimer is the Lord of Darkness."

A malevolent smile turned Grey's face ugly. "Mortimer! The thieving bastard! I knew it, but had no evidence. How long have you known?"

Frightened of Grey's black mood, Rowena thought it in her best interest to lie. "I've only known since yesterday, when I overheard Jaime and Gaylord speaking about the ship due to arrive tonight."

"Tonight?" Grey asked sharply. "Where?"

"In a cove about five miles from the keep where the cliffs give way to woods and sandy beach. The natives call it North Beach. They'll be bringing the smuggled goods back to the keep in wagons. That's all I was able to overhear."

" 'Tis enough, my lady." He gave her a suspicious look. "I confess I am curious, though. Why are you betraying your lover?"

Rowena's smile turned nasty. "The arrogant bastard has cast me aside. He hasn't been the same since that pale bitch came into his life."

Grey quirked a dark brow. "Are you by chance referring to the Lady Aleta?"

"Aye," Rowena sneered. "Even though she has been betrothed to you, my lord, Jaime is still obsessed with the witch. He has banished me from his bed. I warned him I would seek vengeance but he listened not."

"Undone by a vindictive woman," Grey muttered beneath his breath. "How fitting." Aloud, he said, "I am in your debt, my lady. And if 'tis any comfort, Aleta will soon be my bride and beyond Mortimer's reach forever."

The night was moonless, perfect for what Jaime had in mind. Low clouds rolled in from the sea and a fine mist rose from the ground. The hour struck midnight just as Jaime made his way down the long spiral staircase. Gaylord was waiting for him in the hall.

"I am ready," the old man said. Jaime sent Gaylord a sharp glance, thinking he had never looked older or more frail than he did now, with his bent form shrouded in a black cloak. It gave him pause for thought, suddenly realizing that Gaylord was much too old to be engaging in this kind of activity. Intuition warned him to leave Gaylord behind this night.

"Not this time, my friend," Jaime said, clapping him on the shoulder. "Tonight you remain at the keep to direct the wagons when they arrive. I know the men-at-arms are aware of what's going on but I have been reluctant to involve them in my illegal activities. Should any of them awaken, see that they remain in the garrison until the smuggled goods are hidden away in the secret chamber."

"Nay, Jaime, I will accompany you as I have always done. 'Tis bad luck to change now."

"Do as I say, Gaylord," Jaime admonished. Abruptly he turned and walked away, before Gaylord's arguments swayed him. Risking his own life was one thing, but placing an old man in peril was another.

The smugglers were already gathered on North Beach when the Lord of Darkness arrived. They were but waiting for him to signal the ship anchored out in the bay. Once the lanterns were lit to alert the ship, they anxiously awaited the arrival of the first boatload of goods. Jaime sat his prancing stallion, alert, watchful. His senses told him something was amiss. Though he saw and heard nothing out of the ordinary, every nerve ending screamed of danger.

The first rowboat had already been unloaded and another had taken its place. The smugglers worked quietly, efficiently, quickly stacking the barrels and chests on the pristine beach to await the wagons. Jaime breathed a sigh of relief when the last boat had been unloaded and the ship's captain paid and sent on his way. When he heard the creak of wagon wheels some of his apprehension diminished, even though he knew danger still existed until the smuggled goods were stashed safely beneath his keep.

The wagons rumbled onto the beach and Jaime turned to watch the shrouded drivers direct the horses alongside the stacked barrels. A premonition of something dark and sinister pumped through Jaime's body with every beat of his heart. Something was terribly wrong! Jaime dismounted, took up a lantern, and approached the first wagon with caution. The driver appeared nervous and when he suddenly looked up, Jaime knew!

His voice exploded through the silent night in shrill warning. "A trap! Run, run!"

Men scattered in all directions, having been schooled by Jaime to flee instantly at his warning and ask questions later. Immediately all hell broke loose as dozens of armed men leaped from the wagon beds, swords drawn and ready for battle. Jaime scrambled for his mount when he saw additional men materializing from the woods surrounding the beach. Though his own flight was seriously hampered, he noted with satisfaction that most of the villagers had slipped away. His warning had come in the nick of time.

Whirling on his heel, Jaime spotted his stallion and tried to reach him before the revenuers were upon him, and found himself face-to-face with Evan Grey. Grey stood poised before Jaime, sword in hand, six men ranged around him, all armed and ready to skewer Jaime at a moment's notice.

"Your dangerous game is up, Mortimer," Grey sneered. "Or should I say, Lord of Darkness?"

"So I see," Jaime said with a calmness that infuriated Grey.

"If you're wondering how I knew your identity, let's just say a very beautiful lady told me."

Though Grey deliberately omitted her name, Jaime knew he was referring to Aleta. "Give your lady my regards," Jaime said with icy disdain.

"Oh, I shall, I shall. Meanwhile, she'll be pleased to know that you will finally reap your just rewards for your nefarious deeds. And the King will thank me for halting the loss of taxes to his coffers. Your arrest and execution will be a fitting end for a traitor's son. Fate has decreed that the son should die in the same manner as the father."

"Bastard!" Jaime snarled, lunging for Grey. If he ever got his hands around the man's throat he'd not let go until all the life had been squeezed from his worthless hide. Unfortunately Jaime never got to within arm's length of Grey. Two men stepped forward. Using the hilt of their swords, they felled him with vicious blows to the head. Jaime fell heavily to the wet sand, cursing Aleta with his last conscious breath.

Aleta's wedding day approached with frightening speed. Prevented from leaving the town house, she languished in splendid boredom in her chamber. She was grateful that Lord Grey hadn't returned after she had attacked him for trying to rape her, but she had tasted her father's wrath for her insolent behavior. When he learned what she had done he had struck her across the face with such force she had carried the mark on her cheek for over a week. When she told him that Grey had tried to bed her before their wedding, he seemed shocked but did not apologize for striking her.

" 'Tisn't as if you're a virgin," he had said. He had refused to look her in the eye, as if shamed by what had taken place. "You had no such qualms about bedding Mortimer."

And now, with only a week remaining before the wedding, Aleta came to a realization that stunned her. She had often wondered why Jaime's seed failed to thrive in her womb but she wondered no longer. She knew without a doubt that she was expecting Jaime's child. She hadn't had her woman's time in two months; her breasts were tender and nearly every morning she awoke so nauseous she barely made it to the chamber pot.

She knew her father would be livid when he learned of her pregnancy and she could only guess at Lord Grey's reaction. Would he be angry enough to break the betrothal? she wondered hopefully. Nay, she decided. There was more, much more, than a man wanting a woman behind his proposal. Something that involved secrets of which even Jaime was unaware. More than simple greed fueled Evan's hatred for the Mortimers, she decided astutely. Dark secrets lurked somewhere in the deep past. Secrets known only to Evan Grey.

Two days before the wedding was to take place, Lord Somerset summoned Aleta to attend him in the hall. "What is it, Father?" she asked hopefully. "Has Lord Grey changed his mind about the wedding?"

He sent her an exasperated glance. "Lord Grey has returned to London in triumph. The Lord of

Darkness has finally been captured and awaits execution in the dungeons at Whitehall."

A look of utter dismay crossed Aleta's features. "The Lord of Darkness?" she gasped. "Are you certain, Father?"

"Aye, daughter, but 'tis unnecessary to reveal his name, for the knave is well known to you. How long have you known about Jaime Mortimer?"

"I—I don't know what you're talking about." Never would she betray Jaime, even if the whole world knew his secret. "Is he well?"

"As well as can be expected under the circumstances, my dear, until the King returns to London to order the execution. 'Tis quite a feather in Evan's cap. You should be proud of your future husband."

"Proud that the man I love is in prison awaiting execution? Nay, Father, perhaps Jaime broke the law, but much worse has been done to him. I can't marry Lord Grey. If you love me you won't insist upon this farce. I don't love him. I belong to Jaime."

"Love," Somerset scoffed. "What do you know about love? I didn't love your mother when we married, yet we dealt well enough with one another until she died giving birth. 'Tis a pity your brother perished with her."

"Why did you never remarry, Father?" Aleta asked curiously. Though he had mistresses aplenty she wondered why he had never felt the need to take another wife and produce a male heir.

Somerset hesitated, then decided to tell Aleta the truth. "I have no need for a male heir," he informed her. " 'Twas settled between Lord Grey and myself after the Mortimer brat disappeared and was considered dead. I betrothed you to Lord Grey with the intention that he was to become my heir. Don't thwart me in this, Aleta. You must admit I have been a most indulgent father and required little from you except your obedience."

"And I have been a most dutiful daughter, Father, but I cannot obey you in this. I love Jaime."

Somerset's temper exploded. "How can you love the knave? When the King sanctioned the marriage between you and Mortimer, you begged me to intercede. What has he done to you to capture your loyalty?"

Aleta opened her mouth to speak.

"Nay, do not tell me, for I already know. Obviously the man is a master at seduction and has turned you into a shameless hussy, bound by hungers of the flesh. Mark you well, daughter, I strongly advise that you save all this misguided passion for Lord Grey."

"Nay, Father, I cannot marry Lord Grey," Aleta persisted stubbornly.

"You have no say in the matter. Evan will be here directly to make the final arrangements for the wedding. That's why I sent for you."

As if on cue, Evan Grey strode into the hall, his steps jaunty and confident. Even from a distance Aleta could see that capturing the Lord of Darkness had bolstered his ego and nourished his arrogance. He stared hard at Aleta before greeting Somerset effusively. Only after greetings had been exchanged did Evan turn to Aleta and say, "My lady, you look ravishing. I look forward with relish to our wedding day." His voice held a note of menace that frightened Aleta. She knew he had neither forgotten nor forgiven her for attacking him and that he intended to make her suffer.

Inhaling sharply, Aleta said, "There will be no wedding, my lord."

She had expected violence but Grey merely gave her a smug smile. " 'Tis a pity, my lady, that I must wait two days to begin your lessons in humility and obedience."

"Since both you and Father insist upon ignoring my wishes, I am forced to divulge the reason I cannot become your wife." She paused meaningfully, then blurted out, "I am carrying Jaime's child."

Grey turned a deathly shade of white, which slowly changed to mottled red. "Bitch!" he lashed out cruelly. "If you think carrying Mortimer's seed inside your soft belly will change my mind, you're sadly mistaken. He may have plowed you first, but I will be the only one to get legitimate children on you. The bastard you carry may never live to see the light of day. And if it does by chance survive the womb, then I will personally see that it is smothered at birth."

"Nay!" Aleta cried out, appalled. Never had she known such terror. "Not even you could be so cruel!" She turned to Somerset, her eyes wide with fright. "Father, I beseech you, do not allow this travesty."

Somerset frowned in consternation. He and Grey had perpetrated some dastardly deeds in their time, but even he wasn't convinced that murdering an innocent child was the right thing to do. "Such drastic measures aren't necessary, Lord Grey," he contended. "Should the child survive we need only find it a good home."

"I will decide what's best for my wife," Grey said with cold cunning. "Have you forgotten so soon that we are in this together?"

Somerset recognized a warning when he heard one. He and Grey were deeply involved in past mayhem and he couldn't afford to anger the man. "'Twill be as you say, my lord," Somerset said, bowing to Grey's logic. "Aleta will be yours to do with as you please, but know that I will be most unhappy if she is harmed."

"Your concern touches me." Sarcasm dripped from Grey's voice. "I have waited a long time to wed Aleta. 'Tis up to her how much force is necessary to make her into the obedient wife I desire."

"I will kill you before I'd allow you to harm my child," Aleta declared with quiet determination. "I would have him live to know his father."

Grey laughed harshly. "Then they will greet one another in hell, for Jaime Mortimer is a condemned man with one foot already in the grave."

"I want to see Jaime," Aleta demanded.

"I think not. We will be married in two days as planned, and you and your father will leave immediately for Somerset Castle in Wales, where you will remain until the birth of your child. The thought of bedding you with another man's seed growing in your belly sickens me. I want nothing to do with you until you have dropped your bastard."

Aleta's heart leaped with sudden joy. A reprieve, she thought gleefully. Any number of things could happen in seven months. She could escape her father's estate; Jaime could escape the hangman's rope; the King could intervene . . . God had given her hope where none had existed before. With enough faith anything was possible.

Aleta's faith did not stop the wedding between her and Evan Grey. She was married in her fa-

ther's London town house with no one present but
the priest who performed the ceremony, her father,
and the Somerset housekeeper and bailiff, who
served as witnesses. Though the church court had
granted the annulment, Grey thought it best not to
bring undue attention to his marriage. When the
King returned to London he would find the deed
already done.

Aleta had stubbornly resolved to withhold a reply to the marriage vows but her silence had angered Lord Grey to such an extent she feared his
violence. In the end she gave reluctant consent in
a voice so low the priest had to ask her to repeat
it. In a surprisingly short time the final words
were spoken and Aleta found herself the recipient
of a blessedly brief but brutal kiss, bestowed on
her by a bridegroom who seemed more angry
than pleased.

Within an hour of the ceremony Aleta was on
her way to her father's remote estate in Wales.
Grey's parting words were directed at Somerset.
"Guard her well, Somerset. Send word if
something—unexpected should happen to the bastard she carries. Otherwise I will remain in London until she drops the brat. When I return to
Wales I do not wish to be reminded of my wife's
previous marriage, if you get my meaning."

"Perfectly," Somerset agreed.

"I will leave the details to you." He turned to
Aleta, a sneer on his face. "You have many months
in which to think upon the various ways you can
please me. Take advantage of them, my lady, for
when we are finally united I expect complete and
total surrender."

* * *

Wallowing in filth, his head bloodied, his body battered, Jaime tried to adjust his eyes to the blackness of the tiny cell, unrelieved by light of any kind. How many days had he been here? he wondered bleakly. The first days had been a blur in his mind. So had the journey from Wales to London. He had been beaten severely, bound and gagged and dumped into the back of a wagon. The trip had been a nightmare from beginning to end. He recalled little of it except for the pain and almost daily beatings ordered by Evan Grey. Food and water had been offered infrequently, just enough to keep him alive for the hangman. But the worst pain came with the knowledge of Aleta's heartless betrayal.

Suddenly Jaime cocked his head. Attuned as he was to the utter silence of the dungeon, the sound of approaching footsteps reverberated loudly in the cavernous passages. Since he had already been given his first and only meal of the day, he had no idea who was coming or why. Was he to be executed without a trial?

The door to his cell swung open and Jaime flinched at the sudden burst of brilliant torchlight.

"It reeks like dung in here," Grey observed, wrinkling his nose in disgust. "But somehow the foul odor and filth clinging to you seem fitting."

Jaime recognized the voice immediately and a surge of raw hatred rushed through his abused body. Had he the strength he would have lunged for the man's throat despite the dire consequences. "Do you enjoy gloating?"

"Aye, it does my heart good to see justice done. But that's not the reason for my visit. I thought you'd enjoy knowing that I have just come from my marriage ceremony. Aleta and I were wed this very day and I wanted to bring you the good news personally. But you of all people can appreciate the fact that the bedding took place long before the ceremony. Do I have you to thank for my lady's passion? She's like a bitch in heat. She cannot get enough—"

Mustering the last of his meager strength, Jaime lunged at Grey. He was struck down by the guards before his first blow fell.

Chapter 15

Evan Grey had expected King Henry to be angry, but he had no idea the monarch would be absolutely livid when told of his marriage to Aleta.

"You *what?*" Henry bellowed when Grey explained that the church court had set aside the marriage between Aleta and Jaime Mortimer. "Why wasn't I informed of this?"

"Sire," Grey said ingratiatingly, "you were so involved in planning your trip to France for your upcoming wedding that I thought it best not to trouble you with the court's ruling. The decision was reached on the grounds that Mortimer waited overlong to claim Aleta, and it was ruled that Lord Somerset was justified in betrothing his daughter to another since everyone assumed Mortimer was dead. Lady Aleta was immediately affianced to me and we were wed one week ago."

Henry slanted him an oblique look. "Nothing that goes on in my kingdom is unimportant. I should have been notified. And now you say that Jaime Mortimer is the smuggler known as Lord of Darkness?"

"Aye, Sire," Grey said gravely. "The thieving bastard is in the dungeon awaiting your pleasure."

"I'm surprised you didn't take it upon yourself to order the execution," Henry said sourly.

Grey turned a dull shade of red, not at all pleased with the king's put-down. "You wrong me, Sire, for you know I have your best interests at heart. I had hoped you'd be pleased with the knave's capture."

"And so I am. 'Tis a relief to have a source of income restored to me. I have great need of the taxes."

"Shall I call the scribe to draw up an execution order?"

"Nay, I would speak with the man first," Henry said thoughtfully. "I was quite impressed with him that day he burst into the chapel to stop your wedding to Lady Aleta. And I must admit the questions he raised concerning his father's guilt have intrigued me."

"Jaime Mortimer is a madman whose wild accusations should not be taken seriously," Grey protested. His greatest fear was that some irregularity would be found in Lord Mortimer's conviction and subsequent execution. In all these years no one had questioned the charges against the man, or the court's decision—not until Jaime Mortimer had appeared from nowhere to claim his father's innocence.

"I'm not so certain Mortimer is as mad as you say," Henry mused thoughtfully.

Grey blanched. "Wha—what do you mean, Sire?"

"What? Oh, nothing, nothing. Let us speak a moment about your wedding to Lady Aleta. I take it she was agreeable to the match?"

Unable to look Henry in the eye, Grey mumbled, "Lord Somerset was most agreeable. He wants what is best for his daughter."

Henry realized Grey was dissembling but did not pursue the matter. There were still a few weeks left before he sailed for France and he fully intended to investigate further. "Where is your lady now, Lord Grey?"

"In Wales, with her father, Sire. London is not to her liking." He delivered the lie smoothly, smiling obsequiously.

"Rather unusual to be separated, isn't it? New bridegroom and all."

"I'm quite eager to join my lady, Sire, as soon as all the loose ends are taken care of here in London. I strongly urge you to consider a quick execution. The Lord of Darkness has been a thorn in our sides for a long time."

"Hmmm, aye," Henry said, stroking his smooth chin distractedly. He wanted to give the matter further thought before issuing orders. And he wanted to speak personally to Jaime Mortimer.

Grey left shortly afterward, not at all satisfied with the way the conversation had gone. Henry seemed far too taken with Mortimer for his liking. The execution had to take place without delay, he told himself, else he'd be hounded the rest of his life by Jaime Mortimer. Not merely because of Mortimer's claim that his father was innocent, but because of the way Aleta had been taken from him.

The cuts and bruises had begun to heal on Jaime's body but he still wallowed in the most squalid filth imaginable. What little water allowed him was carefully hoarded for drinking purposes.

Food was meager at best, and what there was of it was unfit for human consumption. But he forced himself to swallow the watery gruel for what little strength it offered. What he needed was good rich beef broth and red meat. What he got was slop.

Nursing his aching head, still tender from the clubbing he had received, Jaime's anger escalated with each miserable day spent in the damp dungeon. Mostly his anger was directed at Aleta, for the way she had betrayed him after making him believe she cared for him. He thought she was quite adept at lying, and a wonderful actress besides.

In order to keep his limbs strong and supple, Jaime made a habit of exercising long hours in the tiny, airless cell. He was lunging with a make-believe sword when he heard footsteps echoing down the passageway. When they stopped before his cell, he tensed, recalling the painful results of his last visitor. Had Lord Grey returned to torture him? This time he was in better shape to defend himself.

The heavy door creaked open on ancient rusted hinges. When his eyes adjusted to the sudden burst of light, Jaime was stunned to see King Henry standing before him. "Your Majesty," he said, dropping to one knee.

"Rise, Mortimer," Henry ordered, shocked by Jaime's pitiful condition. But he should have expected as much, knowing Grey's penchant for cruelty.

Jaime rose with difficulty, staggering slightly from the effort.

"You look terrible. I trust you have learned something from your mistakes. Smuggling is a crime against your King and your country, and the punishment is most severe."

"You are right, of course, Sire," Jaime said, his bruised lips spreading into a mischievous grin. "But smuggling *does* pay well."

Henry frowned. "Aye, I suppose it does, at my expense. Taxes from the brandy and sundry goods you smuggled throughout the years would have financed another excursion into France. Or provided my bride with rich gifts due a woman of her high rank. Catherine is a king's daughter; she deserves the best. But England is forever in debt," he complained sourly, "no thanks to men like you. Lord Grey is clamoring for your head and I can't blame him."

"Evan Grey is a lying bastard who has stolen everything of mine. Now he even has my wife. Once I am dead he will never have to worry about skeletons coming out of the closet to haunt him. There will no longer be a Mortimer to point a finger. May I ask, Sire, if you have investigated the charges against my father?"

"That's one of the reasons I have come to see you personally rather than order your execution immediately, as Grey insisted," Henry said. "A secret investigation has uncovered possible misdeeds on the part of the accusers. There is also evidence that the judges were bribed."

Incredible joy gave Jaime a much-needed lift. "You've proven that my father was innocent?"

"Nay, but there are irregularities that merit further investigation," Henry allowed.

Jaime's face fell. With his luck he'd probably be dead and buried long before the truth came out. "As you well know, my time on earth is limited."

"You should have thought of that before you

took up smuggling. With Grey and Somerset clamoring for your head, 'twould seem your charmed life has run its course."

Despite his words, Jaime could tell that Henry was reluctant to order his execution. They genuinely liked one another and had developed an empathy that first time they had met. If there was some way— Suddenly Jaime went still as an idea as outrageous as it was preposterous came to him. It could succeed, he believed, if Henry was as greedy as he thought and the kingdom as strapped for money as the King intimated.

"Not necessarily," Jaime said confidentially. "We could strike a trade, Sire. One beneficial to both of us."

Henry's interest was definitely piqued. So was his curiosity. "What kind of trade? 'Twould seem you have little bargaining power, but I am willing to listen. Anything that benefits the kingdom is of interest to me."

Jaime cast a sidelong glance at the guards ranged behind Henry, making his desire known that he wished for a private word with his king. Clearly intrigued, Henry ordered the guards outside the cell. When they were quite alone, Jaime approached the king so they could speak in low tones. But evidently the stench of his unwashed body was too much for the monarch, who held his nose and waved him back.

"That's close enough, Mortimer, your stench offends me. Say on, I can hear you."

Jaime bowed, smiling ruefully. "I have no wish to offend, Sire. Nor do I wish to swing from the end of a rope. The trade I speak of is my life for a king's ransom in gold and silver."

Henry's eyes sparkled greedily. "Gold and silver? The first time I set eyes on you I could have sworn you were as poor as a church mouse."

" 'Tis what I wanted you to think, Sire. If I appeared as a wealthy man, you would have been suspicious. Smuggling has paid very well indeed. 'Tis all yours, Sire, in return for my release and a promise to continue the investigation into my father's innocence. He was too honest to commit treason."

Henry's eyes narrowed thoughtfully. "Grey and Somerset would be livid if I dealt with you. I could order a thorough search of your keep, you know, and find the gold myself."

Jaime smiled wryly. "You would find nothing, Sire. No one but I knows the hiding place." Not quite true, but the King need not know otherwise.

"Great wealth, you say?" Henry repeated, keenly fascinated by the thought of adding to his wealth.

"Thousands of pounds sterling, and gold aplenty. Think what you could buy for your future wife. And all the wars you could finance."

"If I do accept your trade," Henry said slyly, "I want your solemn oath that you will never again engage in smuggling. You will return to Wales and remain there until I send for you. My investigation of the charges against your father will continue, but you must tell no one and say nothing until all the facts are thoroughly evaluated and the guilty parties identified."

"And what of my wife?" Jaime had no idea why he was inquiring about Aleta, for she was a faithless bitch whom he was better off without. If only his heart would listen to his head.

"I'm sorry I did not learn of the conspiracy against your father before Lord Somerset obtained the annulment of your marriage. I've had much on my mind of late, and my journey to France to claim my bride is consuming more of my time than I'd like. Had I been informed of the annulment, I might have been able to stop it, but since Grey and Lady Aleta are already wed there is little I can do. The terms I outlined are the only ones available for the trade you spoke of."

Jaime didn't need to think twice before accepting. Once he was out of this infernal dungeon he would get Aleta back, and on his own terms. Lord Grey hadn't seen the last of him, nor had Aleta. And once she was back in his keep he'd make her damn sorry she had betrayed him. Punishment took on many forms and he'd find one to fit the sin. Perhaps a beating, or confinement, or—or— making love to her, endlessly, until she begged for mercy. It was a heady thought, one that sent his senses reeling.

"I agree to your terms, Sire," Jaime acquiesced.

"Then follow me. You will be given clean clothes and allowed to bathe before your journey to Wales. To make certain you uphold your end of the bargain you will be escorted to your home by my own guard, who will see that the riches you spoke of are delivered safely into my keeping. If the captain of the guard finds you have been less than truthful, you will be returned for immediate execution."

"I think you will be pleased, Sire," Jaime returned with quiet conviction. "And I am most grateful." Of course it would strip him of all his wealth, but having his life back was worth it. And one day, he silently vowed, one day he'd regain everything that had been stolen from him by Evan Grey and Lord Somerset.

Before Jaime left London the next day he had learned from Henry that Aleta was no longer in residence. She had been sent to her father's estate in Wales to await her husband's pleasure. Jaime's heart thudded painfully against his breast. Nearly as old and as remote as his own keep, Somerset Castle lay less than ten leagues from Criccieth. Was it his punishment to have Aleta so close yet so far, knowing she was no longer his?

Henry had also informed Jaime that he had advised Evan Grey to remain in London during the investigation into the treason charges against Clarence Mortimer since he and Somerset had been the principal accusers in the case. It did Jaime's heart good when he thought about the anguish Grey must be suffering while waiting for the outcome of the investigation.

The journey to Criccieth keep proved uneventful. Jaime's strength was slowly returning, for which he was grateful, and with clothes loaned to him by Henry, he felt almost human again. Following the King's direction, Jaime had been guarded closely. But as they daily grew closer to the keep, Jaime realized he would soon be a pauper, and the idea did not sit well with him. Unfortunately there was nothing he could do about it.

They camped early on the day before their expected arrival at the keep, and with a start Jaime realized they were very close to Somerset Castle. The urgent need to gaze upon the place where Aleta dwelled was so palpable it was like an ache deep in his gut. He wanted—God's blood, he wanted to gaze upon Aleta's beautiful face, to hear the sweet sound of her voice . . . to love her. But since that was impossible he'd settle for a chance to look upon the place where she lived. Finding an excuse to slip away from the King's men wasn't easy.

Since they hadn't had fresh meat for the last two days, when Jaime offered to hunt for their supper, his offer wasn't declined out of hand. The captain of the guard, an experienced soldier and astute judge of character, gave him a hard look and asked, "Fresh meat would be welcome, lad, but can I trust you?"

"I know these woods, Captain. I give my solemn oath not to try to escape. What purpose would it serve? I'd given my word to the King and I don't intend to dishonor the Mortimer name by breaking my promise. Allow me to hunt and I will return with fresh meat in time for supper."

"I'll send a man with you."

"Nay, more than one man traipsing through the woods would scare off game."

The captain rubbed his chin in indecision. " 'Tis true, but if you aren't back by dark we'll come looking for you."

Elated despite the captain's stern warning, Jaime nodded, spurred his mount, and rode off.

Aleta had cried herself to sleep so many nights she no longer had tears to shed. Each day she waited in unrelenting misery for word to reach them that Jaime had been executed. But thus far no messenger of death had arrived at her father's remote estate. Was Jaime already dead? she agonized. Surely not, she tried to tell herself, else she'd know it in her heart. How he must hate her, thinking that she'd betrayed him. How she longed to tell him of their child, to watch his face when he learned he was to be a father. Would he be happy?

Or would he hate the child because he despised the mother?

Aleta's one consolation was that she had not been confined to the manor. Since Jaime was incarcerated and awaiting death, Lord Somerset saw no reason to confine his daughter. Besides, he reasoned, letting her ride her palfrey might help rid her of the child Lord Grey intended to do away with at birth. The thought of murdering an innocent child did not set well with Somerset. He'd much rather see Aleta miscarry through natural means than have to do away with the babe himself. In fact, he would absolutely refuse to do it when the time came.

Each day Aleta ordered her palfrey saddled and insisted upon riding alone. She didn't ride far, wanting no harm to come to the babe she carried, but she spent nearly the entire day secluded in a remote glen, remembering every precious moment she and Jaime had shared. During those times she never thought of Jaime's death, only his life, his vitality, and the brief peace they had known as man and wife. Nor did she concentrate on her future as Evan Grey's wife. If she allowed herself to dwell on her marriage to Grey, despair would surely kill her.

As was her habit, Aleta had her palfrey saddled and waiting shortly after breakfast. After stuffing the pockets of her warm cloak with fruit, cheese, and bread, she rode from the keep before her father, who was an indolent creature, had arisen. In order to protect her child she rode at a slow pace, arriving at her favorite spot where a bubbling stream bisected a wooded glen.

Choosing a shady tree beside the stream, Aleta stretched out on the ground beneath its leafy branches, thinking that soon the leaves would be falling in anticipation of winter. Well into her fourth month of pregnancy, Aleta was still slim enough to fool those who did not suspect. Her breasts were somewhat enlarged and her waist an inch or two thicker, but she suspected she was one of those fortunate women who didn't swell and become ungainly until late pregnancy.

Gazing upward into the hazy sky, Aleta's dismal thoughts carried her to the dungeon where Jaime was being held. Was there no escape for the man she loved? she wondered bleakly. She had never felt so incredibly helpless in her life. When the sun was a blazing red ball high in the sky, Aleta munched distractedly on her lunch, not really feeling hunger but aware that proper diet was necessary to bring forth a healthy child. She didn't dare dwell on the fate of her babe once it was born. Despite his faults she knew her father loved her and wouldn't allow her newborn babe to suffer at Evan's hands. Even if the babe was given away Aleta harbored the hope that they would be reunited one day.

She had no intention of living with Evan Grey as man and wife. She would escape him, she vowed, as soon as she was safely delivered and capable of caring for herself and her child. So many thoughts flew through Aleta's brain that she soon grew weary. Pulling her cloak closely about her, she fell into a deep sleep. She slept heavily, unaware that the sun was slowly sinking in the west, due to shorter days that signaled the approach of fall and winter.

As Jaime neared Somerset Castle he spotted a deer. Since he had promised Captain Hancock that he would return with fresh meat, he didn't hesitate as he gave chase through the woods, thinking to double back later for a look at the castle. Nocking an arrow in his crossbow, he took aim just as the fleet animal crashed into a secluded glen bisected by a lazy brook. The arrow found its mark, felling the deer with one clean hit in a vital spot.

Kneeing his borrowed mount, Jaime sped after the deer, breaking into the glen with a thunder of hooves and triumphant whoop. Startled from sleep by the commotion, Aleta sat up, blinking in dismay when she saw a deer fall not three feet from where she sat. She saw the rider a moment later when he crashed through the trees. Attempting to get out of the way, Aleta jumped to her feet.

Jaime didn't see Aleta until he was nearly upon her. When she leaped to her feet he yanked brutally on the reins, sawing the poor animal's mouth until he reared in protest. It wasn't until the animal skidded to a halt that he realized it was Aleta who stood before him. His first response was one of incredible joy, which slowly eroded into unrelenting rage.

Aleta stared at Jaime as if seeing a ghost. She had imagined him either incarcerated in the darkest dungeon at Whitehall, or dead. Seeing him now—strong, healthy, and scowling at her with unrelenting hatred—was too much for her as she began a slow spiral to the ground. Spitting out a foul oath, Jaime leaped from his mount, catching her before she hit the ground.

Aleta's eyes opened slowly, aware that Jaime's glowering features were mere inches from hers, staring down at her with loathing.

"Jaime." His name left her lips on a breathless

sigh. With shaking hand she reached out to touch his face. Jaime inhaled sharply, her touch so unnerving he jerked backward.

"Are you disappointed to see me alive?" he asked nastily.

"Disappointed?" Aleta looked puzzled. "Nay, my lord, overjoyed. How did you escape?"

"It matters little how I escaped your *husband's* brand of justice," he said. " 'Tis fate that I should find you alone. While I was rotting in my dismal prison I dreamed constantly of all the various ways I would punish you should I be lucky enough to live."

Aleta's eyes were huge saucers in her pale face. "I did nothing wrong." Her shaky denial brought a frown to Jaime's face.

"You betrayed me, my lady!" he thundered. He reached for her, yanking her against him with a jolt that rattled her teeth.

"Nay, Jaime, I love you."

"Love? Bah, 'tis Grey you love. Is he a better lover than I?" he taunted. "Can he make you writhe and cry out? Why, Aleta, why did you do it? Did you hate me so much you wanted my death?"

Aleta was sobbing now, unable to bear the brunt of Jaime's hatred. "I—I don't hate you at all. I told you, I love you. It wasn't I who betrayed you."

Jaime stared down on Aleta's golden head, bowed beneath the weight of her misery, and was visibly shaken. No matter what she had done, he still wanted her. He was sorely tempted to take her up on his horse and steal her away from Grey now if the King's men weren't breathing down his neck. Where could he take her? Grey would converge on the keep with an army if he was stupid enough to take her there. Until Jaime possessed decisive proof that his father was no traitor and he regained the Mortimer title, there was no place in the kingdom where he and Aleta would be safe.

"You must believe me, Jaime," Aleta insisted when he continued to stare at her in a strange manner. "I swear that I did not betray you."

He wanted to believe—God's blood, he wanted to believe. But it was too farfetched to assume that one of his friends or fellow smugglers had betrayed him. "Nay, my lady, swear all you want, I cannot believe you. You are wed by Grey now, just like you've always wanted."

"I do not want Lord Grey!" Aleta cried, clearly upset. "'Tis you I want, Jaime, truly."

"Lies! All lies!" Her words angered him so greatly he raised his hand, intending to beat her as she deserved, as he had dreamed of doing during all those brutal beatings he had endured.

Aleta went still, powerless to stop Jaime from doing her serious harm. Instinctively she closed her eyes and crossed her arms over her stomach, hoping at least to protect the child she carried. With Jaime feeling about her the way he did, she feared telling him she carried his child.

Aleta's stoic expression and white face effectively diffused Jaime's terrible anger. He had never struck a woman in his life, and though Aleta deserved it he couldn't bring himself to administer the first blow. With a cry of dismay, his arms fell helplessly to her shoulders, pulling her hard against him. She felt small and soft and vulnerable, making him want to protect her, not hurt her. His mouth covered hers with brutal hunger, crushing her to him with almost desperate need. The hard ravishment of his mouth sent Aleta's stomach into a wild swirl.

His kiss, at first angry, ground hurtfully against Aleta's soft lips, his tongue a thrusting, insolent sword. Forced to endure his punishing kiss, Aleta whimpered softly. Then suddenly, inexplicably, his kiss gentled, becoming more urgent and demanding than brutal. His hoarse groan told Aleta he wasn't as unaffected as he seemed by their kiss. When he bore her to the ground, she uttered a small cry of protest. Though she wanted Jaime desperately, she didn't want him to take her in anger.

"Nay, Jaime, not here, not like this."

Jaime's face hardened. "Aye, my lady, here and now. You are still my wife. As far as I'm concerned our marriage was legal and binding. I care not if Grey has tasted your sweetness, you were mine first. I will make you forget you've bedded Grey. 'Twill be my name on your lips when pleasure seizes you. I want you to remember this day always, my lady, and remember me, for one day you will be mine again. It defies logic that I should still want you, but I do, my lady, oh, aye, I do."

"Jaime, Evan never—" Her words died in her throat as he covered her mouth in another searing kiss that rendered her helpless to resist when he began undressing her. The rush of cool air against her heated flesh was her first indication that Jaime had removed all her clothes.

"Don't lie, Aleta, it ill becomes you," Jaime murmured against her lips.

He searched her face for the space of a heartbeat before moving down to capture a pink nipple, sucking it deeply into his mouth while his hand seared a path across her stomach to her thigh.

"You've put on weight," Jaime taunted, hefting an ivory breast in his hand. "Or mayhap you've become more womanly." His hand outlined the curve of her hip. "Aye," he observed wryly, "definitely more womanly."

While Aleta pondered his words, Jaime swiftly stripped off his clothes, coming back to rest full-length atop her. Then his lips were tantalizing the tips of her breasts again, which had swollen to their fullest. He suckled hungrily, sending currents of desire through her, before blazing a path across her stomach to her thigh. Aleta felt the moist tip of his tongue questing upward along the inside of her thigh and surged against him, seeking an even deeper intimacy. Grasping her buttocks in both hands, he lifted her into the hot wetness of his mouth. Aleta cried out as his tongue parted the golden hair at the juncture of her loins, thrusting into the pink folds of delicate flesh, finding the tender bud of her desire.

Instead of pushing him away, Aleta wound her hands into the rich darkness of his hair and pulled him closer—closer still, fearing she would die if he stopped. Aware that she was hovering on the verge of climax, Jaime thrust one finger inside her, then two, working them relentlessly as his tongue continued to ravish her. Aleta grew rigid, then began shaking uncontrollably as she exploded into so many pieces she feared she'd never be whole again.

Rising above her, Jaime paused, mesmerized by the look of raw pleasure on her lovely face. "Does Grey do that to you, Aleta?" Her answer was lost in a strangled moan as he thrust into her savagely, his throbbing shaft an instrument of sweet torture. She felt herself stretching as her tightness sheathed him perfectly, and intense pleasure spiraled through her again. With a will of their own her arms surrounded him; her hands caressed his back, his shoulders, the taut mounds of his buttocks, flexing and unflexing as he thrust and withdrew, thrust and withdrew.

Stunned that she could respond again so soon after her violent climax only moments before, Aleta met and matched his strokes, striving to reach those golden heights where only Jaime was capable of sending her. She squawked in surprise when he abruptly changed their positions, bringing her atop him. Spreading her legs, he placed them on either side of him so that she straddled him. The subtle movement pushed him even deeper inside her.

"Ride me, Aleta," he urged, gasping from the restraint he had placed upon himself.

The turbulence of his passion surged around her, making her vibrantly aware of her own desire, sending it soaring. And when he lifted his head to suckle her aching breasts, she tumbled into a chasm of pure erotic sensation. Flooded with wave after wave of incredible rapture, she soared to previously unknown heights of raw sensual pleasure.

Seized by a shattering splendor, Jaime rode her to the crest of his own blissful completion.

Chapter 16

❦

Shaken from an encounter that was neither planned nor expected, Jaime set Aleta aside and rose unsteadily to his feet. When he began pulling on his clothing in short, jerking motions, Aleta was puzzled by his anger. Rising slowly, she found her own clothing and with trembling hands began dressing. When she finished she darted a glance at Jaime, not surprised to see him scowling fiercely at her.

"What have I done?" she asked softly.

"You mean besides betraying me?"

His words wounded her deeply.

"Once again you have bewitched me with your beautiful face and seductive body."

"I am no witch."

"Witch or seductress, 'tis all the same. Did you cast your spell upon Lord Grey?"

"Jaime, please, you must believe me. No matter what you think of me, know that I would never betray you. Furthermore, I find marriage to Lord Grey distasteful. For reasons you know nothing about I cannot remain with Evan. Take me with you, I beg you."

Aleta's words stunned Jaime. The terror and

pleading in her blue eyes were so very real he almost believed her. Almost but not quite.

"One day, my lady, you will be mine again. But not now, not while I am a virtual prisoner of Henry's personal guard."

"A prisoner? How so? Where are your captors?"

"Surely you don't think I was able to escape from that dank pit of hell I had been consigned to, did you? Nay, my lady, I struck a bargain with Henry. My life for all the wealth I have accumulated through smuggling."

"You are truly wealthy?" Somehow Aleta never quite believed Jaime's claim to great wealth.

"Beyond your wildest dreams. Or rather, I *was* wealthy. Not a farthing will remain once Henry gets his hands on it."

"I don't care, Jaime, truly," Aleta insisted. "There is a very good reason why you should take me with you now." She was thinking of the babe she carried and Jaime's reaction when he learned he was to become a father.

"Reason or no, where would I take you, my lady? Without money I cannot pay my men-at-arms to protect you. My keep can't be defended against attack by Grey or your father and—" He paused meaningfully. "—stealing you away at this time might anger Henry and hinder my efforts to vindicate my father."

Rage seethed within Aleta. Vengeance so consumed Jaime that he had room for naught else in his life. No room for her, and surely no room for a child. Telling him about the babe now would serve no purpose, she decided sadly. She would find a way to escape Evan and keep her child, and Jaime be damned.

"Your cause!" she spat scornfully. "Everything

you've done since we've met has been for your own benefit! If you are so blind that you can see nothing else, I want nothing to do with you." Deliberately she turned her back, refusing to watch him leave.

"I must go, Aleta, before Captain Hancock sends his men searching for me. I promised to return with fresh meat before dark."

"And I must return home before Father comes looking for me. Good-bye, my lord, I—I'm glad you've not been separated from your head." With measured steps she walked to where her palfrey was hobbled. Jaime followed.

"Aleta, wait!" He grasped her arm, spinning her around to face him. "What is the reason?"

"What?"

"You said there was a reason I should take you with me."

"Forget it, Jaime, 'tis nothing," Aleta replied airily. "You wouldn't be interested." Indeed, she thought sadly, she could love him to distraction and he still wouldn't be interested in her or their babe.

"Believe me, my love," Jaime declared with such fierce conviction that Aleta was inclined to believe him, "if there was any way I could protect you and not lose Henry's friendship I'd carry you away with me immediately. You're mine, Aleta, and I don't give up what's mine easily. If Henry's investigators had worked more quickly, I'd be more powerful today than either your father or Grey. But soon the truth will be out and my title and property restored to me."

" 'Twill be too late." Biting her lip, she looked away.

Confused by her words, Jaime grew apprehensive. He had no idea what she meant. "Nay, Aleta, for I will think of a way to prevent Gray from touching you again. I may be penniless now, but I am not helpless. This raging lust I have for you rides me mercilessly. Until we meet again, my lady, do not forget our meeting in this secluded glade."

Then she was in his arms, experiencing the sweet torture of his kiss, feeling the hard crush of his body. Breaking off abruptly, he turned on his heel, swung the dead deer across his saddle, leaped behind it, and rode away.

Leaving Aleta behind was the most difficult thing Jaime had ever done. He knew he loved her still, even when he had good reason to hate her, but his practical nature had won out when he would have thrown her onto the saddle and carried her away. With nowhere to go and no place to hide, the King's men would catch up with him within hours. And perhaps land him in the dungeon again. Or cost him his head.

Jaime knew Grey was likely to remain in London, having been ordered by the King not to leave the city while the investigation was being conducted. Which meant that Evan wouldn't return to Wales to claim his bride any time soon, giving Jaime time to consider his options where Aleta was concerned.

Criccieth keep had changed little in the time he had been gone, Jaime decided as he and his guards rode past the crumbling curtain wall.

" 'Tis a sorry mess," Captain Hancock remarked, eyeing the keep with open disdain. "Seems unlikely these ancient ruins will yield the wealth King Henry expects."

Jaime said nothing, preferring instead to watch the look on Hancock's face when the caskets of gold and silver were removed from the secret room beneath his keep.

Jaime's knights were clustered in the bailey to greet him. Gaylord stood at their head, looking worried. "God's blood, Jaime!" the old man cried. "We had word that you had been cast into the dungeon, awaiting execution!"

"I was," Jaime said grimly, "and still would be but for the King's mercy."

Gaylord looked incredulous. "I don't understand. God knows you have little reason to expect the King's mercy."

" 'Tis a long story, Gaylord, which I will explain later. My friends here—" He motioned toward the King's guard. "—need food and drink to sustain them for the trip back to London."

"You return immediately?" Gaylord asked Captain Hancock.

"Aye," Hancock said gravely. "After our business is finished here we have no reason to linger." He sent Jaime a meaningful look while keeping a wary eye on the great number of men-at-arms milling about. More than enough to send his lesser number of men fleeing for their lives should their master order it. But Jaime's honor was at stake. He was bound to relinquish his fortune as promised.

Dismissing both Gaylord and his men-at-arms, Jaime led Captain Hancock and his men into the keep and down to the storeroom. Pushing several barrels of flour and salted fish aside, he pointed out an iron ring embedded in the floor. Two men leaped forward, lifting the door aside and peering eagerly into the darkness.

"A torch," Hancock ordered brusquely. When

the torch was placed into his hand he carefully descended the stairs, into the pit where Jaime's wealth had been stored. Two men followed. In quick order several small caskets were handed up to those waiting above while Jaime looked on with stoic resignation. Losing his wealth to the King was nothing compared to his life.

When ten small caskets rested on the storeroom floor, Hancock and the companions ascended the ladder and began examining the contents with great excitement. Jaime watched, a puzzled frown creasing his brow. He knew for a fact that there should be twice ten and more stowed away in the secret room. But since Hancock seemed more than pleased with the yield, he said nothing. In short order the caskets of gold and silver were loaded into the wagon that had accompanied them and a guard set to protect it. Then the rest of the guards entered the hall to partake of the generous feast Gaylord had ordered prepared.

Somewhat leery of the large numbers of men-at-arms at Jaime's disposal, Hancock opted to leave for London immediately. He feared a night attack by Jaime's small army despite Jaime's vow to obey the King's order to surrender his ill-gotten gains. In fact, the sooner Hancock left this crumbling pile of rocks the better he'd feel. Facing wild Welshmen was preferable to fighting Jaime Mortimer and his army, which were obviously highly trained and itching to fight.

Jaime waited until Hancock and his men disappeared into the woods, then indicated that Gaylord should follow him to his chamber. With the door closed to ensure their privacy, Jaime asked, "What in God's name happened to the rest of the monies hidden in the secret room?"

"I wondered if you'd noticed," Gaylord said with a pleased smile. "Am I correct in assuming that you promised the King your wealth in exchange for your life?"

"Aye. Fortunately the King has no idea he's to get less than half the wealth I've accumulated. What happened, old friend?"

"When I learned you had been incarcerated and awaited execution, I grew desperate. For days I searched my brain for a way to save you. Though the men were willing to storm London I doubted the wisdom of doing so. I knew it would take cunning rather than a show of force to set you free. That's when I decided to take half your wealth and bribe every important person in London, if necessary. Henry's personal guard earn slim wages and most would jump at the chance to earn a little extra for looking the other way while you slipped away.

"I realized that time was growing short and intended to leave for London tomorrow, bearing caskets of gold and silver and taking half your men with me. The caskets had already been loaded into the wagon before you arrived in anticipation of our early departure tomorrow."

"God's blood, Gaylord, are you telling me that a veritable fortune sat under the guards' noses all the time they were here and they didn't even know it?"

"Aye, so it was."

"Once again I am in your debt, my friend," Jaime said huskily. "Nay, you are more than friend. You have been a father to me since my own father's death, teaching me when I knew nothing, preparing me for the day I will become the Earl of Flint. That day may arrive very soon, Gaylord."

Gaylord grew excited. "What has Henry learned?"

"He is close to uncovering a plot instigated long ago to destroy my father. As we suspected, Father was falsely accused in order to strip him of his title and wealth."

"Close? How close?" Gaylord questioned eagerly. There were things he knew about Clarence Mortimer but hadn't told Jaime yet. The time was approaching, though, when Jaime must be told.

"They still do not have the names of the instigators but Henry promised he'd have them very soon. Of course we both know who was behind those false accusations. But until Henry has substantial proof he has advised me to hold my tongue, return to Criccieth, and keep out of trouble. He has promised to send for me when the time is right."

"Praise the Lord," Gaylord said reverently. "But—what of Lady Aleta? Did you see her in London?"

Jaime's features hardened. "Aleta is Evan Grey's wife. They were married before my release."

Gaylord looked stricken. "Then she is lost to you."

"Nay!"

Jaime's fierce shout of denial startled Gaylord.

"I will have her back, Gaylord. She is with her father at Somerset Castle, not ten leagues from here. For some reason known only to Grey, he sent her away shortly after their wedding day. I—I have seen her; she is well."

Gaylord looked astounded. "God's blood, Jaime, how did you manage that?"

Jaime's cheeky grin revealed more than his words. "'Tis a long story. Suffice it to say that just yesterday I spoke at length with Aleta." More than mere words passed between them, he thought but did not say. But his body and mind recalled every ecstatic moment of their passionate encounter in that secluded glen.

"Did she tell you that she is innocent of any wrongdoing where you're concerned? 'Tis my opinion that Lady Aleta isn't capable of betrayal."

"When I want your opinion I'll ask for it," Jaime said sourly. "Name another who could have betrayed me."

Gaylord rubbed his chin thoughtfully. "Rowena, mayhap."

"God's blood, Gaylord, Rowena knew nothing about the Lord of Darkness."

"She was a sly one," Gaylord observed. "A woman scorned hath no conscience. She would have betrayed you without a moment's hesitation. Did you see her the morning after you banished her from the keep?"

Jaime shook his head.

"I thought not. Neither did I, or any of the men. I'd put nothing past the jealous witch."

"You've given me much to think about, Gaylord," Jaime declared. "After you've seen that the caskets are removed to a safe place we'll talk again."

Realizing that he had been dismissed, Gaylord left the chamber, happily aware that he had planted seeds of doubt about Aleta's guilt in Jaime's mind. At least he hoped he had.

Back and forth, back and forth, Jaime's long strides carried him from one end of the chamber to the other, his mind working furiously. Was Gaylord correct? Had he misjudged Aleta? Did she truly love him? If there was a hint of truth to her words, he had done her a grave injustice and left her in an appalling situation. She had begged him to take her with him yet he had disregarded her wishes and ridden off. At the time it had seemed the prudent thing to do since he felt unable to protect her from Grey or her father. Would he have left her had he truly believed she didn't want Evan Grey?

The longer he brooded the more he realized that he had to learn the truth. He had to see Aleta again, before Grey arrived at Somerset Castle to claim his bride. He couldn't bear the knowledge that a bastard like Grey had already possessed the woman he loved and intended to do so again and again, planting his children inside her. Suddenly, with a clarity that was previously lacking, Jaime knew exactly what he had to do.

He had made a grave error leaving Aleta yesterday. Though he had suffered the pangs of hell, when he left her he had genuinely thought he had done right under the circumstances. But he should have taken his chances and run with Aleta to the coast, where they could board a ship bound for Ireland. Thanks to Gaylord he still had half a fortune left, enough to hire an army and rescue Aleta, and to hell with King Henry. His mind made up, he left his chamber to tell Gaylord of his decision. The very next morning he sent men throughout the countryside, to gather the mercenaries they'd recruited to storm Somerset Castle. He also instructed Gaylord to hire a ship to carry them to Ireland.

Aleta had arrived home so late the day she had encountered Jaime in the glen, looking so disheveled, that her father had refused to allow her to ride out again. He hadn't accepted her flimsy excuse for her delay and decided he could no longer trust her. She had kept to her rooms for the next two days, claiming illness. Something was amiss, Somerset surmised, but he knew not what.

Several days later Somerset received distressing news. A rider arrived from London bearing a message from Lord Grey. In it he explained how the King had thwarted their plan for Jaime's short future by allowing him to buy his way to freedom. Aleta had entered the hall while Somerset was reading the missive and was startled when he let loose a string of curses that singed her ears. She knew immediately that the letter contained news of Jaime's release from prison and waited patiently for her father to relay the message to her. She didn't have long to wait.

"God's toenails, Aleta, the knave is a wizard! How could Henry be so stupid as to allow a criminal his freedom? The man deserves to swing from the end of a rope, or have his head lopped off for what he has done."

"Who are you talking about, Father?" Aleta asked with feigned innocence.

"Mortimer, that's who! Not only that, Henry has appointed a special commission to investigate the treason charges brought against his father all those years ago. 'Tis insane, that's what it is! Lord Grey has been ordered to remain in London."

"Perhaps Clarence Mortimer really was innocent?"

Somerset's face turned from red to purple, so great was his anger. "By all that's holy, daughter, you have no idea what you're suggesting. Or what that investigation could prove. This whole mess could blow up in our faces."

Aleta blanched. She hadn't wanted to think her father was guilty of falsely accusing an innocent man but she was slowly arriving at that opinion. "Are you saying that you and Lord Grey are involved in Clarence Mortimer's trial and execution?"

Somerset sent her a quelling look. " 'Tis nothing for you to be concerned over, daughter. You were a mere child when all this took place. Needless to say your bridegroom won't be arriving at the castle any time soon and I am stuck here in virtual seclusion until the birth of your child." He stared purposely at her stomach, which was finally showing subtle signs of pregnancy. "For a time I began to doubt you really were increasing but I can see now that you weren't lying. For your own protection, 'tis best that you remain inside the castle."

"Are you forbidding me to go riding again?"

"Aye. With Mortimer on the loose there's no telling if or when he'll turn up here." He sent her an assessing look, recalling her late arrival some days past. "Or have you already seen the knave?"

"I doubt Jaime gives a damn about me, Father. You're wasting your time speculating whether or not he'll come here to see me."

Before many more weeks had passed Aleta would learn that her thinking was not only flawed but completely inaccurate.

Within two weeks Jaime's army swelled as men arrived at Criccieth keep. Most of them were mercenaries willing to do almost anything for a price, but some were villagers who rallied to Jaime out of loyalty. But even before that, men had been put to work building catapults, siege machines, and ladder-like apparatuses for assaulting walls, while others worked with the armorer, fashioning weapons. When told they were to attack Somerset Castle, those who balked were sent packing and those who remained began a program of vigorous training. Given the great numbers of men on hand, Jaime reckoned on another two weeks before all phases of preparation were completed.

Icy fingers of dampness clung to his hair and skin. A cold mist rolled in from the sea, giving the landscape an almost eerie appearance as Jaime rode at the head of his army on a gray, dismal day in early September. A day fit for neither man nor beast, Jaime thought drearily as his army crawled slowly toward Somerset Castle. Ten leagues was a long way for men to drag siege machinery, he reasoned, but by nightfall he fully expected the bulk of his army to be camped outside the castle walls. And if the unsuspecting Somerset refused to relinquish his daughter he'd find his castle under vigorous siege.

Rain fell at sundown. Not heavy sheets of drenching water but a misty drizzle that produced enough moisture to make everyone miserable. As predicted, Jaime's army reached the castle shortly after nightfall. Refraining from building fires so as not to alert those within, camp was set up in the woods surrounding the ancient castle. Jaime slept little that night, thinking about Aleta and how very much he wanted to apologize for believing she had betrayed him. Then he would love her. Love her so completely that she'd forget Evan Grey had ever possessed her.

Good fortune seemed to shine on Jaime the following morning as he stood before the iron portcullis protecting the entrance to the castle. The day was bright with promise; even the sun seemed to smile down on him as it rose in glorious splendor in the eastern sky. Jaime took it as an omen as he moved into position where he could easily be seen by those patrolling within the bailey. His army had materialized from the woods, ready to storm the castle at his command. A grim smile curved his full lips as a great cry rose up inside the castle and men rushed hither and yon, arming themselves.

"Show yourself, Somerset!" Jaime called through the portcullis.

After a long delay, Lord Somerset appeared outside the keep, clad for battle in chain mail and sporting an impressive array of weapons. "What do you want with me, Mortimer?" he shouted back.

"Need you ask? I've come for my lady. Send Aleta to me and my army will leave peaceably. Resist and I promise you much blood will be shed."

"Aleta is no longer your wife," Somerset declared.

"Ask Aleta whom she prefers," came Jaime's smug reply.

"My daughter has no say in the matter. She was legally wed to Lord Grey and shall remain so." Somerset's mind worked furiously. He had no intention of engaging in a long battle with Jaime Mortimer. He knew his castle could hold indefinitely under siege but he hadn't the stamina to confront a younger, more cunning opponent.

Over ten years ago he had listened to Evan Grey and his father and was so intrigued by what he could gain from the very wealthy Lord Mortimer that he had immediately joined forces with the

Greys to falsely accuse Mortimer of treason. King Henry IV had been so incensed over the rebellion in Wales at the time that he had accepted the flimsy evidence and after a brief trial had ordered Mortimer's death. It wasn't until after Mortimer's execution that Somerset had learned the real reason the Greys wanted to bring the Mortimers down. When young Jaime Mortimer couldn't be found, Somerset and the elder Grey had struck a bargain to betroth Aleta to Evan, thus assuring Somerset's silence and cooperation.

Everything would have gone as planned if Jaime Mortimer hadn't shown up to foil their plans at a most inopportune time. Somerset's share of the Mortimer fortune had come at a time when he had needed it most, allowing him to pursue an indolent life in London instead of living off his land in remote Wales. He wasn't about to lose it all now to a man who had literally risen from obscurity to challenge him.

"Call off your men, Mortimer," Somerset replied, an idea already forming in his mind. "I will bring out Aleta so she can tell you herself how happy she is to be Lord Grey's bride. You may be quite surprised by what you learn."

The moment Jaime had appeared outside the castle walls, Aleta could barely contain her excitement. She wanted to rush out immediately but her father had cautioned her to remain inside until he learned what Jaime wanted. Though she didn't say, she already knew what that was. He wanted her, and the thought made her heart soar with joy. He loved her! She had known it all along. It had just taken him a long time to adjust to the idea. Even though he still thought she had betrayed him, he loved her nonetheless. Happiness bubbled through her like intoxicating wine.

Breathlessly she watched Jaime and her father speaking, and when Lord Somerset turned to reenter the keep she ran to meet him. "What does Jaime want, Father?" she asked eagerly.

"Need you ask, daughter?" Somerset growled brusquely. "The arrogant bastard seems to think you prefer him to Lord Grey."

"I do, I do," Aleta trilled. "Please, Father, let me go to Jaime. I want no blood shed between you and the man I love."

"If Evan was here he'd squash Mortimer's pitiful army like an insect beneath his feet. If you go with Mortimer now, there is no place you can hide where Evan won't find you."

"I'll take my chances," Aleta said stubbornly.

"Nay, daughter, I won't allow it. You can speak with Mortimer but you will say only what I tell you to say."

"I won't do it," Aleta persisted.

"You will, else I'll instruct my most accurate archers to slay him where he stands before the portcullis."

A swift intake of breath effectively conveyed Aleta's dismay. "You wouldn't! Where is your honor?"

"I have too much to lose to think about honor. Do you do as I say?"

Aleta believed him. Too heartsick to speak, she searched her mind for a method to foil her father's diabolical machinations. Surely Jaime wouldn't fall for her father's ruse, would he? Perhaps she could signal him somehow, make him understand she was merely following her father's orders. Jaime loved her, didn't he? She must trust him to realize she was being forced to do her father's bidding. Time, she thought desperately, she needed time. But her time had run out.

"Well, what is it to be?" Somerset asked impatiently.

"I will do as you say," Aleta answered, unwilling to risk Jaime's life.

Somerset smiled, nodded, then said abruptly, "Take off your dress."

"What?"

"Take off your dress, daughter, I want no mistake made about your pregnancy. Unlike most women in your condition you are not overly large and I want Mortimer to see for himself that you are carrying Evan's child."

"Father! You know very well 'tis Jaime's child I'm carrying."

"Aye, but I'm willing to bet Mortimer doesn't know it. As hotheaded as he is he'll believe what you tell him. Now then, off with your dress."

"I refuse to parade around in my shift before all your men," Aleta declared in a stunning display of courage.

"It isn't too late to order my archers to take aim on Mortimer," Somerset warned ominously. "Even now they are poised on the wall awaiting my direction."

Aleta blanched. "Nay, Father, I will do as you say." While she removed her outer garment he told her what she was to say.

"Jaime will not believe it," Aleta declared shakily. But she feared he would.

"Aye, daughter, he will, if you are convincing enough." Once her dress was removed he looked approvingly on the small protrusion of her stomach pushing through the shift. Grasping her hand, he dragged her out the door to within a few feet of the portcullis where Jaime stood waiting.

Jaime was shocked and angered when he saw Lord Somerset pull Aleta through the bailey in her shift. What could the man be thinking? he wondered, visibly shaken. He was so enraged it took every bit of his iron will to keep from ordering his army into an all-out attack.

"What's the meaning of this, Somerset?" he roared, searching Aleta's white face. "Why are you parading your daughter before your men in her shift? Are you punishing her for preferring me to Lord Grey?"

Somerset smiled cunningly. "Look at my daughter closely, Mortimer, and tell me what you see."

Jaime's eyes lingered on Aleta's agonized features. "I see a woman terrorized by your cruelty. Release her, my lord."

"Look closer," Somerset urged, pushing Aleta forward. The abrupt motion swept her shift against her protruding belly, leaving no doubt about her state of approaching motherhood.

Jaime's face turned a startling green beneath his tan and a choking sound gurgled up from the depths of his throat. Aleta was pregnant! His heart leaped. Was it his child she carried?

"Now do you understand why Aleta prefers to remain with her legal husband?" Somerset smiled nastily. "His seed found fertile ground on their wedding night, while all the months you and my daughter were wed failed to produce fruit."

With stricken eyes, Jaime stared at Aleta, silently begging her to deny her father's words. But her gaze remained downcast, refusing to respond to his unspoken challenge. Not satisfied by Aleta's silence, Somerset goaded her cruelly.

"Speak, daughter, tell this misbegotten knave whose child you carry."

" 'Tis—'tis Evan's child." Her voice was so low Jaime had to strain to hear her.

"Louder, daughter," Somerset ordered. "Tell him to leave and never bother you again."

Jaime's eyes never left Aleta as she finally raised her head. When their eyes met he saw pain, and pity, and something deep and profound that defied description. It was almost as if she were trying to convey a silent message to him. Her lips were bloodless, her face drained of all color. She gave an almost imperceptible shake of her head, but it was so fleeting Jaime thought he had imagined it.

Aleta bit her lip to keep from screaming out the truth to Jaime. She looked at her father, saw his warning glance, and gave the answer her father demanded. " 'Tis true, Jaime. The child I carry belongs to—to Evan. So you can see that attacking the castle would serve no purpose."

"Why didn't you tell me this the day we met in the glen?" Jaime raged.

Somerset glared malevolently at Aleta but said nothing. It was the first he had heard of any meeting.

Aleta searched her brain for a reply that would somehow convey special meaning to Jaime. "It would have betrayed my reason."

Jaime's eyes narrowed. She spoke in riddles. His brain was too muddled, his shock too great to make sense of her words. "Mayhap your *reason* all along was to make a great fool of me."

"Nay, Jaime, I—"

The rest of her sentence was lost as Jaime whirled on his heel, leaped onto his huge black stallion, and thundered off.

Chapter 17

Jaime returned to the keep in a black rage. His first act was to pay off and dismiss all but the original twelve or so of the vast numbers of men who had rallied to his cause. His next was to call for a keg of brandy. Shutting himself in his chamber, he proceeded to get roaring drunk.

Devastated by the knowledge that the woman he loved was carrying another man's child, nothing or no one was able to reach Jaime during those dark days. Barely touching the food carried to him by the faithful Gaylord, he refused to speak of Aleta or even acknowledge Gaylord's questions. What Gaylord learned, he learned from Sir Giles.

As for Jaime, he wallowed in self-pity, his thoughts so destructive that confining himself to his chamber was the only way he could keep from racing to London and committing murder. Though he remained in a drunken stupor for an entire week, his mind refused to drown in its alcoholic bath as his thoughts returned again and again to Aleta and how she had bewitched him with her sweet lies of love.

Love! Bah! he thought derisively. All the while she was begging him to take her with him, insisting that she loved him, she was carrying another man's child. Hadn't one man been enough for her? And to make matters worse, he had fallen completely, irrevocably in love with the little witch. So much in love that he had been willing, nay, eager, to abandon his mission to prove his father's innocence and flee with Aleta to Ireland.

Jaime had sunk so low that when Gaylord barged into the chamber at the end of the week he hardly recognized the man he had grown to love like a son. So great was Gaylord's disgust with Jaime's slide into self-destruction that he immediately banished what remained of the brandy and ordered food and a bath. While waiting for his orders to be obeyed, Gaylord began haranguing Jaime, accusing him of giving in to weakness when it was strength he needed.

"You're a fool, Jaime Mortimer," Gaylord muttered darkly as he threw aside the tapestries that covered the windows, letting in light and fresh air. "The room reeks of alcohol and the foul stench of dissipation. Rouse yourself, lad, a visitor awaits."

"Send him away, I'm in no mood for visitors," Jaime growled around his swollen tongue. "God's blood, Gaylord, I need a drink." He reached for the jug sitting on the table beside the bed and found it empty. Sending Gaylord a black look, Jaime sent the jug spinning across the room, where it shattered against the wall. It was exactly how his head felt. "Get me a bloody drink!"

"Nay, Jaime," Gaylord said with quiet determination. "You've had enough, lad. A messenger has arrived from the King. I've sent him to the kitchen for a meal so you've time to gather your wits before greeting him."

"I don't give a damn about the King," Jaime said sourly.

Moments later a servant arrived, bearing a tray of food. Jaime looked at it cross-eyed and gagged. "Up, Jaime, up, I say," Gaylord prodded relentlessly. "'Tisn't like you to grieve so over a woman. You're a man of action, Jaime, not a drunken sot deceived by false words."

"False words? Ha, little you know about it."

"I know enough, lad. What's more, I believe none of it."

Forcing open his bloodshot eyes, Jaime glared up at Gaylord. "You didn't see Aleta, Gaylord. She is definitely carrying a child. Lord knows I wanted to believe it was mine, but I heard her quite clearly when she said that she carried Grey's child."

"And you, like a fool, believed her. I've never known you to be so gullible. But then again, you've never been in love before," Gaylord added cryptically. "Get up, I say! There's much to accomplish before you are fit to greet the King's messenger."

Gaylord finally got through to Jaime. Rising fully clothed from the bed, he swayed dangerously before finding his balance.

"You haven't changed your clothes in more than a week," Gaylord charged, eyeing Jaime's stained tunic with disgust. "Food first," he said brusquely, "then a bath."

"I'm not hungry." Jaime's growling stomach belied his sullen words. Why couldn't Gaylord just leave him alone? But Gaylord would not be dissuaded. Before Jaime knew it he had been first coerced, then bullied, into sampling the tasty array of food prepared for his benefit. After he finished he gave grudging acknowledgment to the fact that his stomach did feel less queasy with food in it. If only his head would stop pounding.

By the time Jaime stepped out of the bath he felt almost human. Since shaving demanded a steadier hand than his, he allowed Gaylord to shave him and trim his long hair into a semblance of order. By the time he was ready to greet the King's messenger he looked more like himself than he had in over a week. When he would have left his chamber, Gaylord detained him. The old man's face was grave, his words spoken from the heart.

"Jaime, I'd advise you to think carefully about what happened at Somerset Castle before drawing a conclusion. Things aren't always what they seem. Perhaps Lady Aleta was as much the victim as you were. She is but a helpless woman controlled by her father and Lord Grey. What alternative did she have but to do and say as they directed?"

"You have been my conscience and my mentor for many years, old friend, but this time you are wrong. You, too, have been bewitched by Aleta, perhaps more so than I since you are ever eager to rally to her side."

" 'Tis true I have grown inordinately fond of Lady Aleta, but 'tis you who have always been my main concern. I have nurtured and guided you these many years, lad, and I have not led you astray yet. Wise men seek the truth before jumping to conclusions that could destroy their lives." So saying, he turned abruptly and hurried from the chamber.

Jaime lingered a moment more, mulling over Gaylord's disturbing words. *Do you think me a wise man, old friend, or am I the fool you accused me of be-*

ing? he asked himself. It didn't take him long to decide to follow Gaylord's sage advice. Instead of wallowing in self-pity, pickling his brain in strong drink, he should have tempered his rage long enough to think clearly about Aleta's words and what they might have implied.

'Tis true Lord Somerset could have used excessive coercion to make Aleta say what she did, he reflected, and the child Aleta carried could in truth be his. Perhaps the reason she mentioned, the one she did not want to betray, had to do with the child she was expecting—his child. It was the same reason she had referred to at the glen, but he had been too obtuse to realize it at the time. Cursing his vile temper, Jaime finally left his chamber to receive the King's messenger.

The missive from the King was concise and told him nothing beyond the fact that he was to present himself without delay at Windsor Castle. The messenger could add little enlightenment to the message since he wasn't privy to the King's reasons for the summons. Gaylord and Jaime exchanged glances, both aware that the summons was directly related to the investigation into the conviction and execution of Clarence Mortimer.

"I will leave immediately," Jaime said, eager to speak to Henry. He had waited more than ten long years for justice to be done.

"Will you go alone?" Gaylord queried.

"Half the men-at-arms will accompany me. The other half will remain with you at the keep. When I return I shall be Lord Jaime Mortimer, Earl of Flint, with all my father's holdings restored to me."

"God willing," Gaylord intoned reverently. "And let's hope Evan Grey, Somerset, and all those involved in the conspiracy against your father will be duly punished for their crimes."

"Perhaps I'll learn at long last what inspired such a dastardly act," Jaime mused thoughtfully. "Something more than greed had to drive the men responsible. Neither Somerset nor Grey were poor men, and both held titles. Although at the time the elder Grey was a minor baron with a small estate, both he and Evan were considered decent men. That's why no one suspected them of supplying false information about my father."

Gaylord said nothing, merely nodding at Jaime's supposition. The old man was torn; torn between telling Jaime what he knew about his father or waiting to see if the truth would one day come out. He opted to wait.

"I will prepare for our move to Mortimer Manor," Gaylord said with great relish. " 'Twill be a welcome change from Criccieth keep."

"Aye, Gaylord, Mortimer Manor will be ours once again. And when I return I fully expect to have learned the truth about the child Aleta carries."

Jaime's journey to Windsor Castle was a hectic race through crisp autumn days and clear cold nights. Anxious to reach Windsor Castle, he spared neither himself, nor his horse, nor his men. He arrived in the midst of a grand gala, yet another festivity in honor of the King's upcoming marriage to Catherine of France. The celebration, attended by everyone of importance at Henry's court, was well under way when Jaime walked unannounced into the great hall. In the midst of the spectacle sat Henry, surrounded by lords and ladies of the realm. Evidently a great feast had just

taken place, for the tables were still overflowing
with remnants of the scrumptious meal and a
place in the middle of the room was being cleared
for the entertainment.

Realizing that his chances of speaking privately
with the King this night were remote, Jaime contented himself with viewing the festivities from a
dark corner, unwilling to involve himself in the
kind of debauchery that was known to take place
at court when the King was in residence. The entertainment this night was rather dull and Jaime
was on the verge of asking one of the servants to
show him to an unoccupied room in the vast castle
when he spotted Evan Grey.

With his head cocked attentively toward an attractive lady, Grey acted nothing like a married
man, which sent rage spiraling through Jaime. Not
a woman present in the great hall could hold a
candle to Aleta. When the woman smiled at Grey
in open invitation and exited the hall soon after,
the eager scoundrel waited but a few minutes before following discreetly. Jaime watched in disgust
as Grey ascended a winding staircase. He withdrew from the shadows, intending to follow Grey,
when Henry spotted him from across the room
and motioned him forward.

"Mortimer, welcome," Henry greeted jovially.
Casting a wistful glance at Grey's rapidly departing back, Jaime joined the King with marked
reluctance.

"I received your message, Sire," Jaime said as a
seat was made available for him beside the King,
"and came as quickly as I could."

"I'd say you flew," Henry jested. "Regrettably I
must ask you to be patient a little longer. As you
can see, we are in the midst of a celebration. I

leave in a fortnight for France to claim my bride, and I want this matter cleared up before my departure."

Jaime frowned. "I will try to be patient, but as you well know this matter has been close to my heart since I was a lad of fifteen. Not that I'm not grateful to you for your investigation, Sire," he quickly added.

"Then another few hours won't hurt," Henry said as he turned his attention to the entertainment taking place in the center of the hall. "Meet me in my rooms for breakfast and I will tell you all that has transpired in your absence."

"Can you not at least tell my if my father's innocence has been proven?" He had come too far, risked too much to let the moment pass without a positive response.

Henry stared hard at Jaime before saying, "Your father's honor has been restored. But in doing so, men in high places have been implicated in a vicious plot to discredit him. We will speak further of this tomorrow."

Victory had never tasted so sweet. His eyes shining in gratitude, Jaime said, "May I be excused, Sire? I have much to think about, and the journey from Wales has left me weary beyond belief."

"Seek your bed, Mortimer," Henry said dismissively. "Ask one of the servants to direct you to an unoccupied room."

Once Jaime had spread out his belongings in the tiny room he had been given, he grew restless. All he could think of was Evan Grey sporting somewhere in the castle with a woman, unaware that he was about to be exposed. He couldn't wait to see the look on the knave's face when told he was to be stripped of the title he had stolen from the Mortimers. Though Henry hadn't mentioned any names, it was no mystery to Jaime who had been behind the dastardly plot. Since the elder Grey had died a few years ago, the blame now lay entirely with Evan, since he had been the one who had benefitted most. Henry IV had awarded the vast Mortimer holdings and title to Evan Grey.

Leaving his room, Jaime wandered down the empty hallways in search of a servant. Finding sleep impossible, he suddenly realized that he was hungry. And once he found something to eat he wanted to check on his men to make certain they had been properly fed and bedded. The tinkling sound of laughter drew his attention to a door that hadn't latched properly. He would have passed without giving it a second thought if he hadn't glanced through the slim opening and seen Evan Grey sprawled atop a nearly nude woman reclining on a divan.

Jaime's temper exploded when he heard Grey's response to the woman's question concerning the adequacy of his wife. "My lady can't begin to satisfy me like you do, my love. Her pathetic efforts are truly laughable. But enough of my wife," he said, shoving her skirts above her waist. "Your hot little mouth has given rise to this terrible itch between my legs."

The woman squealed in delight as Grey sank his manroot deep inside her. It was at that moment that Jaime burst into the room. Leaping to his feet, Grey turned ashen when Jaime interrupted his rendezvous, a murderous expression on his dark features.

"What the hell are you doing here?"

"I am here at the King's bidding," Jaime declared. "Your days are numbered, Grey. Exposure is at hand and all your ill-gotten gains will be lost to you."

Grey looked stunned. "I don't know what you're talking about."

Suddenly the woman jumped up, sent Jaime a terrified look, and scooted out the door. Grey made as if to follow.

"Let your whore go, Grey, this is between you and me."

"I have nothing to say to you, Mortimer."

"I think you do. Did you know Aleta is carrying your child?"

Jaime's words stopped Grey in his tracks. Turning to Jaime, he smirked slyly. "You're jealous! Is that what this is all about, Mortimer?"

"Jealousy has nothing to do with it," Jaime insisted harshly. " 'Tis Aleta I want to talk about. Does she carry your child?"

"You saw her?" Grey had hoped Jaime would never find out about Aleta's pregnancy, but, since he had, he intended to use the knowledge to his own benefit.

"Aye." The knuckles on his clenched fists turned white and Jaime fought to contain his great rage.

"Then the evidence speaks for itself."

" 'Tis not so simple," Jaime declared, aware that Grey was deliberately taunting him. "Tell me that Aleta is carrying your child. 'Tis most important that I hear you say the words."

Grey's thin lips curved upward into a cunning smile. "Ah, perhaps you think the child is yours. If you're waiting for me to confirm or deny your suspicion, you've got a long wait coming, but I sincerely thank you for teaching my lady all those little tricks. She pleased me greatly, though I am reluctant to admit that she damn near wore me out with her insatiable demands. Who would think that a passionate wildcat lurked beneath such cool beauty?"

Jaime's fragile control shattered. "You bastard!" he shouted, leaping for Grey's throat. "Henry knows of your false testimony against my father, and very soon everything you have gained through lies will once again be in Mortimer hands. You are doomed, Grey, and I couldn't be happier."

Fists flying, Grey fended off Jaime's telling blows as they fell to the floor in a tangle of arms and legs. Grey would have been pounded to a bloody pulp if two knights who happened to be passing by and heard the ruckus hadn't rushed in and broken up the fight. Panting raggedly, wiping blood from his battered face, Grey cast Jaime a venomous glance and left the chamber in a great rush. When Jaime roused himself enough to give chase, Grey had disappeared in the darkened hallway.

Cursing violently, Jaime knew that Henry would be livid when he learned what had happened. He should have held his tongue no matter how much Grey had infuriated him. Since he was unlikely to encounter Evan Grey again this night, Jaime returned to his room, his thoughts on Aleta and what Grey had told him. But perhaps for the first time in many weeks he was thinking clearly. Until he learned otherwise he would consider everything Grey said to be fabricated.

King Henry quaffed deeply from his cup of ale, smacked his lips, and said with a hint of reproach, "You've had a busy night, Mortimer." Jaime had just joined Henry in his rooms where the King sat chewing morosely on the substantial breakfast he preferred each morning.

Jaime met Henry's dark scowl squarely, realizing that he had earned the King's displeasure. "I'm sorry, Sire, but Lord Grey goaded me beyond human endurance."

Henry's exasperated sigh did not bode well for Jaime. "Sit, man, you give me indigestion towering over me like an avenging angel." He shoved a last morsel of kidney pie in his mouth, chewed thoughtfully, swallowed, then set his fork down, shoving his plate away. "Would that you had employed more discretion in the matter."

"Evan Grey has been the bane of my existence for years. Pray do not keep me in suspense, my lord. What have you learned about my father? Has your commission proven his innocence?"

"Aye, Jaime, 'tis as you suspected. There were two men besides the elder and younger Grey involved in the conspiracy against Clarence Mortimer. As you know the elder Grey died some years ago. Another man, Lord Barlow, disappeared, but my investigators were able to find him, in the nick of time, I might add. He lay dying of a serious illness and passed on shortly after he gave a deathbed confession involving Lords Grey and Somerset in a conspiracy against your father. They falsely accused your father of treason and seized the Mortimer property and wealth for themselves."

"But why?" Jaime asked curiously. "Neither Grey nor Somerset had reason to hate my father."

"My investigators implied that the Greys were the instigators of the plot, driven by some imagined or real grudge they held against your father. The others were inveigled to join with them after being promised a share of the wealth. Lord Barlow was quite vocal about being cheated by Somerset and Grey, insisting he received little or nothing for his efforts. After my father bestowed the Mortimer title and properties on Evan Grey, he decided to keep most of the wealth in his own treasury. As you well know, England has always been strapped for money."

"Did Lord Barlow receive nothing of value?"

"Only Lord Somerset received a share, after a deal was struck to betroth Evan Grey to Lady Aleta. Barlow was given a worthless property from the estate."

Jaime stared at Henry in stunned silence. He suspected there was more behind the Greys' obvious hatred of the Mortimers but had no idea what.

"Times were unsettled while all this took place," Henry continued, "and my father was in the midst of a rebellion in Wales. When Lord Mortimer was accused of leading the rebellion by three respected men, the King had no choice but to charge your father with treason. I've gone over the transcripts of the trial and the testimony given was indeed damning. Father wanted the matter brought to conclusion quickly and after a brief trial your father was convicted and duly executed. I'm sorry, Jaime, but no blame can be laid to my father, whose duty was to put down the rebellion and execute the leaders."

"I agree. Blame does not lay with the King." Dredging up old memories had been painful for Jaime. "The Greys, Somerset, and Barlow, driven by greed and some deeper need, gave false testimony. Before I kill Evan Grey I will learn what drove them to seek my father's life."

"Nay, Jaime, justice will be done, but not by

you. I have ordered Lord Grey's arrest and requested that he be brought to me for questioning.
You must realize that all this took place many
years ago, and it may be too late to find enough
witnesses to reopen the case. The most I can promise is that as of this very day your title and holdings are to be restored to you. I can't return the
monies seized by my father, for it has all gone to
finance those infernal wars that have plagued England. But any wealth Grey and Somerset have accumulated these past ten years shall be yours."

"I would like to be present when Lord Grey is
questioned, Sire," Jaime requested. If possible, he
wanted to wring the truth about Aleta's pregnancy
from the man.

"Aye, I'll leave instructions that you be notified
when Grey is questioned. Now, while we're waiting for Lord Grey to be apprehended, let us go to
the great hall and inform everyone of your good
fortune. Word travels fast. Soon all of England will
know that your title has been restored. Henceforth
you will be known as Lord Jaime Mortimer, Earl
of Flint. 'Tis most fortunate that nearly every nobleman in the land is present at Windsor Castle
this day, for they will spread the word far and
wide."

The news was met with more than a little curiosity and a great deal of speculation as to the fate
of the previous Earl of Flint, Lord Evan Grey. Most
people present offered congratulations, but some
withheld judgment, waiting to hear what had
transpired to bring a powerful earl like Lord Grey
down. Though some recalled the rebellion that led
to the infamous transfer of the Mortimer title to
Evan Grey, many did not.

Henry was introducing Jaime to one of his barons when he was interrupted in mid-sentence by one of his knights, who indicated the urgent need for speech. Excusing himself, Henry pulled the man aside, giving him permission to speak. Jaime was close on Henry's heels, certain that the knight had news of Grey.

The knight's words sent a shiver of apprehension sliding down Jaime's spine. "Sire, Lord Grey is nowhere to be found. The castle has been searched thoroughly and no one has seen him since last evening. We finally found a stable man who recalled seeing Lord Grey riding away from the castle as if the devil was after him."

"God's blood!" Jaime roared. " 'Tis my fault for letting slip that he had been found out. Did the stable man notice in which direction he was headed?"

" 'Twas full dark, my lord, and the stable man was more interested in seeking his bed than in one man's comings and goings."

Henry scowled darkly. He didn't like having his plans thwarted. He was leaving the country in a fortnight and wanted this matter cleared up before he left. Henry V wasn't a man known for his mercy. He could be cruel and vindictive toward those who tried to escape his justice. "Alert the guard immediately," he ordered brusquely. "My guess is that he's fled to London."

The knight bowed, turned, and hurried off to do his King's bidding. "Do not despair, Mortimer," Henry said when he and Jaime were alone. "The bird has flown but he can't have gone far. We'll scour London until we find the scoundrel."

Jaime took his leave as soon as possible. Henry might think that Grey had fled to London, but Jaime wasn't so certain. It was true that Grey could easily lose himself in London's underground, but Jaime's guess was that Evan Grey would flee the country, though not without his wife. Convinced that Grey would head directly for Wales and Somerset Castle, Jaime made plans accordingly.

When told that Jaime intended to go to Wales to reclaim his ancestral home, Henry gave his blessing, along with an official document restoring Jaime's title and property.

" 'Tis wise that you leave the matter of Evan Grey to me," Henry said, unaware of Jaime's motives for going to Wales. "You are much too hotheaded for a confrontation with Grey. I employ men who are experts at extracting the truth from recalcitrant men."

"I fear Grey will flee the country." Jaime's greatest worry was that Grey would leave England and never be found. He wanted to make Henry aware of the possibility.

"I suspect as much myself," Henry agreed, "and have taken steps to halt Grey's flight should he be so disposed. Every important seaport in England will be watched, and should he try to book passage he will be apprehended and returned to Winsor Castle."

Jaime was pleased. The remote possibility existed that Grey would try to leave the country from an English port. It was good to know that the King's men would be on hand to apprehend him. Meanwhile he would go to Somerset Castle and stop Grey's flight from that direction. He loved Aleta too much to let her go without a fight.

Aleta, languishing in exquisite misery in her chamber at Somerset Castle, was convinced that

Jaime believed she was carrying Evan Grey's
child. There was no doubt about her advanced
state of pregnancy now, for her stomach had
swelled dramatically during the past weeks. No
word had been received recently from Evan Grey
and the remoteness of Somerset Castle left them
without communication of any sort from London
or Windsor Castle. For all they knew, London and
its environs could have vanished from the face of
the earth. And the way Aleta felt she didn't care.

Jaime hated her, her father thought more of his
own welfare than hers, and she was married to a
man she despised. *Oh, Jaime,* she lamented silently.
*I had to lie to spare you. Lord knows I tried to convey
the truth to you. Surely you must know that I was
forced to confess to something that was utterly false.
But no matter, I will protect our child with my dying
breath and solemnly vow to escape Evan before I am
forced to submit to him. I love you, Jaime Mortimer,
and will never love another.*

The following day Evan Grey arrived at Somerset Castle. He rode like a maniac through the iron
portcullis and immediately ordered the grill lowered. After a brief consultation with Lord Somerset, every available knight was ordered into full
armor and placed on alert.

Consumed with curiosity, Aleta left the sanctuary of her room to learn for herself what had
brought Lord Grey to Somerset Castle and why he
had arrived without escort. It wasn't like Evan to
travel alone through dangerous country or arrive
without fanfare. What she saw when she walked
into the great hall shocked her.

Never had she seen Lord Grey so disheveled or
distraught. He looked as if he had ridden without
respite, stopping for neither rest nor food. His

once-elegant attire was grimy and travel-stained
and he was covered with mud and road dirt. His
face was drawn, his eyes those of a madman, wild
and unfocused. He and her father were engaged in
vigorous disagreement when Aleta joined them.
Conversation came to an abrupt halt when they
saw Aleta.

"What is it?" she asked, aware that something of
great portent had occurred. "What has happened?"

Grey turned bloodshot eyes on her, lingering
with obvious loathing on her protruding stomach.
"The bastard has found us out," he spat contemptuously. "The next step is for the King to place us
under arrest."

"God's blood, Grey, say no more!" Somerset
warned. He looked pointedly at Aleta, drawing
Grey's attention to the fact that Aleta knew nothing about their underhanded dealings.

" 'Tis too late, my lord, for soon all of England
will know of our efforts to destroy Lord Mortimer
all those years ago."

"Why now?" Somerset lamented. "Many years
have passed since the deed was done. Why did
Mortimer's heir appear from nowhere to foil our
plans? Everyone thought the child had died soon
after his father's execution."

By now Aleta knew exactly to whom and to
what Evan and her father were referring. Somehow, some way, for reasons known only to them,
they had provided false information that had sent
Jaime's father to his death.

"How could you, Father? Were you so desperate
to share in Lord Mortimer's wealth?"

"You don't understand, daughter," Somerset

tried to explain. " 'Twas a pact between Grey and myself."

Aleta turned on Grey, her eyes spitting fire. "Have you no conscience? Only a vile, despicable bastard would send an innocent man to his death. I hope you rot in hell for what you've done."

"Bitch!" Desperation had driven Grey as far as he could go as he balanced precariously on the edge of sanity. "Whore! Take your repulsive belly where I won't be reminded that you've spread your legs for a Mortimer."

"You're not half the man Jaime is!"

Staring at Aleta as if she were a poisonous snake, Grey's slim hold on reality snapped. Raising his arm, he slapped her across the face with his open palm, sending her flying.

Stunned by the vicious blow, Aleta picked herself off the floor with difficulty. When Grey took a menacing step forward, Aleta cringed and crossed her arms over her stomach to protect her child. But before Grey's second blow was delivered, Somerset stepped between her and her tormentor.

"Brutality is unnecessary, my lord," he advised sternly. It was one thing for him to reprimand his own daughter but quite another for someone else to abuse her. Especially in her delicate condition. Somerset might be greedy, and cruel in certain matters, but his daughter had always been obedient, respectful, and undeserving of Grey's cruelty.

"Have you forgotten, my lord?" Grey sneered. "Aleta is my wife to do with as I please."

"Not while you're in my home. Only a coward would brutalize his wife."

During the weeks he and Aleta had dealt closely with one another, Somerset realized that the child Aleta carried would be his grandchild no matter who had fathered it, and he began to look forward to its birth. Somerset blood flowed through the child's veins, and since Aleta was his only offspring she was the only one capable of providing him with heirs. And no matter what Lord Grey said or ordered, he would not allow Aleta's child to be destroyed. Or Aleta hurt, for that matter.

"You're too soft," Grey spat. Suddenly the wildness returned to his eyes. "If the King finds us we'll both be forced to confess to our crime. Who would have thought we'd be undone by a man we both thought had perished as a child."

"I should have never joined forces with you, your father, and Lord Barlow," Somerset complained bitterly. "I had just lost my wife and my mind was disturbed. I became greedy. But you, my lord, had much more to gain from destroying the Mortimers."

"Aye," Grey muttered darkly. "Revenge. Everything that Jaime Mortimer was to inherit belonged to me."

Aleta's curiosity got the best of her. Still shielded by her father's bulk, she peeked around him and asked, "How could that be?"

Grey's piercing gaze settled on Aleta. "None of your business, wench." He turned his attention back to Somerset. "I don't know how long we have until the King's men arrive. According to Mortimer, our conspiracy has been exposed. I didn't wait around long enough to learn what Henry intended for me."

"Jaime was at Windsor Castle?" Aleta asked, elated. "What did he say to you?"

Grey laughed harshly. "He wanted to know whose child you carried. He entertains the idea that the child is his."

Aleta inhaled sharply. "But the child *is* Jaime's. What did you tell him?"

"Nothing. It amuses me to let him wonder about it the rest of his life."

"What are we going to do?" Somerset's brow wrinkled worriedly. "I have no intention of letting Henry drag me to London for trial."

"I've already thought of that," came Grey's smug answer. "Before I arrived I stopped off and made arrangements for a ship to pick us up two days hence at North Beach. I don't dare return to Grey Manor, but we'll have plenty of time to pack everything of value in Somerset Castle before we meet the ship."

"Where are you going?" This from Aleta, who had no intention of leaving English soil.

"To France. I don't intend to remain long enough to sample the King's justice, and I'm sure your father feels the same."

"I'm not going with you," Aleta insisted stubbornly.

"You're my wife. You will go where I take you."

"I want my child born in Wales." She turned pleading eyes on her father. "Please, Father, don't make me go."

" 'Tis not for me to say, child. A wife must follow her husband. If you're worried about being treated harshly by Lord Grey, fear not, I will be with you to see that you do not suffer at his hands."

"I suggest that you both start packing immediately," Grey said. "Since the majority of the men-at-arms are loyal to me, my lord, dispatched here from Grey Manor to guard Lady Aleta, I will inform them that they are to escort us to the coast."

"I pray that we are gone before Henry's men come for us," Somerset whispered anxiously.

Chapter 18

Jaime reached Somerset Castle a day behind Evan Grey. He had stopped briefly at Criccieth keep to inform Gaylord of everything that had transpired at Windsor Castle.

"It gives me great pleasure to address the new Earl of Flint, my lord," Gaylord said, grinning hugely. "Ah, Jaime, 'tis been a long wait, but worth the effort. Do you claim Mortimer Manor immediately?"

"Nay, Gaylord, I fear Grey intends to flee the country with Aleta. 'Tis my belief that he is at Somerset Castle. If so, my lady is in grave danger. He knows what taking Aleta with him will do to me. Especially if she is carrying my child like I suspect."

"Ah," Gaylord said, smiling, "so you did heed my words. What would you have me do, lad?"

"Claim Mortimer Manor in my name. Take our valuables and anything else you deem worthwhile. I know not when I will join you, but when I do my lady will be with me."

" 'Tis impossible, Jaime!" Gaylord cried, aghast. "You've dismissed all your mercenaries but for twelve knights. 'Tisn't enough to storm a fortress as strong as Somerset Castle. And there isn't time to raise another army."

"I will take my knights. They are good, brave men, trained to fight against overwhelming odds."

" 'Tisn't enough, lad." Suddenly Gaylord's face lifted. "The villagers, lad. There isn't a man among them who wouldn't give his life for you. I'll send word immediately."

A few hours later Jaime rode at the head of a ragtag army of peasants and knights, some mounted, but most on foot bearing a collection of arms, including stout cudgels, swords, and crossbows. During the night they moved into place and by early morning they were hidden in the woods surrounding Somerset Castle.

Jaime recalled the last time he had been separated from Aleta by the iron portcullis and heard her tell him she was expecting Grey's child. It had been the lowest point in his life. This time he wasn't going to give up so easily, or let anger rule his head. No one was going to take Aleta from him.

Jaime scanned the castle walls, noting the increased guard along the wall walks. It would appear as if Somerset was expecting company. And if Jaime was correct, Evan Grey was inside those walls. Keeping well out of range of arrows, Jaime revealed himself at the edge of the woods, cautioning his men to remain concealed. Alert guards within the castle saw him immediately and gave the alarm. A satisfied smile curved Jaime's lips when both Somerset and Grey came rushing out of the keep. Immediately he signaled to one of his knights, whose instructions were to ride to Windsor Castle and inform the King that Lord Grey was at Somerset Castle.

Cautiously Grey approached the portcullis, followed by Somerset.

"Where is Aleta?" Jaime called loudly across the distance. "Have you harmed her?"

"My daughter is well," Somerset shouted back. "What do you want?"

"You are both wanted by the King for questioning in regards to false charges brought against my father, Clarence Mortimer. I suggest you comply immediately."

"Like hell!" Grey snarled. "We'll be gone from English soil long before Henry's men arrive to arrest us."

"I'm not alone, Grey, I have enough men with me to lay siege to the castle and make certain you don't leave until Henry's men arrive."

"I don't believe you," Grey scoffed derisively.

At his words, Jaime signaled his men to step out from the cover of trees. From a distance the villagers, with their crude weapons and lack of mail, were indistinguishable from the fully armed knights. Fortunately for Jaime, Somerset and Grey saw what Jaime intended for them to see. Both men realized immediately that leaving the castle would be difficult in the face of such overwhelming opposition. Once again Grey sought his cunning to get him out of a tight situation. Turning abruptly, he brushed past Somerset and into the keep.

Had Aleta known Jaime was outside the gate with a small army she would have been better prepared. But it so happened she had overslept that morning and had just finished dressing when Grey burst into her room, brandishing a sword.

"You!" Aleta cried, spinning around to glare at him. "What do you want?"

"Come with me." His succinct words sent a chill down her spine. And when he grasped her wrist and began pulling her out the door, she feared he had lost his mind.

"Where are you taking me?"

"You'll see." His eyes glowed with madness and he appeared deeply disturbed.

Though she tried to hold back she was no match for Grey's superior strength. And when he dragged her up the tower stairs she knew true fear. Did he intend to throw her from the parapet? Where was her father?

Grey allowed her no respite as he ruthlessly dragged her up the spiral stone stairway. Panting raggedly, on the verge of collapse, Aleta was thrust out onto the wall walk that circled the perimeter of the battlement. The wind tore at her hair and clothing, stealing her breath away, and the chilling dampness settled deep into her bones. Several of the guards patrolling the wall looked startled by their appearance, but a harsh command from Grey sent them below.

"Why have you brought me here, Evan?" Her teeth were chattering so she could barely force the words past her lips. "What are you going to do?"

"Look down," Grey ordered, pulling her dangerously close to the edge of the battlement. "What do you see?"

Curious as well as frightened, Aleta glanced through a crenel to the ground below. At first she saw nothing. Then she saw him, poised at the edge of the woods a short distance beyond the portcullis.

"Jaime!" A gust of wind tore his name from her lips, propelling it through the air to Jaime's ears. At first Jaime thought it was the screech of a wild bird soaring overhead that he heard, but some sixth sense made him look upward. Then he saw her and the blood froze in his veins.

"Aleta!"

"If you value Lady Aleta's life and the life of the child she carries, you'll send your army away," Grey shouted. "Resist and they die. Heed me well, Mortimer, I'm a desperate man. There's nothing I won't do to leave the country well ahead of the King's men. If you don't comply with my wishes, the next time you see Aleta she'll be a bright splash against the rocks below."

"God's blood, Grey, I knew you were corrupt, but I had no idea how truly evil you were. Threatening the life of a pregnant woman is contemptible."

"I do not make idle threats," Grey warned ominously. " 'Twill take little effort to throw Aleta over the battlement. As for her child, 'tis not mine so I care not what happens to it."

For a brief moment Jaime allowed himself the luxury of savoring Grey's words. Aleta was carrying *his* child, not Grey's. That welcome bit of information made Jaime even more determined than ever to save Aleta.

"What would you have me do?" Jaime's gaze lingered on Aleta's white face; he was frightened by her paleness. From where he stood he could see her shivering and knew that without a warm cloak to protect her she must be suffering unbearably from the icy bite of the wind.

Suddenly Jaime saw a movement along the wall behind Grey and he watched helplessly as a tense drama began to unfold on the wall walk high atop the battlement. Lord Somerset, realizing what was taking place there, had rushed to his daughter's

defense. Almost too late he had come to the realization that he loved Aleta and truly cared what
happened to her and her child. After Evan Grey
had shown up at Somerset Castle the other day in
a state bordering on madness, Somerset was almost persuaded to beg the King's mercy rather
than throw in his lot with a madman.

Aleta saw Somerset long before Grey became
aware of his presence, so intent was he upon
taunting Jaime. Grateful that her father had come
to her defense, Aleta felt relief surge through her.
Deep down he loved her, she realized, despite the
fact that during the past months he'd given her little reason to think so.

Suddenly Grey became aware of Aleta's gaze,
focused on something or someone behind him. He
whirled, relaxing somewhat when he saw Somerset.

"Let Aleta go," Somerset demanded harshly.

Grey grinned. "Fear not, my lord, Mortimer will
never allow anything to happen to Lady Aleta or
his child."

"I said let her go," Somerset repeated. " 'Tis insane to torment her needlessly. I've done some despicable things in my life, but I've never hidden
behind a woman's skirts. And certainly not a
woman far gone with child."

"Bah, Mortimer's get doesn't deserve to see the
light of day. The Mortimers are a cursed lot."

Somerset took a step forward, intending to
wrest Aleta from Grey's grip.

"Come no closer, my lord, lest you cause your
daughter's death."

"Your mind is twisted, Grey," Somerset charged,
keeping a wary eye on Aleta. "Does Mortimer
know why you plotted against his father all those

years ago? Does he know why you would have killed him had you found him after his father's execution? Does he realize that you're his half-brother? Or am I the only one you've trusted with that knowledge?"

Aleta's mouth dropped open and her eyes widened in shock. Did her father know what he had said? Were Jaime and Evan half-brothers? How could that be?

"Aye, we're half-brothers," Grey snarled, "but I claim no kinship with the bastard. His father raped my mother one day when she was just thirteen years old. She was out riding alone when Mortimer came upon her. He assumed she was a peasant because she had slipped away without her maid and he raped her. Even as a young lad Clarence Mortimer was an arrogant bastard. She didn't even know his name and was too frightened to tell anyone what had happened. She had been visiting Grey Manor because she was soon to marry Gordon Grey. When I was born, Gordon assumed I was his son."

Grey appeared to enjoy the retelling of the story he had kept to himself since his mother had whispered the secret of his paternity to him on her deathbed. Somerset had been the only person he had ever told. Not even Gordon Grey knew the truth. The elder Grey, a staunch defender of Henry IV, had been duped by Evan into believing that Clarence Mortimer had actually committed treason.

Finally, Aleta found her tongue. "I don't believe you. You're nothing like Jaime."

Grey sent her a malevolent glare. " 'Tis true enough, my lady. My mother only learned the name of her rapist many years later. She kept the secret until a moment before her death, when she whispered her startling confession to me. I vowed on her dead body that I'd make Clarence Mortimer pay for what he did to my mother all those years ago.

"Had Mortimer been an honorable man he would have married my mother and I would have been the rightful heir to all his wealth. But as it worked out I still got everything, just like it was meant to be. That's why I wanted you, my lady. You were the last link to the Mortimers, the last possession that would have belonged to the Mortimers had they lived. When Jaime Mortimer turned up from nowhere to claim you, I wanted to kill him."

Aleta's head was spinning. Was Evan telling the truth or was he suffering from delusions? Had he gone completely insane? Yet— Yet there was just enough fact in his story to make it believable. Aleta felt certain that Jaime had no inkling of the real reason behind Evan's hatred for the Mortimers.

"That's no reason to take out your anger on my daughter," Somerset declared, having heard the story of Grey's paternity before. "I'm going to take Aleta back to her room. She'll freeze to death up here." He stepped forward, a look of utter determination on his florid face.

Grey's expression twisted into a mask of hostility as his hold tightened on Aleta. "Nay, my lord, our only chance of leaving the country unhampered depends on Aleta. Mortimer will do anything to keep her safe."

"As will I, my lord," Somerset said evenly. Despite Grey's warning, he grasped Aleta's other arm, effecting a tug-of-war between the two men.

Grey reacted in a most unexpected way. Determined to stop Somerset and desperate to keep Aleta where Jaime could see her, he raised the sword he had been holding all this time and ran him through. Uttering a strangled cry, Somerset fell to the wooden walkway.

Aleta made a small inarticulate sound as she tried to pull free from Grey's hold and go to her father. Clutching her about the waist, he pulled her further along the wall walk. Aleta struggled to escape his cruel grasp but desisted immediately when he whispered harshly in her ear, "If you value the life of your child, you will cease struggling immediately."

Far below the battlement Jaime watched the scene unfold with something akin to horror. Never had he felt so frustrated, so damn helpless. When Grey had thrust his sword through Lord Somerset, Jaime's blood ran cold. Was Aleta next? When he saw Aleta struggling awkwardly with Grey he wanted to sprout wings and fly to her defense. Suddenly the struggling stopped and Jaime tensed when Grey looked over the battlement directly down on him.

"See what could happen when I'm thwarted, Mortimer? I've killed once; I'll not hesitate to do so again."

Cold, black fear raced through Jaime. "What would you have me do, Grey?"

"Take your men and leave immediately," Grey commanded. "I'll be watching from the battlement. Unless I see you at the head of the column leading your men away, Aleta will suffer. I'm a desperate man, Mortimer, I do not make idle threats."

He brought Aleta precariously close to the edge

of a crenel, a gap in the wall through which guards could look out and aim arrows at the enemy. Jaime sucked in a ragged breath, fearing that the demented man would throw his love over the side.

"It will be as you say," he called up to Grey. "But if you harm Aleta, there is no place in the world you can hide where I won't find you."

Easing back into the concealment of the woods, Jaime called Sir Giles to his side. The knight stepped forward with alacrity, awaiting instructions.

"Quickly, Sir Giles, change mail with me and don my helmet. Then take my black stallion and ride at the head of my army. Lead them out of sight into the hills and await further instructions."

"What do you intend, my lord?"

"I want Grey to think that we have left as he demanded. I will remain hidden in the woods to await his next move. Leave a man behind to act as messenger. When I have need of you I will send word." Clothing was hastily exchanged and after a cursory inspection of Sir Giles, Jaime said, "You'll do. Go now, but keep your face averted so as not to alert Grey to our deception."

Crouching behind the concealment of thick brush, Jaime watched as his men, with Sir Giles wearing his clothing at their head, retreated from the woods in an orderly fashion. The column stretched out in a long line and slowly disappeared over the crest of the hill. The man left behind to act as messenger joined Jaime and the two settled down to await further development.

Clasped in Grey's cruel grasp atop the battlement, Aleta succumbed to despair. For all she knew her father was already dead, and Jaime, her last hope for rescue, had abandoned her to Evan Grey. Though she knew that Jaime had left in order to save her life, just as she had lied twice before to save Jaime's life, the knowledge did little to allay her fear and grief. What would become of her now?

" 'Twould seem the bastard values your life, my lady," Grey taunted nastily. "How fortunate for you. See," he pointed out, "he rides at the head of his ragtag army."

Then he began dragging her along the wall walk, toward the staircase. When they approached Lord Somerset's body lying so still and white, Aleta begged, "Let me see to my father, he needs help."

" 'Tis too late, the wound was mortal." His voice was utterly without remorse.

"You can't just leave him here for carrion to devour," Aleta screamed, horrified. Nearly at the end of her tether, she perched on the edge of hysteria.

An hysterical woman on his hands was the last thing Grey wanted. He needed Aleta's cooperation if they were to leave the castle this night to board the ship for France. Flinging her aside, he snarled, "See to your father, then. If he still lives my men will carry him to his room where you may see to his wounds. If he is dead as I suspect, he will be buried in the bailey."

Finding herself suddenly free, Aleta rushed to her father, dropping to her knees beside him. She saw immediately that Grey had been right. The wound, a solid thrust through the heart, was indeed mortal. Lord Somerset had died instantly. Aleta was grateful that at least he hadn't suffered unduly. Sitting back on her heels, she glared up at Grey.

"Murderer! You won't get away with this. Jaime will stop you and the King will see justice done."

"Mortimer won't touch me as long as I have you. And Henry can't be bothered; he leaves for France shortly. Come along," he said, dragging her to her feet, "we've much to do before we meet the ship that will carry us away."

"Nay!" Aleta said, resisting. "I won't leave Father like this."

"He will be taken care of," Grey said, losing patience. " 'Tis nearly dusk, there is much to be done before departure." When Aleta still resisted, he picked her up bodily and carried her down the stairs. When he reached her chamber he shoved her inside and locked the door. "I will come for you at midnight," he informed her through the closed panel.

Grey spent the hours till midnight packing all the valuables he found in the castle and overseeing their loading into two carts. He also ordered Lord Somerset's body carried from the battlement and buried in the inner bailey. He was prepared to encounter trouble from Somerset's knights, but since his own knights far outnumbered Somerset's, thoughts of rebellion were quickly quelled. Since most of Somerset's men, and his own, for that matter, were mercenaries, little loyalty existed for the slain man. Power lay with the victor and Grey was clearly the victor.

Tears streamed from her eyes as Aleta watched from the window of her chamber her father being buried in the inner bailey. Though he hadn't been the perfect parent, and was known to put his own interests above those of his daughter, he had been her sire and she had loved him. She mourned him with real tears, dwelling on the early years after her mother's death when they had been close. It was after his involvement with Evan Grey that their friendship had changed. His obsessive greed had brought about an innocent man's death and for that it would be a long time before she forgave him. If she was allowed to live long enough.

At the stroke of midnight Grey came for her. She had dozed off sitting in a chair, fully clothed in her warmest attire. Up until the very last minute she had believed Jaime would burst through the door and rescue her from Evan's clutches. But it was not to be. If not for the child she carried she wouldn't have cared whether she lived or died.

Grey picked up her small trunk and hurried her along, leading her out into the inner bailey. Aleta was stunned to see all the men-at-arms assembled around two carts loaded with everything of value in the keep. She knew her father kept chests of gold and silver at hand and supposed Evan had appropriated those as well. When she hesitated beside a cart, he lifted her onto the seat and sprang up beside her.

Aided by moonlight and torches held by some of the guards to light their way, they slowly exited through the castle gate. From the direction they took, Aleta realized immediately they were heading toward the coast. Had she known Jaime watched from the cover of nearby trees she wouldn't have given in so easily to despair.

Jaime had almost given up in defeat when he saw the portcullis raise and two carts accompanied by a large number of men-at-arms stream from the castle. They passed him so closely he could clearly see Aleta's strained face glowing whitely in the moonlight. Her anguish, so visible on her beautiful face, tore him apart, but there had been no way to advise her of his plans. Did she believe he had abandoned her? Grey, his expression grim and determined, sat beside her, driving the cart. After Jaime had seen him kill Somerset he knew how desperate Grey had become and realized that he would stop at nothing to escape the King's wrath.

When the men and carts turned north toward the coast, Jaime smiled cunningly. From the direction Grey had taken, Jaime knew exactly where he was going. There was a deep-water cove down the coast less than a league away. The Lord of Darkness had used it many times in the past for his smuggling operations when he was constantly changing beaches to confuse the King's men. Certain of Grey's direction, he awakened the messenger, who had been dozing beside him.

Sir Garth awakened immediately at Jaime's touch. "Ride like the wind," Jaime admonished. "Tell the men to meet me at North Beach. The village men know it well and will lead you there. Trust them."

Sir Garth left immediately. Mounting the horse Sir Giles had left behind, wishing he had his own black stallion, Jaime followed Grey, keeping well to the rear. He trailed behind the men and carts for two hours. Then, certain that Aleta was in no immediate danger, he spurred his mount into the woods so he could ride ahead without being seen. If luck was with him he would join his men at the cove long before Grey and the slow-moving carts arrived.

Jaime's men were indeed waiting on the beach when he arrived. Sir Giles strode forward to meet him. "What are your orders, my lord?"

"We wait," Jaime said grimly. "Have the men

conceal themselves in the trees where they can't be seen. At my signal we'll rush out in ambush, cutting off Grey's escape. But advise the men to take great care that my lady isn't harmed," Jaime warned. "She carries my child and both are dear to me."

Gray misty dawn rolled in from the sea and the sky was turning from the darkest purple to pale mauve when Jaime saw the outline of a ship anchored a short distance from the beach in the deep cove. Nearly beside himself with anxiety, his relief was enormous when he saw Grey's men on the path leading to the beach. Two carts followed, one of them carrying Aleta, who was slumped in the seat, exhausted.

Jaime chafed anxiously as the men and wagons wound their way to the beach. By the time they had gathered on the shore, three rowboats had arrived from the ship and were waiting to load passengers and cargo.

When Evan Grey lifted Aleta from the wagon, Jaime gave the signal for attack.

Chapter 19

Resisting wildly, Aleta was dragged from the cart. She knew if Evan succeeded in getting her into the rowboat she'd never return. Never see Jaime again. Might never even live to bear the child she carried. Just then the babe inside her swelling womb made its presence known, and Aleta renewed her struggles.

"Stop fighting," Grey ground out as he hauled Aleta behind him toward the rowboats. "You're only hurting yourself by resisting."

Reserving her strength, Aleta did not attempt to answer as she dug her heels into the soft sand and strained against the pull of Evan's powerful arms. Sobbing from the pain of her futile effort to escape and resigning herself to the inevitable, Aleta could hardly believe her eyes when she saw men rushing out onto the beach from the surrounding woods. Brandishing weapons, mostly crude staffs, picks, and various other farm tools that might be considered useful against the enemy, the men fell upon Evan's knights, whose superior arms and strength wavered beneath the surprise attack.

A violent curse left Grey's lips. He had seen Jaime Mortimer ride away with his men; how had

337

he known where to lay in ambush? How had he arrived here before them? Just to make certain Mortimer had left Somerset Castle like he ordered, he had set a watch on the battlement. Who would have guessed that Mortimer's ill-equipped army would attack with such vigor? Fortunately he had in his possession the one thing that would prevent Mortimer from gaining the upper hand: Aleta. Renewing his efforts, he gave a vicious jerk on Aleta's arm, dragging her toward the water's edge where the rowboats bobbed in the surf.

As he neared the water's edge, Grey gaped in horror when two of the rowboats pulled away from shore. Obviously the sailors were unwilling to become part of a fight that did not concern them. The third boat, a little slower in reacting, had yet to be launched back to the ship when Grey reached it, dragging Aleta behind him. Throwing her into the boat, he leaped in after her, ordering the sailors to pull toward the ship. Anxious to escape what was quickly becoming a rout, the oarsmen bent their backs to the task.

Jaime parried thrust after thrust in hand-to-hand combat as he fought his way to Aleta's side. Despite the villagers' lack of arms, they were accustomed to fighting and attacked Lord Grey's knights with vigor and cunning. And Jaime's knights were all brave men, well-armed and loyal. Already Grey's men were falling back beneath Jaime's surprise attack. He had lost sight of Aleta soon after he had engaged in battle and frantically searched the dark beach for her. Only a slim crescent of moon and several lanterns lit by Grey's men before the attack aided his search.

His heart flew into his mouth when he finally saw her. He could tell that she was resisting

wildly, but her strength wasn't sufficient to stop
Grey from picking her up and tossing her bodily
into the rowboat bobbing in the surf. Making short
work of the knight who had engaged him in combat, Jaime sprinted toward the shoreline, screaming Aleta's name.

Dazed as she was, Aleta heard Jaime call her
name and responded by rising unsteadily to her
feet, reaching out to him. The rowboat was quickly
gaining speed now, retreating from the shore into
deep water. Jaime poised at the water's edge, preparing to cast aside his heavy armor and leap in
after Aleta and Grey. But Grey, true to his villain-
ous instincts, rose to his feet and pressed the tip of
his sword against Aleta's breast.

"Come no further, Mortimer!" he yelled across
the small stretch of water separating him from
Jaime. "Step into the water and Aleta will be fish
bait."

Jaime froze, his face a mask of hatred and rage.
"Bastard! Harm Aleta and my child and I'll travel
to the ends of the earth to find you."

Grey laughed harshly, noting with glee that the
stretch of water between him and Jaime lengthened with each stroke of the oars. Soon the rowboat would be lost in total darkness as it rode the
crest of dark waves to the ship waiting to carry
Grey away. Aleta must have realized it too for she
screamed and jerked backward to escape the cruel
prick of Grey's sword, setting the tiny boat to
rocking. Grey reached for her, intending to subdue
her and confine her to the bottom of the boat.

Perched on the horns of dilemma, Jaime
watched in growing panic as Aleta's pale face
grew smaller and smaller in the darkness. When
he saw her jerk backward, rocking the boat precar-

iously in her struggle, he knew a moment of profound fear.

"You little bitch!" Grey snarled, trying to control Aleta and at the same time prevent the boat from capsizing.

" 'Ere now, mate, wot the 'ell are ye tryin' to do?" one of the sailors cried as he grasped the sides of the boat. "I can't swim."

"Neither can I!" gasped the shipmate as Aleta and Grey struggled and the small boat rocked furiously.

Suddenly the small boat listed to the right, hung a breathless moment on the brink of a wave, then capsized, flinging its occupants into the hostile depths of the churning sea. The two sailors sank like rocks, fear preventing them from making even the slightest effort to save themselves. Despite the heaviness of her dress and petticoats, Aleta fought to keep her head above water. As a child she had swum often in the sea, and though she hadn't attempted it in years she hoped her strength would hold out long enough for her to tread water until help arrived from shore.

Suddenly Grey's head bobbed up beside her, his eyes wild as he fought to remain afloat. Then he saw Aleta and his expression filled with hatred. She flapped her arms wildly to escape him, but he reached out desperately and grasped a long golden strand of her hair. "I won't die alone," he rasped harshly. "If I can't have you, neither will Mortimer."

"Can't you swim?" Aleta found the strength to ask.

"Nay." It was his last word as he slid beneath the surface. Aleta managed a large gulp of air before he tugged her after him, his closed fist clutching her hair.

Down ... Down ... The water grew bitter cold, and so black Aleta felt as if she had entered the darkest pit of hell. Struggling violently, she tried to get Grey to release her hair, but even in death he sought to deny her life. Her lungs begging for breath, Aleta knew she was dying, knew she'd never give birth to Jaime's babe, and knew pain far greater than that of having her lungs burst from lack of air. And as blackness and despair dragged her deeper into acceptance of her fate, she bade a silent farewell to the man she had grown to love despite enormous odds. Then, with the endless void of death approaching on silent wings, she knew no more.

The moment Jaime saw the rowboat capsize and Aleta disappear beneath the surface, his frozen limbs found life again. His hands shook as he unbuckled his sword belt and threw his weapons aside. His chain mail and helmet followed quickly. Bracing himself for the icy plunge, he dove into the frigid water, his strong, determined strokes carrying him toward the overturned boat bobbing in the waves. Nothing mattered now but Aleta. She couldn't die, he needed her too much, loved her too desperately.

Jaime had reached the boat now, his eyes frantic as he searched the dark surface of the foaming sea. Nothing. Not only had Aleta disappeared but so had Grey and the two sailors. His mind and heart screaming in protest against injustice to the innocent, Jaime took a deep breath and dived beneath the surface, praying that the current hadn't carried Aleta too far from the capsized boat. It was like looking into an inky world of darkness, Jaime thought as he scrabbled in the murky depths for the woman he loved.

His bursting lungs forced him to resurface. Vaguely aware of the mauve streaks of dawn turning the sky from black to gray, he quickly looked around to make certain Aleta hadn't bobbed to the surface, then he sucked in a deep breath and submerged again. This time he dove deeper, nearly to the rocky bottom before he saw Aleta, her hair floating around her like a golden shroud. Subduing the urgent need to rise for air, Jaime grasped Aleta around the waist, intending to pull her with him to the surface. That's when he realized that Grey lay in the water beside her, one hand entangled in her hair. But by then his lungs were ready to explode and reaching the surface with Aleta was a driving force within him. Delaying another moment meant sure death for both of them.

Adrenaline pumped through Jaime's veins as he slowly, painstakingly inched upward, dragging both Aleta and Grey with him. He broke surface with not a moment to spare as he sucked in great gulps of air. Once his own needs were fulfilled, he turned his attention to Aleta. Her face was as white as death, her breathing nearly nonexistent as he searched for signs indicating that she still lived. Grey's head bobbed up beside him and he saw at a glance that his hand still clutched her hair. Cursing Grey's evil purpose, Jaime tugged viciously, but Grey's fist remained tightly clenched, as if that golden strand in his hand was his lifeline. Jaime tugged again, determined to free Aleta and get her to shore as soon as possible. It was imperative that he press the water from her lungs before it was too late. He gave a cry of triumph when the hank of hair tore free from Grey's fist. Then Jaime started for shore, towing Aleta behind him.

Coughing and choking, Grey suddenly came to life, reaching out and clutching Aleta's skirt in passing. "Mortimer, don't leave me." The frantic tugging on Aleta's dress nearly dragged Jaime under. "Save me, I can't swim."

Jaime heard Grey's frantic plea but he knew he couldn't save them both. The choice was easily made. Aleta was his love, his life. Desperate to get Aleta to shore immediately, he released the tape holding her skirt and pushed it down her hips until it floated free. He looked back only once. Grey was staring at him, his mouth gaping in horror, his fingers clutching air as he slowly sank beneath the surface for the last time.

With strong, steady strokes Jaime cut through the water, desperation lending him incredible strength. Before he reached the shore Sir Giles waded out to meet him, taking Aleta up in his arms as another knight rushed forward to help Jaime.

"She's dead, my lord," Sir Giles said as he lay Aleta gently upon the sand.

Jaime's cry was an anguished denial of the terrible blow fate had dealt him. "*Nay!*" Shoving Sir Giles aside, he knelt beside Aleta, turning her onto her stomach. Then, straddling her thighs, he began pressing her back, forcing the seawater from her lungs. He grunted in satisfaction when a stream of water gushed from her mouth. After several minutes he rolled her onto her back, placing his ear against her chest.

Nothing. Growing desperate, Jaime placed his mouth over hers, forcing his own breath into her mouth in a frantic attempt to give her life. He had no idea if it would work but he was willing to attempt anything to save his love.

" 'Tis no use, my lord," Sir Giles observed, placing a restraining hand on Jaime's shoulder.

Shaking free of the knight's hand, Jaime did not bother to acknowledge him, so distraught now that he would have kept it up all day had there been a need. Aleta couldn't die. No one had ever meant more to him than Aleta and the child she carried.

The sky had turned to pale-gray now, with streaks of morning sun visible in the east. Someone brought a blanket, placing it over Aleta as Jaime continued his lifesaving tactics. He was cold, bitter cold, but refused to succumb to discomfort when Aleta's life was in jeopardy. Nothing mattered to him, not Sir Giles's words, or the fact that his wet clothes were growing stiff from cold. All he saw was the blue tinge around Aleta's lips and her shivering body. Through a haze of painful memories he recalled the softness of those red lips, the sweetness, the warmth of her responsive body.

Trembling from exhaustion, Jaime fought against the terrible knowledge that Aleta was dead, refusing to abandon her to cruel fate. He was sobbing openly when he sat back on his heels, finally forced to admit that his love had left him. Grasping her limp body in his arms, he pulled her hard against him, his arms tightening like steel bands as he hugged her desperately.

Suddenly another spurt of water gushed from her lungs and she began coughing and gagging. After a few choking gasps, she began breathing on her own. Jaime made no effort to hide the tears of joy that rolled down his cheeks. He was too happy to worry about displaying weakness before his knights and friends. It was one of the few times in his life that Jaime allowed real emotion to crack the hard shell behind which he had hidden most of his life. And he wasn't embarrassed.

When Aleta was breathing on her own, Jaime found a moment to ask Sir Giles, "What of the battle? Have we suffered many casualties?"

Sir Giles smiled. "Lord Grey's men were subdued easily enough despite their superior weapons and strength. Seems they hadn't the enthusiasm for prolonged combat after their lord left them to fend for themselves. What are your orders, my lord?"

"Take the prisoners to Mortimer Manor. No longer will my home be known as Grey Manor. 'Tis mine now. Leave several knights to escort my lady and myself home. I want to make Aleta comfortable as soon as possible, she's in desperate need of care."

"I pray all will be well with Lady Aleta and her babe," Sir Giles said. Though she seemed to be breathing now, a few minutes ago the knight wouldn't have given the plucky lady one chance in a million of surviving.

Frantic over Aleta's failure to regain consciousness, Jaime gathered her into his arms and carried her to the nearest cart, where he placed her gently in the back. Then he climbed in beside her, cradling her in his arms so as to protect her from being jolted about in the wagon bed. She was shaking now and her teeth chattered so loudly he feared she'd become ill with ague. Only moments ago he had been so close to losing her that he couldn't bear the thought of losing her to illness.

It was a long ride to Mortimer Manor. They

stopped once along the way to borrow blankets
from a nearby manor and continued on. Aleta remained unconscious. Jaime prayed that Gaylord,
who had knowledge of many things, would be
able to help his lady. His one consolation was that
thus far there were no signs that Aleta might lose
their child. When a weak sun sent down fingers of
warmth, dispelling some of the cold, Jaime re-
joiced. It seemed like a sign from above, promising
a rosy future for him and Aleta.

A few hours later Aleta sighed and opened her
eyes. Disoriented at first, she waited until the mist
cleared from her vision before trying to make
sense out of her thoughts. The last thing she recalled was being pulled into the cold, murky
depths of the sea by Evan Grey. Then death
claimed her.

Or had it? It seemed impossible that she had
somehow cheated death and survived. Looking
up, she saw sky. And sun. And the worried face of
the man she loved. She blinked, and blinked
again. Jaime's face floated above her, his eyes
filled with concern, and something more. Love. He
loved her. She could see it clearly now. Had it
been there all the time?

Heartfelt relief shuddered through Jaime when
Aleta opened her eyes and stared at him. When
she remained silent for several tense minutes he
feared shock had erased memory from her mind.
Did she not know who he was?

"Aleta." Her name was a sigh upon his lips as
his arms tightened around her. "I thought I'd lost
you."

She opened her mouth to speak but no words
came. Her throat was sore from all the salt water
she had swallowed and regurgitated. She could

only look into his eyes, telling him by her expression what was in her heart.

"Nay, don't talk," Jaime advised, placing a finger against her lips. "Rest now, my love, we'll be at Mortimer Manor soon. No one will ever hurt you again."

Aleta's eyes grew wide with fright, suddenly recalling Lord Grey's cruel attempt to drown her. She opened her mouth again, this time managing to whisper, "Evan?" Jaime knew exactly what she was asking despite her lack of words.

"Fear not, my love, Evan Grey will never hurt you again. He's buried in a watery grave and the sea rarely gives up its dead."

She paled visibly and slumped in his arms. When Jaime spoke to her next, her eyes had closed again and she had drifted into sleep.

Mortimer Manor, erected by Jaime's great-grandfather, was one of the most modern manors in Wales. It lay a few leagues from Flint, a town of many souls, most of whom recalled with fondness Lord Mortimer and his young son. When the wagon clattered over the drawbridge and stopped before the thick wooden doors, Gaylord rushed out to meet them.

"Thank God," the old man said when Jaime jumped out of the cart, cradling Aleta in his arms. When he saw Aleta collapsed motionlessly against Jaime's chest, a worried frown crossed his brow. "What's wrong with Lady Aleta?"

"I pray 'tis nothing more than exhaustion," Jaime said as he carried Aleta into the manor. Gaylord preceded him, leading the way up the stone staircase and holding the door open to the master chamber. Jaime laid Aleta on the bed, his heart pounding from fear as he watched the shallow rise and fall of her chest.

"What happened, lad?" Gaylord asked anxiously. "You're both soaking wet."

"Evan Grey was at Somerset Castle, just as I suspected. When I informed him that he was wanted for questioning by the King and demanded that he release Aleta to me, he decided to use Aleta as hostage. He ordered me to leave else he'd throw my lady from the battlement."

Gaylord's eyes grew round. "You left Aleta in Grey's keeping?"

"Aye, I had no choice. I hoped Lord Somerset would intervene since Aleta is his only child."

"Did he?"

"He tried, but unfortunately he was slain by Grey. I sent the men into hiding and remained nearby to keep watch on the castle. Grey emerged just past midnight with carts loaded with valuables and a small army of men. Aleta was with him. I was so certain Grey was going to meet a ship at North Beach that I immediately sent word to the men to meet me there. We were laying in ambush when Grey arrived.

"A short but fierce battle was waged, but somehow Grey managed to get Aleta into a rowboat. When I tried to follow, Grey threatened to kill Aleta. I'm still not sure what happened but there was a struggle and the small boat overturned. Because of the darkness I had a difficult time finding Aleta. Vindictive to the end, Grey had dragged her under with him. Thank God I found her, just when I despaired of ever seeing my lady again. She regained consciousness briefly but has been like this ever since."

"What of Grey?" Gaylord asked sharply.

"Dead. And good riddance. Seems he couldn't swim. 'Tis Aleta I'm worried about."

"You say Lady Aleta awoke briefly?"

Jaime nodded.

"Did she speak?"

"Aye, a single word."

"Was she coherent?"

"Aye, but she was awake so briefly 'tis difficult to judge from a single word. Needless to say, I'm deeply concerned about both Aleta and the child she carries."

Gaylord placed a gnarled hand on Aleta's brow. She felt cool to the touch. Too cool. " 'Tis in God's hands now, but her strong pulse bodes well for her. I'll summon a tiring woman. Your lady needs to be stripped of her wet garments and warmed. I'll order hot broth sent up immediately."

"See to the broth, Gaylord, I'll take care of Aleta's other needs," Jaime insisted, his hands already fumbling with the fastenings on her dress. Gaylord nodded and left the room.

Lifting Aleta's limp body in his arms, Jaime quickly stripped off her sodden garments and wrapped her in a fur robe he found at the foot of the bed. He paused briefly to rest his hand on her swollen stomach, amazed that the child she carried still clung tenaciously to its nourishing nest. Then he sat down beside her, recalling with fondness all the reasons he had discovered for loving her.

A short time later Gaylord returned with a steaming bowl of broth, which Jaime painstakingly fed to Aleta a tiny sip at a time. Though she still refused to open her eyes she dutifully swallowed the hot liquid, leading Jaime to believe she was more aware than she let on. Setting the bowl aside, he softly called her name.

"Aleta, you're safe, my love. Wake up."

Aleta frowned, unwilling to leave the hazy world of beautiful dreams. Jaime was in her dream, and their child. It was a boy, with hair as dark as his father's and just as handsome. Jaime was speaking to her, telling her how much he loved her and how grateful he was for the child she had given him.

"Aleta, can you hear me?"

"Of course I can hear you," Aleta croaked hoarsely, unaware that she had spoken aloud.

"Open your eyes, my love. Look at me."

Why did Jaime want her to look at him? she wondered distractedly. Why must she open her eyes? She felt safe in the dream world, where nothing and no one could harm her or her child. Why wouldn't he leave her alone? But Jaime was so insistent Aleta finally gave in to his urging and opened her eyes. The first thing she saw was Jaime, smiling down on her. The next thing she noticed were surroundings totally unfamiliar to her. Since she had never seen the master chamber when Evan had brought her here she had no idea where she was.

"Where am I?"

"'Tis your new home, my love. I've brought you to Mortimer Manor. Our child will be born in my ancestral home."

At the mention of their child all those painful memories that she had been trying to avoid came rushing forth and her hands flew to her stomach. The comforting bulge below her waist brought a relief so profound the ability to speak left her. But

Jaime was astute enough to realize her fears and alleviate them.

"All is well with our babe, Aleta," he assured her. Of course he had no idea if his statement would remain true hours from now, or even the next day, but he prayed it would. Time and again Aleta had proven her strength and strong will.

Despite her weariness, Aleta's eyes glowed with happiness. "How did you manage to find me in the water? Evan tried to drown me. He couldn't swim, you know?"

"God was with me," he said with a touch of faith he hadn't known he possessed. "As for Evan—"

"He's dead," Aleta said, her voice devoid of all emotion. "'Tis a fitting end."

Jaime looked at her curiously. "King Henry was onto him; he would have been punished for giving false evidence."

"I know."

"I'm sorry to tell you this, my love, but your father was also involved in the conspiracy against my father."

A look of pain crossed Aleta's pale features. "'Tis too late. Evan killed Father when he demanded that Evan release me from the battlement. I watched him being buried in the inner bailey. Father wasn't a bad man, Jaime, just a greedy one. I think in the end he repented of his crime against your family. I also felt he was beginning to look forward to his first grandchild."

Tears rolled down her cheeks and Jaime gathered her into his arms, offering comfort. He seriously doubted Lord Somerset felt the kind of guilt Aleta described, but he was her father and Jaime wasn't going to destroy the love she felt for the man.

"I know, love, I saw it all. It's over," he crooned into her ear. "Henry has returned to me everything that Grey and his cohorts had stolen. When you are well enough, we'll be married again so no one will question our child's legitimacy. I regret all the unhappiness I've caused you, but if you haven't guessed by now that I love you, 'tis time I told you. After you came into my life, no other woman meant anything to me, no matter what Rowena tried to tell you. I never bedded the wench after we were married."

"And I never betrayed you. I loved you too much."

Suddenly Jaime grew thoughtful. "I should have realized that Rowena was the one who had betrayed me. She and Grey were probably conspiring together all along. I wish I knew what drove the Greys to conspire against my father. I've always felt there was more to it than simple greed. But if I'm right, I fear the reason died with Grey and your father."

Aleta paled. *She* knew the reason. Evan had blurted it out, never suspecting that she would see Jaime again to tell him. But did she dare tell him? Was it necessary that Jaime know that Evan Grey was his half-brother?

"What's wrong, my lady, why are you so quiet? Your face is so pale it frightens me. Are you in pain? Is it the babe?"

"I—I was just thinking about something," Aleta said guiltily. She was determined not to tell Jaime what she knew until she spoke with Gaylord. Surely the old man must have been privy to all the family secrets. If he was deliberately keeping the knowledge from Jaime, she wanted to know why. "As for the babe, he is well. See how strongly he kicks?"

Taking his hand, she placed it upon her stomach so he could feel the strength of his child's will to survive. She watched his expression change from wonder to utter delight. "He's a fighter," Jaime said proudly.

"Or she is," Aleta added.

" 'Tis no matter, I'll take either."

When Aleta's eyes began to grow heavy, Jaime realized he was tiring her. There were still so many things he wanted to say, needed to tell her, but they would keep. Pulling the fur robe up to her chin, he bade her sleep. Then he sat beside her until she drifted off.

When Aleta awoke several hours later it was dark and Gaylord had taken Jaime's place beside her. When the old man saw her stirring and noted the way her eyes darted about the room, he said, "I sent Jaime off to bed. He hasn't had a decent night's sleep in days. The only way he'd go is if I promised to sit beside you and call him the moment you awakened."

"I'm glad you're here," Aleta said softly. "I need your advice."

"My advice, my lady? What can I help you with?"

" 'Tis Jaime. I learned something quite disturbing from Lord Grey and I don't know if I should tell him."

Though the only light in the room came from the hearth, it was bright enough for Aleta to see Gaylord's expression grow wary. "Perhaps you should tell me what it is you learned."

"How long have you been with the Mortimer family, Gaylord?"

"Since I was a very young man. I was the bailiff of Mortimer Manor before Clarence married Jaime's mother, and remained so until Jaime and I were forced from the manor." Gaylord had a good idea what was coming next but preferred to wait for Aleta's explanation. He had known the day would arrive when the truth came out and had dreaded it.

"You must know a great deal about the family," Aleta prodded relentlessly.

Gaylord sighed. "Aye, there were no secrets I wasn't aware of."

Aleta hated to disturb the old man, especially if his memories were painful, but she felt duty-bound to do so. It wasn't right to keep a matter of such grave importance from Jaime.

"Then you must be aware that Evan Grey and Jaime were half-brothers." There was no easy way to say it except to state it directly.

Gaylord's narrow shoulders slumped and his entire body seemed to collapse inward. "Aye, I suspected it."

"But Jaime doesn't? Why haven't you told him?"

"Because not even Lord Mortimer knew for sure. He saw Lady Grey but once years later and few words were exchanged. He was shocked to learn she wasn't the peasant girl he had thought all those years ago. He had been a young lad on the verge of manhood at the time and feeling his oats. Had he known the consequences of his rash act, he would have made it right long ago.

"When he confided in me he was shamed, and made me promise never to tell Jaime what he had done to that young girl. But now that you know, a great weight has been lifted from my shoulders. 'Twill be your decision whether or not to tell Jaime."

Chapter 20

Jaime opened the door to Aleta's chamber and quietly entered. He had expected to see Gaylord sitting at Aleta's bedside and when he didn't anger surged through him. Gaylord had promised to remain with Aleta while he caught a few hours of much-needed rest and the old man rarely if ever broke his word. What Jaime didn't realize was that Aleta, having awakened feeling much improved, had urged Gaylord to seek his own bed, insisting she was well enough to be left alone.

Aleta heard the door open and turned her head. Before he had departed, Gaylord left a lit candle on the nightstand, and in the flickering glow Aleta recognized Jaime's powerful form. Her breath caught in her throat as she recalled the strength of his arms, the persuasion of his kisses, and the depth of his passion. She had missed him dreadfully, wanted him, needed him. When Lord Evan had made her his wife, she'd felt as if her life had ended. The one thing that had kept her sane was Jaime's child that she carried inside her. And her greatest fear was that Evan intended to destroy her child once it was born.

Jaime crossed the room in swift strides, naked but for the hose he had drawn on upon awakening. Though several hours remained before dawn, a strange urgency had driven him to look in on Aleta. He had to see her again, to look upon her beautiful face, to know that she was well. Losing Aleta now, when he had so much to offer her, when he loved and needed her so fiercely, would render everything he'd worked for all these years worthless.

Jaime paused beside the bed, wishing he could tell Aleta everything that was in his heart but knowing that it would be cruel to awaken her after all she'd been through. Words would come later, he decided, after Aleta was out of danger.

Her heart bursting with love, Aleta watched Jaime approach. Bare-chested, his legs bulging with thick muscles, he stood before her in the dim light like an ancient warrior. His shoulders were broad, his torso powerful, his belly flat and firm. His inky hair clung to his neck and shoulders in silken waves, framing his handsome features. He was so blatantly male, so magnificently masculine he made her breath catch in her throat. Fearing he would leave, Aleta reached out to him, whispering his name.

Jaime groaned and dropped to his knees beside the bed, his name on her lips the sweetest sound he had ever heard.

"Why aren't you sleeping, my love?" His voice was soft with tenderness.

She touched his face, savoring the satiny smoothness beneath the bristly stubble that he hadn't taken the time to remove. "I've done nothing but sleep since I arrived, and I'm no longer tired. Sit beside me."

Jaime hesitated. Sitting beside Aleta when he wanted her so desperately was the worst kind of torture.

Aleta noted Jaime's reluctance to join her on the bed and her heart sank down to her toes. Did he still accuse her of betraying him? Was he hesitant to touch her because he assumed Evan had bedded her? Did she want him to love her so badly that she had dreamed he had whispered words of love to her?

"I—I don't know if I can lie beside you and not make love to you," Jaime admitted. "And I'd die before hurting you in any way."

Aleta couldn't help but think Jaime was only mouthing those words so as not to hurt her feelings. "Please," she whispered shakily. She had been through so much she couldn't bear the thought of losing Jaime. She leaned forward and pressed her lips to his breastbone, and was pleased by the wild thunder of his heart beneath her lips.

It was almost more than Jaime could bear. A groan of surrender slipped past his lips as he stretched out beside her. For years he had practiced self-control, and though it wouldn't be easy with Aleta he could do so again.

"Hold me, Jaime, I've been so afraid." The plea left her lips on a ragged sigh. "I feared Lord Grey would destroy our child, but I would have killed him had he attempted it."

"Did the bastard hurt you." Jaime asked through clenched teeth. He didn't really want to know the details, but he needed to know if Grey had hurt her during those times he had bedded her.

"Nay. Evan sent me with Father to Somerset

Castle almost immediately after the wedding. He couldn't bear the thought of bedding me while I carried your child."

Raising up on his elbow, Jaime searched her face. Had he misunderstood? Was Aleta telling him that she had never submitted to Grey? "It matters not that Grey has bedded you, my love, for I know it wasn't what you wanted."

"Didn't you hear me? Evan never made me his wife in the true sense of the word. I left for Wales immediately after the wedding ceremony."

Jaime was stunned. "But Grey came to me in the dungeon and taunted me about how wonderfully you made love and how passionate you were."

"He lied, Jaime. There is only one man who can rouse me to passion, and that man is you."

His arms tightened around her, holding her as if she was more precious than gold and silver. "It wouldn't have mattered, love, but for your sake it pleases me that you weren't forced to endure his attentions. We can put all that behind us now. We have a whole lifetime ahead of us to raise our children in peace and contentment."

"What about the Lord of Darkness?" she asked anxiously.

"The Lord of Darkness ceased to exist when Henry sought my promise to give up smuggling. The villagers have earned a good living through smuggling all these years and because of it have escaped poverty. I don't regret what I've done, but I won't go back to it. I have all I need right here at Mortimer Manor. My one regret is not having discovered the reason for the Greys' hatred. For years the Greys and Mortimers existed in harmony. But after Evan's mother died things changed. If only I knew—"

Aleta realized that if she intended to tell Jaime about Evan, this was the time. But her mind refused to form the words. What purpose would it serve? she asked herself. Then the moment was lost when Jaime raised her chin and kissed her. Gently at first, then so fiercely his body trembled from the effort to control his passion. But restraint was the last thing Aleta wanted right now as she kissed him back with a fervor that shocked Jaime.

Her mouth opened, inviting his tongue, and Jaime moaned as he accepted her invitation. Against his better judgment, realizing where it would take him, his hands roamed beneath her bedgown. Her breasts were fuller, he realized immediately, and her waist certainly thicker, but she had never looked or felt more beautiful to him. His hands rough with urgency, he pulled aside the edges of her bedgown, baring the creamy mounds of her breasts to his gaze. Leaning down, he nuzzled, then kissed, the satin smoothness of her neck and breasts, drawing his tongue across the turgid nipples with tiny dancing flickers that brought a gasp from her lips.

As if realizing where this was leading, Jaime drew back, his dark eyes glowing with repressed passion. But Aleta would have none of it. She had waited too long for this day. "My lord, please," she whimpered, pulling his head back down to her breasts.

"I don't think I can stop if I continue," Jaime warned harshly. " 'Tis been too long since I've loved you."

"There's no need to stop."

"The child . . ."

"He's fine, truly. If he hasn't been dislodged by

now, nothing will harm him. Love me, my lord, love me with your all heart and soul."

"Nothing would please me more," Jaime groaned. Then he was removing her bedgown, marveling at the fine texture of her skin, the shapely perfection of her long legs, and the creamy smoothness of her thighs. "You're so beautiful. I'm the luckiest man alive."

"And I'm a most fortunate woman," Aleta sighed, tugging at his hose. Jaime obliged instantly, slipping his hose over his hips and tossing them aside.

"Everything about you is perfect. I think I fell in love with you the first time I saw you. Do you remember? You called me a peasant with dung clinging to his boots."

She felt his gaze slide over her like a hot scorching wind. "You have to admit you were arrogant beyond belief. I had every reason to resist marriage to you. But that was before I fell in love with you."

"And I with you," Jaime said, his dark eyes glowing as he lowered his head to suckle the tips of her breasts. She gasped in delight as his tongue trailed a path of fire to the jut of her hipbone and beyond. His cheeks felt deliciously rough against the smoothness of her flesh and she shivered with uncontrollable anticipation. And then, his lips upon the sweet bulge of her stomach, he spread her thighs and knelt between them. When he circled her navel with his tongue then slid his lips lower to kiss the fleecy cleft between her legs, Aleta stiffened and cried out.

"Jaime, I can't bear it!"

"It makes me happy to give you pleasure," he whispered against the moist warmth of her flesh.

He still wasn't convinced it was safe to make love to Aleta, but there was more than one way to give her pleasure even if he received none himself. "Relax, sweet, just concentrate on what I'm doing to you."

Aleta's answer was a low moan as his lips pressed against the velvet heat between her legs, his tongue a ravishing sword of fire and delight as it thrust into her. Grasping her hips, he raised her up to him, feasting voraciously on her tender woman's flesh. Unable to stop herself, she arched against his mouth and cried out, shamelessly grasping his head to bring him even closer.

Rapture exploded through her, filling her body with a sweet throbbing so intense, so incredibly profound it was almost unbearable. Raising his head so he could watch her face in the throes of passion, Jaime received almost as much pleasure from seeing Aleta convulse from the force of her climax as he would had he joined her in the blissful journey. When he moved from between her legs to lie beside her, Aleta sent him a startled glance.

"Jaime, aren't you going to . . ."

"Nay, my love, I don't want to hurt you."

"It will hurt me more if you don't finish what you started. You can't harm the babe, if that's what's stopping you."

Tentatively she reached out, resting her hand on the taut ridges of his flat stomach. His flesh jumped beneath her touch. Encouraged, her small hand moved slowly downward to the rigid thrust of his manhood, still needy, still wanting. Her fingers curled around him; she was amazed at his control and determined that he should experience the same kind of pleasure he had just given her.

When she slid her palm experimentally up and down the length of his staff, Jaime's tormented gasp gave her courage to do something she'd thought about many times but never had the audacity to try.

Rising on her elbow, she leaned over him, daring to place a kiss on the velvety tip of his staff.

"God's blood, Aleta!"

When her mouth opened and took him inside, he nearly flew off the bed. After several torturous seconds he lifted her up by the shoulders and pressed her down on the bed. Looming above her, his eyes as dark as obsidian, he asked raggedly, "Are you sure, my love?"

"Aye, Jaime, I want you."

Realizing that he could not mount her comfortably and rather than risk harming the child, Jaime rolled her onto her side and stretched out behind her. "Raise your leg, sweet."

Perplexed but trusting Jaime completely, Aleta raised her leg. Sliding between her thighs, he rested her leg on his hip, spreading her more fully to accommodate him. The breath hissed through her teeth as she felt his great length prod between her legs then slowly, oh so slowly, fill her. The feeling was utter rapture and a small cry slipped past her lips. Jaime froze, thinking he had hurt her.

"Do you want me to stop?"

"Nay! Don't stop! Love me, Jaime, please love me."

"Forever, my love," he gasped as he slid deeper inside her. Then further speech was impossible as Jaime's mind and thoughts were consumed with the love he felt for the precious woman in his arms.

His thrusts were slow, deliberate, wanting to

bring Aleta pleasure again before he sought his own. Aleta thrust back against him, accepting the bold force of his manhood and returning it in kind. She was gasping now, drawn deeper and deeper into the magic of Jaime's loving. When his hand came around to search amid the golden fleece at the juncture of her thighs, Aleta held her breath, wondering what he would do next. Then he was parting her, searching for and finding the tiny nub of flesh that was the font of her femininity. His erotic stroking sent her very close to the edge.

They were both breathing very hard now, both profoundly aware of the naked passion driving them. Yet passion was just a small part of the wondrous magic between them.

Aleta's thoughts shattered as rapture splintered through her. She screamed Jaime's name, unable to repress the need to cry out. Vaguely she felt Jaime stiffen, felt the heat of his breath against her neck, heard him shout out at the pinnacle of his climax.

Smiling contentedly, Aleta slept. Jaime curled around her and held her close as exhaustion claimed him. He awoke again at dawn, shocked to find Aleta bending over him, spreading tiny, nipping kisses across his chest. When her tongue flicked out and licked his flat male nipples, Jaime hardened instantly. With the swiftness of a cat, he flipped her over, gazed deeply into her eyes, then thrust inside her.

Hours later when Gaylord looked into the room, he saw the lovers entwined in blissful sleep, and quietly closed the door behind him.

A pale wintry sun rode high in the sky when Jaime opened his eyes to greet the day. Recalling instantly the passionate night he had shared with Aleta, his eyes sought out the woman sleeping peacefully beside him. She was curled up against his side like a contented kitten and Jaime couldn't ever remember waking up feeling so good. His first inclination was to make love to her again, but he quickly put that thought aside, recalling with relish that they had made love twice during the night, and this despite the fact that Aleta was still weak from her struggle with Evan Grey. He frowned, silently chastising himself for letting his lust rule his good judgment.

Aleta stirred, snuggling closer to the warmth of Jaime's big body. Pure frustration brought a groan from his lips, bringing Aleta fully awake. She opened her eyes, looked up at Jaime, and smiled blissfully.

"Don't look at me like that, my love, else I embarrass myself like an untried youth who can't control his urges."

"I wouldn't mind."

"But I would. I meant it when I said I don't want to do anything to harm you or our child. Twice in one night is enough exercise for a woman as heavily pregnant as you are. Just let me hold you a while longer before I greet the day properly."

Aleta sighed happily. "I was so afraid you'd think that Evan was the father of our child. That's what he wanted you to believe, you know."

Jaime had the grace to look guilty. "I must confess I believed it at first. Until Gaylord set me straight. He also was the one who insisted that you didn't have it in your heart to betray me. The more I considered his words the more I realized that Rowena had played a vicious game with me.

One day I'll find the little witch and drag the truth from her."

"Rowena was jealous," Aleta said thoughtfully. "When she realized she couldn't have you, she wanted revenge. That's why she was so eager to help me escape when you locked me in the keep."

Jaime flushed. "Can you forgive me for that? I was so damn wrong. I just knew you hated me and intended to betray me when you learned about the Lord of Darkness."

"I loved you, my lord. I've loved you for a very long time. I would have never hurt you. By then I had discovered what Evan was really like and wanted nothing to do with him."

"Will you marry me, my lady?"

He was so serious that Aleta's heart went out to him. "I'd be most happy to marry you, my lord. Whenever you say."

"Henry is in London preparing for his departure to France. What say you we leave for London as soon as you're able to travel so that the King and all the lords and ladies of the realm can attend the wedding of the Earl of Flint and his chosen bride. I'll send a messenger immediately telling Henry to expect us. Do you think our babe will wait that long?"

"Aye, there's plenty of time."

Suddenly Jaime grew thoughtful. "Perhaps Henry has learned more about the conspiracy against my father. I can't get it out of my mind. I wish now that Grey had survived to provide the answers I seek. I may never know what drove the Greys to turn against the Mortimers."

His words, so solemn, so utterly devoid of understanding, moved Aleta deeply. How could she keep the secrets Evan had carelessly imparted when she knew she had the answers Jaime thirsted for? The solution was simple: she couldn't. Jaime deserved to know the truth, no matter what Gaylord's reason for withholding it all these years.

Praying she was doing the right thing, she sucked in a calming breath and said, "I have the answers you seek, my lord."

Uncertain to what she was referring, Jaime sent her a puzzled look. "What answers do you mean, my love?"

"I know why Lord Grey hated the Mortimers. I know the reason he conspired against your father and drew both his father and my father into his evil plot."

"God's blood, Aleta!" Shooting into an upright position, he dragged Aleta with him. "You knew and never told me?"

"I haven't always known," she explained hastily, suddenly wary under his fierce gaze. "Evan told me everything when he held me prisoner on the battlement above Somerset Castle. I—I wasn't convinced it would serve any purpose to reveal the facts to you now. None of the participants are alive and you've already regained all that you lost after your father's death."

"No earthly reward could ever compensate for the death of an honorable and loving father," Jaime said darkly. "Had Gaylord not been so resourceful, I wouldn't be here now to reclaim my birthright. Tell me, my lady, tell me what you know."

"I know you loved your father, Jaime, and I refrained from telling you immediately because I didn't want you to think less of him."

"What in bloody hell are you talking about? I

knew my father, knew he would never do anything dishonorable. If Grey said otherwise then he lied. Out with it, Aleta, what did the bastard say?"

He wasn't aware that his fingers were digging into her upper arms until Aleta winced and said, "You're hurting me."

Immediately he released her, his expression contrite. "Forgive me, my love, I didn't mean to be brutish. I promise to listen to your words and judge for myself whether or not Grey spoke the truth."

"What do you know of your father's youth?"

"Only what Gaylord has told me. I was young when I lost my father and youth does not lend itself to confidences. I do know that he achieved knighthood under the tutelage of Lord Blakely. He spent his early years in England, returning infrequently to Wales for short visits. He was betrothed to my mother when he was fifteen and my mother five. They married when he was twenty-six. Mother was sixteen. After marriage they made their home at Mortimer Manor, where I was born."

"Were the Mortimers and Greys always friends?"

"Neighbors and acquaintances but never close friends. Yet strange as it may seem, until Evan's mother died the two families dealt well with one another. What are you getting at, Aleta? Of what importance could my father's youth have in what transpired later?"

Aleta knew Jaime well enough to realize he was growing impatient. "Bear with me, Jaime, I'm trying to explain in the best way I know. Did you know Evan's mother?"

"Vaguely; she rarely traveled with her husband and son. She seemed a shy, private person, not the kind to make friends easily. She lost several children after Evan was born and remained in frail health. She rarely came to Mortimer Manor though she was invited often enough. The only time she did come she and Father appeared uncomfortable with one another. She never came again."

"Let me tell you a story," Aleta said softly as she searched her mind for the right words. "One day a handsome youth was out riding. He chanced upon a lovely young girl who had slipped away from her tiring woman, mistook her for a peasant, and raped her. You must realize that the lad was very young at the time, and feeling his oats. The girl had no idea who the lad was and was too shamed to tell anyone what happened. A short time later she married the man she was betrothed to and bore him a son."

During the telling of the tale Jaime's expression turned from open skepticism to outright disbelief. "Nay, my father would never do such a thing! He was an honorable man. Evan Grey was a liar who knew not what he was talking about."

"Evan claimed he was your half-brother. He said neither he nor his father had the slightest inkling until his mother confessed to him on her deathbed. It wasn't until years later that she learned the name of the man who had raped her. By then they were both married and she saw no purpose in revealing the truth."

"God's blood! It would explain many things." Though he didn't want to believe he and Grey were half-brothers it would at least make sense out of all that had happened. "It seems unbelievable that Lord Grey would make Evan his heir if he knew he wasn't really his son. The elder Grey had several bastards he could have left it to."

"Evan insisted the elder Grey didn't know, that he was the only one privy to his mother's death-bed confession. I think he deliberately kept the truth from the man he had always assumed was his father."

Now Jaime was truly puzzled. "Then why did the elder Grey incriminate my father when he was innocent?"

"According to Evan, he convinced Lord Grey that Clarence Mortimer really was a traitor. The only person he took into his confidence was my father. He and the other man involved were to share in the Mortimer fortune."

"What else did Grey tell you?" Jaime asked tightly.

"Nothing. I've told you everything." Deliberately she refrained from mentioning the fact that Gaylord was aware of the truth.

Jaime was quiet a long time, not quite convinced but aware that Grey had no reason to lie to Aleta.

"Jaime, it doesn't matter. You must think no less of your father for something he did in his youth." She couldn't bear the terrible anguish he seemed to be suffering and her arms went protectively around him. "Forget the past. I love you. We have our whole lives ahead of us."

Jaime's dark eyes searched her upturned face, seeing someone more dear to him than his own life. What had started out as a marriage from hell had changed into a relationship based on love. Though trust had been lacking at first, he had never doubted his love for Aleta, not even when he had tried to deny to himself that Aleta meant more to him than any human alive. That she loved *him* was incredible. They couldn't have gotten off to a worse beginning. For weeks Aleta had taken great delight in telling him how much she hated him.

Jaime was silent so long Aleta grew alarmed. "Jaime, did you hear me? I love you."

Her stared at her, then the corners of his mouth tilted upward into a brilliant smile, transforming his face from darkness to light. The breath caught in Aleta's throat as she was struck anew by the handsome man who had once been called Lord of Darkness. If the villagers could see him now, she thought dreamily, they would call him Lord of Light.

"If you love me half as much as I love you I'd die a happy man."

Suddenly the child resting inside Aleta's womb gave a mighty kick, making his presence known to both parents. For a moment Jaime looked startled, then he laughed, placing a hand on the mound of her stomach. Jaime's laughter transfixed her; it was the first time she had ever heard him laugh aloud.

"Our son—"

"Or daughter."

"Aye. Our son or daughter wants attention. Either that or he or she is protesting being squeezed so tightly between us. Perhaps I should leave you to rest." He kissed her nose and eased himself from bed.

"I do not really want to rest, my lord." The husky quality of her voice stopped him in his tracks. Clutching his arm, she tried to drag him back into bed.

"Aleta . . ." He regarded her tenderly, aware that he had probably exhausted her last night. He'd never do anything to endanger her life or that of their child. "I don't think . . ."

"Humor me, my lord. One kiss is all I want, then you may go about your business while I loll in bed the rest of the day."

"How can I refuse so pretty a request?" Jaime teased as he bent his head. The banked fire smoldering in the depths of her blue eyes should have warned him, for the moment their lips touched he was lost.

Groaning in blissful agony, he lifted his head and growled, "Witch. I surrender. Do with me as you will."

"Remember those words, my lord," Aleta said provocatively as she rolled him atop her, "for I shall always demand your surrender."

"Just as I shall demand yours," Jaime whispered raggedly as with one bold thrust he made them one.

Epilogue

It was the kind of wedding Aleta had always dreamed about. Resplendent in blue brocade trimmed in ermine, sprinkled with precious gems, and wearing the Mortimer family jewels, Aleta felt like a princess beside her prince. Her tall, cone-shaped *hennin* and silken veil all but covered her silvery tresses, which hung loose and flowing to her waist.

Unlike their first brief ceremony where Jaime wore the trappings of a peasant, this time he had garbed himself in finery more in keeping with his station in life. Bowing to the fashion of the day, he was dressed in peacock colors of brilliant green, violet, and yellow. His doublet was of velvet and his hose, one green and one yellow, showed off his muscular legs to perfection. Large silver buckles decorated his shoes and he wore a sword with jeweled handle strapped about his waist.

The King's chapel was the setting for the ceremony, attended by nearly every nobleman in the country. Since Aleta no longer had a father to give her away, a beaming King Henry performed the honors. The Bishop himself was on hand to join the young couple and Henry had ordered a grand feast afterward to honor the newlyweds.

If anyone thought it strange that the bride was far gone with child, no one mentioned it. Instead, the guests concentrated on the radiant beauty of the bride, the proud bearing of the groom, and their obvious happiness.

Once Henry had received word of what had happened on that deserted stretch of beach in Wales and learned that Aleta and Jaime wished to be married in London, he had gone all-out to make their wedding a gala affair. He stood on the sidelines now, beaming as the Bishop pronounced Jaime and Aleta man and wife. An astute judge of character, Henry was glad he had befriended Jaime Mortimer that day the young man had brazenly interrupted the wedding of Lady Aleta and Lord Grey. Learning that Mortimer had been the Lord of Darkness had been a significant setback that they had surmounted, and he felt reasonably certain now that the smuggler would never resurface to cause him to regret his decision.

The moment the ceremony was over and the guests moved into the great hall to partake of the wedding feast, Henry drew Jaime aside for private conversation. Due to leave for France at the end of the week, he had a startling bit of information to pass on to Jaime before he left.

"I'm most grateful to you, Sire," Jaime said, "for making my wedding memorable."

" 'Tis nothing, Lord Mortimer. Just seeing your lady's radiant face is reward enough. Do you recall our conversation of several days ago when you told me how it came about that the Lord of Darkness was captured by Grey and his men?"

"You mean about my false impression that Lady

Aleta had betrayed me when all along it was Rowena Howard?" He grew angry just thinking about it. "Aye, I recall." Upon arriving in London Jaime had regaled Henry with the entire story.

"You'll be interested in knowing that Sir Guy, Rowena's brother, is one of the knights who will accompany me to France. I just recently took him into my service. He asked me to find a husband for his sister before we left England. Seems the young woman is too much trouble for him to handle." He smiled slyly. "Do you have any ideas?"

Jaime's eyebrows shot up in surprise. "Rowena is in London?"

" 'Twould seem so."

Jaime grinned widely. "A husband, you say?"

Suddenly his eyes fell upon a fierce, violent-tempered Scots border lord whom he had just met—a man as wild and untamed as the country he represented. Lord Cullen MacDonough had been in London several weeks, seeking Henry's help in putting down a small rebellion. A man of middle years, he had gone through several wives and currently was without a spouse. Rumor had it that MacDonough, a fiery redhead with a flaming beard, was a merciless warrior and harsh disciplinarian whose crude manners left much to be desired. Jaime had spoken to him several times since arriving in London and thought him a perfect mate for a vindictive witch like Rowena. Marriage to a man like MacDonough would be just punishment, Jaime thought gleefully.

Henry saw the direction of Jaime's gaze and grinned in obvious approval. "Lord MacDonough seeks a boon. I've a sudden notion to grant it if he agrees to my terms. A private wedding tomorrow in my chambers should be easy enough to arrange. Forgive me if I don't invite you."

"Are we missing out on something?" Aleta chose that moment to join Jaime and Henry. She looked from the King to her husband, wondering why they both appeared quite pleased with themselves.

"Nay, my lady." Jaime smiled, placing an arm around her shoulders and pulling her close. "You and I will be occupied with more important things and have little time to devote to other matters." His eyes sparkled mischievously and Henry laughed outright at his sexual innuendo. "I have plans that include only the two of us. 'Tis our wedding night, after all."

"You must tell your lady our little joke," Henry advised, grinning with devilish delight. "I'm sure she'll approve."

"Later," Jaime said, his eyes never leaving Aleta's face as he turned her toward the stairs leading to their chamber. "Much later. Shall we retire, my lady?"

Aleta blushed furiously. "Aye, my lord, but I warn you, I shall want to know about the joke King Henry spoke of."

"And I warn you, my lady," he advised, his eyes glowing with a savage inner fire, "'twill be later, much later, before you're ready to listen."

Aleta squealed in surprise as he swept her up into his arms and started up the stairs. A moment later she had forgotten all about Henry's joke and was purring in perfect contentment.

Ice & Rapture

CONNIE MASON

Winner of the *Romantic Times* Storyteller of the Year Award!

Cool as a cucumber, and totally dedicated to her career as a newspaper woman, Maggie Afton is just the kind of challenge brash Chase McGarrett enjoys. But he is exactly the kind of man she despises. Cold and hot, reserved and brazen, Maggie and Chase are a study in opposites. But when they join forces during the Klondike gold rush, the fiery sparks of their searing desire burn brighter than the northern lights.

___4193-6 $5.99 US/$6.99 CAN

SHADOW WALKER

CONNIE MASON

Bestselling Author of *Flame*!

"Why did you do that?"

"Kiss you?" Cole shrugged. "Because you wanted me to, I suppose. Why else would a man kiss a woman?"

But Dawn knows lots of other reasons, especially if the woman is nothing but half-breed whose father has sold her to the first interested male. Defenseless and exquisitely lovely, Dawn is overjoyed when Cole Webster kills the ruthless outlaw who is her husband in name only. But now she has a very different sort of man to contend with. A man of unquestionable virility, a man who prizes justice and honors the Native American traditions that have been lost to her. Most intriguing of all, he is obviously a man who knows exactly how to bring a woman to soaring heights of pleasure. And yes, she does want his kiss...and maybe a whole lot more.

_4260-6 $5.99 US/$6.99 CAN

FLAME
CONNIE MASON

"Each new Connie Mason book is a prize!"
—Heather Graham

When her brother is accused of murder, Ashley Webster heads west to clear his name. Although the proud Yankee is prepared to face any hardship on her journey to Fort Bridger, she is horrified to learn that single women aren't welcome on any wagon train. Desperate to cross the plains, Ashley decides to pay the first bachelor willing to pose as her husband. Then the fiery redhead comes across a former Johnny Reb in the St. Joe's jail, and she can't think of any man she'd rather marry in name only. But out on the rugged trail Tanner MacTavish quickly proves too intense, too virile, too dangerous for her peace of mind. And after Tanner steals a passionate kiss, Ashley knows that, even though the Civil War is over, a new battle is brewing—a battle for the heart that she may be only too happy to lose.

_4150-2 $5.99 US/$6.99 CAN